D0482202

A DREDGING IN
SWANN

A DREDGING IN
SWANN

A SEB CREEK MYSTERY

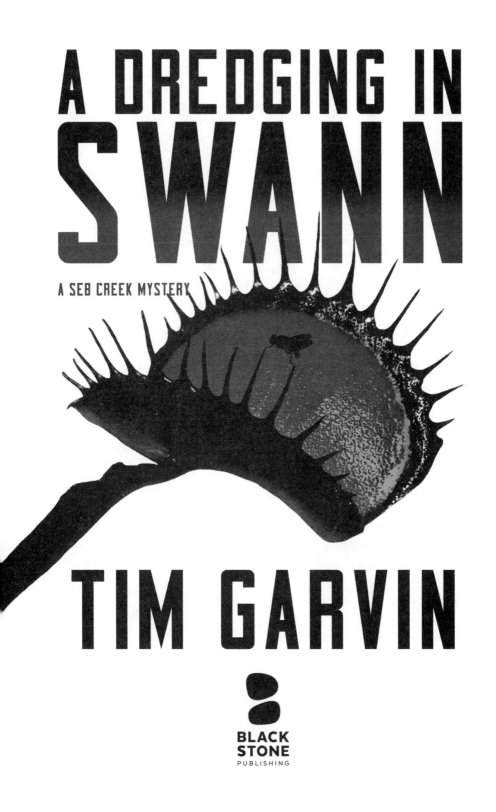

TIM GARVIN

**BLACK
STONE**
PUBLISHING

Copyright © 2020 by Tim Garvin
Published in 2020 by Blackstone Publishing
Cover and book design by K. Jones

All rights reserved. This book or any portion
thereof may not be reproduced or used in any manner
whatsoever without the express written permission
of the publisher except for the use of brief quotations
in a book review.

The characters and events in this book are fictitious.
Any similarity to real persons, living or dead, is coincidental
and not intended by the author.

Printed in the United States of America

First edition: 2020
ISBN 978-1-9825-5084-4
Fiction / Mystery & Detective / General

1 3 5 7 9 10 8 6 4 2

CIP data for this book is available
from the Library of Congress

Blackstone Publishing
31 Mistletoe Rd.
Ashland, OR 97520

www.BlackstonePublishing.com

For Cynthia

MURDER AND MERCY

If Leo Sackler had written to the parole commission to say he was sorry for killing Hugh Britt, they would have likely let him go. After all, he was past seventy, had kept a fleet of prison service trucks in fine repair for many years, and releasing him would have saved money. But they were wary of a man unable to submit to public regret, who, despite the state's appeal-proof case against him, tediously maintained innocence. Parole Commissioner Henrietta Cross, dean of the cosmetology department at Swann County Community College, particularly mistrusted him. She was past seventy herself and had not only been a resident of Swann County when the murder happened, but had known the victim, Hugh Britt. She had also known his father, Marshall Britt, and also the irrefutable facts of the case, how Hugh and Leo had fought publicly on the Britt dock over the concealed magnets on Hugh's fish scales, how Hugh had gaffed Leo through the biceps and thrown him back into his boat, how four hours later Leo and his skiff had been stopped by the marine patrol for speeding in a no-wake zone, headed away from the Britt fish house. The patrol had noted bloody footprints in the skiff—fish blood, said Leo—written him up, and let him proceed. But Hugh's body was found axed to death the next morning, and the sheriff found Leo and his boat on Cat Island the next afternoon, covered in cattails. It wasn't fish blood, after all. It was Hugh Britt blood, and they found an axe in the water thirty yards from the dock.

The prosecutor could have gone capital, since Leo was a black man and Hugh was a white man and rich, but also since Leo had returned to the Britt dock after the fight, which meant forethought. Or they could have gone second degree, an angry murder, since it no doubt was, Hugh's forehead being cleaved twice through to the brain. In the end they split the difference and went first degree with a life sentence, which in 1969, the year of the murder, was forty years to a parole hearing. In North Carolina a parole hearing means they look through your file. They looked through Leo's file in 2010, 2013, and 2016, in each case absent that needful letter of regret, and in each case denied.

Then, early in 2017, Germaine Ford died and made a news and internet sensation by leaving her Sable River farm and fortune to the long-forgotten, unrepentant convict Leo Sackler. She had never married, and cousins descended to protest. But Germaine had been careful, enlisting a psychologist and an eminent Raleigh lawyer in the will's preparation, and the bequest held up in superior court.

A reporter for the *Raleigh News & Observer* interviewed Leo in prison. Mr. Sackler, how come she left you her land and money? Were you lovers? Was it guilt because she killed Hugh Britt? Which everybody was thinking.

Leo, a celebrity inside and out now, smiled and said he had never met the lady, didn't know a thing, but that God grinds fine.

Then the governor, in one of her last acts before leaving office, let him go through a grant of executive clemency.

Two days after his release, Leo appeared at the lawyer's office with his daughter to receive the keys to the Ford lodge, where, in days long forgotten, he had spent three years of his youth. The day after that he bought a vintage 1954 pickup, three bicycles for his grandchildren, and, because the lodge was empty except for a single rolltop desk, four truckloads of Sears furniture.

THE SCOFFLAW

Sebastian Creek's shift was going long, involving an interview with a bottle-cut victim at the Spartanville emergency room and now a stop-by at Smitty's Sportsbar where the fight had gone down. The bar had formerly been the TrimTease, a just-out-of-town strip joint on the off-limits sheet at the Marine base. The new owner, Chuck Handley, was worried about getting his own black mark with the provost marshal and also downhearted because it was fairly early on Saturday night, and his bar had cleared when his customers learned the cops were coming.

Handley tossed a credit card onto the bar. He said, "His name is Carl Peener, which I know because here's his credit card, which he left on the bar when he ran off."

Kate Jersey, the crime tech, a middle-aged woman with a sheriff's cap jammed over a pile of silver hair, was dusting Peener's section of the bar. She shook out a zip bag and fingertipped the card into it. She said, "You might have told me you had that, Mr. Handley. I would have said, great, but don't touch it."

Handley said, "I guess I was waiting for Seb."

Seb pressed the plastic over the name, Carl Peener, and shrugged at Kate. He and the bartender had gotten connected a month ago when Handley's testimony to internal affairs backed Seb on a bribery charge.

Seb, who had spoken to the victim in the hospital, said, "They were arguing about politics?"

"Yeah, but it was the other two guys that were arguing. Peener just butted in, told them they were fools for being on any side, everything's rigged, that type of deal. Next thing I know, I'm down at the other end, a bottle breaks, and he stabs the guy and takes off. I ran out and saw his van. It was white and had something about furniture on the side. Now look here—this is extraordinary for us. This is way out of the ordinary."

After Seb got the description—big guy, ponytail, mustache and sideburns, gray sweatshirt, little bit bald, maybe a biker—Kate, who had been on the phone with the card company, said, "He's from Atlanta."

Seb used a booth to write it up on his laptop, then sent it to the incidents section of the sheriff's office. A moment later his phone dinged—the night magistrate had issued a warrant, and it had been forwarded to the state police. Seb called Fernando, the shift lieutenant, to alert him about the warrant and the advisability of a few motel checks, and also that Peener had probably fled for home. The victim had been cut only on the palm of his hand, so the DA would likely not press for extradition, which Peener, who impressed as a felon, would likely know. Kate had packed up and left, dismissing the deputy at the entrance.

Handley had his cleanup guy in early and was arranging chairs with him. Seb, talking fast because he had formed a daring, ardent plan for the rest of the evening, and because a storm was forecast, assured the bartender that the incident would probably not provoke an off-limits black mark since it was not part of an atmosphere of badness, and he, a sheriff's detective and former Marine MP, would testify to that if the provost marshal inquired. He began to leave, then impatiently remembered he should make a courtesy call to the Georgia state police, in case they wanted to notate the scofflaw's sheet, if he had one. He did, they informed him, for minor possession, motorcycle theft, and punching out a female, and they thanked him.

Then he was done. His daring plan was to drop by the Fairchild pottery studio on the way home and ask Mia Fairchild for a get-acquainted coffee date, hopefully the next morning at the Inlet Café, if she could make it by eight. Seb had met her six months before when he picked up his then-girlfriend, Charlene, from a pottery class. The studio was at the end of Willow Road in patrol section two, and two weeks ago, when it was burglarized, the lieutenant had assigned the case to Marty Jerrold, the section-two detective. In the hallway after the briefing, Seb had asked Marty for the case, and Marty had said, sure, but look, how about take these motorcycle thefts too, three of them, different houses but definitely-probably connected, so really one case. Which Seb had done, despite Marty's smirk-hiding straight face.

As Seb left the bar and entered the parking lot, he received a double jolt. The first jolt was from a neon-lit pile of trash flickering in a wind eddy beside the bar's dumpster, a perfect IED hide, except this wasn't a street in Iraq where trash piles sometimes exploded. That kind of jitter hadn't happened in a while, a year maybe, and he flashed that it was his coming Mia gamble, his keyed-up wanting, which killed calm and left him exposed. He closed his eyes and stood, took some breaths.

When he opened them, he got his second jolt, Squint Cooper, exiting his SUV and coming toward him with a computer tablet. He was a man in his sixties, broad-shouldered and lanky, with a bald top and crown of silky gray hair hanging to his collar. He wore a white T-shirt and a denim jacket and stood three inches taller than Seb's six-two. Seb exhaled slowly, steeling himself for a session with Squint, a man known for contempt, rough humor, and a bullying brilliance.

Squint stopped in front of him, wearing his customary slant smile which said, everything's a joke and so are you. He said, "I called your dispatch, and she told me you were out here on a call. Somebody got stabbed?"

"Cut with a bottle. Is this important? Because I've got to—"

"Well, you got a minute, don't you?" He held the tablet between them and woke the screen.

Seb said, "A fast minute."

Squint, intent on the screen, said, "How's Gretchen? I saw on the web where she's back in Italy leading her tours." A sudden wind gust whipped his long hair into a neon-silvered halo.

Seb made a smile. He said, "C'mon, man. I got to move." The Cooper and Creek families had become oddly intertwined, first because when he was a Marine CID sergeant, Seb had arrested Squint's son, Cody Cooper, for possession with intent. A few years later Squint dated Seb's mother, Gretchen, and together they arranged a romance between Seb and Squint's daughter, Charlene. Cody had been locked up for two years, a circumstance which did not daunt the love affairs, neither of which lasted more than a few months anyway.

Squint said, "All right. But kindly tell Gretchen her pal Squint conveys his regards. I hope she enjoys the Colosseum, where she'll be on Monday. Now look at here." He held the tablet sideways and touched the start arrow. A video began, a drone's view, the camera passing over a T-top fishing boat in gray-green water.

"This is from that eco fucker Peter Prince. He was drone-snooping my hogs this afternoon, and he posted it to the web." The camera swung over an island, then a strip of water, then another island occupied by a solitary tent, an orange octagon bubble.

Squint said, "I had a tent just like that. Or else it's mine, which it might be." He stroked the video forward, then let it play again.

The camera showed treetops now, then the long metal-rippled tops of hog barns. It moved down a road, then showed the farm's dead box, a black metal dumpster overflowing with hog carcasses. Squint stroked again, and the camera showed two miniature figures below, one aiming a rifle. "That's me shooting at it. See how he's zigzagging?" The camera lolled and waved across the sheds below. He stroked the video forward to a blue van driving along a gravel driveway. "That's Jorge. I sent him after it in the van, but he lost it over the pine barrens." Squint tapped the tablet and closed its case. "And yes, I had some misfortune. The fans in my number three shed went down and fifty-three near-finished hogs asphyxiated from ammonia poisoning. No one's fault or else God's. Now there it is for all to see. Fifty carcasses in the dead box. He flew over just around noon. I come to lodge my complaint. I want a deputy on this. Which I have complained before to no avail."

Seb, who had called Prince several weeks before at Squint's behest, said, "He doesn't scare. He knows the law better than we do." As a tweak, he added, "He's a fearless crusader." Then, instead of lecturing Squint once again on the ambiguity of North Carolina's drone surveillance law—or asking the question that naturally occurred to him—what happened to your backup fans?—he asked, an attempt at diversion, if Squint had listened to the Shaun Davey version of "The Parting Glass" yet.

Hell yes, he had, and he was coming as usual to the Sunday-evening singing practice, but couldn't the sheriff stake out the farm just temporarily?

Seb said, "Squint, we've been through all that. The sheriff won't spend deputies on violations of a vague-ass law. Did you get a drone?" A month ago, Seb had advised a counter-drone strategy, whereby Squint's drone would follow Prince's back to Prince's sneaky launch site, then submit the video to the district court, thus providing enough evidence for a judge, if he was so inclined, to charge Prince with a drone-snooping misdemeanor and impose a $250 slap on his high-minded wrist.

Squint said, "I'm not taking up drone flying, but if one fine day we find his LZ, somebody's going to the emergency room."

Seb said, "So long, Squint. Tell Cody and Charlene I say hello. Now I got to get home before this storm."

He patted Squint's shoulder and walked to his Honda. Behind him, he heard Squint's SUV start and crunch through the lot onto the road. He opened the trunk, removed his jacket, and shrugged out of his shoulder rig, then stowed it and his nine millimeter in the trunk vault. It was eight thirty now, possibly too late for a drop-by at Mia's, especially on a Saturday night.

He was going to do it though. As Seb got behind the wheel, he felt his heart start and felt the adrenaline flush of female fear. Like high school, he thought, but it was a good true normal fear, way more welcome than an IED flutter. The black plastic was still glinting in the wind beside the dumpster, just a scrap of bag now, an ordinary harmless muteness, but five minutes ago a portal back to Anbar and the day-to-day staying-alive fury. He breathed. He was going to see this woman. It was selfish, because what did she know of wild war on the other side of the world, but let it be selfish. Sometimes it was brave to be selfish.

As he swung around in the parking lot, he glanced down the alley behind the bar and in the security light above the bar's rear door saw a white van and a big guy climbing into the driver's seat. Seb gunned the Honda down the alley, squeezed between the vine-tangled chain link and the van, then angle-parked in front, blocking the van. The guy could have backed up, but in the side mirror Seb saw the door open. The guy got out. He had a mustache and ponytail and heavy sloped shoulders. He came forward.

Seb swung out of his car and held up his hands, hesitating the man's forward progress. He said, "Carl, did you hurt that bartender?"

THE FLYTRAP PIRATE

Cody Cooper snugged into his sand chair, packed a pipe, and lit up. Across the channel, over the barren outer island, he could see a little piece of ocean and above that a line of black clouds spiking soundless lightning. Maybe the clouds were coming toward him, maybe headed out to sea. Hard to know. The lightning was beautiful and silent, like a painting.

Probably he should put the tent back up before hard dark, since it was complicated, full of tabs and rods and grommets, and had been hard enough to assemble in daylight. And it would be a gamble to sleep in the open, in case the storm was coming toward him. But right now he wanted to cool out after the hard slog of all-day digging, and also after his momentary panic. The panic happened when he returned with the flytraps and saw the bright orange tent. When he put the tent up that morning, it was a figuring-out challenge, a pride thing, and only when he got back with the flytraps did he realize, *fuck me*, the tent was like waving an orange flag at the Marine patrol. Five minutes ago, he had grabbed it down, madman fast, and stuffed it under a bush. Putting the tent up in the daylight was his malformed mind working in sections again, leading him astray.

He had scouted the Marine canals the day before, looking for patrols, but it was a wilderness training area, and he hadn't seen any. That morning he'd cruised up the waterway, finally found the water tower, then found a bushy bump of island a few hundred yards south and threw up his tent.

Then he took the boat to the mainland and, fifty feet from the shore, as remembered from ten years ago, he found the pod of Venus flytraps flourishing in a luscious green carpet all around the water-tower base.

And amazingly, and also sort of sad, he found the cracked gray remnant of his homemade bungee cord, still hanging from the tower's walkway a hundred feet up. He had made the cord out of bundled latex tubing in his senior year in high school, and it had worked fine, first for trees and then for bridges, earning him a coveted daredevil reputation. The water tower had been his last jump and drew a cheering, jeering, fifty-kid audience, which provoked him into a too-horizontal swan dive. The spring-back shot him into the descending pipe, ending his daredevil career with a hospital stay and several visits to the dentist. He had been modeling himself after Sam Patch, the famous New Jersey leaper, who, just like Cody, made a last, crowd-goaded jump, except that Sam had not survived.

Cody toked, then began letting the Ka-Bar battle knife somersault from his fingertip into the sand, trying for a perfect stick. He had shortened the knife by grinding its broken tip and now used it as a flytrap digger. It was one of his prize possessions, since from time to time it wafted into his mind the image of his barracks buddy, Kenny Bartol. In Iraq, he and Kenny had been trapped in their blown-up Marine transport truck for three hours, which is how Cody had broken the knife tip, trying to pry open a smashed first aid kit. Kenny was in a frenzy about his leg stumps, and when Cody finally got the kit open and tied him off, Kenny had turned white, then started to mumble, then died. Cody started drugging after that, and the Marines kicked him with an Other Than Honorable. He kept the Ka-Bar though, and from time to time as he dug flytraps he sent Kenny good wishes, in case he still existed somewhere.

The water-tower flytraps had produced a mighty haul, four full pillowcases. And he had only thinned the pods, leaving enough to reseed for next year, in case he was still in the business. Which he wouldn't be, he hoped. He would have a nest egg by then and be able to have an achievement. He could have a restaurant, or he could buy a small piece of land and have a paintball course. Or he could start a nursery, with the paintball course in back, a combination thing, which was a smart idea that he would have to remember, but then it was gone, and he couldn't get it back, except to feel that it was some good inspiration for the future, now vanished in the marijuana mind-dance. He should have a notebook to capture achievement ideas, which often came when he was stoned, and which he needed since he couldn't get a decent job because of his prison stint.

He toked again, and Keisha floated up with her happy pixie face. His attention was currently centered on Keisha as a promising life companion. And it was a combination nursery–paintball course! Keisha could help, sell tickets and water plants. He considered writing *nursery and paintball* in the sand to remind himself tomorrow morning, but the storm was coming, he could see it closing now, and rain would wash the words away, and it was dark, and fuck, and he had to put the tent up.

He popped up from his sand chair and dragged the tent back to the flat place, and what a complicated motherfucker, and which part was the floor, and then it was up. Some irresistible intelligence in him had risen and mastered it. His mind was in sections, yes, but now and then a good section prevailed, or also it was luck. He tossed in the flytrap pillowcases, got his sleeping bag from the boat, and his pack with the energy bars, flashlight, water bottle, and book, and tossed them in.

He stuffed another pipe, then went back to his sand chair to wait for the storm, remembering that he had forgotten some important idea, something about plans for the future, which he had thought of writing in the sand, and should have, since it was gone.

BIG DOG

Leo Sackler woke that morning and felt the free-from-prison gladness come again, waking him with its ordinary kindness. He was drifting on gladness, is how he thought about it. It was like a hungry man, a starving man, and now he's in a food-everywhere place, and the food is not tricky. You turn and there it always is—at your fingertips, at your elbow, right up on you everywhere—only it's freedom instead of food, the gladness of freedom, deeply better than food—to be free every morning and anything whatsoever to do. First go out on the porch, urinate off the porch into the morning trees and sun, then cross the big room into the big kitchen, fry a plate of eggs, eat them all or not, have toast, a pot of coffee, then out to the well, free to work or not to work. But definitely work.

He had been out seventeen days, but he hadn't found the letter until the second week, so he had only been digging out the old well for five days. But he was already down more than fifteen feet. She didn't say how deep the well was back in the day, but if it was thirty feet and the digging went soupy and he had to hire help, he would hire help and just be the video man.

He learned he had a knack for the new things, even after forty-eight years absent from the world. He had heard about the iPhone but had never seen one, and when he left the phone store with his daughter, Virginia, and they sat in his truck and she explained and taught, he focused hard through the gladness and found it all simple to see. He was going to be able to live in this new world.

Now it was getting toward noon. He had made a dozen trips up and down the ladder, made another foot at least, might make another before the rain came. When the rain came, he would stop working. It came to him he could get naked and walk around in it, leave on his tennis shoes and do a rain scamper like a child. That's just what he would do. It would be foolishness, because it would not be enough, not even to wash him. But it would be partway enough, and he would most definitely do it.

He felt the shadows deepen, then felt a patter of clods on his hair and neck. He stuck the shovel hard in with his boot and looked up to see another little clod rain coming. It scattered on his forehead and eyelids. He was ten feet below the man on the surface, a tall man with the morning sun behind him, a shadow man in jeans and a baseball cap.

The man said, "What the fuck you doing down there?"

Leo said, "Don't be throwing clods down on me, please, sir. You want my attention just call down. What I'm doing is just what it look like. I'm digging my well. How can I help you?"

"I come to see you. I went through your house, saw all your stuff. I could have had my way with your goods. You're Leo Sackler?"

"Yes, sir. How can I help you?"

The man stepped sideways out of the sun, and the hole brightened, showing Leo's brown face, polite, irritated, and fear-suppressed. The man moved again, and the hole redarkened. The man said, "I like your truck. That's a honey. How much you pay for that? I know they ain't cheap."

"How can I help you?"

As Leo put his foot on the ladder's bottom rung and started to climb, the man kicked the top rung, and the ladder jumped halfway across the well before it clattered back on the brick wellhead. One of the rungs collided with Leo's forehead. He dabbed his skin for blood, but it was dry.

The man said, "They say you a millionaire today."

Leo unstuck the shovel and dropped it across his shoulder. The spade could be a shield, if it came to that. He said, "Speak your piece."

The man said, "I'm going to start you at a thousand dollars a month. That's no more than a mosquito for a man like you. I'm the big dog in the neighborhood, and no man is safe but through me. From burglars or arsonists or snipers neither. That's my pronouncement to you. Best advice, do not get squirrelly. What's your answer?"

"What's your name, son?"

"You call me son, I'm the one looking down? A thousand a month for peace. What's your answer?"

"Let me think on it."

"You already thought on it. What's your answer?"

"All right, then."

"You got my thousand to start?"

"No, sir. I must go to the bank."

"I'll be back tomorrow. Don't get squirrelly."

The hole brightened again as the man vanished. Leo swung the shovel down, folded his hands on the handle top, laid his forehead across them. He had been thinking of the lovely rain. Now he thought of a gun, thought of the bank, thought of the young deputy that had been coming around. He craved to sit, but the buckets were already full of mud and couldn't be inverted. He leaned against the well wall and let his head fall onto his chest, deeper and deeper.

ALLEY FIGHT

Peener stopped, and Seb said again, "Did you hurt that bartender?"

Peener said, "No, I didn't. I did borrow three twenties from him, since I needed gas money. The motherfucker gave my credit card to the cops. I bet you got it."

"Yes, I do. I'm with the sheriff." Seb reached behind him and slipped the handcuffs from his belt. He said, "Get on the wall, Carl. I got to hook you up."

Peener said, "I'm not going with you."

"Yes, you are. You stabbed a guy."

"I was defending myself."

"Get on the wall, Carl."

Peener smiled and shrugged. "Let me see your gun."

Seb said, "If I see yours, you'll see mine."

"I don't carry one. Being a felon."

Seb nodded, then said, "I locked mine in the trunk." He added, a between-men comment: "Where I can't get to it."

Peener made an appreciative laugh. "Well, damn, son, we got to tussle." He came forward in a boxer's shuffle, fists up.

Seb retreated past the hood of his car, put the Honda between him and Peener. He scanned the gravel for a weapon. He was back in Anbar now. He had put on the battle jacket. He would think later, he would think honestly: it felt good, it was also home.

Peener said, "C'mon, chickenshit." He came around the Honda.

Seb ran to the rear of the van, tried the door, a tire iron, anything. It was locked. He moved between the van and the bar. Peener circled the Honda, then crossed between the vehicles, went into his stance again. He said, "C'mon, dawg, let's fight it out."

Seb walked forward, the handcuffs in his right hand. He feinted with his left, flinching Peener's concentration, then whipped the handcuffs hard across the broad face. Peener shouted with pain, lurched back, and as he straightened, Seb kicked him perfectly between his thick thighs. Peener said, "Fuck," and hunched. Seb spun him and pushed him hard toward the wall. The rear door swung open—heavy metal rear door, Handley the bartender coming to see—and Peener went face-first into the edge with a bad sound. He was down and out.

The incident took forty-five minutes to clear. Kate was back for the scene, and since Seb was a participant, she took the investigation too, Seb making sure she got clear and detailed testimony from Handley that he had opened the rear door himself, just at an unfortunate moment for Peener. The EMS guys had taken Peener to the hospital, a skull-deep gash on his forehead and seeing double, and already complaining about police brutality.

It was going to be the third complaint against Seb this year, and the State Bureau of Investigation would open a case, since that was the promise the new sheriff had made when he got elected. That was why he got elected. He had beaten an old boy incumbent of twenty-four years, some of whose deputies had been terrorizing the citizenry, white and black and poor, and had finally shot a good old boy in a trailer-park tussle for a Taser, supposedly. One deputy was fired and two quit, but all without charges, so it wasn't enough to settle the outrage, and the new sheriff vowed to bring in the SBI to investigate deputy misconduct. Swann County was way off I-95, the notorious Iron Pipeline for drug transport, so corruption wasn't the issue, at least for that election, though it might be soon, with heroin use and overdose death spiking. No, what was on the county's mind, and on the Raleigh paper's mind, and on the nation's mind, was police brutality.

There were two main bad parts for Seb in the incident. One was that the new sheriff was his former Marine Corps boss, the provost marshal of Camp Henderson when Seb had been a CID detective. So if the sheriff didn't hammer his old sergeant, the press could sniff favoritism.

The other bad part, the worse bad part, was that a month ago bartender Handley had testified to internal affairs that Queeny Barker, a black male transvestite, had indeed fallen to her knees in front of Seb as he entered the bar to arrest her for soliciting, seized his buttocks, and shouted, "I'm gonna suck my Sebby's dick." It wasn't the dick-sucking shout that mattered, it was the buttocks seizing, since Queeny claimed to the booking sergeant that she was a victim of police corruption and injustice, having paid Seb one hundred dollars and still been arrested, just look in his back pocket, which Seb did, removing the bill and handing it over for evidence. Queeny, who was bipolar and bad with her antivirals, had gone from HIV to AIDS a year ago and was still locked up, having been refused bail for her soliciting charge in order to protect the public. So now it was the same bartender backing him twice, first with Queeny, now with Peener. Plus, two months earlier, a dealer selling near a middle school swore that Seb had squeezed his testicles to make him reveal the location of his stash. In that case, Seb had only seized the testicles, a squeeze being unnecessary. Peener would be Seb's third complaint in less than a year and trigger an SBI investigation. The press would love it. The sheriff would hate it. The public would frown.

Back in his Honda, he had to decide: go see the girl or brood. So go see the girl. It wasn't ten yet, and he knew she sometimes worked late, who knows, even on a Saturday night, and he could breathe on the way. Definitely the fight had been a joy—except poor Peener, with his concussed brain and split forehead, which Seb didn't yet but might later, maybe, feel something about—so don't hide the joy, but put it on the shelf with the other wrong joys, where he could see it and watch it and take its measure, everything being measured now and for the last several years against the joy he had felt in Iraq when he had died for six minutes.

And there she was, lights on in the studio, bent over her potter's wheel, raising a slender cylinder. She looked up, puffed back a lock of hair, and gave him a bland oh-it's-you expression. Two weeks earlier, in his initial interview with her about the burglary, he'd mentioned that he and Charlene were no longer together. The conversation then had gone from professional to friendly to interested, which was not professional, so then back to professional but with a memory of interested. He had watched her knowing smile come and go and had gotten a wise feeling from her.

Now she sat up straight, waiting. After a short no-progress report concerning the burglary, he made his eight o'clock coffee offer.

She said, "Oh."

He said, "If you can make it."

The kind wise smile came. She said, "No Charlene?"

"No, no. We're friends, but …"

She said, "Okay."

He felt a joy burst and gripped it back. It would be an upwind challenge. She was a halfway famous artist and might be an I-don't-date-cops type besides. But he had gotten his *yes*.

He extended his hand to shake, smiling away her muddy-handed shrug. They shook, and he wrung his hands together to dry the clay, holding his face sober, not gathering her appreciation with a look. He had gotten his *yes*, a great valuable main thing.

Back in his Honda, he breathed and breathed. Don't hope was important. But hope was important too.

SIMPLE TRUE GUYS

Seb headed home to Swanntown on the Marine cut through the base. The expected storm had arrived. The thunder altered from booming to banging and occasional lightning jagged into the swamp, illuminating the asphalt and dashboard. Rain made a frenzy on the windshield, and his Honda rocked, but he knew the road and stayed at seventy a few seconds longer, past smart. He had been expressing himself with speed.

Now he let up and coasted to fifty. He had done well, he thought. They would have coffee together, out on the inlet dock on the water. The storm would be through by then, and there would be the cool morning sun on her auburn hair. Then he thought, no, he had blown it with that wet-clay handwringing bullshit. Why not a smile there, at least a goofy shrug? Instead his sober soldier self, his squared-away, upstanding self. In some ways, with women every man was screwed from go, and not just emotion-hiding soldiers. Men fell in love with softness and beauty and slants of smile and teasing comments, which came from the other world, housed in that fairy body and face, which danced around you, seeing your exposure and dismay and considering both surrender and indifference.

Maybe he wasn't ready. But he longed. So he was. Anyway, she had agreed to coffee.

The fight joy had subsided, though not enough yet to feel any Peener sympathy. Besides, who knows, the door opening might have saved Peener an even worse beating. Seb had put on the battle jacket.

His first deployment had been during the invasion, and when he returned, desperate for an anchor, he married Glenda, his college girlfriend. Four years later he was redeployed into the Surge, where, for him, the killing began. First, he shot at some guys on a balcony, then at some guys in a street, then for certain killed a guy behind a propane tank, then for certain two guys on a stairwell. His last kill, just before his own death, had been a teenager, a boy crawling through the scrub with an RPG. Seb had picked him up from his post in an irrigation ditch, got him centered in his four-power, and just before he squeezed off saw the kid irritably slap a mosquito on his temple—then Seb put a bullet through the same spot. When they advanced, he steered past the body and force-fed himself a glance at the kid's dead eyes—somebody's kid, somebody's brother, and under the battle hate his heart woke. The boy had been alive. He had slapped a mosquito.

The next day Seb caught an RPG fragment through his armpit into his aortic arch. When they got him to the hospital his pulse was 180 and the pressure almost gone. Then he was gone, and he came up out of his body and saw the doctors and nurses working over him and then went down a tunnel of glorious light, and there was his dead father, who had killed himself, now benign and kindly—and he saw his whole life go by like shuffling cards. And he saw some others that shined, and then one of the shining ones came forward and said, *you have more to do*, and embraced him, and the love that went through him and around him showed Seb everything about life that he would ever know. Then he woke up in the hospital, and they sent him home.

Glenda found him one night in their backyard, sobbing. She laid her hand on his shoulder and said, "Seb, maybe you should get some help." He wanted her commiseration, but also, and more deeply, he felt her commiseration as pain. The love was gone, the angel love and her love too. Now it was the ordinary world of courtesy and chatter, which had no view into the world of blood and death. He blamed her and blamed himself for blaming. More oppressive yet, he had begun to sense the agonizing indifference of everyone to everyone.

In war, where one moment you are speaking to a friend and the next he is a ragged corpse, where the missions come one after another, where entire families die at checkpoints and mortared markets, where he had killed a boy slapping a mosquito—in that finality something more brutal even than war was revealed, that through all life, and in all hearts, there existed a secret current of indifference, and when you returned from battle, filled with jitters, dreams, and flashbacks, and tried to reenter normal life, you felt the smooth walls of that indifference like a coffin. Normal life denied you readmittance, first with useless solicitude, then with silence. You could not emerge from the numbness that had protected you, and the military that had trained that numbness into you was incompetent to free you from it. Rage built, and helplessness, and despair. If you escaped booze, drugs, suicide, and jail, you redeployed fast because you needed the clarity of war, where your enemies were simple and true and over there, the guys shooting at you, and your friends were the simple true guys beside you shooting back.

Then Glenda confessed her affair. She wasn't in love either, she said, and maybe never had been. Anyway, he was changed, she said, and what did he expect? He was behind a wall.

After they divorced, to free himself from the combat cycle, he applied to the Marine Criminal Investigation Division, and his last deployment had been stateside at Camp Henderson, just outside his home county, where he had been a CID sergeant under Henry Rhodes, now the new sheriff. He moved back to the barracks, unmoored. When his enlistment was up, he left the Marines to finish college.

To supplement his income, he formed a rock band. He began to take long slow walks in the woods around Raleigh, and on the walks began to sing, not rock songs, but hymns and slow-cadenced folk ballads that his mother, a music teacher, had taught him as a child, songs in which human emotion had been purified and distilled. Feeling began to reemerge. He thought more and more of his near-death experience, learned it was called an NDE, that thousands had had them, in the past and especially now, since the sixties, when cardiovascular resuscitation became possible. They were the same in every era and culture—a tunnel or river, dead relatives, angels or Jesus or Krishna, and always love and welcome. He eventually saw the indifference of the world that had tormented him more evenly and recognized it in himself as well. He graduated and took a job with his old commander. Battle fever was a jacket now, a dangerous jacket, no doubt, but you could take it off, and there was a closet for it, and you could close the closet.

His mother, who was then dating Squint Cooper, the famous Silver Star–recipient hog farmer, sensed the change in him, and invited him to dinner, and also invited Squint's daughter, Charlene. Seb hesitated. After all, when Seb was a Marine MP, he had sent her brother, Cody, to the brig. But she was bright-minded, and it hadn't mattered. Charlene was pretty and willing, and they'd dated for a few months. It was like a movie though, his front self saying the words, his behind self watching and wanting solitude, sometimes wanting to run.

Then he met Charlene's pottery instructor, Mia Fairchild. Something in him thawed. Something woke and wanted. He picked Charlene up at the studio three times, then told her he needed a break. He was not ready, he said, and hoped he was lying.

THE M416

When the storm neared, Cody left the sand chair and lay on top of his sleeping bag to watch the lightning strikes out over the water. Next thing, a seventy-five knot wind was raking his campsite. Seventy-five knots, he learned from his sister the next day, was hurricane force. The tent went flat and started flapping like a pinned bird. Which meant he had missed a tab or grommet in the stoned tent erection he had been so proud of. Or else his dad had bought a cheap tent. If Cody hadn't had the foresight to get his body flattened on the floor, the tent would have kited into the night.

When the rain started, it was horizontal and bullet-hard, and, since the net window was blown tight across the top of his head and bald spot, it stung like crazy. This was the point, he would think later, that fate started.

He wrestled the window sideways, so that now it came down beside his face. That was when the first chopper blasted over, the engine noise almost blending into the storm, but lower pitched and noticeable. Then the twin lightning strikes came, big-time fatefully, and the glare showed the blacked-out chopper and also something big tumbling from the underslung cargo net. Then blackness again.

It was super vivid, so maybe a hallucination. He had toked two bowls that evening, but he didn't hallucinate on weed, unless it was laced, and he did not lace his weed. But he had anointed one baggie with a sprinkle of nic-otine from Charlene's e-cig stash—product research—then got the baggies confused. So maybe he had just made a discovery—hallucinogenic nicotine marijuana. Five seconds later, still wondering whether he had hallucinated or seen something amazing, a chopper dropping its load into the drink, he saw a second chopper roar over, also blacked out. A few seconds after that the campsite was bathed in pearly white, and he heard the whumping concussion of the explosion. And he saw, very clearly, twenty yards out in the creek, wheels down, the load sticking up like a timber snag, the M416 trailer that had dropped from the net.

A HANGING

The Honda had climbed back to sixty, and now a massive gust slapped it into the opposite lane. Seb corrected and slowed again. The wild, brave wind matched his mood. He started the song "Four Strong Winds," holding the wheel with his right hand and cupping his ear with his left to hear above the racket of rain.

"*Four strong winds that blow lonely …*"

Then the sky on the ocean side blossomed amazingly white yellow and brightly endured, so definitely not artillery or a lightning strike. An instant later, even over the rain crash, he heard the rolling thumps of explosions. The green rectangle of mile marker six flared past in his headlights. He lifted the radio mike.

"Lori, how copy?"

A female voice crisped through the speaker. "Lori. Go ahead, Seb."

"I'm on mile six of the Marine cut. I just observed a major explosion on the sea side. In the swamp. I think it's an aviation crash. You better call the base."

"You stopping?"

"No. It's hell and gone in the swamp. I couldn't see it, but the sky lit up, and I heard it. Call the Marines. Tell them mile six."

"It's not artillery?"

"It was fuel."

"Copy that. Out."

It would be an accident. They wouldn't waste that much fuel in training. Unless they might. Some battalion commander gets an idea. So maybe an exploded fuel dump for some wild-hair reason. But likely choppers. It would be choppers. And violent flaming death.

Lori called him back three minutes later.

"Sebastian. How copy?"

He lifted the mike. "Go ahead."

"It was a chopper, or two choppers. I spoke to the provost watch over there. They're going frantic."

"Jesus."

"Where are you?"

"I'm about to leave the cut. Going home."

"Well, you got to turn around."

"They want me out there?" He began to slow, looking for a turn-around.

"This is unrelated. I just got a call from Deputy Garland. He was on patrol out near Twice Mile and went to check on Leo Sackler, which he's been doing, I guess."

"That got the Ford place?"

"Right, that got the Ford place. And he found Leo hung by the neck in a hole. Randall's securing the crime scene."

"He's dead?"

"Randall says he is definitely dead."

"It's not a suicide? It's a crime scene?" Seb had stopped the Honda and now backed into a chained-off gravel road, then swung back onto the asphalt in the opposite direction.

"Well, you're the detective. It might be Randall's wishful thinking."

"What do you mean, a hole?"

"Randall says Leo's been digging a hole out there. I guess it's real deep. And now he's hung in it. From a ladder or something. Randall was talking fairly fast. I called Lieutenant Stinson, and I'm fixing to call the rest of the squad. And the sheriff. I had you as on call, which the lieutenant said was right. By the way, he thinks you're going to be on courthouse duty for a while because of your fight. Are you okay?"

"I'm fine. And, just so you know, I did not violate the man's civil rights. I'm turned around. ETA in ten minutes. Tell Randall to stay out of the hole. Tell him to get out his plastic sheet and cover everything he can. Is it raining in town?"

"It stopped. It's probably still raining on Randall though. The sheriff will love that. About the plastic."

"I know he will."

Seb crossed the Fleming Ferry gate in the rapid-pass lane, went eleven miles west along Sable River Road to Twice Mile Road, then a short stretch to the Ford farm gate, a rust-covered arch of ornate blacksmith-twisted iron. The gravel road made a soggy crunch, but the rain had stopped. He passed under the straight-line canopy of oaks, the typical Southern passage to the manse, which was a two story, many windowed erection of peeled logs and copper roofing, a hundred feet wide and half as deep, set on the bank of the once pristine Sable River inlet. The inlet was currently being despoiled by farm, lawn, and parking lot runoff, and also, three years ago, it was inundated with twenty-five million gallons of Cooper Farms hog shit, which flowed down Council Creek past the lodge and into the inlet, resulting in a million menhaden and spotted trout deaths and an uproar of lawsuits.

He turned left in the gravel parking area, and his headlights jounced at a brown Swann County cruiser parked beside a red Ford pickup, shiny and ancient, the swollen rear fenders like matronly hips. Randall emerged from the cruiser with his leather investigation logbook and hailed him. He was an early twenties black man, a six-month deputy, just released to his own patrol. His gym-bulked size was evident even under his slicker.

He was at the door when Seb's car stopped, backstepping as the door opened.

As Seb got out, his flashlight glanced Randall's large-jawed face, which seemed to Seb intent with first-murder excitement. He would not know about the chopper crash then. Seb considered mentioning it, but that would mean exchanging rue, which he was not inclined to do with this eager youth.

Seb said, "Randall Garland?"

"Right."

They shook hands and said it was nice to meet each other.

Seb said, "You tape it off?"

"Well, I started. Then I thought I better get that plastic down. I was halfway into it and here come the rain and wind. What we need is stakes too."

The new sheriff had used part of his welcome money for replacement items for the patrol car trunks: flares, tape, and blankets, plus—the sheriff's innovation—a roll of four mil plastic for outdoor crime scene preservation, just in lucky time to protect the death scene of the mysterious Leo Sackler.

"Did it blow off?"

"Half of it did. It's plastered all over the trees."

"We going to be in the woods?"

"No, just the side of the house. You won't need boots."

"I was thinking chiggers and ticks." It was middle May, and Seb had seen the unmowed grass on the lawns as he entered.

"Oh, man. I been in there already. You got any bug spray?"

Seb retrieved a spray can from his door panel, sprayed his cuffs and ankles, and handed the can to Randall.

Seb said, "Anybody in the house?"

"No. I knocked, then I went in and made a sweep. It was unlocked." Randall sprayed his cuffs, then wrote briefly in his logbook. "I got you in at ten thirty-four."

Seb replaced the bug spray in the door, retrieved his flashlight, then rummaged for a pair of latex gloves, and slid them on. He calculated. Ten hours before his coffee date with Mia. Give him a few hours at the scene, he might get home to sleep and shower. Or sleep in his car, get a toothbrush at a 7-Eleven. They started across the gravel.

Seb said, "That's his pickup?"

"Yep."

"Looks like a high-priced antique."

"He paid twenty-five thousand for it. It's a '54 F-100. He and his dad used to work on them."

"Lori said you were out here checking on him. You get to know him?"

"A little. I'm on area two patrol, and I think, well, what if he gets victimized? Maybe those Coopertown boys think he's got some of that money in the house. So I wanted to show the cruiser for visual deterrent."

"How many times?"

"This is my fourth trip."

"You shoot the shit with him?"

"Sort of. Nice place, nice view, that kind of stuff. Nice truck."

"You usually come after dark?"

"No, just this time. I had come in the daylight, and I wanted to slow roll Coopertown in the dark."

"Did they see you?"

"In the daylight they did. This evening a few guys had fires going under the bathtubs in Elton's yard. Before the storm."

"You ever run into visitors out here?"

"Never did."

They left the graveled lot and crossed through the knee-high grass of the side lawn. A mound of red-brown earth came in view, coursed with rivulets. Beside it was a round hole, six feet in diameter, and above the hole a multipurpose ladder was cocked in a V. At the top of the V hung three lines of thin nylon rope. Two were relaxed and led to the handles of five-gallon plastic buckets upended near the mound. A third bucket lay on its side some yards away. One rope was taut.

Randall said, "Last time I come out here, he was down there digging. He said he was going to dig out the old well."

A handled rod with some type of clamp at the end leaned against the ladder. In a moment, Seb placed it. A selfie stick. Which likely meant a phone somewhere. The top of another ladder emerged from the dark of the hole. Beside the hole, a stepladder lay across a sheet of clear plastic. Another plastic sheet made a pearly cummerbund around the trunks of a stand of pines twenty yards away.

The woolly white top of a head came in view. Seb circled, flashlighted the dark-brown face, slack jaw, brown tongue, open eyes. The face and clothes glistened with rainwater. The rope looped around his neck and under his right armpit, so that the arm was erect over his head, elbow bent, the wrist and hand dropped near the opposite ear, like a dancer's move. Below, a shovel lay crosswise on the uneven mud. He wandered the light methodically over the bottom. There was no phone visible.

Randall said, "It's brick on the sides down there." The deputy shined his flashlight on the wall. "You can make out the bricks."

Seb said, "Why was he digging out the well?"

"I asked him, and he said, 'Everybody needs water.'"

"How did he say it?"

"What do you mean?"

"Did he say it sly, like that's not the real reason, but I can't tell you the real reason?"

"He said it more friendly. He wanted the whole family to move in with him, so maybe he needed water. Or maybe he wanted something to do, like a guy glad to be out of prison. Like why he bought that old truck. That's what I thought."

"Did he say how old the well was?"

"No, but it was grass on top. He had to cut through the sod."

Seb said, "Did you check for a pulse?"

"Well, I couldn't get down to him, and I didn't want to pull him up in case I would mess things up. I laid down and touched his cheek, and it felt like cold putty, so I thought, well, I guarantee he's dead."

"I suppose you laid that ladder on the plastic."

"Yeah, because a while back, man, the wind was—"

"It would have been better just to have gone back to the cruiser, Randall. If it's a crime, I'm going to need clues."

Randall threw his arms halfway wide. "Well, I wondered. But the rain was coming hard, and I was thinking, maybe I'll save a footprint. There's some dirt under there."

Seb raised the light slightly so that Randall's face emerged from shadow. The face was strained, earnest for fairness but ready for blame.

After a moment, Seb said, "Maybe you're right." When the flashlight gleamed Randall's face again, Seb saw the strain had relented to relief. He said, "I was on the cut going home, and I witnessed two choppers exploding in a fireball over the swamp."

"Oh, my God!"

"That's all I know. Lori says they're responding over there. About fifteen minutes ago."

"Oh, man."

"We need to start a grid search. We're looking for a phone."

MISFORTUNATE FIND

Cody scrunched in his tent, waiting out the wind. He didn't want to catch a flying branch in the face and also didn't want to wade the creek with busy lightning. Ten minutes later the lightning stopped, and the wind was down to a thirty-knot gale. He shrugged around under the sodden nylon until he found his flashlight, then backed out the door and beamed the light around. Several of the tent pegs had come out of the sand and some of the cords were whipping around, but most still held. He saw that Charlene's aluminum boat, which he had tied to a bush, had come completely out of the water, five-horse motor and all, and lay streamed on its bowline a few feet from the tent. If he had tied it looser, the prop could have bashed him in the head.

He crossed to the water and aimed the flashlight across the canal, and there it was, the M416, standard little military trailer, crisscrossed with straps, and under the straps its cargo, two six-foot-long cases stenciled with FIM-92.

The fate part of his finding the M416 had started years ago, in Kuwait, when he and Kenny Bartol had been the only two guys in his company selected for Stinger training. A squad of low-altitude air defense guys had driven them into the desert and let them each shoot down a drone, so that now, standing on the water in a wild gale, Cody knew exactly what he was looking at.

His heart raced, and he was instantly full of prickling danger and panic hurry. He would have time, since those choppers had crashed, definitely, and that's where the Marines would be, swarming the wreckage. Then again, the pilot might have radioed, *lost my cargo, heading back.* That right there was why they crashed, probably, one guy turning and the other guy right in his face.

Later he would wonder: Did he even consider not taking them? He had not. The section of his nature that made the extravagant swan dive off the water tower now started him across the canal. Except he was barefoot, so he turned and trotted back to the tent and rummaged out his tennis shoes, and also—good thinking—his trusty Ka-Bar. He knew military straps and buckles, but right now needed shortcuts, all and any.

A JIGGLE OF
CROSSED BEAMS

The headlights of a car emerged from the oak lane and drove to the edge of the lot in a hot gleam. When the lights doused, Randall's flashlight revealed a civilian sedan. A short heavy-bottomed man got out, set a leather bag beside his feet, opened an umbrella, then started toward them.

Seb spoke to Randall. "I should have brought that bug spray, if I was thinking. You mind getting it? Car door." Randall and the wide man passed on the grass.

Seb said, "Randall's getting you some bug spray."

The man's round face opened. "That's a good idea." He set down his medical kit, found a pair of gloves, and slid them on.

Seb said, "You got here fast."

"I was on the way home when I got the call." He closed his umbrella and played his flashlight over the corpse. "That's Leo Sackler, as was reported to me. The plot does thicken." He was gray-haired, in his sixties, and when he bounced his head, his cheeks flounced like satchels, and his neck accordioned.

"Randall couldn't reach him for a pulse, but he touched the face and said it was cold."

"Oh, he's dead. You don't hang on a rope with your eyes open and tongue out unless you're dead. Here's a poem: *They told me, Francis*

Hinsley, they told me you were hung. With red protruding eyeballs and black protruding tongue. Evelyn Waugh. I have finally found occasion for it. But perhaps you deplore banter at a death scene."

"So far it's not banter. Banter takes two."

The coroner brushed Seb's face with his light. "Well put, sir."

"Thank you."

"My wife wants to come sing with you. She's a contralto. With major pipes. She doesn't have PTSD though, unless I gave it to her. Do you ever use ringers?"

"We haven't, but it's something to think about."

"She'd blow your socks off. She was a ringer back home at the Hartford Episcopal choir, also the African Episcopal. Why'd I say back home? This is home." The coroner, Walt Carney, was one of the many relocaters from the north that had flooded Swann County in the last decade for the weather and prices.

Randall returned with the bug spray and sprayed Carney's proffered ankles. Another cruiser entered the lot, and a tall middle-aged sheriff's officer got out. He was slender and dark, his stride a mix of rolling elegance and discipline.

Randall said, "This is Lieutenant Fernando, my shift commander."

"I know Jose," said Seb.

Fernando said, "You got a murder?"

Seb said, "We're just starting. All I need is Randall. The investigation squad's on the way."

Fernando appraised Randall. "Tape it and keep it clear. The press will be descending. Doug Baker has been notified."

"Doug Baker …"

"The public information officer."

"Yes, sir."

Fernando played his flashlight onto the plastic-wrapped trees. "That's your plastic?"

"Yes, sir. The—"

"I'll tell the sheriff we need stakes."

Randall slumped his gratitude.

Fernando said, "I interviewed that Peener guy at the hospital, Seb."

"How is he?"

"The doctor said he's okay. But he's going to file a complaint."

"It was by the book, Jose. The bartender just happened to open the door." To Randall and Carney, who were listening intently: "I got in a fight arresting a guy." To Fernando: "Kate got the testimony. So that's the same bartender backing me up twice. Bad, but there it is. Oh, well."

Fernando said, "I talked to the sheriff, and he instructed me to notify the SBI."

"Is he putting me in the courthouse?"

"He didn't say. I talked to him before this murder." Fernando looked back to the corpse in the well. "Our deceased here has got a daughter over in Amboise and a son in prison. The daughter works at the town hall. The wife remarried long ago. I'm heading over to notify the daughter right now. If you want to talk to her tomorrow, I'll let her know."

"Tell her I'll get to her sometime before noon. Provided I'm still on the case. Text me her number, will you?" He thought of Mia and their coming meeting. The paper wouldn't have anything yet about the fight or complaint. It would soon though, all about the cop with serial brutalities. Her green eyes had gazed in a straight way.

Fernando said, "I'll leave you guys to it. Update me on the half hour, Randall."

"Yes, sir."

Fernando spoke to Seb again. "You don't need another patrol for the press? I expect you'll get the satellite vans out here."

Seb said, "Randall looks big enough to handle them."

Which earned more Randall gratitude.

As Fernando walked back to his cruiser, Carney said, "That lieutenant sings with you, doesn't he?"

"He does," said Seb.

"Has he got that bell note, that mariachi bell note, you know what I mean?"

"I do know, and he does."

"You don't look like you got in a fight."

Randall said, "That's what I was thinking."

Seb calmed off a pulse of battle joy. He said, "It wasn't much. The poor guy went headfirst into a door and got hurt."

There was a polite silence.

Carney said, "What's the weather going to do?"

"Clear the rest of the night."

Two more sets of headlights entered the lot as Fernando's cruiser pulled out, and an ambulance and sedan parked next to Carney's car. Two blue-shirted technicians emerged from the ambulance, and a woman stepped out of the sedan. She opened her trunk, hung two bulky SLR cameras from her neck, and lifted out her camera bag.

Seb said to Randall, "Looks like you've got bug spray duty. After that, let's tape it off." As the three newcomers approached, Seb said to the men, "You guys hang out in your van, if you will."

The two ambulance guys said they would and turned back. The woman waved her flashlight across the corpse. She said, "Is that an accident?"

Seb said, "I'm investigating."

She set her bag down and began to check camera settings, then startled back as Randall crouched at her side and began to spray. "What the hell, man!"

Randall said, "Bug spray. High grass."

"Well, ask, my goodness. I don't do deet, and that's deet, I bet."

Seb said, "Might be better than two hundred chigger bites. Detective Barb Addario, meet Deputy Randall Garland."

Barb said, "Well, spray me, Randall. But next time use your words."

"I apologize." She presented her ankles one at a time to be sprayed. She was a short, black-haired woman, midthirties, athletically built, a bulky awkward-looking pistol fastened to her belt.

Seb lifted the stepladder and set it aside. Then he and Barb carefully peeled up the plastic and handed it to Randall. Seb inspected the newly uncovered earth. It was wet, heavily rained on, hardly different in appearance than the exposed side. It was barren of footprints.

Barb began taking flash pictures, depositing numbered yellow markers as she worked. She said, "Seb, hit his face with your flashlight so I can get focus. So what do we think? Murder, suicide, or accident? Looks like an accident. With his arm that way."

Carney said, "That's what I halfway conclude."

Seb said, "I have some doubts."

Barb lowered her camera. She and Carney waited. Seb said, "That rope is tied off short here on the ladder."

Barb began shooting again, her flash strobing the corpse like a funhouse tableau.

Seb said, "Suicide, you don't put a rope around your armpit. And an accident means he got tangled in a lasso." Seb beamed his light on the unattached bucket. "The rope went to that bucket, don't you think? Then somehow he got hung in it."

Barb said, "He could have been pulling himself up the ladder, kind of a helper rope. Probably not."

Seb said, "It's too short for a safety rope."

Carney said, "Maybe he was getting it around his waist—as a safety rope—and he fell in."

"You wouldn't tie a safety rope off that short. You loop it and feed yourself down."

"You would. Maybe he wouldn't."

Barb said, "Oh, boy. Criminal investigation in action." She was working the perimeter of the hole, dropping markers, shooting, stepping, shooting, stepping.

Seb said, "I'm wondering why he didn't start swinging and get back on the ladder. With that rope under his arm, he wouldn't have been unconscious right away, would he?"

Carney said, "He might have panicked and run out of breath. Or out of blood to his brain. That rope's hardly a quarter inch."

"Will the autopsy show he fell?"

"It might, if his neck is broken. But it might not. He could have fallen by stages, grabbing the ladder and whatnot."

"In that case, he would have started swinging, wouldn't he?"

"Maybe he started to fall and tried to grab the top of the ladder and bam, six feet straight down. Even if it didn't break his neck, it might have knocked him out."

Seb said, "You want me to conclude accident, don't you? I'm starting to think you killed him."

"Now that's some good banter," said Carney.

Barb said, "I'm done up here." She let her cameras hang and switched on her flashlight. "This is so interesting. We have no idea what happened, but pretty soon we'll have a theory. And it could be complete bullshit since we don't have a time machine."

Carney said, "The commission is way too cheap for a time machine." His flashlight swung to collect their smiles. At the last county commissioners meeting, Carney had lobbied for one of the new CT autopsy scanners, proposing a regional death investigation center, a moneymaker, but the commissioners had declined, resulting in unaccustomed tension when Carney lamented the range of their imaginations.

Barb said, "This right here is exactly why innocent people go to jail. We get a theory and stick to it. They better not call me, because I'll testify everybody was so mystified a detective accused the coroner." She too moved her light to collect smiles.

Another car entered the lot. As it parked, the lights doused, and the door swung open before the car stopped moving. Marty Jerrold, a short blocky man in his early forties emerged in a yellow T-shirt, shrugged into his weapon rig, then snatched a plaid sport coat from the car seat and thrust into it as he approached. He wore his brown hair close-cropped. His belt ran under his round stomach like a sling. He switched on his flashlight, brushed the beam over the three figures at the well mouth, then paced around until his beam illuminated the death mask. He said, "What happened? Did he fall?"

Barb said, "That's just what we've been discussing. Chime in, Marty. Did he fall, make a bad job of suicide, or did someone hang him? Start detecting."

Marty threw his hands wide, a gesture of affable drama. He said, "Who caught the case? Seb, right?"

"I'm on call, so I caught it."

"Goddamn. My section, and you catch a famous whodunit. You got my case. I hope you're satisfied."

Seb gave the impression of thought, then nodded. "I *am* satisfied."

Marty played his beam over the corpse. "I'm voting for accident. That's a selfie stick. You find a phone?"

Seb said, "Not yet. Randall's doing a grid search. It might be in the house." He went over their discussion—a safety rope, a slip and entanglement, the problem of the ladder being available and not used.

Marty said, "Unless his neck is broken. Which I vote it is. Not because I don't want you to have a career-builder in your second year. I'm just detecting."

Seb had spent only a year in patrol before being promoted to detective corporal. His early promotion had raised eyebrows in the department, and a few hackles.

Marty said, "There's a shitload of murder motive though. This dude has got major money."

"Had," said Barb.

Another car entered the lot. Two men emerged and approached, following flashlight beams.

Marty said, "We beat the brass, so good start anyway."

Lieutenant Stinson, the taller of the two men, played his light over the corpse. He was in his forties and wore a plain brown shirt with STINSON stenciled over the pocket. Sergeant Morris, younger, shorter, and wider, wore an identical shirt stenciled with MORRIS.

Marty said, "Did you guys have to forfeit?"

Sergeant Morris said, "The league let our teammates roll the last few frames. It's going to screw up my average though."

Stinson said, "Where are we, Seb?"

Seb restated their conclusions, and lack of them, plus the unfound phone.

Stinson said, "Here's how we go—Seb, you're the lead, so you get to boss these guys around on your first murder. Can you do that?"

"I can."

Marty said, "He'll be enthusiastic."

Stinson said, "I suggest somebody for the phone records, somebody for the bank and lawyers, somebody for the prison, somebody for known associates, somebody for the canvass."

Marty said, "That's more somebodies than we got."

Stinson said, "You guys are working for Seb, okay?"

"Sure," said Barb.

Marty said, "Fine."

Stinson said, "I talked to the sheriff about Peener, Seb. And just so you know ..."

Seb said, "Fernando told me. I'm going to be investigated."

"Yes, you are. I recommended courthouse duty, but the sheriff said leave you on this murder."

Barb said, "What's this?"

Marty said, "Investigated for what?"

Seb said, "I got in a fight, and a guy got hurt." He briefed them, the bar fight, the alley fight, the door, Handley twice.

Barb said, "Well, that sucks."

Marty said, "I need to hear more about this fight."

Stinson said, "You're finished with the photos, Barb?" When she nodded, he said, "Let's get him out of there. Can we, doc?"

Carney said, "I been thinking that over, and here's my recommendation. One guy—I'm thinking Deputy Randall—pulls him straight up out of the hole, very gently, by the rope. Barb videos to make a record. Otherwise, you have to go down and stamp all over everything down there."

Randall, who had heard his name, approached. "It's taped. I can pull him up, no sweat."

They spread a sheet of plastic, and, while Barb videoed with the on-camera LED, Randall pulled the body smoothly from the well.

It was the corpse of a tall rangy black man, narrow shouldered and light framed, in a sodden mud-stained white T-shirt and baggy jeans. His face was long and age-creased. His dark tongue bulged between perfect false teeth. His hair was thick, like a crest of dirty foam. Carney knelt in the sodden earth, stroked the eyelids across the swollen eyes. He severed the rope with a scalpel and arranged the cut section alongside the frozen arm. A faint smell of feces became evident. As Carney bagged the hands, he said, "I'm guessing eight to ten hours, by rigor and temperature. Let's get him in the shop, and I'll be more certain."

Barb said, "If it's a murder, oh boy."

Carney said, "That's what I told Seb, the plot does thicken."

Seb held his breath against the feces odor, knelt, and patted the jeans. He removed a ring of four keys, zipped them into a clear evidence bag. There was no phone.

Stinson gestured for the blue-shirted ambulance techs. They approached with a body bag, laid it beside the corpse, and unzipped it.

Randall handed one of the men the bug spray. While they sprayed their ankles, he glanced apprehensively through his assembled superiors, hesitated, then said, "Doc, why not put his tongue back in his mouth before they close him up?"

Carney raised his eyes from the corpse to gaze attentively at Randall. Then he nodded. "Why not." He removed a wooden spatula from his kit, knelt, and prodded the tongue back into the mouth. He closed the jaw, held it for a moment. When he released, the mouth opened, but the tongue stayed put. He exchanged glances with Randall, who nodded his thanks. They watched the medical techs lift the corpse onto the bag, then begin tucking the feet, shoulders, and head inside.

Seb looked at Randall. "He was a decent guy, was he?"

Randall said, "I don't know if he was. He was to me. You think someone killed him?"

"I'm wondering."

Carney said, "You think he was digging for something?"

"Maybe treasure," said Barb. She videoed the zipping up of the corpse and turned off the camera. Inky blackness closed around them, and all seven switched on flashlights. A jiggle of crossed beams followed the para-medics and their long black burden to the ambulance.

Seb said, "Everybody heard about the chopper crash?"

STINGER

The case on the right side was bashed in and crudded with sand where the initial impact had been, but the other case was perfect, sitting a foot out of the water. Several of the plastic missile beds between the cases were empty, but three missiles remained, buckled into place. Cody cut away the nylon straps of the good case, hauled it free, and shoulder-carried it across the creek to the sand. He flipped the buckles and opened it, and there they were, new-looking and fine, a gripstock, launch tube, and battery pack for the FIM-92, the man-portable surface-to-air-missile known as a Stinger. He closed the case and secured the buckles, then trotted to his boat and in five fast heaves grunted it across the sand and into the water. He tossed the flytrap pillowcases between the seats, then stuffed the clothes and food into the sleeping bag and crammed it and the tent into the bow. He toted the launcher case across the sand and laid it down sideways in front of the driver's seat.

Then he needed to calm, get his heart rate down so he could think. In a few hours there would be guys all over the campsite, guys that would definitely be thinking, picking up bits of this and that and sending it to labs. So search. Hurry, but take the time. With his beam on high he began a sand-kicking, baby-stepping grid search, found a few tent pegs, which they could have maybe traced to the surplus store, where they could have gotten his father on a video, who knows these days, found the matchbox he had tucked under the tent, found the paperback he was reading, some thriller from his sister's house. With his sister's fucking name in it. Found a Venus flytrap, right there on the sand, the one he had been fooling with and had tucked under the tent beside the matches. Which would have been like saying, over here, guys, it's Cody Cooper, the Venus flytrap poacher recently nabbed in Brunswick County.

He finished the search, then sank to his knees to breathe, trying to calm. Then he grid-searched once more and found nothing. Footprints though, fuck! He fished the Ka-Bar from the front pocket of his jeans, unsheathed it, hacked off a four-foot branch of leafy scrub, and started brushing sand. He had come from the boat to the tent site, then to the water and waded, and that was it. No, he scouted the island. But that was before the rain, so the footprints would be washed out. So boat to the tent, tent to the water. He brushed and brushed, one-handed, using the flashlight, backing right to the boat, getting every last single mark.

He stepped into the boat and shoved off with an oar. He was stoned, goddammit. What was he forgetting? He set the motor into the water, pulled the cord, once, twice, set the choke, pulled, and the motor kicked into its purr.

Two minutes later he was entering the inlet—and realized he had forgotten the fucking missiles. He turned around, nosed back into the creek, cruised to the trailer snag, and loaded two of the three missiles into the bottom of the boat, then realized, good Christ, fingerprints! He stripped off his T-shirt and spent ten furious minutes rubbing every surface he could find, once, then twice, then three times. He loaded the third missile and sat for a moment, trying to think. Nothing came. One thing for sure, if he hadn't forgotten the missiles, he wouldn't have remembered about fingerprints. Wild-ass fate.

PRECIOUS BOX

Seb came awake to a knuckle rap on the driver's window. He switched on the key and hit the window toggle. Kate Jersey, the crime scene tech, leaned down. Her tan one-piece was streaked with mud.

"We're signing out, Seb."

"What time is it?"

"Getting toward dawn."

"You get anything?"

"Fingerprints. Couple of crappy footprints in the hole. Rain washed everything up top."

"The phone?"

"No phone, and no prints on the selfie stick. But here's a good clue. No fingerprints on the top of the ladder either, where you have to grab it going up or down."

"Wiped?"

"Maybe wiped. But he had a pair of gloves down in the hole, so maybe just gloves."

"What about the middle part of the ladder?"

"What a detective. Yep, lots of fingerprints there. Also, not certain about this, but my impression is the ground was smoothed before the rain. Not even any contours. But that's a guess."

"Anything in the truck? Like a phone?"

"Nothing. A box of Kleenex."

"So maybe we got one, maybe not."

"That's it. We finished the house, and the stable back there. It's full of old firewood. The TV vans are come and gone. Doug Baker kept them away from you at great personal cost, so you owe him big-time."

"What do you hear about the chopper crash?"

"Twenty-one dead."

"Jesus."

"I know it."

"Anything else in the hole?"

"Just mud. We probed for the phone and did not hit the top of a treasure chest."

"How deep did you go?"

"Two feet about."

"Where's Randall?"

"He's in his cruiser, failing to stay awake."

"Okay, Kate. When will I hear from you?"

"This afternoon. I'm going home to get a nap. You look nicely rested."

He met her eyes. "I'm going to be investigated."

"I know. I was careful with my report, Seb. I think you'll be good. The sheriff left you on this case, right?"

"That might be bad though. Start the SBI thinking favoritism."

"Start the reporters thinking, is what I thought. Look, me and Ernie are out of here. We'll come back for the gear."

She joined a tall man carrying two evidence cases. He handed her one, and they crossed to separate cars.

Seb spoke into his radio.

"This is Seb. Who copies?"

A man's voice came back. "This is Bob, Seb. What's up?"

"I need a deputy out here to relieve Randall."

"On the way."

Randall's cruiser was still parked near the lawn, and beyond it, on the grass, two silver tripods of lights had been switched off. The ladder and grass and dark of the hole had begun to emerge in dawn. Randall, still wearing his rain slicker, was slumped onto the wheel in the front seat. Seb rapped him awake. Randall sat up and snugged his cap, then got out and leaned against a fender, waking more. The radio murmured hip-hop.

Seb said, "Go home, man. Good job tonight. I called for your relief. Just leave me the logbook, and I'll hand it off. I'm going to do the house again."

"If you need me, I'm fine."

"No, man. Go home and sleep. First thing tomorrow, I want you to start a canvass, all the farms, all the homesteads, all the trailers, except leave Coopertown to me. And leave Cooper Farms to me too. I know Squint Cooper, and I'll see him tonight. From you, I want any traffic— foot, bikes, cars. Call me when you're halfway done and report. Sleep four hours then up and going again, okay?"

"Okay."

Seb waved him out of the lot. The scene had widened in the gray light—the pine forest at the edge of tall grass, the bulk of the log lodge and its wide lap of gravel, lines of white and pink azaleas on the brick walks. Death and darkness again disappearing into life and light. The routine submergence. In two hours, he would appear before Mia, who would ask, what is your job? He would say, I am the sandman. I put the past to sleep.

After Stinson and Morris left, Seb conferred with Barb and Marty and handed out assignments. In the morning, Barb would start the court order for phone records. Marty, still play-griping, would contact the prison system for records and a list of Sackler's associates. Seb would start with the daughter. Stinson had rescheduled the morning briefing for eleven-thirty. Since the scene was isolated, and there was no witness canvass to perform, when CSI arrived, Barb and Marty left for home.

Seb had walked the house already and walked it again with the techs. When grogginess took his concentration, he retreated to his car to sleep. It was unlikely to be a forensic solve anyway. It would be a whodunit dig. If it was murder. Before he slept, he browsed databases for the Sackler name. The oldest child, Virginia, whom he would interview today, worked at the Amboise town hall. Her brother, Marshall, was doing federal narcotics time. Raymond Charles, Virginia's husband, was an addict and had disap-peared. All three fell into the who-benefits category.

He crossed to the pine porch that ran a hundred feet along the entire front of the lodge. A row of knee-high red clay pots were lined against the log wall. At the end of the row, fifty-odd topsoil and cow-manure bags were neatly stacked. The ornate handles of the double doors were hazed with whitish fingerprint dust. He laid the logbook on the entranceway decking, then fished a pair of latex gloves from his jacket pocket and slipped them on. He slid on a pair of Tyvek booties from the crime tech box and pushed through into the cavernous great room.

A balcony crowned three sides. Hallways led to the wings on both floors. A fireplace and stone wall rose to the vaulted roof, and beside it a wide stairway curved upstairs to the balconies. The fireplace, he noted, was clean of ash.

The room was filled with a jumble of furniture—couches, chairs, dressers, tables, beds—some still in cartons. Three bicycles were propped against a wall. Fingerprint dust lay like mildew over likely surfaces, the mantel, wooden accents on the furniture, a single beer bottle on an end table.

He stopped beside the fireplace and closed his eyes for a moment to see if he could tell what he thought. He thought murder but couldn't tell whether it was hunch or the love of chase that pulled. Both probably.

He browsed the halls, circled through each empty room. In the kitchen, he opened the empty refrigerator, then opened the freezer side and found several packets of seeds—spinach, lettuce, tomato, watermelon, cantaloupe. Through the kitchen window he noticed the stable Kate had mentioned.

He left his booties beside the back door and crossed the overgrown lawn on a stone walk. The stable was a single-slope open-front wooden building with four stalls. In one, a new lawn tractor was parked out of the rain. The others were halfway filled with dusty stacks of firewood. The left wall had a built-in shelf filled with odds and ends, a few lamps, a rusted cross-cut saw, ancient-looking wrenches and hammers, empty picture frames, a tin Phineas Brothers tobacco box. The box's top was ornate and colorful and embossed with a large PB. It was dusted with fingerprint powder, and, unlike the other items on the shelf, it was not covered with natural dust. He held the base of the box and popped open the hinged lid. It was empty.

As he closed the lid, he saw the white edge of the photograph protruding from a crack where the shelf met the wall. He lifted it free. It was a small, crisply focused black-and-white shot of a middle-aged black man and boy in a skiff, both smiling at the camera, the boy self-consciously, the man benignly. Seb placed the photo in a plastic bag and slid it into his jacket pocket.

He started away, then turned. There was an oddity. The flooring of the stable was dusty gray boards, rough cut in one-foot widths, and covered with the debris of time—pebbles of clod, brown leaf pieces, bits of bark. The board nearest the back wall was shorter and the smattering of its detritus cover had shifted, so that one side was clearer than the other. He found a handleless sawblade on the shelf, slipped it between a crack, twisted the teeth into the edge, and pulled. The board came up, revealing a hole. On its bottom lay a dirty white towel. He lifted it free, shook it open, and draped it across the woodpile. He inspected the hole with his phone's flashlight. It was empty, but just deep and long enough for the tobacco box. He took a photograph with his phone. The murder hunch strengthened.

CAT ISLAND

Cody had started down the inlet, heading toward his sister's dock, then thought, what the fuck, haul the launcher back to my trailer, stow it in the bedroom, tell my sister not to go in there?

He needed to stash it. He needed to bury it. He needed a fucking shovel. He could bury it on a beach though, just with his Ka-Bar to cut sand, the way he built his sand chair. Sites flashed through—the island with the Civil War fort, or Cat Island, or just any unnamed island in the marshes—but they would see the boat track and his footprints, or if he branch-brushed it, still it would leave a disturbance. Who came ashore here, our missile thief? Then an idea came, and he swung the boat around and headed back down the inlet toward the ocean.

Ten minutes later he was nosing up Cat Island slough. He had passed a couple of flounder skiffs back in the creek mouths, one with two guys, a poler and a guy in the bow gigging with a lantern, the other with one guy doing both jobs. If investigators found them on the inlet in the morning—unlikely anyway, since most giggers had jobs—they could report, yeah, we saw a skiff, so what? Some gigger changing water, so what?

A hundred and fifty yards in, his high beam picked up the timbers of the Cat Island wharf, stuck into the beach like giant black and gray splinters. Back before the war, when the island was still private, somebody had built a fishing resort and boat dock. After the resort folded and the island was gifted to the state, hurricanes blew the buildings off, and the wharf had been nibbled to sticks. There was still a broken pier section sticking out toward the water and a place under it where high school kids made fires, drank beer, and smoked dope, which fifteen years ago Cody himself had done. And always a confusion of footprints.

He nosed in, locked the motor up, then hopped out and tugged the boat firm. He shouldered the case and trotted up the beach, spraying light ahead of him. The sand was bumpy with rained-on footprints, and directly under the wharf overhang were two firepits, each circled with stone, no doubt ferried in by enterprising kids. Between them the sand was sodden and melted-looking, but nicely disturbed, so just right. He positioned himself between the firepits and began to cut with his Ka-Bar. In ten minutes he had made a six-foot-long, foot-and-a-half-deep trench. Cody tipped in the case, rubbed it into place, then ran for the missiles and carried all three to the trench in an arm cradle.

He arranged the missiles in the hole, covered them with his sleeping bag, then pushed sand across them, thinking—too late—that sand in the delicate works could make them inoperable. But it was hurry hurry.

Then, as he was pouring water over the sand with the plastic bailing pitcher, a cold feeling swept through him. He thought, what does it matter if they are inoperable? What am I going to do with them? He stopped and straightened his aching spine to his six-four height. The grass had worn off, and the world seemed ordinary and dull. He combed sandy hands through his thinning hair, and thought, fuck, fuck, fuck, I stole three Stinger missiles.

A SONG FOR LEO SACKLER

Seb saved the master bedroom for last. It contained a single sheet-covered bed with a light blanket neatly folded in front of two pillows, a floor lamp, three cardboard boxes with clean clothes, jeans, T-shirts, a sweatshirt, underwear, socks. A fourth box contained dirty clothes. He dumped it out and felt the empty pockets of the single pair of jeans. Three car magazines, each swollen with dog-ears, lay beside the bed.

An old rolltop desk sat against a bay window, half blocking the view of the gray-green inlet. The cover was up and the drawer pulls and desktop had been dusted. In one of the desk's folder slots, Seb found a torn-open ten-pack of manila folders, and beside it three folders with contents. In each folder he found a printed CSI form noting that the contents had been scanned into electronic case file 05172017-02.

One folder contained a single sheet, a prison form documenting Sackler's release from Carteret Correctional Facility on May 3, 2017. The second held papers related to the purchase, for $26,400, of a 1954 Ford pickup from Brawlie's Antique Cars. It was red-stamped with PAID. The third contained receipts with date and time printed. Which meant they could pull security video. Seb paged through them—Lowe's for the pots and soil, Sears for the furniture, bicycles, clothes, riding mower, and a few kitchen items. The last receipt was from Verizon. Sackler had opened an account the day after his release and purchased two new iPhones.

Seb turned, glanced around the room for electrical outlets. There were several, but none charging a phone. He crossed the room and swept his hand behind the bed. He felt the receptacle and charger cube and followed the wire to a phone that had been slipped under the mattress. He bagged it, then swiped it through the plastic and found it was unlocked. He surfed to the camera and opened the stored items. There were no pictures but several videos. He opened the last one. After some blurred camera shaking—Leo getting the selfie stick positioned—the picture stilled and showed the well and ladder descending into the dark. An off-camera voice said, "Down buckets. Down buckets." Three white plastic buckets tumbled into the picture with a drumming racket, their nylon ropes trailing into the murk. Leo's feet appeared at the side of the frame and he began to descend the ladder rung by rung. He wore jeans and a dirt-stained white T-shirt. Seb noted he gripped the ladder sides and was not wearing gloves.

Leo stopped halfway down and looked up at the camera. His face gleamed with sweat. He kicked one leg to the side, then the other. He said, "Nothing in my hands, little friend. Nothing up my sleeve." He continued down. At the bottom, his white-topped head began a rhythmic dipping and weaving. The sound of shoveling was heard.

Seb closed the video and surfed back seven files to the first video. It opened again with blurred shaking as Leo positioned the phone on the selfie stick. The picture again showed the top of the well, then the buckets cascading into the darkness. Leo's voice started off-screen and continued as he entered the frame and began to descend the ladder. Again he stopped halfway down and gazed upward. He said, "You got to go on and on like an ant. An ant don't think about the hole he's digging. He just thinking about that little bit of earth he got. Just hoist it up and carry it up and lay it on the pile and go back down and get his self another one. Don't think an inch ahead. He's digging his self a home." He paused, then nodded, looking intently at the camera. "That's what I'm doing, little friend. I'm digging my home, just like a little ant." He descended into the murk and sounds of digging were heard. Seb swiped the video forward. More sounds of digging. Seb blanked the screen and tucked the phone into his jacket pocket. Crime scene would have to watch every minute of every video.

His phone rang. On the screen he saw Sheriff Rhodes' name.

"Hey, Sheriff."

"You still on the scene?"

"I'm about to log out."

"What do we got?"

Seb described the scene, the approximate times, the tobacco box, his inconclusive conclusions. "The empty tobacco box and no fingerprints on the ladder, those are the main crappy clues for murder. Plus a missing phone. Maybe it's an accident, but there's plenty of motive. The house and land alone have got to be worth a bunch of millions. I'm at the puzzling stage. Also, I found a second phone in the bedroom. He had a receipt for two of them." As he reported about the video of Leo speaking to the camera, he realized he should not have mentioned the second phone. Kate and Ernie had not found it. He said, "It'll be a long siege for Kate and Ernie. You talk to them?"

"Kate gave me a verbal. She also told me about the fight. Now you tell me about the fight."

Seb gave the details, the handcuff swipe, the kick, the door. He said, "I know you notified SBI. I'm good."

"You're good?"

"I am."

"Well, I'm not. I've become a politician, you know."

"I know it."

"The press will be snarling."

Seb let a moment pass. He said, "Well ..."

"I'm not throwing you to no damn dogs, Seb. I left you on the case, didn't I?"

"Yes, you did."

"You know why?"

"Because nobody's going to push you around."

The sheriff laughed. "And also, I trust you. Except it would have been good had you not struck him with your goddamn handcuffs."

"Well ..."

"I heard you reported the chopper crash."

"I did, yeah."

"I'm on my way out there right now. The FBI called me."

"What are they doing in it?"

"Remains to be seen. Can you get me something this afternoon? I got reporters calling."

"I'll get you something, but it's going to be investigation ongoing. It's a whodunit and also a what-is-it. Fernando did the notification last night. I'm seeing the daughter today."

"He called me."

"How'd she seem, did he say?"

"You mean did she confess? She did not."

"I'm seeing her around ten. But first I have an important romantic meeting. Coffee at the Inlet Café with my future wife."

"Really? Jennifer will be happy and disappointed at the same time." In April, at the all-department picnic and softball tournament the sheriff's wife had taken a motherly interest in Seb's love life, or lack of one, and made suggestions.

Seb said, "I'll come in after that and do my report. Kate and Ernie are finished and gone."

"Okay. Go fall in love."

"I hope I do. By the way, do you know the history of all this business at the lodge? I mean the murder back then? You being my considerable elder."

"Not really. There was a will dispute, and the Sacklers had to move. I only know that because it was in the newspaper after Germaine gave him the lodge. Leo Sackler lived at that lodge when he was a kid, you know."

After the phone call, Seb entered the bathroom. The mirror had been dusted and several strips of prints removed. A large white towel hung over the shower bar. Inside the cabinet were a toothbrush, toothpaste, a bottle of aspirin, a bag of safety razors, deodorant, two bars of unopened soap, and a second toothbrush, still in its packaging. He hesitated, but not long. He removed the new toothbrush from its packaging, ran a line of toothpaste across the bristle, and brushed his teeth. He lathered with the bar of soap, washed his face, then dried with toilet paper. He undid his short rubber-banded ponytail, finger-combed, and refastened it. He sniffed his pits, wiped the deodorant bar with toilet paper, and applied it through the neck of his

T-shirt. He inspected himself. To avoid the hassle of a daily shave, he kept his beard stubbled. It could have used an electric razor pass but would do.

As Seb began to leave the bathroom, he stopped, returned to the sink, laid his hands on it, lowered his head, and willed a pulse of half-fake gratitude for the use of the toiletries. Leo Sackler's face swam up, the face he had consciously imprinted, a black, sweat-streaked, playful face, saying *little friend* to the camera. The gratitude trued. The person inside the face was gone. But the seeds in the freezer and red clay pots on the porch and the bicycles in the great room remained and yearned. They could not be satisfied but could be quieted. He could tell Mia when they were old, on a beach, I am the sandman.

As he walked down the long hall, he felt the urge to sing, and he sang in his timbrous tenor:

> *"Oh, all the money that ere I had,*
> *I spent it in good company.*
> *And all the harm I've ever done,*
> *Alas, it was to none but me.*
> *And all I've done for want of wit,*
> *To memory now I can't recall.*
> *So fill to me the parting glass.*
> *Good night and joy be to you all."*

He finished the song on the manure-and-planter cluttered porch in the new bright day. A patrol car rolled up the gravel drive, Randall's relief.

A BUNDLE OF STICKS

Cody lived behind his sister's house on Loman Creek. A year ago, Charlene had hired a private detective to track him down in Phoenix where, after being released from military prison and a stint working his dad's hogs, he had been homeless for two years. She sent him a bus ticket and settled him in a trailer near the garage.

She came down the walk from behind the house while he was pulling the boat onto the dock.

She said, "Damn, Cody, you're going to hurt yourself."

She was a short, wiry woman, in her early thirties, a counselor at one of the county high schools. She wore jeans and a white T-shirt under a red lumberjack shirt, unbuttoned and tied at the waist. Her brown hair was bundled beneath a Duke Gardens baseball cap.

He gave a last pull. The boat came out of the water and onto the dock with a metal *clump*. His sister came to stand by his side. They gazed at the sandy bilge and the bulge of orange tent crammed in the bow.

He said, "No school today?"

She cocked her head. "There's no school on Sunday. I thought you might a got blown away. Looks like you about did."

Cody said, "The tent blew down right around me. I barely got my traps inside."

"Traps? What are traps?" She disapproved of his poaching—she was unaware that it had gone felony—but permitted it if undiscussed. Mainly, it wasn't dope. "I thought you were going to be out a few days. You get wrecked?"

"Pretty much. The boat blew right up on the sand."

"You probably didn't hear. Two helicopters crashed last night on the base."

He said quickly, automatically, "I didn't hear them."

She looked at him curiously. "I mean hear about them. Why? You weren't on the base, I hope."

"No."

"They were all killed. It might have been some of my kids' parents. I'm waiting to find out. What are you doing with the boat?"

"I'm going to clean it. I'm going to pull it back to the hose."

"The hose will reach the dock."

"I know, but I'm wanting shade. I'm fixing to work on this boat, Charlene. I'm fixing to paint it."

"You're going to paint my boat?"

"I'm going to paint it and sell it."

She smiled and punched his shoulder. "You're in a nice mood for getting wrecked."

"Yes, I am. This day I have turned the leaf, Charlene. For some god-damn reason, I have, and I believe it."

He did believe it, in a way. As he drove the boat up the inlet toward his sister's dock, a massive fear knot had tightened in his chest. Somehow they would track him. They would be ferocious in pursuit. They would comb the campsite. Satellite cameras might have followed him. They would ask fishermen, people in the shore houses. They would find him, detain him, and put him in a room. They would stalk and loom. They would slam the table. They would glare and shout. And then, as he imagined it, as he felt their hatred flash around him, he began to relax. Something in him rose and became calm and calmly withstood. Their hatred was a test and initiation. And he thought, maybe in the back of my mind that's why I took the missiles, to draw down a big chunk of purpose and stand inside it and let the world fall away harmless. It *was* fate, in a sense, that had selected him to find that launcher, that had plunked it down in front of Cody Cooper, of all people, who could recognize it, whose life had gone bad from childhood violence and war and drugs and thousands of wasted days, and who had now wakened in an unexpected and exalted way. He had come into possession of a Stinger system, and the entire United States military and police would rise in fury to seek him. He was in the eye of a hurricane and felt its strange, wild calm.

So what to do? Keep the missiles for a week, then return them. Leave them somewhere, send a note. Except how to reach the island again? There would be searchers. Sell the missiles. Which was how to get caught. How would you sell a Stinger missile anyway? Put an ad on the dark web, STINGER FOR SALE, NORTH CAROLINA? You would probably get inquiries. It was bad thinking. He could contact the base today. Not by phone, even public phone, because of all the cameras these days, so email through a tor client, which he had used during his weed-selling days. Except after Silk Road went down in an international bust, there were rumors that the NSA or CIA or both were buying tor exit nodes in Romania and Bulgaria and the *stan* countries to track the Russians and ISIS, and were now able to follow server bounces, whatever the fuck that meant, and, main thing, the dark web was maybe not so dark anymore.

Then just leave them buried. Hide the boat in the garage. If they got him in a room, be calm and strong. He could sit unmoved while they uselessly frenzied. He could be reborn in their hatred. Let that happen if it was happening.

His sister said, "Cody, if you have turned the leaf, I am so happy. I don't believe it for a minute, but in case it's true, here's a congratulations hug from your sister." She embraced him, laying her brow against his chest. She said, "You smell like marijuana, so this leaf turning must be recent."

He returned her embrace, then held her at arm's length and smiled down. He said, "Do you have to give up grass when you turn the leaf?"

"Yes, you do."

"Reach into my jacket."

She patted his jacket pockets with both hands, then twisted a hand into one of them. She drew out a baggie of grass and thrust it under her tied shirt. "Is this the one you sprayed with nicotine?"

He said, "You know what I thought at first? I thought that nicotine had made me …" He stopped. He had started to tell her that he thought the nicotine made him hallucinate, then realized that led to witnessing a trailer fall from one of the helicopters, then realized that he could have casually told her about that and about the missiles, just talking on the dock, making conversation, and suddenly the bright confidence he had felt a moment ago was replaced with terror.

She said, "What? Did you just see a ghost?"

He tried to shake his head but was only able to jerk it a little. He was enclosed in terror. He shut his eyes and said, "Fuck, fuck, fuck."

She slipped an arm around him and drew herself into him. She said, "Honey, don't fret. Don't do it. You know what? I'm going to make us breakfast. I'm going to make us bacon and eggs, and I got these great croissants at the store. And no, it's not Dad's bacon. C'mon inside with me. You just went white. C'mon inside." She gently pushed, but he was rigid.

He said, "The boat …"

"You really want to paint it?"

"Why not?" Cody saw her startle and realized his voice was too loud. He made his voice normal and said, word by word, "You go up, and I will come after I unload the boat."

She briefly tightened her arm around his waist and released him. "Okay, honey. Give me ten minutes."

She crossed the dock, glancing back once with a cheery worried smile, and went up the stone walk to the house. He was in robot mode now. He had been this way before in his homeless period, where life is dark, and each dark force means to starve, infect, or rob you, and you have to ox forward and not flinch.

He unscrewed the motor mounts, detached the gas line, hoisted the motor onto the dock, then heaved the five-gallon gas can beside it. He carried the motor and can, one in each hand, back to the detached garage, lifted them over his head, and slid them onto a piece of plywood in the rafters. At the dock, he laid the bow rope over a shoulder and trudged the boat up the path, through an ivy-covered trellis, and left it beside the coil of hose. Now he had the scrambled tent to deal with. And he had to get the traps out of the pillowcases and cover their roots with wet paper towels for transport. His passion for the flytrap business had withered to a chore. Terror had faded, but confidence was gone too. He was a bundle of sticks now, moved by invisible strings.

It was possible he would live the rest of his life in prison.

SPONGING IN THE YURT

He said, "You know why I'm a cop?"

Mia perked her eyebrows, which meant, you think I'm already interested? Or it meant, how did you know I'm already interested?

They were sitting on the outside dock section of the Inlet Café, formerly Frank's Seafood Collective, where the shrimpers, crabbers, and netters had off-loaded only a few years ago, before the fishing went bad from imports and a souring inlet. The fishermen, many elderly and without boats now, continued to collect in the mornings around an inside corner table.

She was tall, only a hand's width shorter than his six-two, and wore her auburn hair in a ponytail with a front ruff to cover her broad brow. Her nose was generous and straight, her mouth expressive, her cheekbones high and precise. It was an attractive, intelligent, patient face and why he was here.

The rising sun was still low over the inlet marshes, haloing her hair, and in the shade of the umbrella her expression was, I know what this is, this start and trial, and I'm comfortable, so be comfortable. They drank coffee, both declining something to nibble. After she had sketched about her family in Ohio—her older brother, her amiable divorce—he had sketched too—his mother a music teacher, currently guiding a group of retirees around Italy, his perished father, his New York librarian sister, then a skim of his three deployments, his divorce, his new career with the sheriff.

Then: "You know why I'm a cop?"

"Why?"

"Damn, I hoped you could tell me."

They smiled.

He said, "I majored in criminal law at State."

"But why?"

"I took an elective when I was a sophomore. And also I had been a cop in the Marines. And I thought, hey, that could be a job."

"What was your major before?"

He looked briefly into her eyes, showing her he valued the question. "Kind of a mix, but a lot of music courses. In college I was in a band."

"What kind of music did you play?"

"Well, when I had my own band, it was music that you could get your voice into. Creedence, the Stones, Springsteen. And Dylan. We were a cover band and played for money. Lounges and weddings."

She nodded.

He said, "You're thinking, does this guy write songs? Is he a creative man?"

She smiled. "He reads minds, at least."

"I do write songs. And one day, if there is another day for us, I will play one for you. On my trusty Gibson."

"I bet you miss it."

"Well, I still sing. I'm director of the Pass the Salt singers."

"Oh, my. That was you. I heard you sing 'Danny Boy' at the high school. I was too far away to really see you. I actually cried. That was lovely."

"That was a good night for me. I just happened to be in voice, and I … I was …"

"You were feeling emotional?"

"I was."

"Anything in particular?"

He saw she was prying. He was glad. He said, "Nothing in particular, just feeling deep. So then, in good voice, feeling deep, and 'Danny Boy.' All good."

"That's a nice way of saying that. Do you ever cry when you sing?"

"The eyes may wet, but the throat must ignore. But we don't discourage tears. Just the opposite."

Her head lifted a fraction as this settled. She said, "I read the handout. So everyone in the group has PTSD?"

"Yes, they do. Me too, so no sudden moves."

They smiled again.

He said, "I can talk about it. I don't mind. So, sometime. But I was always into singing. My mother's a singer. After I left the service and went back to school, besides singing in the band, I started to sing by myself again. But only songs with feeling. That's what we sing in Pass the Salt. To slow down the savage energy. The Mongol warriors, after they got home, the women would take them into a yurt and sponge them down. Talk softly to them. I bet they sang to them."

"Good God, I just feel like crying myself."

He saw she wanted to touch him but was shy. He reached and lightly touched the back of her hand with one finger.

She puffed a sigh. There was a pause while she considered. In the end, she changed the subject. She said, "And now you're a detective."

"Right."

"You must have made detective fast."

"You are entering a sensitive area."

"Really?"

"Some think I should have undergone a longer stretch in patrol. My old commander hired me. Sheriff Rhodes."

"But you passed the test."

"A rigorous test which only the few may pass." This landed flat. Jokes about ego were still ego. He said, "Forget I said that."

"I'm sure it's true. Are you going to catch my burglar?"

"I have my eye on a nest of criminals. They have to make a mistake."

"Really? We have a nest of criminals in Swann County?"

"More than one. They work odd jobs, then do crime when they get lazy. Or too strung out."

"Meth?"

"And heroin. And pills."

"The opioid epidemic."

"Yes."

"So what mistake will they make?"

"They will pawn your pots or your scale."

"I bet they can use the scale."

"They probably already have one, which is why they took yours, because they recognized it."

"So wait."

"The alternative is to handcuff somebody to a tree for three days. They'll pawn something eventually. They'll say, damn, where'd all these pretty pots come from? I bet we could pawn them. Then I will arrest them, put them in the system, and effect reform."

She made a smile and head cock. "Are you a cynic?"

"I am in my head. But not in my heart."

"An optimistic cynic?"

"That's right. You know something?"

"What?"

He had been relishing the quiet steadiness of her mind and wide green eyes. He urged to tell her and also not to. But he had started. He said, "You are good company."

"Really?"

"So far."

"Oh, no. Now I have to live up to myself."

If they were a month into their friendship, he would have leaned to kiss her. She might evaporate though. Nothing true was rushed. He said, "So how did you become a potter?"

Also because of a stray college course, she said. She had been an English major for the love of books, but fear of the cold world after graduation built, and she loved pottery next and sensed money, so it became her minor, then her life.

He said, "I love your pots. First time I saw them was in Greenville at a craft fair. Then when Charlene took your class, I met you again. I looked you up on the web and saw all your awards."

"Oh, yes. I must list them for all to see. Did you see me at the craft fair?"

"I bought four mugs from you. And when your burglary came in, I asked for the case. Had to bump another detective."

"You rascal. But if you really cared, you'd tie someone to a tree."

"If it'll move things along, I will."

They smiled, settling into it.

He said, "I like your pots. Lots of grace, mostly white, little marks of color to set off the space."

She raised her eyebrows in appreciation. "Well, thanks."

There was a pause, while both waited for a topic. She said, "The radio said there was a suspicious death last night," then made a chuckley I'm-so-trite grimace, which, since that was her news, told him, first, that she didn't disdain cops and, second, that she hadn't heard about the helicopter crash. He had been uncomfortably aware that they were courting in the wake of a tragedy. That she did not know about it was an easement. That he had not mentioned it was an omission.

He said, "There was. Leo Sackler. The one who inherited the Ford place."

"Oh, my God. I guess I wasn't paying attention. Was he murdered?"

"I don't know yet. Probably."

"Is his daughter Virginia?"

"She is."

"I know her. She took a class with me."

"When was this?"

"Two years ago about. Are you the detective on the case?"

"Yes. I spent all night on the scene."

"Then you had to come and meet me. You should have just called."

"I slept a little in my car."

"They said he was found hanging in a well."

"He was, yes."

"So that's what you do."

"I'm afraid it is." He could tell the sandman riff now. But she was thinking about dead bodies, and horror. He said, "That part's over, the death scene. It *is* awful. We don't crack jokes. Much. Every time I see a dead body, I think, well, they didn't expect that. Then there's some guilt. I get to keep living." He could tell her that he had died, that you don't die, that nobody dies. She would be a perfect person to tell.

"That's so true."

"It can quiet you down. And I do let it."

They exchanged smiles. The war could come back up, but neither invited it.

She said, "I bet it makes you want to sing 'Danny Boy' sometimes."

He would think back on that comment, on her quiet empathy for this stranger, and know that was when need started toward love. He smiled. He said, "I sang 'The Parting Glass' this morning. Do you know it?"

"No. I'm sure it's lovely." She frowned an unspoken question.

"They had taken the body away. I was alone in the house."

The waitress filled their coffees again, the third time.

Mia said, "We'll have to stop talking and pee eventually."

It was going well. That was in the air. They could be a couple.

She said, "Why the name Pass the Salt, by the way?"

"Well, we needed a name, and everybody was coming up with stuff. We got it down to Pass the Soul, Dude. Then Ahmad, who is our hip-hop enthusiast, said, no, man, Pass the Salt, Dawg. And we all said, damn, that's it. Except we shortened it."

"From hip-hop to 'Danny Boy' is quite a journey."

"It is for Ahmad. He's always bugging me to develop some rap stuff. He got shot in the throat. He can hum in tune, but his voice is fairly raspy. But we like good hummers. We take everybody."

The mention of injury paused the conversation. In a moment, she said, "Your group was very enjoyable."

"Good. Good. We work at it. It's important to us."

She reached across to touch his hand, as he had touched hers, with one finger. She said, "I won't ask you about the war. And how you healed. Or thank you for your service or something, which I think must sound awful on some level. Kind of a box people tick off when they meet a soldier. We should have yurts and sponges."

A joy laugh erupted from his chest. He laced the fingers of her hand, the one that had touched him, through his and held it between them, eye level, palm to palm. Then he laid the hand on the table, patted it to rest with two hands, and sat more erect. He was chagrined but careless. He wanted to lean forward, toward love, but refrained. He smiled. He said, "Do you sing, by the way?"

"Yes, I do. I can even harmonize."

He almost said, *I see you can*, but then was glad he didn't. Nothing true was rushed.

A LEAF AS BIG
AS THE MOON

He told his sister he had turned the leaf, so at breakfast she was revved. She threw in a smirk now and then to prove she wasn't a pushover, but Cody could see that was just her tapping the brake on hope. It touched him and also wore him out.

First she went on about yoga. There was a yoga class starting up in a week at the Y. It was the stretching style of yoga, not the contortion style, and there was some kind of special breathing to it. One of her PTSD books had a chapter on yoga. Many had benefited from its ancient benefits.

Then she mentioned the Pass the Salt singers. So what if Seb Creek sent him to prison and broke her heart. He was a good guy, and the singers were always recruiting, and they were doing great important work, everybody said so. She hadn't heard Cody sing for years and remembered him singing with their mom when he was little. They sang "Down in the Valley" and "Silent Night" so sweetly, did he recall that? A lot of the guys in Pass the Salt had been druggies or drunks, according to Seb, who always asked about Cody. And yes, Dad has joined the group, and here was her insight into that—you don't have to forgive him or anything, but just to stand up in a group and be indifferent to him would be therapy. Think about that. Standing there and singing, giving yourself to singing, which is giving yourself back to life right there in the midst of the oppressive force of Dad, who by the way, told me not a week ago he is willing to forgive and forget. Doesn't that sound like him, him thinking *he's* got to forgive? He said he knows you hate him and doesn't blame you, so that's something. But, Cody, if you just hold those beatings in with hateful resentment and on top of that have PTSD and drug addiction, we know where that leads.

She made another smirk, a loving one. "I do not know if you have turned the leaf, sweetie. I wish I could get inside your heart and turn that leaf for you. I would heave that sucker right over, if it was big as the moon."

He cut himself another nugget of scrambled eggs and scraped it onto his plate. Her energetic supplication had ended by forming a kind of invisible lap in the room, a love-lap which yearned and expected. He felt it as a burden. He must say something undisappointing. He said, "Well. I hear you. I hear that." He forked eggs into his mouth. He nodded his head.

She said, "Boy, I have fixed you up, haven't I? You have to admit, your big sister has just fixed your life."

This was gay irony meant to let him off the hook. It went straight to his heart. A sob exploded, then a covering laugh. He sat bewildered.

She took her plate to the sink and stood for a moment watching the water erode the syrup into the drain. She said to the cupboards, to the world, "We will get this fixed, Cody. There is no doubt of that."

Cody nodded. She had always been his ally. After their mother's death when he was eight and she was twelve, she had comforted him. When the beatings began, she had comforted him. She meant him well. Her plans were good.

Except that he had stolen three Stinger missiles. Except that the hounds of justice would soon be snarling at the door.

SHINING MAN

On the way to Amboise, Seb spoke to Lieutenant Fernando on the phone. Virginia Rubins, née Sackler, had not wept during the death notification, Fernando said, and that morning had gone to work as usual at the Amboise town hall. It was Sunday, but the entire staff had reported to help with scanning the backlog of old files into the town's new database.

Now, as Seb sat across from her over the gray government table in the documents room, he noted the skin beneath her eyes was smooth with cosmetics, either her custom or something to hide rings of sleeplessness. All through Seb's report of her father's end, she maintained a *po*lice-in-my-face stiffness. Her attitude might come from, *one*, I did it, and I best be careful, or *two*, they think I did it, and I best be careful. Either way, *po*lice, we keeping formal. Fernando, since there were only two chairs, stood behind him in a military at-ease posture, which didn't help the mood.

Now Seb swiveled in his chair to halfway face Fernando, gave him a doubtful glance. He looked at Virginia and said, "This guy looks like he's about to arrest us."

That keyed the smirk from Virginia he wanted. He said to Fernando, "I got this, Jose. Give us an hour, say." Then to Virginia, "Jose will give you a ride to make the identification, Ms. Rubins."

Fernando touched his cap and said, "Again, Ms. Rubins, very sorry for your loss." He gave Seb a light shoulder punch and said, "See you tonight, dawg." He strode smoothly to the door, opened it, and closed it silently behind him.

Seb faced Virginia. He said, "If there was an all-round walking contest, that guy would win hands down. His father was a bullfighter, so I bet he got that walk from him." This was not true, at least as far as Seb knew. The true thing was: establish rapport, get information, investigate the murder. Or whatever it was.

Virginia gave him a half smile, which said, charm away but don't expect applause. She was in her midforties with a chunk of straight black hair side-swept and sprayed in place. She wore a blue dress and light-yellow sweater against the building's air-conditioning. She was thin. She kept her hands laced and folded on the table, like a needful dam, either to hold the world out or her feelings in, which could burst through any time, right in front of this white man and embarrass her. Seb and Fernando had escorted her from the front receptionist's desk to the document room, seated her, and Seb had softly repeated the sad, ambiguous tale of her father's death, watching for signs. The only sign was: her mouth opened and her face set. Seb had checked records and made calls on the way to the interview and knew she had worked for the city of Amboise for sixteen years, had three children—two in grade school and one a high school freshman—had been separated from her husband for nine years, and had a younger brother in prison. He also knew she was only two years old when her dad went inside. So maybe she had finished her grieving. Or maybe it was ordinary black-citizen wariness. Or maybe she was a murderer. Except she couldn't have hung him by herself.

"Ms. Rubins, you okay to talk? I'm trying to get a handle on this thing."

"I'm okay. You can call me Virginia."

"Okay. I'm Seb. The truth is I cannot tell if your father was killed in an accident, or if he was murdered, because of the way he was found. We're pretty sure it's not suicide anyway."

Virginia nodded, waited.

"And frankly, there are indications at the scene which push me to think of murder. So if it was murder …"

"I expect you thinking who gets the money?"

"That's a consideration."

"I do, I expect. And my brother."

"Have you seen your father's will?"

"No. I doubt he had one. Mr. Person would know. My father had very little experience of life as you and I lead it." Her head shook as if overtaken with a spasm. Her face worked. She said, "Don't worry. I will do my crying in my own home."

Seb let a moment pass. He said, "Had you been in contact with him since his release?"

"I picked him up at the prison. He stayed with me a few nights, and I took him shopping. Took him to his lawyer, Mr. Person. And the bank. Then I took him out to the lodge."

"Is that Alex Person, the lawyer?"

"It is. He does work for Miss Jean here in Amboise. I gave my father his name. If you want to talk to him, he's in his office over in Spartanville. He and my boss Miss Jean talking back and forth on these records." She hesitated, then continued guardedly. "I have not spoken to him."

"What did your father do at the bank?"

"No idea. He told me to come get him in an hour."

"What happened at the lawyer's?"

"I guess they discussed things. He came out with a folder of papers. And the keys to the lodge."

"What papers?"

"He didn't say. And gave off the idea that was his business. You got to consider my father lived in prison and was about a stranger to me. And I know he felt that too. We didn't want to, but we had that to get over."

"Do you know how much money is involved here?"

"Not exactly. Near five million though. I picked that much up. More with the stocks and that."

"Why was he digging out the well?"

"He didn't tell me. I didn't know about that until yesterday morning."

"He had it dug down fifteen feet. Had you been out to the lodge?"

"Last week Friday, but I didn't see any well."

"It was around the side."

She paused, thought, decided something.

"Okay now, I'm going to tell you something. He said there was a man out to see him yesterday morning. He couldn't see him for the sun because he was down in that well. I was fixing to tell you except you'd think I was making it up, since you're suspecting me."

Seb gave her a truth look. "I'm pretty much not suspecting you. Tell me about the man."

"A man come to see him wanted a thousand dollars a month for security."

"Extortion?"

"Most definite. I don't know what he looked like and neither did my father because the man was in the sun."

"You weren't going to tell me about this?"

"I was looking for a spot."

"This is the spot."

"And I just did. He was a white man, up in the sun."

"How tall? Or if he had a hat? Or an accent?"

"No idea."

"What was your father going to do?"

"He was thinking about paying the man. It was twelve thousand a year, and he could live with that, if it bought security. He didn't know that neighborhood anymore." She paused, pouted her lips. "I was going to tell the lieutenant last night, but I was scared to."

"That we would think you were deflecting?"

"Yes."

"Well, I don't think that. It's a good lead."

"You know who it was?"

"I might. Now then, can you talk to me about the past? About why he went to jail?"

"You just a blank on the history?"

"I skimmed a few articles in the newspaper, but pretty much."

She said, "I wish I still smoked cigarettes. Either a shot of whiskey right about now."

"You want to go get one?"

"No. Miss Jean would think you were arresting me." She took a long breath. "My daddy was the son of Granger and Semolina Sackler, both dead now and with the Lord, most definite." Her face worked. She waited, then went on. "Now, Granger was an oysterman, and he took Semolina off her daddy's tobacco farm. One of my intentions is to have my DNA tested and see about our family. I do so want to know. And I will one day, no doubt." Her mood had softened with memory. Seb nodded and waited. The information door was opening.

She said, "Then here comes Mr. Marshall Britt down to North Carolina from New York wanting to buy land to treat his banker friends to hunting and fishing. This is just after the war, I think 1945. And he hired my grandfather, Granger Sackler, to be his overseer and guide. And he built that beautiful lodge. He was coming and going for ten years or so, but after that he brought his wife and son and moved down. You've seen that lodge."

"I have."

"His wife was Virginia. I'm named for her. The poor woman fell off a horse and died in a day. Marshall Britt was brokenhearted, and who became his friend? Granger Sackler did. My grandfather was not afraid of white men, even back then. Mr. Britt's black employee had feeling for him, and when that starts up everything goes out the window. Black and white go out the window. That's the way we tell it on our side. A year later Marshall asked my grandfather to move into the lodge, not into a slave house beside the lodge, but in the lodge, which he did do, with Semolina, and Leo, my father, who was fourteen years old, and my aunt, Carrie. So you got that picture? Black family packed up out of their little shack house and moved in with a rich white man. Drawing down a nice salary to be keeper. This was about 1960, just before civil rights time. Before she died, Marshall was building Virginia a new house two miles up the Sable. He went on and finished it, and he and his son, Hugh, moved there, but they lived with my family a full year. In that lodge."

Virginia gave Seb a sardonic look. "I'm getting to that murder. I believe that's on your mind."

"I'm waiting and listening."

"You're not writing it though."

"I can remember stories."

She arched her brows. "You may have a tad bit of sense. So Marshall had a will, and then he rewrote that will and gave it to his lawyer, Mr. Bentley Branch, to file it for him. That's because he got cancer and was looking ahead. And he told my grandfather what he wrote, and what it was, he gave my family twenty acres and that lodge. Right on Council Creek. He had a surveyor mark it off. Then Mr. Marshall took his boat out to sea, and when they found the boat it was empty. So that's how he ended himself. He was a prize man. So my grandfather tells Hugh, is my deed coming? And Hugh says, just wait, the estate is settling. A year later the sheriff shows up to the lodge with a paper that says the Sacklers have five days to vacate because the lodge and the twenty acres have been sold to the Ford family of New York City. That was because Mr. Bentley Branch did not file that will. That will was never filed. Marshall had cancer, and I believe Bentley Branch knew where his bread was buttered and that was with Hugh, the heir apparent, who did not contemplate niggers on his land. Even ones he grew up knowing. And that his father loved. That right there may have been the trouble. Just natural, mean-spirited jealousy."

Virginia sat straighter. Her head waved slightly. She said, "That is the black side. Now you must talk to the Branch family, and they will tell you the white side. There was no new will, just a tricky black family making trouble. There was nothing even to contest in court, so my grandfather took his family back to the shack side of Spartanville, which is the black side of Spartanville. They went back to oystering, built them a clam dredge, had a good business, did well, moved everybody down to the Sable in a nice house. I was born there, and my grandfather would show me the lodge from the water, where he lived three years of his life. My daddy and my mother, June, built them a house next to my grandparents. Those were nice days, there on the water. But my father had a sour heart, there is no doubt, and when a chance came he took it. What it was, Hugh had started up a fish house, buying shrimp and oysters and fish, and had him a freezer truck and was hauling up to New York City. My father and grandfather did not sell to him, but their friends did, and they were telling that Hugh was cheating the scales for the black fishermen. They weighed light, not every time, but enough, and word was passing. So my daddy says, let's see about that, and shows up with a skiff full of flounder. And when they weighed in, he searched the scale and finds a couple of magnets tucked underneath. A scuffle breaks out with the scale man, and Hugh comes down from the house and grabs a gaff and puts it into my daddy's arm and hauls him around the dock and throws him into his skiff. Hugh Britt was a large and violent man. This is documented fact and witnessed by various ones, black and white, on the dock that day and written in the newspapers. So then my daddy comes back at night when the boathouse is dark to get that scale and have his proof. And, if you're a white man on the all-white jury, he kills Hugh Britt with an axe, from the front, with his right arm gaffed clean through. Or if you're a black man, he finds him dead. But he walks in blood and leaves footprints and case closed."

Seb said, "What do you think happened?"

"You ask me three months ago, before Germaine Ford's will come out, I'd say I cannot conclude. I told my daddy that whenever I visited, I don't know if you did it, but I love you. I guess I thought he did it, and you know why? Because it was easier than thinking he was in prison on a lie. But I no longer think so because of Germaine Ford's will. Something behind that, and you know the whole county thinks so. Maybe you the one appointed to find out."

"I might be."

"Why you looking so scruffy? You look scruffy for a police."

"I sometimes get loaned to other counties to make drug buys."

"Oh, you do? That's a shame. Busting black children trying to escape the only way they know."

"I agree with that."

"Then you need to clean up."

"Except it's a good look for me, don't you think?"

They half-smiled together.

Seb said, "If Leo didn't kill Hugh, who did?"

"Well, think on it now. The governor lets my daddy loose of jail, and Germaine Ford gives him back her farm where he grew up. And Germaine living there all by herself for fifty years, never married. Don't you think that's a hint in there somewhere? You ever see a picture of Germaine? She was a beauty. Blond hair and slim. She was twenty years old when the Fords moved down, and Hugh was twenty-six. Why'd she give her farm to a convict in prison? Some say, well, she was making up for the treachery of Hugh Britt about the will, and it was her family kicked out a poor black family. No, no. The Fords didn't have nothing to do with that except move in."

"You suspect her?"

"If you don't, you're not thinking."

"Your dad ever say anything to you, when he got out or over the years?"

"He told me what he told that reporter, that God grinds fine."

"What was his plan for the future? Did he have one?"

"Everybody could move in with him. I told him, let everybody get to know him first. His grandkids don't know him, except he's a jailbird. Marshall does not know him."

"You have relatives gathering, smelling money?"

"Aunt Carrie's gone, and she didn't have kids. Some of my friends have called, but I don't talk money with nobody."

"I might come back later for a list of those friends."

"And I might not give it to you. Why would one of my friends kill my father?"

"I don't know. Maybe the money would be easier to get out of you than him."

"You will not get a list from me."

"Your dad bought a lot of stuff when you took him shopping. Where'd you go, Sears?"

"Sears and the farm store. And Lowe's for tools and a bunch of planters. He didn't have no patience to dig a garden and wanted to get growing. Except he started on that well, I guess. Didn't even mow the lawn."

"Where'd you get the desk?"

"He didn't buy the desk. That desk was the only thing left in the house after the estate sale. It was in the bedroom."

Virginia's head dropped, and she stared at her hands. She unlaced and flexed her fingers, then laid her hands in her lap. She raised her head and offered Seb an appraising look. "It has just occurred to me that I am a wealthy woman now. If I don't get arrested. I could have that whiskey right now if I wanted, and Miss Jean could go fish."

Seb raised his eyebrows, an offer.

"I don't want one." She covered her face with her hands and emitted a trembling sigh. She looked at Seb. She said, "Be a good detective in this. You can't right these wrongs, but you can show them to the people."

"I will." After a moment, he said, "Tell me about your mother. I believe she's living over in Duplin County."

"She is. After about four years, she married my stepfather, who raised me and my brother. A man she never loved, but she sealed off my father and kept with my stepfather, who is gone now three years."

"Did your father contact her when he got out?"

"No."

"So they had no contact for all those years?"

"It was one way. He wrote her letters every month for forty-eight years. Can you understand that?"

"I know men in prison do all kinds of things to hope."

"It wasn't even hope. Just like a thread, so he wouldn't fly off into space."

"Did your mother believe in your father's innocence?"

"She did when I was little. When I grew up, it came out she didn't."

"Why?"

"Not based on a fact she knew, or anything he told her. It was the same as me. Better than thinking he's in prison by mistake. She didn't even open his letters anymore. She just put them in the precious box at the top of the closet. That'd be a book of letters by now."

That struck a memory bell somewhere. "A precious box?"

"One of those tobacco boxes. Black folks used to keep their papers in them. Look like they were made for papers. My grandfather had one."

"Has PB on it. For Phineas Brothers. I found one in the stable at the lodge."

"You don't mean it."

"There was a hiding place under the floorboards."

Virginia smiled, flushed with delight. "That was my grandfather's box. I don't know how many times he mentioned it to me. It had a few pictures my grandmother took and some newspaper articles when my father played high school basketball. And money. But he took the money. He left the box on purpose. He said one day we might come get it. And look at here. That day has come, most tragically. I do want that box. Be sure now."

"Someone had dug it out of the floorboards. Did your father know where it was?"

"Sure he did. That's the first thing he would have done is get up that precious box. What was in it?"

"It was empty."

"Well, look in the house."

"I looked. No photos, no newspaper articles."

"Well, then, he moved them. Look in the bank."

"I called the bank. He doesn't have a box there."

Their eyes met for a moment. She said, "Somebody else got into that box then. And no, I do not have them."

Seb drew the photo from his inside jacket pocket and handed it to Virginia. "Don't remove it from the plastic. I found that in the stable. Is that your grandfather?"

"That is Granger Sackler and his son, Leo. Keep care of this now. I want that."

"I will." He took the photo back. "I'd like to hear about your brother."

"I wondered when we'd come to Marshall."

"You were both named for Marshall and Virginia Britt. But you were born after Hugh evicted you."

"So why didn't we hate every Britt there was? See this man right here." She tapped the photo. "We loved what our grandfather loved, and he loved Marshall and Virginia Britt, no matter about their son. Some people have love in them as a natural knack. That's what attracted Marshall Britt. My grandfather was a shining man." Her face worked, and finally, after her capable session of composure and history, her dignity lost its footing, and sorrow broke free. She lowered her head and sobbed. Seb waited, feeling for her, but without rights. After a moment, she lifted her head and palmed tears from her face. Her makeup smeared, exposing rings of purple skin. She said, "All this came because of love, when you think about it. The preachers get that much right. Love and hate must fight it out. Now then. My brother went to prison because he was caught with all that marijuana in that boat and would not tell on his friends, so they took it federal and locked him up for eight years. So he did six years for his friends. If you think a man like that would hire someone to kill his father for money, you best think again."

"He's scheduled for release in three months."

"Will the prison notify him about all this?"

"I can set up a call for you."

"Kind thanks."

"Now I have to ask you about your husband."

"Raymond Charles is back in Chicago and probably dead. His mother don't even know where he is."

"He became addicted to crack?"

"That and other women."

"I couldn't see where you ever got divorced."

"Oh, lord. So you thinking he snuck down here and murdered my father and is planning to show up with his hand out. I expect that would take more sense than he's got left. Last year, his mother told me he weighed just above a hundred pounds."

"I've seen some of that."

"He destroyed himself, poor man." She paused, then added, "I see now I best get myself divorced, in case."

Seb fished a card from his jacket pocket. He said, "Would you be kind enough to email me his mother's address and phone number?"

She took the card, held it between two fingers, and cocked it toward him. She said, "Bark up that tree if you want, but you'll come home to Germaine."

THE HURRICANE
GAUNTLET

In the trailer, Cody dropped the four pillowcases of flytraps on the counter, then noticed a plastic basket of clean, folded clothes on his TV chair: selfless service from his sister. He and Charlene had a deal—she could enter the trailer for laundry but couldn't clean up since that made things hard to find and also incentivized her bitching about disorder. The trailer had become a chaos of glasses, beer cans, whiskey bottles, opened and unopened mail, TV dinner cartons, books, a variety of food-crusted kitchen implements, newspapers and magazines, miscellaneous tools, plus a scatter of screws and bolts from appliances he had dissected. And also some of the appliance carcasses themselves—two radios, two blenders, a microwave oven, and a telescope. In Coopertown, where he lived for a while after prison, working his dad's hogs, Cody was known as the go-to tinkerer.

He cleared the table of dishes and cans, removed the flytraps from the pillowcases, laid them in neat rows on wet paper towels, then gently rolled them into columns. When money was at stake, he could be neat and careful, neatness that would have impressed even Charlene, if she wasn't so anticrime. When Cody learned in Coopertown that flytraps had a nice price, he saw opportunity, and also safety, since flytrap poaching was then only a misdemeanor. His first market was nurseries. If you brought the traps in after hours, they were happy to buy, even after North Carolina upped the poaching penalty from misdemeanor to a class H felony. Hey, the guy swore he was growing them. Then he searched the web and learned that flytrap extract was being used in a new age cancer cure. He made calls, repping himself as the owner of a North Carolina nursery—did they want purebred, natural-grown flytraps from the wetlands of North Carolina, the single place on earth where they grew naturally? They did and paid five times what the nurseries did. He had so far delivered five thousand-trap bundles to two guys in a hotel parking lot. Money was miracle stuff and meant being warm and fed and having things, like a beer when you wanted one, or a TV and the internet, or spending the evening in one of Gleen's scented hot tubs, see if Keisha was around and would join him.

He got busted once, early on, with a couple hundred traps in a backpack, but that was before poaching went felony. He paid the fine but had the record. Eventually, when they discovered the dug-up water tower pods, they would knock on his door.

His cell phone rang in his front pocket.

"Hello."

"Cody, my little man." It was Elton Gleen, starting him off with *little man*, tucking him into his slot. With Elton that was good. It was a safe slot, beside the fire but not burning.

"What say, Elton?"

"I been missing you, little man. Had a job for you too, but it fell on through."

"I'm not too much looking for work."

"Oh, I know you got your thing going. This was just a quick something, help me with a debt. But the man with the money did not cooperate."

"What's up, Elton?"

"I'm just thinking about you. I miss you. I live in the wilderness out here, full of ignorant forest creatures. Pedal your ass over here, and let's light one up."

"I turned the leaf on dope."

"You did? When?"

Cody hesitated, then made the truthful bad answer. "Today."

"Oh, lord. Well, at least come over and hot-tub. I just saw Keisha leave with her mom. She's not working today, and they'll be back. I need to hear an intelligent voice."

Cody hesitated again. Then because Elton could be the right company, the company to end with, if he was ending, he said, "Okay," and closed the call.

Elton Gleen had a soft spot for Cody, since Cody was the landlord's son and smart and also since Cody had gotten out from under, for a while at least, with entrepreneurial moves in the marijuana business and now fly-trapping. Elton owned the best trailer in Coopertown, a fancy double-wide with a front deck, and he kept it and his yard tidy and open for business. He had a double yard too, with four cast-iron bathtubs atop bricked-in gravel firepits and a tarp-covered stack of kindling. His yard was the gathering place for the hundred-odd Coopertown trailer park residents, and for nine bucks you could fill a tub, build a fire to heat the water, choose from an array of scents, and soak while you chatted with your buddies. You could roast hot dogs and marshmallows and, at night, you and your wife or girlfriend could get in and have sex while you soaked, right in front of everybody. If you didn't have a girlfriend, you could solicit one of the gals in trailer five, who, depending on the state of their finances, might oblige for a fee. You couldn't bring your own beer, but you could buy one from Elton's icy cooler. Also wine and whiskey. And some nights, irregular with the employment or larceny of the trailer park denizens and friends, you could join a poker game in the double wide. Now and then the landlord, Squint Cooper, and his business cronies showed up to play table stakes, which cleared the trailer of Coopertowners, except for Elton Gleen, who had won poker tournaments and flew to Las Vegas twice a year, and who won large and lost small.

The trailer park was out of the Spartanville city limits, so the local tavern owners made their complaints to the sheriff, who was interested because Elton also dealt drugs. When the sheriff sent deputies and detectives to interview the residents, they said, booze, whores, gambling, what are you talking about? Then Harvey Clement, veteran outlaw and resident of trailer twenty-three, was busted for bad checks, wired up, and sent back to Coopertown. He vanished, and so far the sheriff had no further volunteers.

When Harvey disappeared, Cody was just out of prison and working for Elton, clearing ash, cleaning tubs, and weed-eating. He believed that Elton had murdered him. A new rug materialized in Elton's double wide when Harvey went missing, a blood-hiding rug, thought Cody, and images of throat slitting and body hauling assailed him for days. He had worked the hogs with Harvey, drugged with him, had even participated in a small orgy with him. He was a good-natured guy and could laugh about his small penis. Harvey told him about Elton's other business, sending couriers to the Texas border to pick up bales of heroin, a run which Harvey himself had made three times.

Now, back from his homeless stretch, Cody still rode his bike to Coopertown every few days to see his girlfriend, Keisha, and also to schmooze with the guys and gals, drawn by dark urges. Coopertown was like hanging with a black guy, is what it was. Simple and no bullshit, down in the stream of easy gliding and what-you-want. Pills and booze and jokes, some just funny and some cruel to test the bottom, to true the brotherhood. When Cody got near Elton, with his dark good looks and big hands and tall strong body, he felt danger trembles. The trembles made him feel alive, no doubt. Like meth though, which strung you out.

He had finished wrapping and storing half the flytraps when he heard three fast fist-bumps against the metal door. He opened it to his father, Squint Cooper, in a blue T-shirt and denim jacket, a cigarette cocked out of the corner of his mouth.

Squint said, "Well, surprise." As he spoke, the cigarette danced like a miniature baton.

Cody had seen his father only once since he returned from his homeless period, on his birthday almost a year ago, at a restaurant dinner organized by Charlene. His father had brought him a tent, a peace offering and bad joke about homelessness. It had been an unpleasant dinner.

Cody said, "Hey, Dad." He waited.

"Let me come in."

"Nowhere to sit." Flytraps covered the kitchen table. He didn't want the bother of explaining, or justifying.

"Well, that's inhospitable. Come on out then." Squint removed his cigarette and boot-crushed it into the gravel. "Let's sit together and confer."

Under the trailer awning were two rusted metal chairs opposite a wooden two-person swing. The house and garage were visible through a screen of pines, and beyond, the small dock and strip of gray-green creek. Squint seated himself in a chair, producing an irritable metal squawk. Cody stepped onto the dirt, closed the door, and sat in the swing facing his father.

Cody said, "What's on your mind?"

"Remember I used to say, what's on your *alleged* mind when you were a kid?"

"Yes."

"Part of the household entertainment, which I am not sure you appreciated."

Cody waited, keeping his face expressionless.

Squint said, "Well, son, a couple of things. First, recall our last conversation, in which you accused me of being a poor father. I have come today to concede it, if I didn't then. Name a sin, and I will acknowledge it. That's my mood. But I make this critical point—childhood is not a factory. It's a fucking gauntlet. Your gauntlet was an asshole giant standing in the way of your nature, offering correction the only way I knew, which was whipping and keeping a short leash. I stand up to being a fool, if I was. But, Cody, you have to stand up to it's not a factory. You come *through* childhood, not *from* it. Trailing clouds of glory, as the poet says. Therefore! I accept blame for the gauntlet, but not the factory. Because it ain't a damn factory."

"Fair point."

"Fair point? Score one for the asshole! The second thing is what the fuck are you doing? You're still flytrapping, aren't you? Feel like lying, go ahead, but I saw that orange tent, the one I gave you for your birthday. I saw it on the internet, out on the base. It was you, wasn't it?"

Cody felt himself pale. He said, "What do you mean, you saw the tent?"

"You were on the base flytrapping. Am I correct? I can see I am. Start off a lie if you want, but there it is. Thing is, I want you to come back to the farm. I'm expanding, and I need help."

"Wait a minute. How did you see the tent?"

"In a video. There's a motherfucker flying drones over the farm looking for violations. And he puts it on the web. I lost fifty hogs the other day and here comes the drone. I showed it to Seb Creek last night, and I recognized that orange tent."

"You showed Seb Creek?" Cody's heart had begun to thud. He leaned forward to prop his elbows on his knees and stare between his feet at the peaceful crumbles of gravel.

"I'm trying to get the sheriff on the case, but he's not interested. They *are* interested in flytrappers though, and they catch you again you're going back to prison. I hope you know flytraps have gone to felony. Plus you were on the fucking base is my guess. They can bring that federal and flat fuck you up, son." He held up two hands, index fingers extended. He said, "So, there it is. One, I accept my gauntlet guilt. Two, I offer a job. Now then, you might want to go back to prison. Some do. You can eat free and read books. But, one day I'll die, and you and Charlene will have to figure what to do with the farm. Might as well get started. I'll put you on management and books, though you might have to work the hogs if I get shorthanded, which I might from time to time. But I'm thinking of some kind of overseer. What do you say?"

"What website?"

"Prince something. Prince video, I think. Don't worry, nobody looks at his fucking website except me. Okay, last thing is, Charlene called me. That's why I'm here. I'll admit it. She's got my arm up behind my back, as she can do. I have been instructed to invite you to the Pass the Salt singers. You might like it, you never know. Wouldn't hurt to get in with Seb Creek anyway, just in case."

"Why'd you show him the video?"

"I told you. To get the sheriff on this drone guy, Peter Prince. Now get off the fucking video. Nobody's going to see that video, and if they do they won't know it's Cody Cooper in the orange tent." He raised his long arms above his head and clasped his hands, stretching. "Christ. You ever get tired of it? I do."

Cody looked up from the gravel. He said, "Of what?"

"Oh, just the problem-solving. Just one problem after another. Everybody dies somewhere along the trail of their problems, and the problems win." He stood. "That's my pitch. So long, buddy." He walked a few steps down the path, then turned. He said, "Think you might come back to the farm?"

Cody lowered his head, then swiveled it to stare at his father. He said, "No. I'm never coming back."

Squint nodded. He said, "I admire that. But you're wasting hate, son. I'm just the hurricane that blew through your life. So-fucking-what. That's the nature of hurricanes. You got to get that much figured out before you're fit to live."

He watched his father stride down the walk, past the garage. He heard the pickup's engine rev, heard it fade.

He rose and went inside to his laptop. On Peter Prince's site, PrinceVideos.com, he found a recent post—HOGS DEAD AT COOPER FARMS. He started the video. It showed the Cooper Farms barns, then cut to the dead box, full of carcasses. It was less than a minute and did not show the swamp, the creeks, the tent, or any of the inlet. It had been edited then. But no doubt the entire video was somewhere, like a gun, hidden but cocked, pointed at his life.

He returned to the kitchen table and began wrapping the flytraps. He opened and closed his jaws, which had tightened and begun to ache in his father's presence. About hurricanes, his father had been right, but also wrong. You didn't have to hate hurricanes to avoid them. He finished the flytraps and deposited the neat bundles in the refrigerator on the flytrap shelf.

Then he sat down in his big TV chair and began to rock back and forth over his knees. There was a video.

A GAFF SCAR

Seb had gotten a text from Lieutenant Stinson moving the briefing to one. He had notes to write up before that, but on the way back to Spartanville, the do-list in his head got past five items, and he pulled into a QuickStop to make calls. He found the number for the federal prison in Kansas on his smartphone, called them, and, after some back-and-forth, a deputy administrator agreed to set up a call between Virginia and her brother.

Then, he found the number of the lawyer Alex Person, whom he vaguely knew from around the courthouse. Then he decided not to call. A visit would be better, since, who knew, Person could have killed the out-of-touch convict to conceal fraud.

His phone dinged with a text from Virginia. She had sent her mother-in-law's name and number, which was part of the do-list, so he called and had a brief conversation with a nasal-voiced elderly woman, who said she had not seen her son for some months and feared for his life, since he was a lost soul, and she was his rock of ages and raft on the stormy sea. And also there was a woman calling three times just this week wanting money owed to her by Raymond Charles and now owed by his mother, Ms. Rubins, so claimed the woman. Ms. Rubins took the position that debts did not transfer from a son to a mother, in any shape or form, and that was right, wasn't it? Seb said he thought so and left his number in case Raymond Charles showed up.

He considered calling the Chicago police, but that felt like busywork at this point, since Raymond Charles did not rank as much of a suspect, down somewhere on the list with brother Marshall hiring a hit man.

Seb swung himself into the passenger seat, opened his laptop, and began to read the articles he had saved that morning from the *Swann Sun*'s archives. Marshall Britt, the New York banker, was first mentioned in 1945 for purchasing several square miles of hunting ground on the Sable Inlet, then in 1950 for building a lavish lodge on the water, and again in 1959 for building Britt House, a mansion at the other end of Twice Mile Road, which traversed the two miles of the Britt waterfront estate. There were stories reporting his wife's death from a horse kick, not from a fall, of finding Marshall's empty boat three years later, and, six years after that, stories about his son Hugh's murder, and Leo's arrest and trial. Most of the murder stories were cursory, but one in the paper's Sunday magazine reported the defense's accusation that Bentley Branch had failed to record Marshall Britt's revised will, and also mentioned a magnetized scale at the Britt fish house as a possible cause of the gaff fight on the dock. Seb wrote the author's name, Jeff Yates, in his notebook.

Germaine Ford appeared in the Style section of the paper in 1966 when her parents moved into the hunting lodge and again in 1967 when her family hosted an extravagant barbecue on the inlet. She was posed between her mother and father, her head cocked, her glance sidelong and off camera, her waist slim in her sundress, her blond hair long and swept over one shoulder. She was beautiful. After the murder in 1969, she did not appear again until her father's obituary in 1984 and again in her mother's in 1989. In 1999, she was mentioned again when hog waste from Cooper Farms, formerly the Britt estate, washed down Council Creek past the lodge. Then three months ago, the front page of the local paper announced her death and bequest to the convict Leo Sackler of the lodge, the twenty now much-prized acres on Sable Inlet, and her bank account. The story was also carried on the back pages of major papers around the country.

The attorney Bentley Branch was mentioned again in his obituary. He was survived by his two sons, Gerald "Bug" Branch and Elver Branch. Bug Branch owned Branch Bail Bonds. Seb knew him.

He closed the laptop, then his eyes, and Mia's face came, at first hard to see, then steadying, like the moon reappearing in calming water. She must be invited and welcomed, like into a house, the porch, the hallway, the kitchen. Eventually the bedroom.

His phone rang. The screen showed the name Walt Carney, the coroner.

"Hey, Walt."

"Seb, got a minute?"

"Sure. You figure it out?"

"What I figured out is your victim does not have a broken neck. He has a broken leg instead. Broken tibia."

"And what do you conclude from that?"

"I'm thinking he fell and got his leg caught in the rungs. I think he slipped between that place where the two ladder halves come together. I looked at Barb's photographs, and that's about a four-inch gap there, and that would be enough fulcrum to break a tibia. How did he get hung? I do not know. Or how's this? He breaks his leg, so he hobbles up the ladder, and gets tangled or something. Hell, I don't know. Anyway, that leg could have been the reason he wasn't able to swing back on the ladder, if he was in pain and panicked."

"Did he have abrasions?"

"He did. On the ankle, so that's why I think he got his foot caught."

"Does the break indicate he fell backward?"

"It does."

"Time of death?"

"Sometime yesterday afternoon. Say one o'clock. Time of death is damn variable though. I'll say approximately one o'clock, but if it comes to it, I can be pushed off that. For one thing, he was hanging in the middle of the air, so no conduction. But by rigor and temperature, best guess, one o'clock."

"Could it have been earlier? Say in the morning?"

"Well, like I say ... Why?"

"He had an unidentified visitor around nine in the morning. Some-body tried to extort him. He called his daughter right after and told her, which is how I know about it. I was wondering if the guy could have still been there and heard the call, and it set him off."

"It's a stretch. Really, it's off the scale. But like I say, no conduction, so it's tough. Also, nothing under his nails. Another little feature is he's got a bullet scar on his right biceps. Through and through."

"It's a gaff scar. He got in a fight when he was a kid, and a guy gaffed him."

"Well, that's just what it looks like. I thought he might have been shot."

"What else? Was he healthy?"

"Good health. No tumors."

"All right, Walt. Fernando will be there in a little while with Sackler's daughter for the identification. Many thanks."

"I'll file the report by the end of the day. Kate just left, by the way. She got his fingerprints. So is it murder?"

"Probably. You want to confess, help me out?"

"Not yet. Hey, what do you think about Emma? My wife. I told her I talked to you about singing, and she's bugging me."

"We're having practice tonight, and I guess I could present it to everybody, see what they say. But, Walt, down deep, probably not. You know, it's kind of a therapy thing."

"Okay, good. Now at least I have some ammunition to resist the formidable Emma. Later."

BUG

Branch Bail Bonds with its open handcuff sign under a triple *B* was across from the new courthouse-jail building. Seb had called Branch's cell and found he was at the jail with his secretary getting a prisoner's signature. They agreed to meet across the street in the bondsman's office.

Seb entered the waiting room and waved to the secretary, a small black woman, who spoke briefly into the phone and held a finger against the receiver as she looked inquiringly at Seb.

Seb said, "I'm supposed to meet Bug. Is he around?"

She gestured to a door. "Go back. I expect he's napping by now. If he's undressed, tell him you didn't ask me."

Seb walked down the hallway to the second door, knocking twice against the wall as he entered. Behind a battered wooden desk, a large round-shouldered man in his sixties swiveled from a computer screen. He wore an unbuttoned green shirt over an orange T-shirt, and his belly mounded beneath it like a gym ball. His face was pink and puffy, and his hair went straight up in a flattop. Seb knew him as the parent of Mickey, one of his high school basketball teammates, and now as a bail bondsman.

"What's up, Seb? Sit."

Seb took one of the two wooden chairs in front of the desk. He said, "You heard Leo Sackler's dead."

"Died of hanging."

"Did you know him?"

"I knew *of* him. Leo was the star basketball player over at Georgetown High School. Before someone bombed it. Our black high school from yesteryear. He was a couple years ahead of me. So where'd you get my name?"

"From Virginia, the daughter. She said Marshall Britt changed his will, and your dad didn't register it. You ever hear that?"

Bug laid his head to the side and gave off a slant smile. "I wondered you didn't mention Mickey. Come right to it."

"Mickey's selling cars in San Diego."

"Last count he was. You probably see more of him than I do with Facebook." There was a silence. Seb out-patiented him. Bug said, "The will that gave the hunting lodge to the Sacklers? So Leo was murdered, and you're looking for motives."

"Don't know yet."

"So did my dad screw Granger Sackler? Probably. The Klan never got much going around here, but if they did, my dad would have joined, pretty sure. He did not like Marshall Britt and that nigger—his words—being friends."

"I always thought Swann County sort of missed all the fuss in civil rights times."

"It did. Folks around here weren't aware enough to hate. They were prejudiced, but that was just the air they breathed. Someone did bomb the high school though. Then the war brought the Marines and the modern world. So you think maybe I killed him? Something to do with my prejudiced father?"

"Well, just to get it out of the way, where were you yesterday afternoon, around one, say?"

"Right here. Ask Maddy on the way out."

"You're asking me to leave?"

"Hell, no. I want to hear about this. Why would a son of Bentley Branch kill Leo Sackler?"

Seb looked into space for a moment, then back. "How about, Leo had proof that your dad had cheated his family and was going to disclose that and ruin the reputation of the eminent Branch clan, which incited you to murder."

Bug's mouth opened, then closed in a smile. He said, "Fuck."

Seb said, "Bug, I got no clue. I really want to ask about Germaine Ford. You knew her, right?"

"I believe she snuck into my masturbation fantasies occasionally. My older brother dated her. Once. She got hooked up with Hugh Britt, and that's what you're looking for, right? All that."

"That's it. Who did she run with?"

"No idea. Except for Hugh Britt, which you already know, I guess. The Fords came down from New York and brought money and a beautiful girl. I'd see her downtown, and it looked like she stepped out of a magazine."

"Did you know Hugh?"

"I knew he was an asshole. He had a preemptory way, you might say. I didn't spill no tears."

"What did everybody think about that murder?"

"Oh, lord, here comes Seb. God almighty, good luck. We all been waiting on you. Ever since Germaine's will come out and give it all to Leo. You're going to be the finger of justice."

"That's what Virginia Sackler said."

"I bet she did. She's got that house and land now. And that money."

"She said Germaine did it."

"When that will came out, that's what I thought. What everybody thought. I remembered she had a black eye."

"When was this?"

"Back then. Sometime around there when Hugh got killed. I didn't see it, but I heard she did. I cannot remember who told me, but I was definitely told it."

"A man or a woman tell you?"

"Can't think, Seb. But there's your two and two make four. They had a physical brawl, and she killed his ass."

"Was Hugh cheating the black fishermen?"

"No idea. Why?"

"That's what the fight on the dock was about, supposedly. When Hugh gaffed Leo Sackler."

"Now I remember. Magnets underneath the scale pan. You know how that's done? You reverse them and tape them down. I could see him doing that. Just a little sneaky meanness he could get in."

"And you don't know who she ran with?"

"I do not. She was only here off and on. She was in college. After the murder she went hermit and became the ghost lady of Swann County. She had housekeepers, and I believe it was various ones of the Land family. You know them? I bailed Junior Land out twice."

In his smartphone, Seb texted himself: *Lands, housekeepers.* He said, "What am I forgetting to ask?"

"No idea. But tell me this—how are the murders of Hugh and Leo connected? I mean, even if Germaine killed Hugh, why does someone kill Leo? Why wasn't he just robbed? Was he robbed?"

"He might have been a little bit robbed."

Bug laughed. "What'd they do, take ten and leave five?"

Seb stood. "Thanks, Bug."

They shook hands across the desk. Bug picked up the phone. He said, "Let me just call my secretary, get that alibi straight." He smiled, hung the phone up. "Tell Mickey if you see him on Facebook he can call his old dad once in a while." He came around the desk. "C'mon, I'll walk you out." Seb preceded him down the hallway. In the reception room, Bug said, "Maddy, tell this man the truth." Then to Seb: "You figure this out, you'll get your fifteen minutes."

A SKILLFUL DISPLAY
OF VIOLENCE

Cody rode past Keisha's trailer, number thirty, and saw her mother's station wagon was gone. He had been her friend for six months, and her boyfriend for four weeks. She was friendly with everyone, but sarcastic only with him, which clued him that she had singled him out. They'd had sex twice, once in his car, once behind her mother's trailer on the grass. One day, if he wasn't in prison, he would marry her, and they could get their own place. Keisha was black, so their kids would be black, so his life would become black, which could be a relief.

He pedaled back to the hot tub yard and leaned his bike against the fence. Mo Stevens and his half brother, Perk, looked across the yard at him, both silent. Three ten-foot benches padded with clip-on seats made the yard's perimeter. Five plastic table-and-chair sets were scattered in the center.

Perk was in a tub with a too-big fire flaming up one side. The Stevens brothers had gradually become Cody's enemies, a process begun by Cody getting involved with Keisha, which Perk, who was half black, did not appreciate, having tried there himself and failed. Mo, who had Cody's old handyman job, had turned against him after Cody mentioned the grass around the Coopertown entrance sign had gotten over the brick foundation, which, he noted as he pedaled past, was where it was again.

Perk passed his hand through the flame. He was a tall, well-muscled young man, just out of high school, down from Raleigh on an extended visit to his older brother, Mo, with whom he shared a father. He wore a sideways baseball cap. His black boxer shorts were a water-blurred hyphen between his bare brown thighs and thick chest. He said, "Do one thing, Cody. Sell me an ounce. I'm heading home tomorrow."

Cody settled on the boat-cushioned bench. He said, "An ounce of what?"

"I know you have some of that twenty-five percent Blue Dream. I know that."

"You know wrong."

Mo said, "You calling him a liar?" Mo was smaller, thinner, in baggy jeans and a pale green T-shirt. He was tilted back in a plastic chair, one foot on a tabletop. He was excitable. He wagged his head. He had gotten off a good one.

Cody said, "I notice the grass up by the sign is long again." He gathered Mo's hard look with an amiable glance. He said, "Just kidding. It is though."

Perk said, "You act like you own the place."

Mo said, "His daddy own it. He on a throne."

Mo's diction, Cody noted, had become blacker as his Perk-bond firmed his anger.

Mo said, "Why you be a dick? Sell the man his ounce."

"I don't sell dope, if I ever did. Where's Elton?"

Mo said, "He's around."

Cody said, "You built that fire too high, Perk. A man cracked a tub that way."

"I built it like I like it."

Mo said, "Like he like it, like he like it. That sound like hip-hop. Why you be a dick, Cody."

Perk got out of the tub on the flameless side, slipped a hand inside his underwear to adjust his genitals, and crossed the grass to sit beside Cody on the bench. He put his arm around the bench back and hard-tapped Cody's deltoid with his middle finger. He said, "One ounce of Blue Dream. I'll take six if you got it, and I want the discount."

Cody watched a trickle of water from Perk's dripping body and shorts creep across the bench top and darken his brown pants. He said, "You're getting me wet." It was interesting. His Stinger-missile problem made other problems boring. He had lost fear. He stood. Perk gripped his forearm and pulled him hard onto the bench again, onto the growing puddle.

Perk said, "We doing business."

Mo said, "Got to, Cody."

"Got to what, Mo? What's he got to?" It was Elton Gleen's fast, country-thin voice. As he left his trailer and crossed the deck, he picked up a bamboo cattle cane from the railing top. He strode through the yard, tapping the bamboo on tubs, chairs, and benches. He wore jeans and a pink tank top that exposed the orange and black of his shoulder-wide tiger tattoo, created in San Francisco by a famous Chinese inker. Elton's head was shaved and on the right side was another tattoo, nine black numbers he had seen on a woman's wrist in a book about the Nazi death camps. He had them done fuzzy, like on the woman's wrist, to express his displeasure with the state and its minions. He was in his fifties, slim-waisted, long-legged, wide-shouldered, with a tanning-bed tan.

Now he stood with his legs spread before Perk and Cody. He said, "The subject under discussion is will Cody here sell off a lid of marijuana. His answer was no, and you two are deviling him. I keep this cane for devils, just so you know. Also, Perk, you dumb shit, you built that fire like a child. That tub cracks, you will haul it off and bring me another."

Perk stood, broader and two inches taller than Elton, who retreated a half step. Perk said, "I'm not hauling shit for you."

"You're not?"

"I don't give a fuck who you are. Don't interfere with me."

"I must and I will. Cody is my friend."

"You best put that cane away, old man."

"No, sir! I need this cane for ones like you."

"Get it out of my sight, or it's going up your ass."

"That's a threat against me." Elton smiled, showing large even teeth. He said, "You a dirty N-word," and emitted a shrill laugh.

As Perk lunged for the cane, Elton stepped nimbly back, lifting the cane to the side. He said, "I'm retreating. Everybody note that."

Perk took a fast step forward. The butt of the cane darted hard into his midsection, folding him. Elton's hand flashed from his left front pocket with an eight-inch sap, which made a *fapping* sound against the back of Perk's baseball cap. Perk dropped silently to the grass, facedown. He did not move.

Mo had put his foot down from the table and now stood. Elton crossed to him, laid the cane across Mo's shoulder like a sword. He said, "What I do not like is feet on the tables, Mo."

Mo ran a hand across his long hair, ducking his head into the motion. He said, "Sorry, Elton."

"Now throw some water on your brother and haul him off. Are you still my employee?"

"Yes."

"Then you'll agree this was all done legal, with a witness. He advanced, and I retreated. Do you agree?"

"I agree."

Mo poured his soft drink gently over the back of his brother's head. Perk got to his hands and knees, then sat for a moment, then pulled himself to his feet using a bench. He stood. Mo gathered Perk's clothes and shoes beside the hot tub, then pushed him forward. They began to walk.

Cody and Elton watched them proceed slowly down the trailer park lane. Elton said, "You're most welcome, little man."

Cody said, "Thanks." He had just witnessed a skillful display of violence. He was not impressed, or interested.

With his cane, Elton scattered the fire beside Perk's tub, then walked to his cushioned Adirondack chair and sat. He said, "I heard those fools on my baby monitor. That Perk needed a whipping before he went back home anyway. The big ones generally do, or they're hard to live with." When Cody didn't reply, he said, "You wouldn't sell him any marijuana, which I was surprised."

"I don't have any."

"Well, things change. You keep flytrapping you'll be back to prison, that's one thing I do know. I wouldn't consider flytrapping much of a career improvement."

Cody could say he was done with flytrapping, that he had seen the choppers, had seen the missiles fall, had stolen the missiles, there was a video. He said, "Well …" Then his mind drifted. He thought of Keisha. He said, "How long ago did Keisha leave?"

"Let's see. I believe it was forty-one minutes ago." Elton let off a spasm of hee-hees. "Love in the young is the engine of life. Cody Cooper, you look glum."

Cody deep-breathed. He lifted his arms and threw out his chest, then fanned them slowly down, exhaling, a seated greeting of the sun. He deep-breathed again. The air could not seem to penetrate him. He said, "What job? What did you want?"

"I needed a collection, but the collectee died on his own hand."

Elton spoke this casually, but with a glance, and Cody felt himself under Elton's measuring. He could ask more, get the details, form judgments, but that was effort and unappealing. He said, "I might just have a hot tub."

"Go on. You should. Except I don't have pine. I'm ran dead out. Things are falling apart around here."

Cody got up and crossed to the scent cabinet. Open boxes of scent packets were stacked neatly on four shelves. He reached behind the eucalyptus box and brought out two green packets of pine scent. He fanned them for Elton. He said, "Two left. My private stash."

Elton laced his fingers behind his head. He said, "Tell you what I'll do. I'll raise you to fifteen bucks an hour. Get rid of that Mo. C'mon, goddammit."

Cody went to the woodpile and began to select kindling. He had been offered two jobs today, when it was too late.

He said, "I just want a tub."

A REALLY PUSSY
HEART SONG

The new county law center was a three-story, block-wide box of red brick with white-painted concrete trim and housed the sheriff's department, the new jail, and three courthouses. As Seb swiped himself into the rear door, a tan SUV stopped in the street. Charlene dropped her arm outside the window and looked across to him.

She said, "Well, I found you. I was taking potluck, and here you are."

"Hey, Charlene." He felt himself tighten. Had she heard about his coffee with Mia?

She said, "You look worried."

He slumped. He smiled.

She said, "Come follow me. I'm going to pull over."

She drove ahead fifteen yards and slid the SUV into a space on the curb. They met on the sidewalk.

She said, "Seb Creek. Give me one hug, and that'll do me."

They embraced. She stepped back and folded her arms determinedly across her chest.

She said, "Don't worry, I'm over caring if you broke my heart. Emotions are so selfish anyway."

It was not about Mia then. They gazed at each other and half-smiled their forgiveness.

She removed her e-cig from her shirt pocket and gave it a puff. She said, "I promised Cody I would quit this if he straightened up. You said it didn't bother you, but I bet it did." She capped the e-cig and pocketed it.

He said, "It didn't bother me."

"Well, something did." She smirked. "Sorry. I'm in another relationship, and I think I got another heartbreak coming already."

He opened his mouth, then waited.

She unfolded her arms, reached with one hand as if to tap his shoulder, didn't, then stood, hip cocked, with an arm akimbo. "I have not come for myself. I've got two poor souls in mind. One of them is my brother, Cody, and the other is a young girl named Rubella Peters. I know ... Rubella. But that's her name, and it's pretty if you forget it's the measles. So Rubella is having trouble at home. She's been coming to my office every week. There may be some abuse there, not the father but his younger brother. I'm digging and don't need you for that. What I do need is you to speak with a man named Elton Gleen. Do you know him?"

"I do."

"Well, last night in the big storm, Rubella did not come home. She stayed all night in the Coopertown trailer park with her cousin and did not call or answer her phone. She called her mother this morning, and her mother called me, and we picked her up in a trailer with a group of young women. And there was Elton Gleen sitting in the living room playing strip poker with Rubella and two more. He had his shirt off, one of the girls was down to her bra and underpants. Rubella only had her shoes off, so I guess she was winning. She's sixteen. We got her out of there, and I told her mother I'd talk to the police, whether or not it was a crime." She waited, then said, "Was it?"

"You probably got her out too soon."

"That's what I thought. I thought you might have a serious conversation with Mr. Gleen though."

"Was it trailer five?"

"Yes, it was. Is it a whorehouse? Because that's sort of what I thought."

"We're not sure. Might be something Elton's got going. I'm going out there today on another matter. I'll have a word with him."

"Thank you. That's poor soul number one. Number two is my little brother, Cody, who you know well, since you arrested him, which I never did blame you for and still don't."

"What's up with Cody?"

"I want you to go see him. I want you to get him into the singers. I know you talked to him that once, when we were dating, but it didn't catch him. You've got to catch him, Seb. You can do this. He'll get into something again. Actually, he's already into something."

"Is he back flytrapping?"

"Don't ask. But right now, he's just like a feather and blowing everywhere. I want you to help him." With one hand, she impatiently forked the corners of her eyes, which had wet.

He thought, she has such heart. Yet he had not emerged to her.

He said, "I'll call him up."

"No, you must not call him up. You must be right in front of him, and tell him a joke, and have a beer with him. Please don't call him."

"He still in that little trailer?"

"Yes. He'll be there tonight for sure. That's all he does is sit in there, like a possum. But he's got a beautiful person inside him. Also, he sings so beautifully. What a fit he would be for you guys. Don't forget that."

He said, "Okay, I'll find some time."

She said, "Well, I've had my hug." She offered her hand, and they shook. As she turned toward her car, she said over her shoulder, "Don't forget about Rubella." She strode to her SUV and drove away.

Seb swiped himself into the rear door. As he climbed the stairs his phone rang. It was Bonnie Miller, the detectives' secretary, who worked until one on alternate Sundays.

"What's up, Bonnie?"

"Downstairs just called. There's a soldier waiting on you in reception."

"I'm just coming up the back stairs."

The Swann County detectives were divided into narcotics, with five detectives, and investigations, with three, plus a sergeant and lieutenant. When he reached the investigations area, the secretary's desk, which sat behind an L of chrome railing, was empty. Five desks lined the wide long room.

Marty Jerrold sat at the first desk, his fingers laced on top of his head, leaning gravely over an open lunch pail. His wife, to counter his expanding belly, had begun preparing him healthy meals. On his way to his own desk, the last in line, Seb stopped and laid a hand on Marty's shoulder.

"Marty, those carrots won't eat themselves."

Marty looked up. He said, "Every meal is a struggle between pleasure and longevity. Write that down. That's wise."

Seb, in wit-swapping accommodation, said, "What's the use of longevity without pleasure?"

Marty said, "Not all pleasure has to do with food, Seb." He looked back at his lunch pail. "Just ninety percent. Doug said the *New York Times* called ten minutes after he issued his press release. I told you this Sackler case was going to be famous." He unlaced his hands and laid them over his sloped chest. "Yes, I can feel it now in my breast, the unhappy warmth of envy."

They cocked their heads together in appreciation of this neat phrasing.

"Where's Bonnie? I just talked to her."

"Taking a leak."

"What did the prison say?"

"They said come on. Tell me about the fight."

Seb gave select details, the handcuff swipe, the crotch kick, the push, the door.

Marty said, "That's why I carry an ankle piece."

And Seb thought, despite himself, then I would have missed that fun fight. He said, "Eat your carrots, or I'll tell on you." He started toward his desk, then turned, backing. "Is Kate in yet?"

"In her lab, I think."

At his desk, Seb called reception on the first floor and was informed that a uniformed Marine had been waiting for him for thirty minutes but had vanished. He went down the hallway to the CSI lab, where he found Kate at her desk typing into a computer. She said, "The only prints on the ladder were Sackler's. We finished the garbage and posted the inventory in the file. Nothing really."

Seb said, "I just talked to his daughter. She had been in the house, so you'll need to print her. I doubt she's in the system. Jose is taking her to the morgue, so you might catch them there." Then he laid the iPhone on her desk.

She lifted the baggie and sighed, stared at it, then looked up at Seb with a flat expression. "Where was it?"

"Under the mattress. I found his phone receipt, and it had two phones on it. The sheriff called when I was still in the bedroom, and I told him I found it. So it's got to be in my report. Wasn't thinking. Sorry."

"Well, Ernie missed it too, so it's only a fifty percent screwup."

"Plus it was three o'clock in the morning."

She dismissed this excuse with a grimace.

He said, "It's not locked. It's got videos on it. I looked at the first one and the last one. It's all him digging. At one point he said, nothing up my sleeve, something like that. So he was looking for something, making a record. So I think we have to keep digging. Think you can get to the videos today?"

She opened the camera app. "How many are there?"

"Well, he's been out a few weeks, and he stayed some days with his daughter. So he's been digging a week maybe."

"There are ten videos. That doesn't seem like enough for a whole week."

"He's probably been erasing them. But here's the thing, Kate—somebody came out yesterday morning trying to extort him."

"Tell me."

"No identification. But Leo told his daughter someone came out when he was down in the well. It's probably on the missing phone, which may be why that phone is missing. Also, he talks now and then to the camera, calls it 'little friend.' So maybe at some point he told his little friend what he was looking for."

"Let me fingerprint it, and I'll get started. Don't worry about your report. I'll blame Ernie, and he can blame me."

At his desk, Seb first wrote the report about the fight with Peener, then began the murder report. As usual, he concentrated on clarity and narrative flow, so that Stinson, his first reader, would be compelled to appreciation, however reluctant. A year of Seb's work ethic had three quarters brought Stinson around, but with looks and pauses here and there he let it be known he had a quarter left to go. He had made a speech at the murder site about the other detectives accepting Seb's lead, but Seb got that it had been at least half duty-inspired. Plus, if it was up to him, Stinson would have put him in the courthouse until SBI investigated.

He had gotten to his arrival at the death scene when his phone rang, and reception informed him that the Marine had stepped outside to smoke a cigarette and was back. On the way to the elevator, he stopped at Bonnie's desk. She was a portly woman in her late fifties with a hard coif of too-brown hair.

Seb said, "Bonnie, do me a solid. Call records and have them pull the Leo Sackler file. Tell them I'm on the way down."

"I will. Was he murdered, do you think?"

"Bonnie, I can't comment on an ongoing investigation."

She smirked.

He smiled. He said, "He probably was. Only way I'll know for sure is catch the killer."

"Lot of money out there."

As he started away, she said to his back, "If you don't get him, call it a suicide."

He left the elevator and entered the spacious reception area. Double doors on the right led to the patrol and dispatch offices. Through a door on the left he saw Martha, the sheriff's white-haired secretary, at her cluttered desk gesturing as she spoke on the phone. She saw Seb and waved a hand erratically, meaning either hello, stop, or come. Behind a glassed window the receptionist raised a finger, then bent it to point to a young man seated on one of the rectangular couches in the waiting area. The man was hunched forward, elbows on knees, intently reading a magazine. His head jerked up as Seb approached, and he stood fast, casting the magazine onto the couch. He was in his early twenties, his face long, the eyes close-set and alert. One side of the upper lip was freshly scabbed. He performed the beginning of a salute, hid the embarrassment of that by falling into an at-ease posture, his hands behind him, then brought his left hand uncertainly to his waist. The stripes on his uniform indicated he was a corporal.

Seb said, "Hello, Corporal. I'm Seb Creek."

They shook hands.

"Hi. Tom Rogers. Captain Delmonico at the brig asked me to come see you. He didn't order me or anything."

Seb said, "About Pass the Salt?"

"Right."

"How long you been in the brig?"

"Just the weekend."

"You get in a fight?"

"Yeah. A bar fight."

"Were you singing in the brig?"

"I was that first night. I was loaded."

"What were you singing?"

"Really? Let's see … I don't know the name of it." He thought, then pronounced evenly, "'Pancho was a bandit, boy. He wore his gun outside his pants for all the honest world to feel.'"

Seb said, "I like that one. You looking for help with PTSD?"

Rogers' face made a faint spasm. He said, "Not really." Then: "I guess."

"Where were you posted?"

"Afghanistan."

Seb's phone buzzed in his jacket. "Sit a second and let me get this. We have a practice tonight. You off duty?"

"I report tomorrow."

"Okay. Sit a minute. Be right with you."

Sheriff Henry Rhodes appeared on his phone's screen. Through the door of the sheriff's office he saw the sheriff's secretary pointing to her phone and nodding to him.

"Hey, Sheriff."

"Where are you, Seb?"

"In reception, staring at Martha. What's up?"

"I need you to report to the Fleming Ferry gate right now. Bill McAllister is on the way to pick you up."

"What's up?"

"I'll let you know when you get here. But I mean now, okay?"

"Lieutenant Stinson called a murder briefing on Sackler in thirty minutes."

"I'll call Stinson, and he can reschedule. Come now."

"On my way."

He ended the call. The sheriff's secretary made the circle-finger okay sign. Seb returned to the soldier, who had remained standing. He said, "You know where the VFW hall is? Down by the inlet?"

"I can find it."

"That's where we practice. Starts at seven tonight. I'll introduce you to everybody. I got to go to the base right now. Maybe you need a ride?"

Seb took Highway 17 south toward Fleming Ferry. Tom Rogers sat beside him without speaking, staring through the windshield, his hands folded in his lap, his thumbs rhythmically stroking. Seb's phone rang, and Deputy Randall Garland's name came up.

"Go ahead, Randall."

"I'm about halfway done with the canvass, just checking in. I worked down Ruin Road on the north side of Cooper Farms. Now I'm headed over to the Lands, and I'll start working down Staunton. Going right by Coopertown. Sure you don't want me to …"

"No, leave Coopertown to me. And leave the Lands too. One of them worked for Germaine Ford, and I need to talk to them. The time of death was around one, by the way, so that's your focus."

"So far all I got is the Parkinsons saw a blue van yesterday, and they saw a Realtor's car a few days ago, they're not sure. They're out on Ruin Road and sit on the porch a good bit. Everything else was local. They don't know the Realtor's name, but they saw the word 'realty' on the side of the car. A white car. They saw the van around noon yesterday. There's six houses on Ruin Road and no one else saw anything."

"Good work, Randall. Leave me the Lands and Coopertown, and email me a little report with whatever else you get. I'll log it in. Before you knock off, okay? Later, man."

Seb glanced at Rogers, who sat upright, staring blankly ahead, still stroking his thumbs. He said, "Can you talk to me a minute?"

Rogers' head turned quickly. "Yeah, sure."

Seb asked if he was married—no—where he was from—Arizona—when his last combat deployment had been—six months ago—did he talk to his folks—now and then—was he in a therapy group at the base—no. Was he diagnosed with PTSD? Hell yes. He can't sleep, his mind races, he's jumpy, he's mad, which is why, like an idiot, he went barhopping and loud talking, to find a fight.

Rogers said, "I don't expect anything from you, by the way. I came because Captain Delmonico said he'd let me go if I would."

"You're hopeless?"

Rogers stared at him. "Delmonico said you got out from under."

"I'm getting there. Everybody in the group is getting there. You want to know the secret?"

"Yeah. Tell me the secret." Rogers' voice was dry, but he watched Seb's face.

"The secret is feeling. Getting your feelings back. I've read all the books, how trauma affects the brain, all the brain talk they do, all the sensory talk. But that's just a map. It's not the place itself. The place is here, right now. Where you are, always right where you are. You get in combat, you drive through bombs, you speed up, and you stay speeded up. Anger is speed, fighting in bars is speed, you can't sleep is speed. You drug much?"

Rogers was silent, watching.

Seb said, "Okay, you drug some. That's you trying to slow down, any way you can. How come you didn't re-up?"

Rogers did not speak, but his brow knit as he concentrated.

Seb said, "Doesn't matter. But me, I was like a lot of guys. I'd try home and then jump back. I got divorced. Couldn't much be in a crowd. Then I discovered singing. Singing has a mysterious property. Only slow sad-ass songs though. What it does, it calls up the deep feelings and helps to cancel the speed. A lot of us didn't have all that much feeling even before we enlisted. Because soldiers aren't pussy, and feelings are pussy, right? Well, it might sound pussy, but everybody in the group's got a case. They either killed people or had friends killed or just got exposed to too much danger for too long. We even got a couple of Special Forces. Everybody's sped up with jump-out-of-your-skin shit. So you found the right guys. Most of us have got our drinking and drugging under control too. So far, we haven't had one suicide. We don't give a fuck what you did or saw or didn't do, and you don't ever have to tell us. Just come sing with us. This is my hurry-up speech, so don't be put off. What do you think?"

Rogers pursed his lips and looked back through the windshield. He said, his voice hardly audible, "Sounds interesting."

Seb said, "I'm the leader of the gang. And as the leader I have a selfish interest in whether you can actually sing. You can be with us anyway, absolutely. But cool if you can sing. So here's your audition. Hit this note." Seb sang a middle C. "Ahhhhhhh."

Rogers frowned, smirked, gazed straight ahead. Then he sang the note perfectly in a tenor voice.

Seb sang another note, a third higher.

Rogers sang the note.

Seb said, "Cool, bro. You can sing. I told Delmonico to send me any-body, but I think he likes to send singers."

Rogers said, "Singers got a little pussy in them."

Seb laughed. "They do, no doubt. So what do you think? You going to show up?"

Rogers blinked several times fast. He said, "Yeah, definitely."

"Very cool. Now then, here's your homework. Get to an internet con-nection and get on YouTube. Type in 'The Parting Glass' and listen to the Shaun Davey version. It's the song at the end of that movie, *Waking Ned Devine*. Listen to that this afternoon. A bunch of times. And show up tonight. That's what we're going to start working on. 'The Parting Glass' is a great song for PTSD. A really pussy heart song."

They laughed. Seb glanced and saw Rogers' face was working against tears. He said, "Bro, we cry like babies when we sing. That's *why* we sing."

Rogers said, "Okay." His voice had thickened.

At Fleming Ferry, Seb parked in the visitor lot. Four black SUVs were waved through the gate as Seb and Rogers approached. Something to do with the crash, no doubt. Rogers made an inconclusive gesture, spoke something inaudible. He started toward the base bus station.

Seb said, "Bro, wait."

Rogers turned.

Seb said, "We got to shake hands, man. Come a day, you will want to embrace me. For now, we shake hands."

Rogers offered his hand, and they shook. Rogers broke into a grin.

Seb said, "Do your homework, Tom. 'The Parting Glass,' Shaun Davey version. Bring that tenor."

BODY BAG HANDLES

Bill McAllister said, "A Stinger's missing. A launcher and three missiles. We got FBI, NSA, Homeland. Even got a squad of Secret Service. The White House has given us two days, then it goes public. As you can imagine, there is a fuckload of panic and a bunch of bossy-ass big shots." He drove his 4x4 truck past the clusters of base office buildings and barracks and into the hurricane-ravaged scrubland of the coast. McAllister was NCIS, a captain. He was in his forties, thick-bodied, and had the puffy contours of a weightlifter that quits lifting but not eating. He was currently assigned to a federal task force and wore his undercover drug-snooping costume, a Stetson atop a scraggle of blond shoulder-length hair, jeans, and plaid sports coat over a white T-shirt. During the last months of his farewell hitch, when Seb was base MP, he and McAllister had busted an assortment of pop-up meth labs, civilian and Marine.

McAllister said, "They flew two choppers out to the beach to shoot drone targets over the ocean. Ever get to do that? It's a kick. So here comes the rain and the big wind, and they're in a hurry to get back to base. The first chopper, Dash One, tries to hover and keeps getting blown off the LZ, and the ground guys can't get the belly net secured. They got two M416 trailers, one for each net, with two missile systems in each one. So four launchers and a bunch of missiles. So they finally get a two-point hookup and lift off. A mile later, one of the holds releases. Some-fucking-how.

The trailer drops into a creek. That's mistake one. Mistake two is for some insane unbelievable reason, the pilot, who's a major, and he flew in both theaters and is way experienced, has a brain fart and makes an unannounced midair turn. He just comes about. And Dash Two is right behind him. They got their hookup first try. So bang, damn near head-to-head. Probably because his hookup took forever he thinks they're a mile behind. But also they're flying instruments and using night vision—that was the exercise—so he didn't have any peripheral. But still. An immense final brain fart. They didn't even radio about the dropped load. We had to puzzle it out. Aviation is very dejected, as you might imagine. They lost six, and the Stinger battery lost fifteen. Plus two Super Stallions."

Seb said, "And a Stinger's missing? What does that mean?"

"They found the M416 in the creek. One of the launcher cases was still intact and strapped in. The straps of the other had been cut, and the case with the gripstock and battery was gone. And three missiles were gone. And no, nobody's thinking a suicide plot and terrorism. We're thinking a pilot's brain fart and a criminal entrepreneur. The background on the pilot is he's a family man, dug in, just bought a new house. So maybe some loose asshole with a boat poaching flounder, and he says, hey, free stuff. Or maybe a Marine out camping, or an ex-Marine with a base pass."

"No ex-Marines, fool."

"Yes, there are. I arrest the bastards all the time."

McAllister slowed and was waved through a gate onto a service road by a cluster of Marine MPs. In a hundred yards they left the road and followed the curving tracks of other vehicles through the grasses between the loblolly and oak scrub. The air was bright and sun-cool, and a light breeze carried salt scent from the ocean across the dunes on their left. The crash site came in view, first a thick scatter of Marine response vehicles and government SUVs, then the burned-out hulks of the three-story Super Stallions, one on its side, both nearly nose to nose, as if the collision had been a death grip, and they had fallen together from the sky. Their carcasses were skeletal, black, and mangled. Soldiers and officers stood in groups watching medical teams work in the wreckage.

McAllister pulled up to the khaki command tent. As they crossed the sand to the flap-spread double door, the hum of generators became audible. Inside, a group of twenty-odd officers and enlisted men and women in civilian suits were littered around several map-spread tables. Sheriff Henry Rhodes detached himself from a group and met them in the tent's center. He said to McAllister, "You filled him in?"

"I did."

"Thanks, Bill. Seb, let's go for a walk."

Seb and the sheriff left the tent, walked a short way across the sand, and stopped. The sheriff had his cap elbow-clamped at his side and now swung it onto his short silver hair. He was thick-bodied man in his late fifties, his wide face now lined and sober, his lips hard-pursed. He gazed into the blue sky and exhaled heavily through his nose. Seb was struck with an impression—the sheriff knew someone on the crews. He was grieving.

A hundred feet away a military-green tractor had finished scraping a flat place in the sand. Teams of Marines trudged from the wreckage with body bags. The bags had handles welded to the ends, so the bodies slumped in wide Cs. The bags, six so far, were being carefully laid in a precise row.

Seb had the fast odd pained impression of the bag's designer thinking of handles—a convenience for the living—how life goes on past death, past twenty-one deaths in this black wreckage. And the men now assembled, the medical teams and officers watching and the corpse-bearers, had only their grim set silent faces for ballast, or else be blown away by meaninglessness. In Iraq, he had seen many of those faces. There they had an enemy to rage against. Here there was nothing, just empty death and a neat line of bodies. They would be in the other world now, something no one here could see or feel or know, not even him, who had been there. He said, "You knew some of them."

The sheriff continued to inspect the sky. He said, "I knew one of the pilots. And his wife and kids." He turned to Seb. He said, "Now here's where we are. NCIS is handling the county search, and they're bringing CID in too. The FBI and Homeland and the rest are going to do airport security, a mile perimeter around every major airport on the East Coast. And databases. All the stuff they do. The White House says two days, then it goes public. Probably that shuts down every airport on the coast, maybe the country. NCIS and CID are going to be out and about in the county, out of uniform. They'll check everyone with a boat, the video feeds, all the launch points. They're going to knock every door on the water. Thirty-one investigators so far and more on the way from Virginia. They found a campsite on an island right beside where the trailer fell. The whole site was brushed with a branch. The main lead is they let a guy out of the brig yesterday with a Dishonorable. He did a year for punching a sergeant. They already had an active shooter threat on him. He's a hard-core survivalist."

"Tom Rogers?"

"No, Grayson Kelly. Why?"

"Rogers just got out of the brig. He contacted me about Pass the Salt."

"CID will get to him. They're talking to everyone Kelly might have jailed with."

"So what are we doing? Warrants?"

A voice behind Seb said, "This your man, Sheriff?"

Seb turned. A tall man in a black suit was gazing intently at him. Amber sunglasses were perched on top of his short black hair. His round face ended in a protuberant chin, like a drip of flesh.

The sheriff said, "Seb, this is Special Agent Lowry."

Lowry said, "I'm the SAC on this operation. Are you familiar with that term?"

Seb repressed a beginning smile. He said, "I forget."

"Special agent in charge."

Seb's smile broke free. He made it into a friendly nod. He said, "Good to meet you."

Lowry's head lifted, pointing his chin. He said, "You're to deal exclusively with the head magistrate." He looked at the sheriff. "Who is it again?"

"Wanda Cromarty," said the sheriff.

Lowry looked at Seb. "Do you know Wanda Cromarty?"

Seb said, "I know her, but not well."

Lowry said, "You don't have to be her personal friend. But there is a need for speed." His gaze uttered impatience coupled with bulletproof condescension.

"I can be quite speedy."

This remark was either insolent or ignorant. Despite himself, Seb let silence mark the ambiguity.

Lowry dropped his amber sunglasses over his gaze. He said, "You, the sheriff, and Cromarty are the only locals involved. You are all working under the Official Secrets Act. Understood?"

Seb cocked his head and frowned a reply.

Lowry said, "It means you're bound to silence. Now and forever."

"Got it."

Lowry turned to the sheriff again. "I want him posted at the magistrate's office."

"Detective Creek just caught a murder."

"I take precedence, Sheriff. Magistrate's office. No delays."

He strode back toward the operations tent.

The sheriff said, "He's under a lot of pressure."

"You really want me camped out at the magistrate?"

"No. I talked to Wanda. I messaged you her cell phone. She'll take your calls. Basically, you're the warrants man. Everyone on the search teams has got your number."

"Our deputies are going to see these guys knocking doors."

"If they do, we tell them a special investigation is underway and to stay clear. I don't know if it's going to take much of your time, but it might."

They turned for a moment to gaze at the line of body bags. Seb said, "I guess I'll shove."

The sheriff filled his lungs and blew his breath. He said, "Where are you on Sackler?"

"You want to hear it right now?"

"I do. Get my mind on something else."

"Main clue so far is somebody came out yesterday morning wanting a thousand a month for security. Straight-up extortion. Leo called his daughter and told her. He was down in the well and couldn't describe the man, except he was white."

"That's an Elton Gleen move."

"I'm talking to him next. But he was out there around nine, so if it was him he must have come back, since Sackler died around one, according to Walt. Also, Sackler had a broken tibia, probably from getting a foot caught in the rungs of the ladder when he fell. Except he had that rope around his neck which would have stopped him from falling. So that's an issue. Also, I found a tobacco tin that might have had money in it. Also, the daughter thinks Germaine Ford killed Hugh Britt, and that's why she left Leo Sackler everything."

"So does everybody else in the county."

"So we got a mystery that goes back to the sixties. Or he was robbed. Or he was extorted and things went bad. Or he hung himself and screwed it up. One of the Land women was housekeeper for Germaine. I'll do that after Gleen. And I want to talk to the ex-governor. See if there was anything behind that grant of clemency."

The sheriff smiled. He said, "Stinson is going to hard-ass you if you make this complicated."

"I know, but I've got to do the diligence."

"The former governor's in the Caribbean with her granddaughter on a sailboat."

"Thanks. I will not tell Stinson you told me."

"Who's got the canvass?"

"Deputy Garland. There's only a few houses out around there. He called this morning and said someone saw a blue van and a realty car, besides the locals moving around. The van was from Cooper Farms. It was out that morning chasing a drone. Then there's Coopertown. I told Randall to leave that to me."

"Look hard at Gleen."

"I'll take a run at him. I should be able to finish my list, unless these guys go search crazy, and I run out of time." Also, that evening Seb had a Pass the Salt practice, which he did not intend to miss. He did not want to mention that though, since it would likely furrow the sheriff's brow, his detective off singing during the first forty-eight of a murder. He would not miss it though. He owed the living more than the dead.

ALIBIS

The two men wore slacks and sport coats without ties. Both were tall, in their forties, one black, one white, both with neat hair and shined shoes. They stood together in Elton Gleen's hot tub yard and announced themselves as federal investigators. They asked if anyone had seen or heard anything noteworthy today or yesterday. Just any little thing out of the ordinary. Anybody out too late, in too early, driving too fast, anybody strange.

Cody had his ears just above the tub water and at first held his head and face stone still. A half hour earlier he had built a careful fire along one side only of his favorite tub, the long two-foot-deep one with the bear-paw feet, and had paid Elton two dollars extra for the double pine scent. If you stayed perfectly still, you could feel the tiny current on your leg hairs caused by the uneven heat. When the investigators appeared in the yard, he sunk down to his nose and ears to hide fear, then popped up again to show innocence, then sunk again anyway, like something was pulling him, which it was—heart-racing panic.

Elton had moved from the Adirondack to a webbed lounger. He gazed up at the two government agents with a clownish smile and let a long, ill-spirited pause continue after their opening inquiry.

Finally, he said, "I have to look over your IDs again. You flashed them too fast."

The black investigator removed his ID wallet, opened it, and held it before Elton's face. Elton read, then looked at the other investigator. The man came forward and flipped open his ID. Elton read. He said, "You're looking for something out of the ordinary? No shit? It's against the law to be out of the ordinary now?"

The black investigator moved a step closer and leaned over the lounger, hands on knees, his face three feet from Elton's, letting his coat fall open to show the pistol. He said, "Don't irritate us, partner. We want to know if you've seen anything unusual."

Elton went cowed. He said, "I get that. No, I get that. Unusual, let's see. I'm thinking." He pointed at Cody. "It's unusual for that mother-fucker to pay extra for scent. He might have come into money."

Dean Fleemer, a short, rail-thin man in a ragged baseball cap and open green shirt, said from the boat-cushion bench, "You cannot remember a smell. I did read that, but don't ask me where. I don't think you can remember a taste either." He nodded and darted an inquiring glance around the yard, an addled effort at topic-changing and peacemaking.

Elton Gleen said, "Dean, shut the fuck up."

The other person in the yard, a muumuu-clad fat woman with bright pink streaks through her thin hair, sat beside Fleemer. She closed her eyes and, as if for privacy, turned her head away to emit a long, contented chuckle.

The investigator came to his full height. He said, "You're Elton Gleen, the landlord?"

"I'm the manager. That motherfucker in the hot tub is the owner, if his dad ever dies. That's the son of the owner."

"Let me get this across to you. We're investigating something and want to know what unusual activity you might have witnessed."

"You're Navy, aren't you? I don't watch that program. Do you have jurisdiction here?"

The investigator said, "How about this, Mr. Gleen? We take you downtown and put you in the box, inconvenience the fuck out of you as an uncooperative witness. How about stand up, Mr. Gleen?"

Elton did not move. He spoke with quiet humility. "Please forgive me, sir. I will be cooperative from now on. Have I seen anything unusual? I have seen several cars leave the trailer park as various ones went off to work. That is not unusual, however. I'm thinking. I come back to my earlier insolent remark that it is unusual for Cody Cooper to buy extra scent, and that honestly is the only unusual item so far today. It's ridiculous to mention about the scent, of course." He held his expression sober and sincere, sweeping the fat woman with a hard gaze when her face started to open with delight.

The other investigator walked to Cody's hot tub and looked down. Cody had sunk to his ears again. The investigator said, "Early for a hot-tub, isn't it? You relaxing?"

Cody pushed against the tub end, raising his head out of the water to reply. At the last minute though, he didn't trust his voice. He nodded.

The investigators exchanged what-next glances. Coopertown was not on the water, and they had been assigned it only because of its reputation. The second investigator said to Cody, "Where were you last night?"

Cody said, "Sleeping," thinking, that must seem true. They can't know that's not true.

"Where."

"In my bed. At home."

The first investigator said, "How about you, Mr. Gleen? Where were you?"

"Also sleeping. Not with Cody though. Forgive me. That shit just pops out. I was sleeping inside my bedroom in my bed."

The second investigator said to Cody, "Why did you buy that extra fucking scent, partner?"

Cody's face went stark. The investigator laughed. He said, "Jamal, let's blow."

The man standing over Elton said, "See you later, you impolite motherfucker."

As the two men walked toward their car, a red Honda pulled up beside their black sedan, and Seb got out. The three men stood together for a moment gazing back toward the hot tubs, talking.

Cody took three deep breaths, then closed his eyes and sunk entirely beneath the water into the black stillness. He could feel his heart thumping and tried to invite the drifting gliding relaxing sensation required for good breath-holding, but the tightness wouldn't release, and he had to pop up after only a minute. When he opened his eyes, standing patiently at the foot of his tub was Seb Creek, the stubble-faced, ponytailed detective that had arrested him six years ago and once dated his sister. He was looking down and half-smiling in a friendly way.

"Hey, Cody."

Cody said, "Hey."

"I saw your sister downtown. She's bugging me about you."

Cody was silent, waiting. He had a powerful urge to slip beneath the water again.

"She wants me to get you into the singers."

Cody sank slowly. His chin touched the water, his earlobes.

Seb said, "We're practicing tonight, seven o'clock, VFW hall by the inlet."

Cody nodded, poking an eye-level ripple across the surface of the water. He poked another one. They sparkled.

Seb said, "Think you might come?"

Cody felt Seb's bland gaze like a spear, pushing into him, pinning him. He said, "I guess … well …" Then he said, "No."

Elton Gleen laced his hands behind his head. "Man, what the fuck anyway. This right here is a disturbance in the field. Two feds, and now Seb Creek."

Seb walked three steps to stand in front of Dean Fleemer. He said, "Hey, Dean." He lifted his head to the fat woman. "Hey, Belle."

Dean said, "Hello, Mr. Creek."

"You know why I'm here?"

"Someone said I took their trimmer probably. Well, I sure did not. I invite you to search my trailer."

Belle said, "You do not, Dean, invite any search whatsoever."

Dean made a slump and bob. He said, "If you got a warrant."

The Fleemers' income came from Dean pushing a lawn mower around nice neighborhoods and knocking doors, followed by Belle in their pickup. A year earlier Seb had arrested him for the theft of a Weed Eater from an open garage, an event fortuitously captured on the homeowner's security video. Dean had done thirty days in county.

Seb said, "I'm not here about trimmers. I'm here about a murder."

Cody realized then that he had been holding his breath and now let it slowly and pleasantly out.

Dean Fleemer said, "I don't know a thing about a murder."

"Where did you have lunch yesterday?"

"What do you mean? I didn't kill anybody."

"Where did you eat your lunch, Dean?"

"What do you mean?"

Belle said, "He means where did you fucking eat. He ate with me, in our home, which is right there, trailer three. Right there." She pointed across the drive to a blue-and-white trailer with a plywood window, a line of three outdoor cookers, and a chain-wrapped, tarp-covered lawn mower.

Seb looked across the benches to Elton Gleen. He smiled. "How about you, Elton. Did you eat with the Fleemers?"

"No. I do not eat with Fleemers." He laughed.

Dean said, "Is lunch against the law now?"

Belle said, "He's checking alibis. Somebody got killed at lunchtime."

"That's right, Belle." Seb crossed the lawn to stand at the foot of Elton's lounger. "You know a guy named Leo Sackler?"

Elton, still with his hands laced behind his head, appraised Seb with disinterest. He said, "Is that who got killed?"

Seb said, "Did you know him? Ever speak with him?"

"Never once. Never saw him with my eyes."

Dean said, "Did he get killed? Who was he?"

Belle said, "He was that black that got the lodge."

Seb said, "Where'd you eat your lunch, Elton? Yesterday."

"I have given up lunch as part of a weight-control regime. Instead, I have a mixture of applesauce, prune juice, and psyllium. I got that from my refrigerator. The rest of the day I spent here and various ones can testify to that. There's two right there."

Belle said, "He was here."

Seb turned to Cody and spoke across the lawn. "How about you, Cody?"

Cody's mouth opened. He tried to think, but his mind tightened. He had been on the Marine base, digging flytraps. He couldn't say that. He could say he ate with his sister. Which could be checked. He was pausing too long. He said, "McDonald's."

"McDonald's out on 24?"

"Yeah."

Seb took out his cell phone, crossed to Cody's hot tub. He said, "Sit up out there a minute, Cody."

Cody pushed himself out of the water so that his thin shoulders emerged. Seb took his picture with the cell phone. Seb said, "In case I have to check your alibi."

Elton said, "You want my picture? Feel free."

Dean said, "Who got killed?"

"Leo Sackler. He was found last night with a rope around his neck. The rope went under his arm, like this." Seb pantomimed the death scene, tracing a line under his arm. "So we don't think it's suicide. We're seeing if it was a murder."

Dean said, "Did someone say they saw me out there or something?"

"Out where?"

"Out where he lives. Where does he live?"

"Right behind the trailer park, about a half mile through the woods. On the inlet."

Belle said, "He's the one, goddammit, Dean, that got the Ford place."

Dean said, "Oh." He added, "Well, I sure did not kill him."

Elton said, "You killed him and robbed him, didn't you, Dean?"

Dean looked at Elton, then at Seb. He said, "He's joking."

Seb crossed to Elton again. He straddled the end of the lounger and sat, forcing Elton to spread his legs and drop his feet onto the grass.

Elton said mildly, "What the fuck, Detective."

"What about the morning? I wonder where you were yesterday morning." Seb kept his voice low, as if between him and Elton. The Fleemers and Cody listened attentively in the quiet of the yard.

"Right here."

"I'm thinking you might have walked over to meet your new neighbor. Just a stroll through the woods."

"I did not."

"And you told him a thousand a month for peace."

"I did not."

"He told his daughter you did. He recognized you, Elton."

Elton let a moment pass. He said, "That's not a dying declaration though, is it? That's hearsay, if I know my law."

"Which I know you do. But what you don't know is that he was videoing everything. Or maybe you do and that's why you took the phone. But did you know he had it set on automatic upload? That video is on the cloud."

Elton let another moment pass. He said, "How about play it for me."

"We're getting a court order. But listen, Elton. I'm on the murder, not the extortion. I'll kick extortion to the side if they're not connected. If they're connected, well then, I can understand your silence. I mean if you went there yesterday morning and then came back and killed him. I can't see you being that stupid, but maybe you went back and something happened, and now we're on different sides. But if you didn't kill him, and only extorted him, and you don't talk to me, we'll take it hard, me and everyone else downtown. Plus it'll be obstruction, which is a five-year crime, and for you probably a shit ton more. So consider—if that video comes in with you on it, even just your voice on it, and we have to go through all kinds of expensive electronic shit proving it's you, that will create intensity and hard feelings. On the other hand, if you relate to me that you had a conversation with Mr. Sackler, and he misunder-stood something—maybe you were offering your services, and he took it wrong—I'm here to understand that."

Elton gave a flat stare, then, as if chest-punched, broke into shrill hee-hees. "Goddamn, that was pretty." He said loudly to the Fleemers, "I love this Seb Creek." He turned a flat stare to Seb. "You must play me the video. Which there is no video. Nobody's a child right here. And I guarantee you, you folks get any sniff of crime on me, you're going to the bank, no doubt. You wouldn't be pressing on me if you had anything. All that about a phone. What's a man doing videoing himself digging a well? Nobody's a child right here."

Seb delivered a lengthy, methodical gaze. He said, "You know what? I doubt you killed him. The timing's off, and it's too stupid for Elton

Gleen. But I'm keeping an open mind. Next subject. I've got to give you a warning. I hate to do it, but I said I would."

"You hate to give me a warning?"

"I do, because I'd rather arrest you. My warning concerns a girl named Rubella—I forget her last name. Her mother and the school counselor found you playing strip poker with her this morning. Recall that?"

Elton smirked. He said, "It's not coming back."

"She's sixteen. If she walks into your trailer naked, you best call 911."

Elton laid his head back and watched the sky indifferently.

Seb stood. He said, "I'll catch you for something one day, if I don't catch you for murder."

Elton said to the sky, "Well, keep on." Then he added, "I got a call from my nephew this morning. He said you beat him unmercifully."

"Carl Peener?"

"He said he's going to sue you good."

Seb crossed again to Cody, who saw him peripherally, took a fast breath, and submerged. When he resurfaced, Seb was standing at the foot of the hot tub, gazing intently at him.

Seb said, "You ever hear a song called 'The Parting Glass'?"

WINDOW COURAGE

Cody sat at Elton's poker table while Elton clattered up a spoon from his silverware drawer. He handed him the spoon and said, "Try it. It will keep you regular as a clock."

Cody lifted the lid of the ceramic teapot, peered in, and inspected the goop, as Elton called it, a cold brown applesauce–prune juice–psyllium jelly. He scooped out a spoontipful and put it in his mouth. It was grainy and tasted pruney. He nodded deferentially. He said, "Nice."

Elton said, "Get some now. Get a glob. It keeps your gut clear and clean. They should use it in the pornography industry."

Cody nodded and took a larger spoontipful.

Elton said, "You didn't get that, did you? Because of anal sex. Which is perversion on top of perversion, in my opinion."

Cody swallowed and nodded. This was his first time in Elton's trailer, the park palace, and he was waiting to see what was what.

Earlier, as Seb Creek drove away, Keisha and her mom had entered the Coopertown driveway in their station wagon, and Seb had talked window to window with the mother, a large black woman. As the station wagon proceeded past the hot tub yard, Cody saw Keisha say something to her mom, and they backed up. So she had said, hey, there's Cody. Cody was the landlord's son and was polite, and so was approved of by Keisha's mom, who did not know his history or that her daughter and Cody were having sex.

Keisha got out of the car and shoved Cody's head under the water. He surfaced and suitably sputtered. He said, "Ms. March, your daughter's trying to drown me."

Keisha said, "I'm baptizing you." She was a trim nineteen-year-old black girl with short hair, a flat, faintly Asian face, and a gap between her front teeth.

That was when Elton Gleen got up from his lounger, produced a towel from his sundries cabinet, and tossed it to Cody, who caught it two-handed before it hit the water. Elton said, "Cody, dry off and come in here. I got to show you something."

It was a command, demeaning to a guy in front of his girlfriend, but Keisha had kindly turned away, pretending interest in the Fleemers' murder account. Cody dried off, wrapped his cutoffs in the towel, and was now seated at the famous thousand-dollar-pot poker table. His bare feet rested on the thick sponge of the blood-hiding rug, and the cheerful face of Harvey Clement fluttered through his mind. He could see Keisha through the sliding glass door. She and her mom were still standing, not settling. Keisha threw him a glance. He lifted his head, but she looked away.

Elton said, "You still eat at McDonald's? I don't consider McDonald's even food."

Cody met his gaze, then let his eyes wander. He didn't bother to speak. Something was coming.

Elton said, "That Seb Creek will get behind you. You saw him sit on my lounger and press on me? That was police work right there."

Cody said, "That was the debt, wasn't it?"

"What debt?"

"The one I was supposed to collect."

Elton said, "I have no idea what you're talking about. Do you have any idea what you're talking about?"

Cody glanced at Elton, then back at Keisha, with her mother, speaking to the Fleemers. He watched her shoulders, her thin arms gesturing. That's why he was here then, in the sanctum, to clean his memory. He said, "No idea."

"That's correct. No ideas. Now then, I saw you freeze up when he asked you where you ate. You said McDonald's, first thing that came to you. But you were out flytrapping, weren't you?"

Cody said, "Yes."

"That's the tangled web of crime, son. Right now, Creek's thinking, why did that fucker lie to me about where he ate? Because what the hell, even Dean Fleemer could see you lied."

Cody looked at Elton. After a moment, he said, "Not necessarily. You knew I was lying because you knew I was out trapping. Maybe he thought I hesitated because I couldn't remember where I ate." This was a clear, faintly defiant, un-Cody-like response and left an odd disquiet in the room. And Cody thought, it's because of Keisha, who again glanced through the glass door at him. She was sending courage.

Elton folded his arms and leaned against the counter. He pursed his thin lips into an air kiss. He said, "Well." He let a moment pass. He said, "How many traps did you get?"

Cody stared at Elton. What was it then? Blackmail? Maybe a flytrapping partnership. Let me hold you in my wisdom and be your guide. For a fee. Keisha had looked away but now looked back again. Their eyes lingered together.

Cody said, "You know why those feds were here?"

"No, I don't."

Cody let a silence go. He lifted the lid of the teapot and tested its perfect fit. It was a white, handmade teapot, tall with a long spout, like a watering can. It had several rose-colored marks at the base and one at the top on one side but not the other, which seemed odd, then right. He said, "I bet I know."

"What do you know, Cody?"

"I stole three of their Stinger missiles." Cody sent a one-hand-clapping wave to Keisha, and she trilled fingers back.

"You did?"

Cody glanced at Elton, then into the air. He felt his body pressing into the chair, heavy and clear. He was seated at the famous poker table and had made a famous bet. He said, "When those choppers crashed."

Elton swung his arms out of their fold, retrieved the teapot, and deposited it in the refrigerator. He put his hands behind him and leaned against them on the counter. He said, "Let's hear it, little man."

Later Cody would see how it had happened, how he'd been at first exalted by the theft and fate, then fear-stricken and numb, then unsettled by his father's bullying apology, then, through the glass door, had imbibed Keisha's assurance and grown strong again and spoken truth, spoken it to wild man Elton Gleen, who he might be in league with about a murder, if Elton had actually killed the black man, and who could now destroy him, which made the truth worthy and strong. Plus, when he thought about it, Elton was the natural refuge for this kind of truth, the dug-in criminal.

So he told it. About making an island camp, about the storm over the ocean, then the wind and lightning and the falling trailer. He even told that he had buried them, the water he had poured to cover his traces. But not where. Sense had reemerged.

Elton said, "Will they shoot?"

"Yes, they'll shoot."

"Cody Cooper, you either hit a jackpot, or you're in one. How much can you get for a Stinger missile?"

"I'm not selling them."

"The fuck you say."

Cody did not respond. His eyes shifted around the kitchen, then again through the glass door. Keisha was getting into the station wagon with her mother. She closed the door, looked at him. She clap-waved, and he clap-waved back.

Elton pulled up one of the folding chairs, reversed it, and sat astraddle. He leaned, forearms braced on the chair top. He said, "Cody, look at me."

Cody looked away from Keisha at Elton's thin lips. It was like pulling out of one dream into another.

Elton said, "They got a prison in Colorado for guys that do terrorist shit. It's like eight-by-eight cells, twenty-four hours a day, one guy by himself. Solitary forever. They don't give a shit if you go crazy. They just feed and water you until you die. They watch you so you can't kill yourself. Just sitting right here, hanging out, we cannot imagine that. We go outside, have a conversation, get in the tub, smoke a doobie. But right now, as I am speaking, there are guys in those cells. And now you have told me about your amazing crime, you dumb motherfucker. Which I don't know if it's true. But if it's true, what the fuck, Cody. I got to pick up the phone. I'm not going to Colorado."

Cody's brow furrowed. He gazed at Elton intently. He did not know what exactly he supposed would happen next with Elton, but it was not, let me call the police. It was, here's what's next, here's what to do. Really, he hadn't supposed anything. It had come out for another reason, a mystery reason, a destiny reason. He flash-considered strolling into the kitchen for a drink of water, say, then rummaging a knife out of a drawer. That did not attract him though, a bloody miserable fight. Also, Elton was flashy strong. He said, "I wish you wouldn't."

"We're sort of friends, Cody, but I don't owe anybody life in an eight-by-eight cell."

"Forget I mentioned it."

"Can't be forgotten, Cody. Is it true?"

"No."

"Don't lie, motherfucker, or I'll pick up that phone."

"Okay."

"Is it true?"

"Yes."

Elton's face stretched in a smile. "Fucking Cody Cooper's got Stinger missiles."

Cody watched. Something was coming. What was next was coming. One tension began to release. There was another one beneath it. There was heavy weight beneath it. He had invited it.

Elton said, "What would somebody pay for a Stinger missile?"

Cody shrugged. He tried to hold his face normal, but it throbbed.

Elton said, "Ten million dollars is what I think. That'll do anyway. And I guarantee you the terrorists have got the money. The question is, how do we contact them? Look at me, Cody."

Cody lifted his head, which had fallen forward.

Elton said, "Don't fade on me, dawg."

"Okay."

"Can you contact the terrorists? Secretly?"

"No."

"Then I have to make that phone call. Can you contact them?"

"Maybe. Probably."

"Probably's bullshit. We can't run with probably. Can you contact the terrorists?"

"Yes."

"How will you do that?"

"They have websites. Get on a tor client and write them an email."

"Let's do it. Can you do it now?"

"No." Cody began to undream. He began to think. "You don't have a tor client, and we can't download one now. They'll be watching for that. Anybody downloads tor now the FBI would come in five minutes."

"Really? Good to know. Then what do we do?"

"I have tor. Thing is, it may be compromised these days. Nobody knows anymore."

"Explain that, Cody. Be quick and be right."

Elton drilled him with a stare. The stare said, I need to know the chances. Bad chances, I call the cops. Cody settled, gathered, and lied: "I can do it. I can get to some clean exit nodes. And I haven't updated my tor for years. So it hasn't been compromised." This was drivel. He watched Elton's head move slowly up, then slowly down, a nod, the reluctant acceptance of odds.

Elton said, "I have three burner phones. I get the least sniff you are bullshitting, I call the police and crush the phone."

Cody said, "That's cool." You fool.

Elton said, "So what do you think, put a note on a terrorist forum? Stinger for sale?"

"Definitely not. They'd think it was a sting."

"Then what?"

"We send ten emails to ten sites. Tonight. On tor. After they respond, we get them in a game chat. We use a private squad in *Battlefield*. That game has Stinger missiles, so the NSA snoopers won't alert even if their algorithms catch the word 'Stinger.' They'll just think, well, it's *Battlefield*, that's normal conversation."

"That's good. That's really good. So how do we convince them we got the goods?"

"Send them a photo on tor."

"How do they know they're not talking to a cop? How do we know we're not talking to a cop?"

Cody had spent hours imagining this problem during his internet drug-selling days, the problem of masking. Two guys approach in the dark, neither certain of the other's identity. There was no good solution. It was something about existence itself, that everything was surfaces, and underneaths were always dark. But he had a sale to make. He said, "We divide the goods to build trust. First they get a missile. Then they get the battery pack. Then the gripstock. Then another missile. Then another one. Finally the launch tube. We never touch money or meet them in person. Never. We leave a missile somewhere and that starts it off."

"They wouldn't show up. I wouldn't. It would be a sting."

"Good point. So we send part of a missile to them. We send it to some Arab country. The explosive part. The cops would never do that. Any cop that did that would be prosecuted. So that starts off the trust."

Elton's stare wandered and softened. He said, "Cody Cooper, dawg, I knew you were smart, but you are the smartest fucking guy I know. And I never knew that. You been hiding that. That's how smart you are, motherfucking Cody Cooper."

Cody gave off a half smile, thinking, way smarter than you.

IF A FLY

It was early afternoon, and so far Seb had not gotten a single call from the missile theft investigators, which either meant no leads or else warrants were unnecessary due to cooperation. Or maybe they had picked somebody up. The two NCIS guys he had met at the trailer park said half the team was searching the swamp, the other half door-knocking and running boat and fishing permits, and so far nothing.

Seb had missed the murder briefing, but Stinson called, and, with a dry edge, informed him that the sheriff had alerted him that Seb had been pulled off to a need-to-know investigation on the base. Stinson had made assignments himself, sending Barb to Lowe's and Sears for video, and okaying Marty's prison visit. Both detectives had also begun reaching out to their informant network. Narcotics had sent a detective to the briefing and were reaching out to their network as well.

Seb informed Stinson he was only the warrants man on the base investigation, was so far unused, and was full time on the Sackler case. He had only half finished his written report, so he reported his day, the daughter, Virginia Sackler, and her extortion testimony, her addict husband and his mother in Chicago, her brother in a federal pen in Kansas, the iPhone videos, the broken leg—which Stinson already knew about—Randall's canvass and the white realty car, the need to start digging out the well, his interview with Elton Gleen at Coopertown, and finally his own review of the 1969 murder history. He said he had Bonnie pulling the old files and did Stinson by any chance know the detective on the Hugh Britt murder?

Stinson, without answering, said, "Let's don't fool around with ancient history yet, Detective. You got a good lead. Let's work it."

"I'm working it. But it's got a time discrepancy. Elton was there at nine, and Sackler died four hours later."

"I talked to Carney. He can't be sure."

"No, but it's a bad percentage. Also, you don't kill the guy you're trying to extort."

"Unless you're trying to intimidate him, and things go bad."

"But the other thing is the well. Something's in that well, and that brings up the history. Looks like it was filled in way back. Possibly around the time of the Britt murder."

"You're the lead investigator, Seb, so I'm not telling you to stand down. But it seems to me you damn near got a smoking gun."

Seb heard the dismissive tone in the lieutenant's voice, which said, how about we solve a simple robbery-homicide and stop running a hot-shot mystery. He said, "I know. Also, I forgot to mention, there might be a drone video of the area around the time of the murder. There's an environmentalist overflying Cooper Farms, and he might have caught some road traffic out there. I'm looking into it."

Stinson said, "Okay. And no, I don't know who handled the Britt murder. Likely dead and gone. So let's browse the warrants and door-knock Coopertown. Let's get some people in the box. Maybe somebody saw Elton taking a walk. Frankly, even with Gleen involved, I'm half inclined to think we're spending time on an accident."

Seb said Coopertown was on the list. Presently though, which he did not mention, he was on his way to interview the Lands, one of whom had worked for Germaine Ford—both parties in the ancient history, out-of-favor, hotshot murder theory.

Stinson set a briefing for ten the next morning, and they disconnected.

As Seb turned onto Staunton Road, he called Bonnie and asked her to hunt up the ex-governor's satellite phone number. She said, why not, I'm just sitting around typing reports. The previous year, the investigators' intelligence officer had retired, and Bonnie, after attending several semi-nars, had taken over her duties, with a pay bump, but not, she occasionally commented, her full salary.

Then he called the lawyer, Alex Person, in case he was still in the office. A receptionist answered and said he was. Seb thanked the woman and hung up without identifying himself.

Stinson was right, of course—Elton was the chief lead. Seb had come away from the Gleen interview with the conviction it had been him at the top of the well. But not that he had killed Sackler. First, it was out of character for a smart criminal. But mostly it left too many loose ends.

As he passed Willow Road, which led to Mia's pottery studio at the western end of the inlet, he recalled the dock there and a guy he knew from childhood, if he was still alive, a Jimmy something, who had a bait shop on a rebuilt barge. It was just before the end of the road, where the studio sat, and maybe he could drop by after the singing, have a talk with Jimmy—see anyone driving past with a boatload of Stinger missiles last night?—then stop by the studio, hey, I was in the neighborhood.

Staunton Road ran two miles along the southern side of the Cooper estate, and as he neared the Land house, Seb rolled up the windows and turned on the air-conditioning. The house, a white wooden box with a low-pitched roof, came in view. Two vehicles, a rusted green van and a small sedan, were parked in the gravel driveway. Beside them sat a gray-white pop-up trailer in the down position. Beneath a bay window a cloud of pink azaleas blossomed. A scatter of croquet equipment littered the lawn.

Seb pulled into the drive and parked behind the sedan. Five hundred feet behind the house, across Council Creek and through a screen of pines, he could see the purple-pink shimmer of one of the Cooper Farms open cesspools, a four-acre rectangle of hog feces the industry called a hog lagoon. Even with the windows up, he could smell the stench. And Christ, he could see a faint rainbow over the field. The automatic sprayer was on. If the breeze was southerly it would drift a shit rain over the house and even a stroll from the car to the front door meant a shower and change of clothes.

As he sat in his car watching the sprayer rainbow and trying to discern wind direction, Josie Land, a small black woman in her fifties, emerged on the front porch, stood with her hands on her waist, and sent out a head cock of inquiry. Seb opened the door and got out. Hog stench was strong, and even if he avoided a shit rain, smell might permeate his clothes. Meaning if he did manage a stop-by at Mia's after the singing, he might need a change. Which meant seven miles home and back. She could be in bed too. Probably a visit was pushing it. Or maybe drive by, see if there were lights on.

Seb stopped at the bottom on the porch steps. He said, "Hi, Josie."

"I wondered was you taking a nap."

"I was checking wind. I could see those sprinklers going."

"Oh, they going today. That's just about how we know rain coming. Mr. Squint start spraying to get ahead. He don't want to get fined." During Hurricane Arthur, one of the Cooper Farms lagoons had overtopped, eroded its berm, and washed millions of gallons of hog shit a mile down Council Creek and into the inlet.

She stopped, offered another head cock, inviting his purpose.

Seb said, "You worked for Germaine Ford, didn't you?"

She said, "You best come on in."

He followed her into the house. As she pushed the door closed behind him, he heard the hushing sound of the neatly fitted seals. The Lands, he knew, had been under siege from hog stench for four years. They laundered and bathed, sealed every window and threshold, burned scented candles, sprayed air fresheners, installed a variety of air filters. When the July heat arrived, the house's white sides wore a moving crust of black flies.

They crossed a small living room with a plastic-covered couch and chairs to an oval wooden table outside a kitchen bar. The wall beside the table was covered with framed family photos. An air-conditioning unit hummed in the kitchen window, and above it, through the top pane, he could see rainbow mist as a sprayer made its pass. He had the vague impression of being in a space capsule on an alien planet. She said, "Please sit. Can I get you a cup of tea?"

"If you're having one. Thanks."

"I would like a cup of tea." She turned the electric stove on under a kettle of water. The house smelled of cinnamon and something else Seb couldn't place and then did—burned sage.

As he pulled out a chair, he said, "I believe that's sage I smell."

"Oh, yes. We have learned to burn sage. I grow it too."

She pulled up a chair and sat across from him, her hands laid palms up on her lap. She gave the impression of a trim bird, upright and perching and attentive. She said, "This about Leo Sackler, I believe."

"It is, yes." She waited. He said, "Where are the grandkids today? On a Sunday."

"They stay in town with their mama's sister on the weekends. She makes them go to church, so we like that."

"How's Jonesy getting on?"

"He's making do. Arthritis don't go with turning wrenches, but he's making do."

"How's the suit going?"

"They don't tell us. They lawyering."

The Lands had joined a class action nuisance suit. Their nuisance allegation was particularly egregious, since Cooper Farms, formerly the Britt hunting estate, had built their waste lagoons a mile away from the water's edge and the Cooper mansion but four hundred feet from the Lands' home. State regulations specified that a hog lagoon could not be built closer than fifteen hundred feet from an occupied dwelling, but when Squint asked for a permit, the house had been unoccupied for more than a year, and a permit was granted. It had been the home of Jonesy's parents, and Jonesy and Josie had been saving for a remodel. When their own home burned, they were forced to move.

"Did you know Mr. Sackler?"

"No, I didn't. But I met him."

"When was this?"

"A week ago. I went out to see if he wanted a maid."

"Did he?"

"He said he would keep me in mind."

The teapot began to whistle. Josie rose, set two cups with teabags on the table, and poured. She brought spoons, honey, and a quart of milk from the refrigerator and sat again. Seb swung his teabag in the water. He said, "I'm thinking somebody might have killed him."

She waited.

He said, "So the Ford lodge is, what, a couple of miles from your house? Make the turn off Staunton to Crandell, left on Twice Mile, and it comes right up. He died around noon yesterday, so I'm out asking did anyone see anything or anybody around noon? Or a car you didn't recognize?"

"I was in this house, and I don't see much in here with these little windows. Or hear much either with these air-conditioners."

"You were by yourself?"

"I was."

He stopped a smile and delivered a brief finger point. "So no alibi."

She said, "No alibi."

They smiled together. He asked about a white Realtor's car, which she had not seen, then asked, "How long did you work for Ms. Ford?"

"Twenty-six years."

"So you started when?"

"Eighty-nine, after her mama died. Before that, Jonesy's mother worked for them."

"She was getting on, and you took over?"

"That's right."

"Your mother-in-law work for Germaine when she got that black eye?"

"I never heard about a black eye. She would have told me."

"Probably before her time."

He asked if Germaine had ever mentioned Leo Sackler. She had not. He asked whether she had inherited anything. Twenty-six thousand dollars, for twenty-six years of housekeeping. They were planning to move as soon as the lawsuit cleared, win or lose.

Seb let a moment pass to collect their attention. He said, "What was she like?" Then he said, "Did you love her?"

Josie smiled. "I like you asking that. Because as solitary as she was, she was never a sharp or hurting woman. Yes, I did love her. That house was like church on Tuesday. Just her and me and quiet."

"Did you cook for her?"

"I did."

"Did you eat with her?"

"I never did."

"She kept things formal?"

Josie tilted her head to think. She said, "You ever know a nun? I never did, but I thought she was like a nun. Have a plan for action and keep inside it. Fold yourself in and stroll along inside yourself. See what I mean? That's not formal like stiffness."

"More like dignity."

"More like that."

"Or depression?"

"She never took to bed or anything, like some do. I was talking to Jonesy—did I ever hear her laugh? I must have, but I cannot remember."

"Did friends come out?"

"Charity friends, best I could tell. She gave to charities."

"No best friend?"

"I didn't see one."

He asked about her schedule. Eight to five, clean up breakfast—which Germaine prepared—make lunch, leave dinner on the table. Sweep, dust, vacuum, clean. He said, "I bet you miss it."

"I ache about it."

"What did she think of your lawsuit?"

"She's the one told us about it. Put us in contact with the Water-keepers and the rest of them."

"She was neighbors with Squint. Was she upset about hogs next door?"

"These hogs right here don't trouble the lodge. That's a mile and half through the woods. But when that lagoon failed, and that hog waste come past the lodge, she sued him good. She called him *that man*. She told me about the nuisance suit and to join up with it. After the house burned, and we moved, I kept a change of clothes at the lodge, but now and then she would catch a whiff of hog on me. She'd get a black look. Not for me. For that man."

"Did you nurse her when she was sick?"

"I did at first. Then a hospice nurse came to live in."

"She died of congestive heart failure?"

"Yes, she did. Her feet swoll up and hands swoll up. We gave her morphine. Then a series of little strokes came to ease her on out."

"I wonder if she went to see the governor before she died."

"Oh, lord, I drove her to Raleigh. It took her fifteen minutes to walk from the car to the governor's office. She needed a deputy to get back to the car."

"How long did they talk?"

"Couple of hours anyway. I went shopping, and a secretary called me to come get her."

"Any idea what they talked about?"

"She didn't tell me. Now ask me if I think she killed Hugh Britt, which folks think."

"Do you?"

"I do not. That woman couldn't kill anything bigger than a fly. If a fly."

THE AFTERLIFE

It was a six-mile ride through the midday heat back to his sister's house, and Cody arrived at the garage sweaty. As he wheeled the bike in, Charlene turned from the back bench where she had been inspecting an open can of paint. She held up a dripping blue stir stick. She said, "Look at here, dude. Plenty left from last time. I broke out the automatic sprayer too, which I think is pretty ready to go, except it might be clogged. But I have mineral spirits in case."

Cody leaned the bike against the wall, bent forward, and wiped his face on his T-shirt. He said, "What are we doing?" Then he remembered. He said he would paint the boat. The thought oppressed. He said, "Oh. The boat."

She said, "I'm holding you to it. And guess what? I ran into Seb Creek. He said he's coming by."

He looked at her.

"Actually, I went by the courthouse and there he was. Don't be mad. I'm a meddler. But he said he would drop by to see you. So in case you have those flytraps all spread around …"

"He's not coming by. I already saw him."

"You did?"

"He came by Coopertown. He's on the murder of that rich black guy."

"Did he ask you about Pass the Salt?"

The weight of his sister's good intentions was like a lead plate in his chest. He said, "I told him no. Sorry."

He glanced away from Charlene's disappointment. At present his only ambition was to get inside his trailer and sit in his chair. On the ride home, at first halfway and then seriously, he began to consider suicide and how to do it—either inhaling water, which was drowning, which he decided wouldn't hurt once you were over the breath-holding part—or jumping off something, which probably wouldn't hurt either but had the nerve-wracking drop—or a gun, which would be messy for Charlene, so do it outside. The word started to run in his mind like a recording, *suicide, suicide*, and he made a note to google it, see where it came from. *Cide* was killing because of homicide, so *sui* must be me or myself. Of course, what if suicide was impossible, and you ended up somewhere else without your body, in an afterlife, which was heaven or hell? With atheist friends, he had always argued for an afterlife, telling them he would either have the last laugh, or there wouldn't be one. Anyway, it was a gamble, in case things continued and the spirit world disapproved of suicide. Besides, when it came down to it, he wanted more life. Not in an eight-by-eight cell though.

So then it was kill Elton Gleen or get rid of the Stingers. Killing Elton would be chancy and difficult. Find a gun—Charlene had a gun—sneak at night, aim through a window. Or walk in, say cold words, fire bullets into him. He falls and dies. Either way was shocking and horrible. Partly it was fear, since Elton was wily and strong, but also it would be completely cruel, the most complete and untakebackable cruelty possible, which you would have to live with and have in your private self for all time. How could you go on a picnic or marry Keisha and have kids if you had that in back of everything? He saw it in the war once, a kid in the mess hall, jokey one day, and the next day he kills himself. Tell her, Keisha, it was him or me. Except it wasn't. It was him or the eight-by-eight cell. So the dilemma was, killing Elton will ruin your life, and not killing him will ruin your life.

So get rid of the Stingers. Elton said, we have to get photos, realistic ones to start the conversation with the terrorists. And Cody said, wait first though. Let the searchers wear out and thin out. On the ride back he had passed a launch ramp and seen the Marine Patrol zooming past, only not with the usual guys in the pilothouse, but with five tie-wearing guys seated in the back. No doubt feds.

Elton had asked where the Stingers were, and Cody had said, somewhere. Which Elton accepted, since it left him out, in case. Maybe start things going in a month, said Cody. Elton said, a week. They agreed on two weeks, so that's what Cody had, two weeks to figure it out.

They would be watching the water. They would set up listening posts with night-vision equipment. Which he could defeat, probably, if he was patient. He would need a trip to the surplus store.

They might locate him before then though. There were two ways. One, they find the dug-up flytrap pods. Two, someone on the water saw him. Also three, they find the video, identify the tent, check the surplus store. That wouldn't be proof though. He had lied to Seb Creek about where he ate lunch, but, hey, guys, I had to, because I was poaching flytraps. I was definitely not stealing your Stinger missiles, in case that's what you're thinking.

A plan began to form. It was vague and difficult and uncertain, and his thoughts continued to drift, sometimes to suicide—deciding on drowning, since Charlene could think it was an accident—sometimes to murder, which he saw he wanted to do and was just a coward about the effect it would have on him. Plus, it could go wrong. Retrieving the Stingers could go wrong too. Also suicide, if there was an afterlife. Just a small thing he had done, just a stoned stunt, and here he was, unable to plan, sliding down a slick pipe to destruction.

He understood better now why he had told Elton Gleen about the Stingers, out of the blue, in a Keisha trance. It had been Keisha, but also he had needed to explode his life. He needed to fuck himself and his old life. And turn the leaf to a new life.

Cody decided to paint the boat. He would sand it first, get all the little flakes in all the little corners, chip and sand and dust it off, then paint it like a madman.

Charlene was still holding the dripping stir stick, watching him with disappointed, hoping eyes.

He said, "I'm going to need a sander and extension cord. And something to scrape with, like a putty knife, if you got one."

She beamed, tucked up both her letdown and enthusiasm, and went to the garage cupboard.

He said, "I'm going to sell this motherfucker when I'm done."

She turned with the sander, brightly, and said, "Well, then, you must do a good job."

OUT-COOLED
AT DEBBIE'S

"I just spoke with his daughter, Virginia. She said she put you in touch with her father."

"She did. Plus I do pro bono work at the prison, and some of the inmates know me."

Seb sat in a plush winged chair across from Alex Person, a small man with a trim gray mustache, thick gray hair, wearing a dark-gray suit. His office was a high-ceilinged room with walnut wainscoting and a modest chandelier suspended over an oak conference table. A bay window looked across the street to the courthouse, and the contrast between the brick-and-concrete government building and the sumptuous office spoke quietly of the needful guidance of wealth.

Seb said, "And Leo ended up not signing anything?"

"His daughter brought him to the office the day he was released. I took him to the bank and got him set up. Then we came back, and I laid out the document he had asked for, which was a living trust with two beneficiaries, his son and daughter. He picked up the pen and put it down."

"He didn't trust you."

"I believe that's right. He took the papers with him to read over. I called him three times, I think. He said he was reading and considering."

"So what happens now?"

"The clerk will appoint an administrator, which will be his daughter, Virginia Rubins, since her brother is in prison. Then it heads into probate. That's what the living trust was for, to avoid probate, which is now upon us with its year of gobbledygook."

"Will you be involved in that?"

"That's up to Virginia. I will offer my services."

"What will that be worth?"

Person made a mouth smile. He said, "A pittance, sir."

"What's a pittance?"

"The clerk will do the math. But less than a hundred thousand. You want to know where I was yesterday afternoon?"

"Sure."

"I was twenty miles at sea with Judge Lainson and his son, Carl. We landed five mahi-mahi."

Seb smiled. "So I can cross you off the list."

"You can." Person dipped his head benignly, indicating his patience with the inquiry. Then his eyes moved to the gold-framed clockface at the corner of his desk, indicating time was money.

"We contract with some forensic accounting guys who will look through all these papers and through the Ford estate. But help me out. If there's fraud somewhere, where's it going to be? Who would have a motive for murder because of fraud? I've heard of probate fraud, for instance. Anyone in your office have anything to do with this besides you?"

"No one. And I had no access to the money."

"No power of attorney?"

"He never signed a paper for me."

"How about the Raleigh lawyer firm that made Germaine Ford's will?"

"That was a living trust as well, and it wasn't a firm, it was Leonard Castle. The ex-governor's personal lawyer."

"Could he have stolen some money?"

Person lifted his head a fraction, his face showing faint distaste, a failed effort at impartiality. He said, "Detective, for what it's worth, I consider Leonard above suspicion."

"He's a friend of yours?"

"Not close, but yes, a friend."

"And you're vouching for him?"

"He has an excellent reputation."

"Okay. But you see what's happening. You guys know each other, and lots of money on the table, and somebody's dead."

Person took a long breath, then nodded. He had collected himself. He said, "You'll have my full cooperation. Send your forensic accountants."

Seb stood. "They'll get in touch. I see you making a good effort not to be offended, and I appreciate it."

Person remained seated. He spread his arms on his desk. He said, "You're doing your job."

"That I am. I'm a paid suspecter."

As he left, Seb found the reception area of the law offices, which had formerly been empty, was now occupied by a young man seated on a couch. Seb approached and sat on the couch edge, angled toward him. He said, "Peter Prince?"

Prince, in his late twenties with short brown hair and a round open reddish face, seemed to pull away from a thought. He laid fingers across his chest and inclined his head, *Me?* He wore jeans and a white untucked shirt with a blue woolen tie knotted loosely at the open collar, a costume broadcasting: making an effort but still me.

"Peter Prince, right?" Seb offered his hand. "Seb Creek."

They shook. Prince said, "Hey."

The secretary spoke from her alcove. "Mr. Prince, Mr. Person is free now."

Prince stood. To the secretary: "Okay, thanks." To Seb: "Nice to meet you. Did you want something?"

"You don't remember me because you never saw my face, but I'm the detective that talked to you a couple of weeks ago about flying drones. In that case, it was drones over Cooper Farms. I recognized you because of your website."

"Okay. Yeah."

"I'm with the sheriff, and I'm investigating a death. I was going to call you today, and here you are."

"What do I have to do with …"

"Look, you got an appointment. Must be important on a Sunday. How long will it take?"

"I don't know. I have to sign some stuff."

"Okay. Look, do this. Meet me at Debbie's when you're done. I'm heading over to get a bite. You know Debbie's?"

"Sure. But what do I …"

"No, no. You don't have anything to do with the death. But you do aerial surveillance, and I'm hoping you can help me. Probably not, but you were in the back of my mind, and here you are. Drone surveillance, by the way, is not my deal. I have no interest there."

"It's not necessarily illegal."

"Good. Maybe you can tune me up on the law. So will you stop by Debbie's? Just on the corner."

Prince thought, gazed away, then back. He said, "Okay."

Debbie's Diner, with red-and-white checked decor retro to the fifties, sat across from the courthouse and served breakfast and lunch for the downtown crowd of lawyers and civil servants. A silent TV set in a corner showed an announcer, then cut to a Super Stallion helicopter taking off from a carrier, a stock shot which meant they had not yet let newspeople onto the crash site.

Seb seated himself at one of the wooden window tables and ordered the grilled cheese–tomato soup combo from a young, pleasant waitress, his only food that day except for two granola bars from a convenience store, and likely his last, except for more granola bars. When he was finished, he sat with coffee and watched the sidewalk. He had planned to spend the rest of the afternoon calling real estate agents, asking about a white car with a realty sign, maybe try to get a satellite call through to the governor. What would she say? My old pal Germaine confessed to murder and wanted me to let an innocent man go?

In two hours he would meet the singers at the VFW hall, and he needed a half hour to get his head right for that, which meant get out of his head and get into a flowing, singing mood. So that gave him an hour and a half, about, unless one of the missile investigators called. How could that have gone down? A flounder poacher finds Stinger missiles in a rainstorm. And loads 'em up. Who would do that? A crazy person, or a wild one. Someone locked into everyday criminality.

He sat with his coffee, thinking of his current collection of pieces. Other than Gleen, he had no suspects, except crooked lawyers, a missing drug-addled husband, and an imprisoned brother. And if it had been Elton Gleen, how to incorporate the hanging, the empty precious box, the mystery in the well? His secretary, Bonnie—he had to call her for the governor's phone number—said, call it suicide if you can't solve it. No, but he could call it an accident. Except how do you break your leg by falling and get hung at the same time? You don't.

So that's where to start.

You break your leg, and some thoughtful person passes you down a lasso to help you up and then snags it around your neck.

Which was how it was done.

You're climbing the ladder, and you slip. Or someone pushes you. You fall, snapping your tibia. The guy calls down, where's the money, and I'll help you. You say, help me, and I'll tell you. So he passes the lasso down. Then, as you're putting it around yourself, the guy jerks it up, around your neck and under one arm. He hauls you up on your tiptoes. Where's the money? And you die that way, because you're an older guy, and it's a thin rope and maybe you hang there a long time. Also, the guy pulls up the ladder so you can't swing over to it. And wipes it down. And takes the phone, which is videoing everything. You tell him where the precious box is, and he cleans it out. And he leaves you hanging. But first he pulls you up and ties you off on the angled ladder. A strong guy.

Seb went over it again. It was solid and reasonable. He should go over it with Carney. They might have a murder theory Stinson would approve.

His phone rang.

"This is Seb Creek."

"Detective Creek, this is Special Agent Lowry. I'm calling to advise you that you are no longer associated with this investigation, but that you are still under the restraint of the Official Secrets Act. Understood?"

"Sure. Why, may I ask? I haven't received a single warrant call."

"You were instructed to remain at the magistrate's office, and you failed to do so."

"I see. How's the investigation going? Any leads?"

"That's need-to-know, and you don't. Goodbye, Mr. Creek."

The phone went dead and immediately rang again. The screen showed Sheriff Rhodes.

"Hello, Sheriff. I just talked to Lowry."

"He told me he was calling you. I saw him hang up."

"He fired me."

"I know. I'm the warrants man now. I called to tell you don't worry about it."

"Is he going to make you camp at Cromarty's office?"

"I talked him out of that."

"How's the investigation going?"

"We issued a warrant for Atlas Storage over on Tremont Road. The soldier they just released, Grayson Kelly, told one of his brig buddies he had a secret hideout and somebody figured it could be a storage unit and started checking and found it."

"They pick him up?"

"No. They found his cot, and some long guns and a bunch of ammo. And five grenades. He's probably still on the water. He could be two hundred miles gone by now. But they're looking. They'll get him."

"Have they settled on this guy then?"

"They're focused on him. Grenades got them excited."

"They're looking where the light's good, sounds like. I mean if it wasn't planned, it had to be random."

"True. While I've got you, what's up with Sackler?"

Seb told him about Elton Gleen, the Lands, the lawyer, the death scene he had just imagined. The coming interview with Prince.

Rhodes said, "So you want to call it a murder?"

"I'm pretty much settled on murder."

"All right. I'll call Doug and tell him to make another press release."

"Reporters been bugging you? Where are you?"

"I'm still on the base. Lowry wants me handy. As for reporters, I recognize their numbers and don't answer. They'll start calling from burners pretty soon."

"They want to know about your detective beating up a citizen?"

"Oh hell, I forgot to tell you. Queeny Barker recanted her bribery charge, and I called off SBI."

"Well, damn."

"So you're back to two complaints, where I would appreciate you remain for the next year at least."

Peter Prince strolled into view on the sidewalk, raised his eyebrows as he made eye contact. Seb said, "Sheriff, let me go. Here comes my interview."

They hung up. Prince crossed the room, sat opposite Seb, and propped his elbows on the table. He laid fingertips across his temples, peering at Seb through palm blinders. He said, "My lawyer just advised me not to speak with you."

"Really? Why?"

"Because the state's brand-new drone law hasn't been tested in court."

"Are you in trouble? Is that why you're seeing a lawyer?" He caught his waitress' eye. "You want coffee?"

The waitress, in her twenties, approached and stood hip-cocked. She said, "What can I get you?" Her face was long but pleasant, made attractive by attentive confidence.

Prince said, "All I want is a glass of cold water with lemon. For that I will leave a dollar tip though."

She said seriously, "Great. That's a seven hundredth of my rent."

Prince watched her retreat to the counter. He said, "I have just been out-cooled. That could be my future wife."

Seb remembered the impression he had gotten from the man a month earlier on the phone, a man affably content with his own superiority. He smiled and waited.

Prince folded his arms. He said, "You asked was I seeing a lawyer because I was in trouble. No. We're starting a new drone website. A place to post your videos. Numerous legal documents must be created, such as who gets the billion dollars when we sell to Google. Soon you too will be able to invest. Check it out on Overflight.com."

"I will. So here's the deal. I talked to Squint Cooper last night, and he accused you of flying a drone over his farm. I did not call you or question you because I don't give a shit and neither does the sheriff. The law reads you can't do surveillance on private property, but you can do newsgathering, and, like you said, until we get a bunch of court decisions refining that distinction, the sheriff's office is on the sidelines. I did, by the way, advise Squint to get a drone himself and try to follow you back to your LZ."

"What did he say?"

"He's not interested."

"Tell him he can also get a drone with a net hanging down. They've been testing them as a way to catch intruder drones. He and the mystery drone flyer could have a dogfight. Instead of trying to shoot it down. If he ever hits one of my drones, by the way, the FAA says he has to pay. That's federal law. That, by the way, is not an admission that it was me overflying Cooper Farms. I will say this though. Three days ago, that asshole forklifted fifty dead hogs out of one of his buildings. He filled up a dead box and left the rest of them lying on the ground. They're still lying there."

"He said a fan system went down."

"Well, that's piss-poor management, isn't it? And he sprays in the rain, and it runs into Council Creek, which he also flooded with hog shit a few years ago. Which is probably why somebody is overflying his wretched-ass hog factory. And because the asshole legislature cut the budget for inspections. And last week passed a limit on nuisance suits."

"Well, that's one subject dispensed with. Now here's another one. I want to find out if this mystery drone-flyer will send me a video of the footage he took yesterday around noon." He held up a hand, forestalling Prince's response. "The very important reason is, there was a man murdered around noon yesterday out at the Ford lodge. You know where that is?"

Prince nodded, waiting.

Seb said, "So the lodge is a short two miles from Cooper Farms on Twice Mile Road. The only two houses out there are on the east side of the inlet, and that's the Cooper house and the lodge. We contacted a few families on the west side of the Cooper land, and have a few leads, but nobody lives on Twice Mile, so nobody to ask. But what if the mystery drone flyer happened to catch some traffic out there around noon?"

Prince said, "The drone would be over the barns which is a mile from Twice Mile Road on the other side of the farm."

"I know, but maybe he caught something on Ruin Road or Crandell, which are the only two ways into Twice Mile. How far away does a drone flyer have to be to stay in contact with his drone?"

"Depends on the equipment." Prince paused, then added, "Also, if he installed relays along the inlet. In that case, he could be miles away."

"Which he might do if he was pissed off at a particular farm."

Prince pouted his lips, a minimal shrug.

Seb said, "You launched from a boat, didn't you? Then you followed your relays down the inlet. Squint showed me the video just after it was posted, and in that version there were a lot of creeks and swamp. Then when I went to look at it, all that was gone. It was edited."

"Can't bore the public with empty frames." The waitress brought a glass of water and set it in front of him. She tried a smile exchange, but Prince did not glance up.

Seb watched her walk away, then said, "So here's the deal. If the drone flyer, whoever he may be, does not send the video to me by tomorrow morning, nine o'clock, search warrants and subpoenas will be issued, and the full force of the law will descend on his hapless ass. I want every frame."

Seb fished a card from his jacket pocket and offered it. Prince unfolded one arm, took the card, and refolded.

Seb said, "Tell him to send it to the email address on the card anonymously."

Prince, who had gone pale, said, "If I run into him."

"Do yourself a favor, bro. Run into him."

THE LAWS OF THE UNIVERSE

Cody was seated on a storage box, flipping the putty knife, practicing doubles. Charlene had brought homemade pizza out to the garage, and they had finished it and opened their second beers. The boat was scraped and ready. He had run mineral spirits through the automatic sprayer, and it was ready too. He would start spraying in the morning, after the dew dried. Charlene had gotten the conversation around to Keisha, where, he admitted, he might be seriously intentioned.

"Are you hooking up?"

He said, "That's nosy."

"I know. Are you?"

"Yeah. A little."

"A little? How does that work?"

"Twice."

"You got some years on her."

"Who cares?"

"I'm not saying anything. It's just her mother's in the picture."

"Her mother likes me."

"You like Keisha?"

"So far."

"A lot?"

"So far. She a hypodermic."

"Oh, Jesus ..."

"I mean she has that effect."

"She gets you high?"

He tried a triple and caught it neatly. He said, "That's right. She puts a needle right into my vein."

They smiled together, both used to and indifferent to his offhand baiting. He said, "If things work out, we might get married."

"Have you talked about it?"

"No, but it's like an open secret when we look at each other."

"She *is* black."

"I noticed that."

"So there's the kid question."

"Fuck the kid question. And fuck anyone who asks it."

"The world does ask it."

"Then fuck the world."

"Sounds like you're feeling ready."

He could reply, but he felt self-pity tears trying to start. He steered. He said, "What's up with your Mike guy? Are you hooking up?"

"A little." She smiled but let sadness through. "I've been waiting on a call. Tap tap tap."

He caught the knife and held it, pointed it at her. He said, "You're a deep well, and he needs to have a deep thirst. If he don't, fuck him and the horse he rode in on."

She was sitting on the overturned boat and now rose and kissed the top of his thinning scalp. She said, "You gorgeous younger brother." She collected dishes and went back into the house.

If he could vanish, would be one solution, but vanish with no memories. Teleport to a new life where he could wake up, and it would be amnesia. What country is this? What food do we eat here? Elton Gleen would actually sell Stinger missiles to Arab terrorists. It was natural to him. It was not evil as much as ignorant. What if Elton saw five hundred terrified people falling toward earth? Could he look them in the eye as they fell, the kids too, and say, fine, where's my ten million? Some guys could, but most probably not. Most guys would have at least a twinge of feeling. Maybe that was mostly what evil was, blanking things out.

Cody went back to the workbench to test the paint. The stir stick glided without obstruction, the paint well-stirred by his dependable sister. It was a deep rich lovely blue and ran like warm honey. He turned the stick, watching the blue fluid fold and flop into the blue pool, the laws of the universe faithfully functioning despite his troubles. There was no trouble anywhere except for his life, and everyone's life. After the boat was painted, he could get a bunch of gas and drive into the ocean, far as he could, many miles, until the gas was gone, give himself to the universe—your problem now.

But don't be an idiot. If he wasn't going to kill himself, he had to solve the fucking problem. He needed a Mylar blanket to defeat their night vision, a ploy he recalled somewhere from his training. First, he needed to google to make sure that was still right.

DETECTIVING

It was five-thirty on a Sunday, and the detectives' area was empty. There were two cardboard file boxes on Seb's desk, and on top of the larger one a typed note:

> *Here is the murder book (smaller box) for the Hugh Britt murder of yesteryear and also the trial proceedings. Also, after much research, I, Bonnie, your servant, figured out how to call the governor and got her number from a very possessive secretary in Raleigh, who also didn't like being bothered on her day off. Dial 011-8816-7690-4511. The 8816 part is the Iridium system prefix of the governor's sat phone, which means she doesn't have to pay a dime for incoming calls. And if you have international calling set up on your cell phone, you don't either, at least to call the Caribbean. Do you? Yes, you do. You left your laptop open on your desk, and I checked.*
>
>

Your faithful gem,
Bonnie
>

> *PS: Incidentally, Zetta in property, being a storage hawk, cleared the evidence box from the Britt murder after Leo Sackler was released and reports that her son is now using the murder weapon (axe) to chop wood. She didn't tell him where it came from.*

A single rose, Seb thought. For her desk tomorrow morning. He clicked open his ballpoint and drew a reminder X on the back of his hand, then lifted the boxes from the desktop and tucked them out of sight—Stinson's sight—behind his trash can. Then on impulse he retrieved the smaller box and browsed the investigation file until he found the lead detective's name: Jason Braughwell. He woke his computer and entered the name in Google with *Swann County Sheriff*. He found the man's 1996 obituary in the *Swann Sun*. He lifted the larger box onto the desk and leafed for the prosecutor's name. The trial and two appeals, all two years apart, were handled by the county district attorney himself, Thomas Felton. Which made political sense, the DA wanting lead on a high-profile sure thing. Seb googled again. Thomas Felton was also deceased. He tucked the boxes behind the trash can again. If he dead-ended, he would read them front to back.

He opened the case file on his computer. He had not gotten back to the Sackler death scene, which meant the report would not be ready for tomorrow's briefing unless he arrived early the next morning. Or be late with it, endure a Stinson frown.

He sat at his desk and gazed into space, a brief consider. He had an hour before he needed to get outside by the water, where he had formed a habit of sitting to cool out before the sing. He could call Barb and Marty, see if they had anything. But he'd see them in the morning. So best time use was call real estate agents for the white car, then the governor, then try to make fifteen minutes for Queeny Barker, who, he learned yesterday, had been transferred to the jail infirmary. But first, on impulse, he shouted long and loud into the empty room: "Kate! Kate, are you here?"

He searched for *Swann County Realtors*, came up with a list of over thirty, and copied them to a Word document. He lifted his desk phone and dialed the first three digits of AAA Realty, then heard:

"Did you just shout my name?" Kate was holding the side of the hall door and leaning into the squad room, gibbon-like.

He said, "That was me having fun on a Sunday. I thought you'd be gone by now."

"Well, I'm not. I have been watching those videos of your murder victim. He's been singing 'Long Tall Sally.' And other hits from the past. He never told his little friend exactly what he was looking for, but he was definitely looking for something. Also, your extortionist wasn't on there."

"You finished them?"

"Just finished them, and I'm leaving."

"How many hours?"

"Five something. It was a one-twenty-eight-gig phone too, and he was shooting high-def. Next question, did the videos upload to iCloud? They did not, because he didn't have Wi-Fi out there and that's the way his phone was set."

"So he never once said, boy, I bet I'm getting close to that money or that body?"

"Sorry. I called maintenance, and I'm meeting two diggers out there tomorrow. So we'll find what we find. Also, Barb sent in video from Lowe's and Sears, and I went through those too. Sackler was with his daughter both times. No lurking felons. Now I'm off to cheer for my husband in a fast-pitch softball game. I would invite you, but it's the first forty-eight. But come anyway."

"Next time. Have fun."

Kate vanished into the hallway. Seb continued to dial. Then he hung up. He had started with the realty agents instead of the governor out of obedience to Stinson. But it had been a long day, and the governor would be more fun, even if she was part of the hotshot theory. He fished out his cell phone and dialed the fifteen numbers. The phone made a series of disjointed tones and began to ring.

"Hello." A woman's voice.

"Hello, this is Detective Seb Creek calling for Governor Lerner."

"This is she."

"Governor, I'm investigating a murder. I wonder if you have time for a couple of questions."

The woman said something to someone else, and a door or cabinet clattered. She said, "I do. I read the *Observer* online so I know about Leo Sackler. Is this about Leo Sackler?"

"Yes, it is."

"Well, fire away. We're anchored in a lovely bay with the sunset on the way, and I have nothing but time. Well, I shouldn't say that, in case you might become envious." She laughed the merry laugh that Seb had heard many times on the news, the laugh adored by her supporters and lamented by her opponents. "The article says it's a suspicious death. So it's a murder?"

"We think it is."

"You want to know about Germaine? And what she told me?"

"That's right."

"Do you know the name Leonard Castle?"

"He's your lawyer."

"You've done your homework. Leonard, Germaine, and I were all in school together at State. You mustn't assume a grand conspiracy. Not at all. Germaine and I were no longer in contact, despite what those earlier articles said. But she knew Leonard was my lawyer and contacted him. She was dying. She told him that Leo Sackler was innocent and could he petition me for a compassionate release. Leonard said, Germaine, how do you know he is innocent? She would not say, but said she would leave a written testament. Have you found that, by the way?"

"No. But there may have been some papers missing at the lodge."

"Really? Oh, goodness."

"A testament, not a confession?"

"Yes. Not a confession."

"You believed her?"

"At first, I did not. I telephoned her after Leonard talked to me. She was bedridden and could barely speak, could barely think actually. I did not know what to make of it all, and neither did Leonard. After all, it was only her word. I will say this though, that when I began to look into the Sackler case with Leonard, I found it was completely circumstantial. In addition, Mr. Sackler had been a model prisoner for forty-odd years. And could have been released if he had admitted guilt. But he would not, and that was impressive. Three days later Germaine appeared in my office. Out of bed and at my door. That's when I believed her. She said she knew the truth and let a man go to prison, and it ruined her life. She wept and pleaded. And I believed her. Either she was telling the truth or was crazy.

And she was not crazy. I did get the idea that she was present at the Hugh Britt murder. That's really all I can tell you. But I am delighted that you have called. It had crossed my mind to call you, or whoever."

"What am I forgetting to ask?"

"If it comes to you, call me back. And if you discover the truth, do please call me back."

He began to call realty agents. All were closed, except for one, whose receptionist agreed to email their agents about white cars and property near Twice Mile Road. He left five messages, noting his list as he went. As he began to dial again, his cell phone rang.

"Hello."

"Hey, Mr. Creek." It was Deputy Randall Garland. "You asked me to call and check in before I knocked. Did DeWitt call?"

"DeWitt who?"

"Press DeWitt. He was the Realtor the Parkinsons saw out on Ruin Road. He sells mostly land and drives a white Prius with a realty sticker on the side."

"How did you learn that?"

"Well, I been calling around as I drove patrol."

"No shit. And you found him."

"Yeah. He said he would call you. He didn't call you?"

"He did not. You got his number?"

After writing the number, Seb said, "Why didn't you call, let me know?"

A silence. Then: "I guess I should have."

Seb intuited. He said, "You didn't want to brag."

"I guess that's right."

"Well, see, Randall, you got to go past bragging, thinking about, alert the detective in case the guy doesn't call."

"Right. I should have called."

"Anyway, you were out detecting today."

"I guess I was."

"In case you ever want to be one, now you know what it is—calling Realtors. Anyway, nice work. It's going in the report even if it hurts your humble feelings."

Randall laughed, and they hung up. Seb dialed the number.

"This is Press."

"Mr. DeWitt. Detective Seb Creek, Swann sheriff's department."

"Oh, Christ. I was supposed to call you. Well, I knew you had my number. I haven't been hiding. It's just been going in and out of my mind. So how can I help?" The voice was loud and fast, the voice of a confident, harried man.

"You spoke with Mr. Sackler yesterday?"

"Day before."

"What time?"

"Morning. Maybe ten."

"What about?"

"Did he want to sell his land and that lodge. He did not."

"Where was he when you saw him?"

"Down in a well. Then he came up and started pulling up buckets of dirt."

"How long did you speak with him?"

"Five minutes. I don't waste time, and his no was no."

"You see anybody else at the lodge?"

"I did not."

"Any cars?"

"There was a pickup. Old-timey."

"Did you go into the house?"

"No. He emptied the buckets and went back down in the well."

"Why was he digging out the well?"

"No idea. I guess he wanted a well."

"He didn't say?"

"And I didn't ask. I dropped my card, and away I went."

"You dropped it into the well?"

"No, I tossed it on the ground."

"What did it look like?"

"It was a white business card. Landman Realty. Which is me."

"Mr. Sackler was killed around one o'clock yesterday. You got an alibi?"

"Let's see. Yeah. I was over in Duplin County talking to Jason Stillson of Stillson Farms. I'm driving, or I'd get you his number."

"I can get it. How long were you over there?"

"Oh, say three hours. Twelve to three, thereabouts. I had lunch with him and his wife and kids. That's fifty miles from Leo Sackler."

"Business meeting?"

"Yep. He's putting part of his farm on the market."

Seb told DeWitt he might have been the last person to see the victim alive and asked him to drop by investigations tomorrow at his convenience and make a statement. He received an *Oh, Christ,* then an *okay.*

QUEENY

Queeny Barker was in the last bed of the long open infirmary ward. The other occupant was a snoring bulbous mound in the first bunk. Queeny had her bed cocked and was sitting up studying an iPad on top of a pillow. She looked up when she felt his approach. On her right cheek, her brown skin had rippled with a pink rash. At the foot of the bed, a leg shackle emerged from the sheet.

Queeny, using her unmodulated man voice, said, "So here you are at last."

"Here I am."

"Do you forgive me?"

"Hell, no."

"Yes, you do. You couldn't no more hold a grudge on me if your life depended on it."

In high school, Seb Creek, the jock, had taken Queeny the queer, then Kevin, under his protection. And had been summoned to bars three times in the last year to arrest her for soliciting.

Queeny said, "It breaks my heart to see you. I don't know why. I'm very emotional right now. Very very."

"They said you have cancer."

"Yes, it's all spread out, tip to toe, no going back. Satisfactory, my dear Watson."

"I will miss you, Queeny."

"Of course you will. Friends miss friends." After a moment, Queeny said, "I wasn't letting nobody fuck me, by the way. It was blow jobs, pure and simple."

Seb said, "I know it was."

Queeny said, "I will say hello to my mama for you."

"Please do that."

"I can feel her waiting. I believe as you grow closer to death you lighten up, and the other world can approach. I feel that and believe it's true."

"I must be a long way from death then."

"Oh, you are. You got a full charge of man force coursing through your veins. That's why I fell for you. Do you forgive me, really?"

"Of course."

"You know why I did it?"

Seb waited.

"Pure self-hatred. And being drunk. But isn't that peculiar? The man who loves me, and that I love, I'm going to plant a hundred dollars on him? Oh, I was ready for you. I had that bill folded over my fingers. I don't deserve any love at all, is what that is. I listened to that bad imp in my head, and you know why? I think it was boredom. I wanted to get back connected with you. And here you are."

Seb smiled.

Queeny said, "You know what I'm sitting here doing? I got this iPad from the nurse, who's my new best girlfriend. I'm studying on near-death experiences. Ever since you told me, I been wanting to, and now my blessing is I can. If I was a youngster, I don't think I would leave my bedroom if I had YouTube. Everything is on YouTube."

"It's a new age."

"It is. If we get to choose, I'll be coming back as a rich white woman."

"Be sure to look me up."

They smiled. Queeny's eyes moistened, and a tear broke loose. "You know what else the nurse told me?"

"What?"

"That you beat up some poor soul and got yourself investigated. That's why I told the truth, to get them off you."

"I appreciate it."

"Am I going to have to worry about you when I'm on the other side? I don't want to be looking down here and worrying. I'll haunt your dumb ass."

"I was making an arrest, and it got physical. He got hurt by accident. I didn't lose it."

"Truth now?"

"Well … my bad imp might have used the occasion."

"Well, I'm going haunt you. If you feel some sweetness, that'll be me."

Seb held out his fist, and they tapped knuckles. Seb said, "I got to go. I got the singers."

"They give me a month about. Do come again."

THE LIGHT BENEATH THE CESSPOOL

The VFW hall where the singers met overlooked the inlet three blocks from the sheriff's office. Seb followed the sidewalk that wandered through the small inlet park. The idea for the singing group had come to him when he delivered a prisoner to the county jail. Three older black prisoners were harmonizing on "The Midnight Special" in the dayroom. The young guys surrounding them wore skeptical expressions but were rapt. The next day he spoke to psychological services on the base, then to Captain Delmonico at the brig. The singing group began to form, at first drawing military males, then military women. Now the sopranos included three female rape victims, all civilian.

He read books on group therapy, Alcoholics Anonymous, and choir training. An ethos of effort and honesty developed. In the talk sessions after each practice, they reported changes in attitude and behavior. Eventually even the men became unashamed of tears. They were invited to perform, both on the base and in town. Psychological services on the base videoed them from time to time as part of a training film for PTSD therapy.

It was Seb's custom on practice days to come early and sit for a while at the park table under the overpass. The loudening-softening shush of traffic above and the green-gray water below were human and ordinary and steadied him. Now, as the table came in view, he saw it was occupied by Squint Cooper, seated on top, slouched over his knees, head down, a cigarette canted in his wide mouth as he peered sideways at Seb.

"Got your spot, I know it," he said. He removed the cigarette, blew the ember clean, dabbed it against his tongue, then pinched it out with a thumb and forefinger. He tucked the cigarette into the breast pocket of his denim jacket. He said, "I hear on the news where Leo Sackler has gone from suicide to murder, and I expect you want to talk to me, so I come early to make myself available. Am I right?"

"You're on the list, as his only neighbor."

"I come to say I can't help, sorry. Never met the man, or saw him either. I'm busy as hell at the farm. We're installing a new system. Guess what? We're going to generate electricity out of hog shit methane. I got a handful of grants. The Department of Energy's going to make me a star."

"Does that mean you're going to cover your lagoons?"

"One of them anyway, to start."

"Cover the one closest to the Lands."

"We're covering the other one." Squint delivered an appraising look. "That's an engineering decision, not mine."

"I was over at Josie Land's today."

"Oh, you were?"

Seb let silence provoke.

Squint said, "Well, I run a hog farm. I offered to buy them out. They'd rather sue."

Seb knew the history. Squint had not offered much, and the suit was recent, a last resort.

Seb said, "I better get on."

Squint said, "Wait a minute. I got a topic to discuss."

"Bring it up after the—"

"No, this is for you. I had a dream, and I believe in dreams. Will you listen?"

"Go ahead."

"I dreamed there was a cesspool under my house, and I could look down and see raging currents of shit. I couldn't get it cleaned out. Too many loose boards or something. Everything tilted. Bad footing." He thrust large hands before his face. "It'd be way boring to bring out I'm a shit farmer. This dream is symbolic. And, oh, Brother Sebastian, it ain't just me. Each one lives in shit or just above and can see it reeking from below, if they ever look, which they don't. We hold our noses." He pinched his nose with one hand and pointed a finger empathically. "Which is repression of self and sets hypocrisy loose as simple ordinary." His expression intensified as Seb's face set in a neutral smile. "You of all people must listen and understand. Then you must answer. For here you are, digging in the heart with song. Digging into those who have been rubbed and drug in death and blood. Can you dig to light, is my question? Can you dose a man with truth and expect good consequences? Or will truth run off his back like water?"

Seb opened his mouth to speak, but Squint continued, holding his thick hands aloft in imprecation. "The problems of life are two—death and desire. Formidable ills, and the prescription is the choking pill of religion, or else, if you're highfalutin, the chicken broth of morality. Well put, Mr. Squint. Then you die and what the fuck. So what is your offer? Sing with Seb and die deeper?"

Beneath Squint's flamboyant egoism, Seb could sense need. But the flamboyance was off-putting, particularly since he had just been with Queeny. He said mildly, "Under the cesspool is light. I testify."

"You testify?"

"Yes."

Squint got nimbly from the tabletop and came to his full height. He said, "Embrace me, Seb. Deep and true as only you can do."

Seb let himself be enfolded, the scent of the tobacco-and-hog-stenched denim part of his general distaste. Squint thrust Seb back and held him at arm's length. "I've taken heart. My fate has been slaughter. The slaughter of the young soldiers of Viet Nam—and some were women, not that it matters if they're throwing grenades. And now I live by the slaughter of hogs." He released Seb, propped his butt against the tabletop, and folded his arms. "Did you talk to that fucker Peter Prince?"

Seb said, "I did talk to him. He mentioned you could get a drone with a net hanging down, and you guys could dogfight."

"If he confessed, you must arrest him."

"It was hypothetical. He was not confessing. Also, you best stop shooting at his drone. If you hit it, you have to pay him."

"Says who?"

"Says the FAA. According to Prince."

"Okay, fine. Now then. I want you to ask my son, Cody, to join the singers."

"I talked to him today. He wasn't interested."

"Charlene make you?"

"She asked me."

"Well, she's god-awful persistent. She's why I'm talking to you. Cody's down in my cesspool, no doubt. Swirling around down there and peering up in accusation. I must sing past him to the light. There was a fellow here earlier. I may have run him off with my conversation. He was pensive and hesitant, and that inspired me like a white sheet of paper. He has since fled."

"You get his name?"

"I can't recall it."

"Was it Tom Rogers?"

"Yes, it was."

"Where is he?" Seb half turned, ready to start up the steps.

"He went into the hall. He's helping Jose set out the chairs."

"What did you say to him?"

"Pretty much what I said to you. About the cesspool of the human mind. I was practicing my delivery."

Seb started up the steps, then turned and fixed Squint with a look. "Don't be swinging your club for exercise, Squint, not in this group. I will ban you."

Squint let his head fall, then bob in a series of nods. "Tell you what. Tell Cody I'm quitting the singers. If he comes, I'll go. That's why I joined, you know. But when I did, he wouldn't. Which learns us the medic's lesson. Tend your own wounds first."

OH, HONEY

Keisha said, "Guess what? I got my period five days ago." She was behind the wheel of her mother's station wagon, driving Cody to the surplus store.

Cody said, "Are you telling me that because you want me to know you're finished with your period or because you thought I was worried about I might have to marry you?"

This tickled her. She leaned across the wide seat to backhand his thigh. "How ever does your mind work! I never can guess, half the time or any of the time."

Cody felt a wave of love for this pixie with the small laughing face and blue nipple-rippled T-shirt—worn for him, no doubt, and delicately illumined in the dashlight glow. They were on the way to purchase the components of Cody's thermal-scope-defeating inspiration—duct tape, three Mylar blankets, and a wide umbrella. He intended to come in from the ocean side and cross the island to the burial site under a Mylar canopy. The bad part of the idea was that if they grabbed him, he would be excuseless. He had considered just driving the boat back to the site, make a fire, roast some weenies, maybe bring some toot, and if they were watching, hey, just hanging out, officers, like I used to do back when. Then, if they were not watching, dig fast and gone. Bad chances though, since even if they only questioned him it could lead to his

Venus flytrap record, and maybe they had found the dug-up pods. That kind of coincidence would break out the metal detectors in a hurry.

So it was the Mylar blanket umbrella cave and a slow, patient sneak from the ocean side. Move ten feet, stop and sit. Move ten feet. Probably take an hour, but definitely take the hour and definitely do not be stoned. Then an hour-long trip back across the dunes carrying the case and the missiles, the missiles in a big enough backpack which he would also have to buy, so add that to the list. And some cord to bind the missiles together so no sound. And a little blanket to muffle them, so add that.

When they got to the surplus store, Keisha would ask, what in heaven's name are you needing these items for? and he would answer, oh, it's a new kind of deer blind I'm trying to invent, where a hunter can just pop it open in a tree and hunker undetected. Since he was a tinkerer after all. He could even say certain theories have deer seeing thermally, which she might believe. Which would be cruel though, to lie extraly to her friendly mind, and which repulsed him to think about.

She warmed him. Charlene liked her too, had made her a cup of coffee when she came to pick him up. They had chatted about her working at Walmart, discussed about Walmart being evil and good, then about Keisha signing up for business classes at Swann County Community College. As he followed Keisha out to the car, Charlene had given him a raised eyebrow, go-get-her-boy face.

So Cody had two fine, kind women pulling for him. As he headed toward lifetime incarceration.

At the surplus store, they loaded the items in a cart. When Keisha inquired, he told the planned-out deer-blind lie, then had to shrug off her undeserved admiration.

Outside, as she was backing up, she said, "Want to go park?"

He lifted her right hand from the back of the seat and cupped it around his face, a palm kiss. He said, "I do."

She headed up Highway 17, then took a road toward the inlet, then a country road, then a brush-clogged road to the water. It was dusk now, and the headlights flared a tobacco barn in a shrub-grown field, then an old cabin with an inlet view. They parked behind the cabin, facing the darkening void of water. She said her high school boyfriend took her here a year ago. Sadly she had broken up with him that very night, and no, he did not get any farewell poontang.

She said, "Let's get in the back seat, want to?"

He pushed himself into the back, listened to her rustling, and when she came over the seat she was naked. She straddled him, and they kissed. She held his head between her hands and kept pulling away and kissing him, then pulling away again and kissing him again. Then she worked his buckle and fly, and he stripped his pants to his ankles and pulled up his T-shirt, and they were naked to naked and kissed and kissed. Then she slid him inside, and they stopped moving and kissing and held for a long time, her fingers delicate on his neck, his hands delicate on her back.

When he began to cry, his chest heaving and bucking against her, she stroked thumbs across his eyes and said, "Oh, honey. Oh, honey."

THE INNER BEING

Everyone had done their homework and thought the Shaun Davey version of "The Parting Glass" excellent, even the whooping at the end, and how about, someone said, throw a few hats into the air, which, when he considered it, Seb agreed added off-the-wall exuberance, plus humor, so bring hats to the next practice. They would make it the final song in their upcoming performance on the base.

Seb divided them up, the bagpipe-emulating drone singers among whom he placed the newly introduced Tom Rogers, to the other end of the room to practice a lower octave plus fifth with Lieutenant Fernando, while he took his experienced on-pitch unison singers, three women and seven men, through the chorus, truing them from the piano keyboard. He had emailed four of the men and Gloria, their big-ranged soprano, a harmony of thirds and fourths, sung a cappella by himself, and now took them through it together, and found they had all memorized it. He added the five melody singers, two women and three men, and when they were blended brought the drones over, and they ran through the chorus three times. It was only trifling muddy. They saw they could do it. They were pleased and happy.

Then he set Fernando up front to sing the two eight-line solos with drone accompaniment, bracketed and ended by the unison chorus. Fernando did not have Shaun Davey's gravel, but his accent added a halfway

Irishy brightness, especially since Seb had worked with him to soften his too-sharp *i*'s.

Then they took a break and went back to their chairs. Seb left the keyboard and stood before them for a few impromptu remarks about the song itself, running down its centuries-long history of revisions, remarking that its current version was, in his opinion, an almost perfectly written lyric. Consider the lines, he said, *There's many a comrade ere I had that's sorry for my going away. And many a sweetheart ere I had would wish me one more day to stay.* See how the two differ, he said, the men and women, the men expressing their usual manly sorrow, but the women—here he gave himself to sublimity—the women, the wells and storehouses of human feeling, how they plead, oh, one more day at least.

The singers nodded and smiled. They recognized this was his effort at therapy, this unashamed making-public of the inner being. This was sponging in the yurt. They were grateful. They were enthused.

They ran through it several more times until the muddiness became musicality, then ran through it again and were done. It was nearing ten o'clock.

Ahmad, a tall, big-shouldered black man, whose throat was scarred with a wound and surgeries, took him aside and made another rasping plea for hip-hop, and couldn't Seb write a little something, because he, Ahmad, now had over a dozen extremely vivid beats plus melodies worked up on his boom box, and did he, Seb, have time for a listen tonight? Seb said he would definitely listen soon, but not tonight. Tonight he had something going.

They gathered their chairs into their customary circle. Seb stood in the center, turning as he spoke. He introduced Tom Rogers again and explained that this was the time they shot the shit, everyone speaking freely or not speaking.

Rogers nodded and shrugged and watched. He and Seb had spoken privately before the practice, Seb inquiring if Tom, during his stretch in the brig, had run into a man named Grayson Kelly. He had not.

Seb addressed the group, noting there were three more practices until their miniconcert on the base, when they would perform "Forever Young,"

"Auld Lang Syne," "The Rose," and now "The Parting Glass." Then he mentioned that the medical examiner's wife, supposedly a fine singer, had expressed interest in performing with them, and was that something they wanted to consider? The proposal was met with silence. He said, "Okay, forget it. Now I need a favor. I want you guys to let me leave early."

Someone said, "Of course."

Someone else said, "What's up?"

Seb said, "I met a woman …" and paused to let the clamor go by. He said, "I don't have a lot of time, and I …" Gloria rose, and, with her hands against his back, pushed him through the circle toward the door. She said, "Go on now. Go. Go."

Then the others took it up, "Go, go, go."

He smiled his gratitude and waved and left.

It was after ten. As he drove along the inlet road toward Willow Creek, he realized he would soon pass Loman Creek Road, where Charlene lived, and where Cody lived in a rear trailer. He was already late for his planned drop-by at Mia's, and as Loman Creek approached he did not slow.

Then he braked hard, making a sliding turn onto the gravel road, and a hundred yards later turned into their driveway and parked behind Charlene's SUV. He walked past Cody's bike, past the garage and upturned boat, then up the path to the trailer. The lights were on. He heard the sound of the television.

He rapped on the metal door. As it opened, he moved his face into the column of spilled light. He said, "Hey, Cody."

Cody said, "What the fuck …"

"I was just heading home after the singers. You got a minute?"

"I told you I'm not going …"

"Yeah, I noticed you did not show up. Hey, you mind if I come in? Get eye-to-eye."

"There's no place to sit."

Seb opened the door wider and stepped onto the first stair. "I'll stand. That's fine."

Cody said, "Hey, man …" But he backed up as Seb stepped onto the trailer floor.

Seb glanced around the labyrinth of miscellaneous clutter. He said, "This place has a lived-in look."

Cody lifted his remote from the chair and paused the TV, which was showing a black-and-white Western. Seb pointed to the screen. "*High Noon*. You know what makes that a classic? Basically, it's because Gary Cooper is not an asshole. Except maybe he could have stayed in town and forgiven those people. I hope I didn't ruin the ending."

"I've seen it. What do you want?"

"I promised Charlene I'd come by, and I didn't think I should count seeing you at Elton's tub yard. So here I am. Your sister says you're maybe getting into something wrong. Right now I'm not a detective, and if a thousand flytraps fell out of your cupboards I wouldn't even notice. She didn't say flytraps. I'm guessing. I hope not dope."

"C'mon, man. You can't just bust in here."

"I'm leaving. Unless you offer me a beer."

"I don't have a beer."

"Okay then. Anyway, I invite you again to Pass the Salt. I need your baritone. So that's one thing. The other thing is, for your sister's sake, who has a big heart for you, do not fuck up. She shed tears of love for you today, Cody. Don't break her heart. That's my message."

Cody smiled. He made a small laugh. He picked up the remote, sank into his padded chair, and started the movie.

He said, "Okay then."

A GIANT MILITARY PROBLEM

As Seb cruised past Jimmy Beagle's Famous Floating Fish House, he spotted a slim figure crossing under the lightbulb on the suspension walkway and thought, that's her, but wasn't sure. He drove the hundred yards to Mia's white barn studio, parked, looked through a window into the darkened gallery, then went down the wooden walkway and opened the door to the attached studio. He spoke loudly, "Mia?"

The studio lights were all on, illuminating her throwing station and a clutter of ware shelves, carts, and canvas-covered tables. No one answered. It was her on the walkway then. She had something in her hands too, something in each hand, and it was beer bottles, definitely, so she and Jimmy Beagle were buddies. Seb and his father had bought minnows from Jimmy years ago. If he wasn't dead, he was old, so why not drop by?

The barge was a hundred feet of rusted steel and had been cut in two lengthwise so that it was only twenty feet wide. It was moored on piers and connected to the land with a suspension bridge and gangway leading to the barge deck. A couple of johnboats with small outboards were lashed to one end. The darkened bait shack sat in the center, and as Seb approached it he saw in the gibbous moonlight the land-facing signboard across the shack's eaves. It had once read JIMMY BEAGLE'S FAMOUS FLOATING FISH HOUSE, hand-lettered red on white, but was faded to unreadable now. At the far end of the deck, he could make out two figures seated on white plastic chairs beside the cleaning counter.

Jimmy's voice said, "Help you, sir?"

Seb started toward them, thinking what to say. He had a plan but had forgotten it. He said, "It's Seb Creek. Is that Jimmy and Mia?"

"Seb?" said Mia.

As Seb approached, he thought he heard Jimmy say, *Is that him?* and Mia say, *It sure is.*

Jimmy rose from his chair. He and Seb shook hands. Seb said, "My dad and I used to get minnows here. Like twenty years ago."

Jimmy nodded. "I been selling menhaden forever and ever. Till the creek closed up. Now if you want my minnows you about got to pole through. Menhaden still here, though not in abundance. That describes me in a fair way." He made a polite chuckle. He was an elderly black man. In the moonlight, his face was like crumpled gray leather. He wore dark pants, flip-flops, and a pale long-sleeved shirt. He gestured with his beer bottle. "I'm about finished with this beer, or I'd pour you a slug."

Mia said, "He can have a slug of mine, if he wants."

Seb said, "I hope I'm not intruding."

Jimmy said, "I believe I'm the one intruding now."

They laughed.

Mia said, "Jimmy and I were talking about the helicopters that crashed. I wondered if you knew some of them."

"The names haven't been released yet. I've been out of uniform for several years, but it's possible."

Mia said, "I've been sad all day. I think because I just met a soldier."

Seb felt for a response. He could make a joke. He didn't.

"Look here," Jimmy said. "I'm cleaning tanks. Let me get to it. Do you mind, Mia?"

"Of course not," said Mia, returning his formality. "Next time."

"Next time, Mia." To Seb: "Nice to see you."

Seb said it was nice to see him again too, and Jimmy walked back to the bait shop fifty feet away. An interior light went on. A window cast a yellow rectangle on the rusty deck, and Mia's face emerged from shadow. She was waiting. She smiled.

Seb said, "I guess I ran him off."

"You did. But he was cleaning tanks when I got here."

"I saw you crossing the bridge."

"I wondered how you found me. Sit down. You want a pull from this beer?" She handed him the bottle. "Drink up. I'm done. I just saw Jimmy's light on. We drink a beer now and then."

Seb drank an inch of beer from the half-full bottle, thinking of her lips on the smooth glass. He was alone in the moonlight with her. He offered the bottle back, but she declined with a gesture.

He said, "It's been twelve hours. I figured that was long enough."

She made a humming laugh. She said, "Have you tied someone to a tree? Or did you come with another intention?"

He said, "I saw some guys today I wish I could tie to a tree. But yes, my intention is to ask you for a date."

"Okay. Let's have a date."

Seb let out a long undisguised sigh. He polished off the beer and set it on the deck. "If I could have a wish, I would wish us ahead about six months. So I would feel braver."

She said, "I'm pretty terrifying." Then she said, "I shouldn't joke. It's hard, starting something."

There was a silence. She said, "I was telling Jimmy about you."

"I thought I picked that up."

"You probably didn't notice, but one of his arms is a little shorter than the other. That's why he wears long-sleeved shirts. He was shot in the elbow in Viet Nam."

Seb looked into the dark bulk of water, then at her. He said, "You wanted to know about war, how it affects people?"

"I didn't want to ask you about it. But yes, I wanted to know, so I thought of Jimmy. I don't know anything about it, except that it's so … different than here."

"You go from the mall to killing strangers in a foreign country."

"Oh, God."

He let a silence go. If he talked, if he let the war come, the passion would come too. He said, "Eventually, if we get to know each other, I'll tell you all about it." He could say, that's why I'm here, and then thought, that's not true though. He was here because he liked her. He smiled at that thought.

She said, "This is such a hard subject to think about. I guess that's why we don't think about it."

He said, "It's the farthest thing from home that we do. From our humanity. Back here, you do a guy a favor, just some ordinary thing you might do, you pass the salt, and in war, that same guy, you shoot him. Or he shoots you. In the singers, we try to reconnect the parts. The savage part that does the killing. That wants to kill, even. And the deeper place that doesn't. Because war cuts you right in two. It's a giant military problem, when you think about it. They can send you to war, but they can't bring you home."

It was time to breathe. He gestured with his hands and now felt her warm hand hold his and squeeze and release. That she released was wise and granted his privacy.

She said, "Do you know the World War I story about Christmas in the trenches?"

"I know it and prize it. It freaked the generals out. But can that be enough about war and Seb? To tell you the truth, I sort of despise talking about it. Not because of guilt or anything, but … I don't know …"

"Because it's sacred. You can't walk there with words."

"Oh, man." He flushed and breathed away tears. One day he would tell her about the land of love and explanation, the place he had visited when he was dead for six minutes. He said, "Is it enough?"

"It's enough, sure."

"I'm basically a happy guy. I want to tell you jokes. And talk about movies."

She touched the back of his hand. She said, "You have an *X* on the back of your hand."

"Yes, I do. That's a reminder to buy our secretary a rose. She did me a favor." He looked at her. She was waiting, offering silence.

He asked her about her work then, about selling at art fairs and about galleries, about the packing and shipment of delicate ceramics. She answered clearly and courteously, but the lightness of the subject contrasted with war and made his questions seem trivial. Finally he was quiet.

Her hand rested on her thigh. He reached and grazed the back of his hand across the top of hers. He wanted to stand and draw her up and embrace her. He resisted. He said, "So how about a date could be we go fishing? Take a boat, maybe go out by the ocean."

She lifted her face into the moonlight, smiled unwillingly. Her face was concentrated.

It was the death of fish, he thought. He said, "It could be that you have an issue with fishing."

"Well, not so much an issue …"

"Are you vegetarian?"

"I am actually. I could watch you fish."

"Watch me kill fish?"

She made a warm smirk.

He said, "I mostly let them go. Did you know Jacques Cousteau didn't fish? He thought it was wrong to kill fish for sport. How's this? We go on a picnic, go out to the ocean."

"We could rent one of Jimmy's boats."

"We could go for an ocean walk, search up some pretty shells. It's cold for swimming, but we could wade."

"Sounds fun."

He said, "So good. Now I better head out. I need to sleep. Unless you want to tell me about your brother."

"Another time. He's quite nice. He's a reporter, and I have two sweet nieces."

They stood. They started toward the fish shack and the walkway behind it.

She said, "We haven't given our date a date. I know you must be busy. I heard on the news the death has become a murder."

They passed the front of the fish house, where Jimmy was bent into a tank. They stopped at the ramp entrance to the suspension bridge. Seb said, "I'm definitely pinched for time. I've been running around all day."

She said, "Do you have a suspect?"

"Lots of them. What's your schedule like?"

"I'm fairly free. I teach on Wednesday evening is all."

"Okay. I've got lots of comp time, so any good weather day we see coming. I look forward to it."

"Thanks for stopping by."

They hesitated, both waiting to see whether a kiss was next.

She said, "Seb, let me kiss you. But don't kiss me back. Just for now."

"Okay."

She leaned, raised her face, and lightly pressed her lips to his. He stood obediently impassive.

She smiled. She said, "Now kiss me back, but just a little."

They kissed. He held her cheeks with fingertips. He felt her warm breath. They parted.

She said, "It's a sign of sincerity to kiss back just a little."

He smiled. He said, "I wouldn't mind kissing back a little more."

She laughed. "That's a sign of something else."

A TABLE OF SPLINTERS

Cody's sister knocked on his door at seven Monday morning, off to school. She kissed him, asked him not to paint the gardenias blue, frowned at the flytraps he was arranging on his kitchen table, and, because she had seen his Mylar-taped umbrella hanging in the garage, told him his deer-blind idea was impressive and a possible moneymaker. He told her he was planning to get some spray paint to camo it up. A lie about a lie. He had altered his plans. A Mylar sneak was too risky. He was going to run.

He phoned his extract buyers and asked them to make an exception, come to him this time, but they wouldn't budge. The overcurrent was, we're businessmen buying from a nursery. The undercurrent was, you're a poacher, and in North Carolina flytrapping has gone felony. So he set up a three o'clock in the Marriott parking lot north of Richmond. That gave him time for a bank run to collect his twenty grand from the safety-deposit box, time for the drive, time for a fast chat with Keisha at Walmart. Take her to the bathroom, show her the stash, inform her it would soon be twenty-five. Then, please Keisha, come to Canada. Canada instead of Mexico because of its beauty and lost northern regions and English. You can go to college in Canada with this amazing amount of money. The reason, Keisha, is that I am a hunted bandit! I have stolen a missile system! An impossible scene to accomplish on a bathroom break. So call her instead. I have fled, Keisha. I am a fool. Meet me in Canada.

He had lost her.

He rolled the flytraps, cold from the refrigerator, into neat thigh-sized bundles, and packed them upright into two waxed chicken boxes. He had twelve hundred flytraps this time, a mighty haul, a bonanza, a useless aching chore. He would flee, flush with money, toward nothing.

One flytrap head had nudged free of its roll, and Cody slid it carefully out and laid it on the wooden table. He pulled the Ka-Bar from its canvas sheath, held it above his head, and drove it down, He missed the half circle of the flytrap head by several inches, worked the knife from the wood and stabbed again, then again, and again. On the fifth try he pinned the head to the splintered tabletop. Unsatisfying. What if he laid his hand, palm up, on the table. He did. He poised the Ka-Bar shoulder height. The blade must enter the palm perfectly into the center, like a nail. He lifted his palm away and drove the knife into the table. He had not reached that stage. It was a possible stage though. In days to come, such a stage could be reached.

There was a rap on his trailer door.

"Cody Cooper!"

Cody crossed the room to push the door curtain aside. It was Elton, standing hands on hips, wearing jeans and a red tank top over the flare of his tiger tattoo. His bald head glinted with oil in the early sun. Behind him stood another man, a large, bulky, frowning man with a mustache and long hair. A thick white bandage crowned his forehead. He had a black eye, and under the eye naked stitches were visible.

"Open up, dawg."

Cody stepped back. Elton climbed the steps, leaving the door open. The large man put a foot on the step and held the door but did not enter. Elton surveyed the kitchen and living room. He shook his head. He spread his hands. He said, "You got yourself a path from the kitchen to the TV chair, and you keep on that path. The rest falls away into depression. I have seen this before, in many a sad life. I could have suspected this in you, but it's a surprise. Is that your laptop?" He gestured to a computer on the table.

"Yes."

Elton crossed the room and lifted the laptop. He pulled the Ka-Bar from the wood. "You been stabbing your fucking table, making splinters."

He tested the edge with a thumb, then slid the knife carefully under his palm-sized turquoise-encrusted belt buckle, blade down. "I will keep this knife temporarily. We got to sit and talk." He gestured toward the open door with his free hand.

Outside on the gravel trailer pad, Cody took a seat in one of the metal chairs.

Elton said, "Come down to the garage. We need some walls, but right here's depressing."

YOU CUT THE CORNER

Seb, who had gone to bed with Mia misgivings, found that when he woke Monday morning, despite a long dreamless sleep, they had returned. He threw off his blanket and sheet and lay in his underwear, letting the chill from the open window flush sleep.

They had talked about war, and he had felt the fist of war clench in his chest. She had been kind, but now could be thinking, do I want to invite this intense soldier into my life? She had opened the subject though. And she had gone to Jimmy, the wounded vet, to ask about war.

And they had kissed. She had asked to kiss him in that soft way, and the silky love feeling had taken them both.

After a moment, he went to the bathroom, then back to the bedroom to stand before the window for his hundred jumping jacks. His apartment was the upper floor of one of Swanntown's heritage homes. Below lay the winding streets of the town's center, stubbornly quaint, but too far off a highway to be much of a tourist lure. Beyond the town, where the sun was rising golden-red in the clear air, he could see Oak Inlet, the scrub-crested strips of island dunes, and beyond that a gleam of ocean. When he moved in two years ago, Mrs. Sutter, his landlord, had inquired about the morning pounding. Jumping jacks, he said. Is that okay? Ah, jumping jacks, she said. It was okay. She was an early riser and said she would hereafter accompany him mentally. Each morning it was a friendly communication, the round, seventyish widow below, aware of his labor, perhaps counting.

After the push-ups and sit-ups, he showered. Then, with an open laptop, he drank coffee from one of Mia's mugs and ate yogurt and Grape-Nuts and toast and began a do-list.

First was the rolltop desk and a careful flashlight search. Either it was too big to move, or it was an antique she thought Leo might value. Or she had left something in it. For instance, the testament the governor had mentioned. That was part of the hotshot murder theory, so not something to mention in the morning briefing with Stinson.

Also, call Kate. She would be out with her well-digging crew. Maybe meet them out there, find a confession, or bloody shoes, or a bloody dress.

Then call Leonard Castle, Germaine's lawyer, ask about the testament, ask about the will. Did Germaine hint at or admit her guilt in the Hugh Britt murder? Unlikely, since wouldn't Castle have contacted law enforcement after her death? Except if she had only hinted.

Get Leo's letters to his wife. Call Virginia Rubins, can she get her mother to release them? Forty-odd years would be five hundred letters. Divide them up. Hours and hours.

Locate the reporter who wrote that Sunday magazine article. What rumors and innuendo did he leave out? If he was alive. So Bonnie again, for the phone number. In the shower, he had scrubbed the X from the back of his hand. A grocery store rose.

What else? The drone video. If it didn't show up, hassle Prince stronger. Likely nothing though, since, as Prince had said, the hog barns were on the other side of Squint's inlet farm.

That was the extent of possibles. After that, door-knocks and a wait for informants. Then a fade to silence and the cold-case cabinet.

When he checked his email, he found a chatty letter from his mother. She was in Italy, leading a tour of Americans through the sites of Rome. Today was the big Colosseum day. He typed a fast reply, mentioned he had met a girl, then deleted that. It would make her restless. She would be back in two weeks, when things would have more shape.

He sent the letter and saw another email had arrived, an anonymous one: Are you a man of your word? I hope so, since I'm trusting the shit out of you. Just in case, I cut the beginning few frames which show some guy in a boat launching a drone. Also, as you'll see, the pilot led them on a goose chase for the fun of it. After the chase, the pilot turned the camera off. The attachment is an MP4 and will run on anything you have. The start time stamp is 11:34 Saturday morning.

Seb double-clicked the attached file, Cooper Farm11.

A drone was flying low over water, then over sand and oak scrub. It passed over an octagon orange tent, which, Seb recalled, Squint had mentioned as like a tent he owned, or maybe even his, or something, then continued, gaining altitude and turning up the inlet, heading west. Seb streamed the video forward with his index finger until the silver roofs of Cooper Farms appeared, three long hog barns, with various outbuildings, then two immense lagoons, one open and purple-brown, the other covered with a pale-green tarp. The camera panned across the farm, then followed a road for several hundred feet, then a side road, and halted over a large metal dumpster. The dumpster lid was thrown back, showing a jumble of hog carcasses. More carcasses were tumbled in a heap beside it. The video descended, slowed, zoomed. Four brown vultures heaved themselves laboriously into flight. Above the carcasses, a swarm of black flies densed and shifted like tiny starlings.

The camera drew back and returned down the road to the farm. Two men appeared below, one bald, one in a blue baseball cap. The bald one lifted a rifle to his shoulder, and the picture shifted abruptly as the drone juked. The camera zoomed, still juking, and showed Squint Cooper and a young Hispanic man, both looking up, Squint aiming, levering the rifle, and firing. In a moment, Squint and the young man strode up the road and into a garage. The camera followed them. A blue van emerged. The camera pulled back, gaining height, then proceeded down the gravel road toward Twice Mile. Behind it, the van pursued. A mile later, a landscaped lawn appeared and in its midst an immense columned home, the Cooper home, formerly the Britt mansion. The camera turned left at Twice Mile, holding a hundred feet above the asphalt, its motion smooth and fast. The van followed. At Ruin Road the drone turned left again.

The van continued behind it for a few hundred yards, then slowed, made a U-turn, and headed back. The camera turned and followed, slowly gaining. The van turned right at Twice Mile, and the camera cut the corner, catching up. At the Cooper Farms entrance the camera, now right behind the van, again cut the corner, first showing the empty gravel road ahead, then looking back. The van had vanished.

The camera gained height and headed across the pine forest. The video closed.

Seb closed his eyes. The van had not returned to the farm, but instead continued down Twice Mile.

Toward the Ford lodge at the western end of the Cooper estate.

At approximately noon.

The evening of the murder investigation, at Smitty's Sportsbar, Squint told him he had sent his employee in the van, Jorge something, to track the drone to its LZ. He found Squint Cooper's number in his phone and pressed send.

"What's up, Seb?"

"The day the drone flew over your farm you said you sent somebody to track it. Who was that?"

"Jorge Navalino. One of my crewmen."

"When did he return?"

"No idea. I was up at the house. Why?"

"Is he around today?"

"Somewhere. I'm up at the house. What's the deal?"

"No deal. Talk to you later." Seb began to end the call then said, "Squint? You there?"

"I'm here. What?"

"The other night outside Smitty's you showed me that video. Recall that?"

"I do. But now he's cut the video down. There's just—"

"I know, but I got the whole thing. And I remember you said something about an orange tent. Remember that?"

"No, I don't."

"There was an orange tent on the sandbars. You said something like, I have a tent like that."

"Well, if I did, I don't remember."

"You don't remember?"

"I don't. What's the significance?"

"I'm surprised you don't remember an orange tent."

"I'm sixty-seven and my brain's gone porous. What's it about?"

"I'm trying to locate where …"

Seb's heart began to beat. A wave of excitement flashed through him. The drone had not crossed the inlet.

He said, "Got to go." And ended the call. He opened his browser and surfed to Peter Prince's website. Prince's cell phone was listed. He dialed.

Prince answered. "Hello."

"Mr. Prince, this is Seb Creek."

"You got the video?"

"I just went through it. Tell me this: you didn't cross the inlet, did you? I didn't see any open water."

"So what?"

"That means you launched on the Cooper Farms side of the inlet. Which is just north of the base. On the same side of the inlet. Which means you flew the drone across the base."

There was silence on the other end of the phone.

Seb said, "Relax. I'm not about that. But you launched from the Intracoastal and cut the corner of the base, didn't you?"

"I knew I never should have given—"

"Hold up. I could give a shit about somebody flying in restricted airspace. That's federal. My business is I need to know *exactly* where you were. Do not lie to me."

"Detective, we're on the phone. Meet me somewhere."

"No time. Here's my guess: You were about two hundred yards past the base boundary in the Intracoastal when you launched. You cut the corner at about forty-five degrees to get to open water. Then you followed your relays down the inlet to Cooper Farms, then went east across the woods. How close am I? If I'm close don't say anything."

There was a silence.

After a moment, Prince said, "Why is this so important?"

"Never mind. I got to go."

Seb ended the call. He found the sheriff's number and pressed send. Let the sheriff tell Lowry. It was possible that a drone video had solved both investigations.

"Hi, Seb, what's up? I was fixing to call you."

"I'm saving you the trip. I just got a lead."

"You did? On Sackler?"

"No, on the other thing. The choppers."

"Really. We just got one here too. Somebody was on the base a couple hundred yards away digging up flytraps."

Seb went cold. "Flytraps? Say again?"

"They found where somebody had been digging flytraps. Under an old water tower. So that could be our guy. They're checking arrests right now."

Seb blew his breath in a long sigh. He said, "Oh, Jesus." His head dropped toward his chest.

"Why? What's your lead?"

He said, "My lead?" His mind would not clear. Seb held the phone against his thigh and inhaled. He brought the phone back to his ear and made his voice matter-of-fact. "I should have called last night—there's a guy I know, and he's got some boats for rent. Jimmy Beagle of Jimmy Beagle's Famous Floating Fish House. He's up at the top of the inlet on Willow Creek. The creek has pretty much filled up, so I doubt he's in any databases, and they'll probably miss him. But I know he rents skiffs because I saw them last night. I was on a romantic tryst with my new girl. It went right out of my head until this morning."

"That the one you had coffee with?"

"It is. Mia."

"And you doubled back on her last night."

"Right. She has a place on Willow Road. She makes pottery."

"Love made you stupid."

"I guess it did. She was out with Jimmy by the fish house having a beer."

"I'll let them know. They haven't found Grayson Kelly, by the way.

But they do know he was planning to go floundering. He told some guys in the brig. That's what he did home in South Carolina."

They ended the call. Seb closed the laptop, shrugged into his weapon harness and sport coat, and went down to his Honda. He started the engine, then slipped out his phone and surfed to the state criminal database. He entered the name *Cody Cooper* and let the phone search while he backed out.

NEW DEAL

Cody, Elton, and the big man descended the slope to the garage. The boat, sanded and scraped, was overturned on sawhorses. The gallon of paint, crowned with blue drippings, sat on the hull. A wide umbrella, duct-taped with a circle of shimmery Mylar curtains, was taped to a clothes hanger and hung from the rafters.

Elton batted the Mylar. He said, "What's this about?"

Cody looked at the big man.

Elton said, "This is my nephew, Carl Peener. He's part of the deal now."

"What deal?"

"The deal where you stole those Stinger missiles, little man."

Cody swung his hands before him dismissively. "I got no idea what you're talking about." He edged toward the boat to pass them. "Listen, I got to …"

The big man put a hand on his chest, stopping him. "You stole some Stinger missiles? How cool is that?"

Elton said, "He's family, and I need him. Next subject, what the fuck is this?" He batted the Mylar again.

Cody backed up. He said, "What the fuck, Elton."

"Cody, we got a new plan. What's this?"

Cody said, "It stops thermal scopes from spotting you." He looked at Peener. Then, committing himself: "For when I go back to the site."

Elton said, "Really." He said to Peener, "You ever hear about that?"

Peener was finger-dabbing the stitches under his eye, He said, "Never did."

Cody said, "Look it up."

Elton said, "Looks like you're painting your boat back blue. Wouldn't it be smarter to paint it red? Or yellow?"

"I guess."

Elton said, "Let's sit down, what say?"

Four webbed chairs hung on nails along the garage wall. Cody removed one, opened it, and sat, letting the casual inhospitality of not offering Elton or Peener a chair hang unremarked.

Elton removed a chair and kicked it open. He sat, laying Cody's laptop on his thighs. They were knee to knee. Cody could lean, reach for his laptop, then seize the knife handle. He shut his eyes for a moment. Joy came, faint then clear. He was free of these people, with their intentions and plans.

Elton said, "What's funny, dawg? You fading on me?"

Cody opened his eyes. He had been smiling. "What are you doing here, Elton?"

"Cody, do one thing. Raise up your T-shirt, up to the neck."

Cody, still half smiling, raised his T-shirt.

"Let me have your phone."

"Not on me."

"Stand up, Cody."

Cody stood. Elton leaned forward, his forehead against Cody's stomach, patted his pockets, swiped through his crotch, ran a hand up his back. He said, "Sit down."

Cody sat.

Elton said, "You know what a habitual felon is, Cody? It's a guy got three felonies, any damn kind. The fourth one, they kick you up four notches, ten years minimum. I got my three. So I pay attention. No offense."

"None taken," Cody said. Then the joy flow spoke. He said, "I liked Harvey Clement."

Elton opened the laptop, faced it toward Cody. It hid the Ka-Bar, which despite the joy, Cody's eyes had swept again.

Elton said, "That's bold talk." His tone was faintly amused, faintly admiring.

"I always felt bad about that. I liked Harvey."

"Harvey Clement wore a wire into my home. I am not afraid to be serious with people. I am being serious with you now. You told me you would send ten emails to the terrorists. Show me on this computer where you sent them."

The joy swirled, making confidence. Cody was knee to knee with menace and unafraid. He was immune. Also, computers were his province. Elton was gazing at a height he could not see. Cody was looking down and unafraid to know it.

Cody said, "I sent ten emails, as I said I would. I used tor so there is no record of that communication on this computer. I did not save it in a Word document for the feds to find." He had sent no emails. He would see Keisha on the way to Richmond. He would say, remember this kiss of love. His gaze wandered across Elton's face, held on the eyes for a second, then rested mild and indifferent on the wide, thin mouth.

After a moment, Elton said, "Tell me what the email said."

"It said I have come into possession of an FIM-92 Stinger launch system with three missiles due to the recent crash of two Super Stallion helicopters in North Carolina, as reported on CNN. I want ten million dollars."

"Did you say you will send a missile as proof?"

"I decided it's better to let that come up."

"Show me a website."

Cody had anticipated. He had searched jihadi websites, seen people kneeling in orange coveralls, seen a cage of people being lowered into a river. If you clicked, a video would start. He had searched, stepping carefully around the videos, until he found a likely page.

He opened the tor browser and typed. He swung the computer around to face Elton. The screen showed a Toyota Hilux pickup with a rear-bed machine gun, parked on a desert road and surrounded by young olive-skinned guys with beards and AK-47s. They were grinning. There was lots of Arabic script. Cody leaned over the screen and pointed. He said, "Hit 'translate' right here. The email button comes up in the upper right."

Elton closed the laptop. He said, "So it's trust Cody."

Cody said, "Trust him to want five million dollars."

"You were sorrowing about Harvey a minute ago."

"Harvey's dead. I'm not."

Elton placed the laptop on Cody's knees and stood. He touched the Ka-Bar at his belt. He said, "I saw you looking at this knife. I don't care if your mind works. My mind works too. I almost went to see your dad."

"Why?"

"A Texas Hold'em tournament is coming up. National. I thought maybe old Squint could stake me. As the price for not telling the feds his son's got their missiles."

"He'd tell you to go fuck yourself."

"Maybe. Anyway, I started thinking—this terrorist bullshit is too fucking complicated. But who else might want a Stinger missile? The cartels is who. And I do business with them. This man right here gets face-to-face with them. And they got rooms of money. So we got a new plan. We're going to get the missiles tonight. We're going to test out your umbrella contraption."

"I'm not going back there now."

"Yeah, you are, because if you don't I pick up a phone. Carl here is going with you, only he's going to be in a different boat, just in case."

"In case I get busted."

"That is correct. So best your contraption does the trick. I'm going for the boat, and Carl here will keep you company. He's got a headache, so don't upset him." Elton removed the Ka-Bar from his belt, grasped the hilt, and tossed the knife to Peener, who caught the handle one-handed. He said, "Let's go back up to the trailer, Cody. You and Carl can watch TV while I get the boat."

Cody sat.

Elton said, "It's what's happening, Cody. Stand up."

Peener, with the knife, started toward him.

"Hey, fellows. How's everybody?"

It was Seb Creek, who had stepped onto the garage concrete from the gravel driveway.

THE MAN ON A RAFT

Seb drove fast out of Swanntown. His database search for Cody Cooper had come up, and there it was, a conviction and fine for misdemeanor Venus fly-trap theft. Which the FBI would already have. As he drove, he searched for flytrap violations in the last ten years. Several pages of names, two hundred maybe. They would distribute the list by email, ten agents, maybe twenty.

His phone rang.

"This is Seb."

"Hey, Seb. Curtis Kelkar. Got a minute?"

Kelkar was a narcotics detective and one of Seb's teammates on the sher-iff's department basketball team. Seb said, "A quick minute. I got a meeting."

"Okay, quick. Carl Peener is out of jail, bailed out by Elton Gleen."

"Elton is his uncle. What'd it cost him?"

"Ten grand."

"I bet that made for some discussion."

"You got time for a few facts?"

"Go ahead."

"We're coordinating with Atlanta narcotics. Peener and his gang—he's got a little start-up motorcycle gang—they're auditioning for the Bandidos. The Bandidos have been looking at Atlanta, and Peener wants to be their guy. So far, they just been stealing bikes, cooking meth, the whole biker deal. Now it appears—this is what we think and what Atlanta thinks—they're connected to a Juarez cartel, which is no doubt Elton's connection, and that's what Peener was doing here, making his uncle's black tar heroin runs. Peener was up in Maryland too, which probably means MS-13."

"Starting a life."

"And they're not stupid. They rent a van, and Atlanta says they have four or five magnetic signs they stick on—drywall, computers, various ones."

"Any residue in the van?"

"No residue. Anyway, that's a heads-up. I saw the pics of Peener. Looks like you won the fight. What did you do, hit him with the whole damn door?"

Seb pulled up to the top of Charlene's entrance drive and stopped. Down the hill at the bottom, he could see Elton Gleen's roll-bar pickup. He got out, eased the car door closed. He removed his nine millimeter, jacked a shell into the chamber, and set the safety. As he came around the corner of the garage, he heard Elton's thin voice: It's what's happening, Cody. Stand up.

He said, "Hey, fellows. How's everybody?"

Elton turned. Cody remained seated. Peener held a knife.

Elton said, "Well, it's Seb Creek."

Seb said, "Mr. Peener, I see you holding that knife. I want you to put it down." He held open his coat. "I got my gun this time."

Peener smiled. He tossed the knife from hand to hand. "Is it a law a man can't hold a knife?"

Seb said, "I feel unsafe." He put his hand over the butt of the nine millimeter.

"Shit, son. Don't be scared." Peener crossed to the boat and clapped the knife on the hull, making a loud *ting*. He said, "How's that?"

Seb said, "Now move to the side, all the way to the side. Elton, you back up there with him."

Elton and Peener arranged themselves beside Cody, who was still sitting. Elton said, "You're ordering free citizens around, Seb. We're all witnessing this."

Seb crossed to the boat and hefted the knife. He walked to the rear of the garage and placed the knife on a shelf. As he turned, he saw the orange tent crumpled between two cardboard boxes. He turned to the three men. "Looks like they got you patched up, Carl. I heard you filed a complaint."

"I damn sure did. I'm suing you too."

"You wouldn't take a potshot at me, would you?"

Peener smiled. "Well, I'm not fixing to warn you."

"I'm worried you might think it's a good way to impress the Bandidos."

"Now that I think about it …"

"Well, Carl, that's a wrong path. Now then, what's this meeting about?"

Elton said, "That's not something you get to ask."

Seb said, "How about you boys go on now. I got to have a private conference with Cody."

Elton said, "You're interrupting a private conference."

Seb said to Cody, "Cody, either they leave or let's go downtown."

Cody said, "They were just leaving. Go downtown for what?"

Seb said, "You heard that, Elton? A property owner has asked you to leave his premises."

Elton said, "Cody, are you asking us to leave the premises?"

Cody said, "I guess."

Seb said, "Be clear, Cody."

Cody said, "Yes, I am."

Seb said, "Off you go."

Peener and Elton crossed the garage. Elton said, "Cody, we'll see you after while."

Seb sat across from Cody. They listened to the pickup's engine start, then heard the gravel grind as it backed up the drive. Seb ran his hands through his hair, re-rubber-banding his ponytail with a concentrated expression. He said, "Those two guys sell drugs, Cody. But trust me, neither one has much career left. Even if you planted the islands again, I doubt they'll be around to pay you."

Cody started, "I'm not …" then stopped as Seb raised a hand.

Seb said, "Good. Smart. By the way, I forgot to tell you, I spoke to your dad last night. What he said was, he will quit the group if you come and sing."

Cody said, "I'm not going to fucking join your singers, for Christ's sake."

"Oh, well," said Seb and waved a hand. He rolled his shoulders back, stretching his chest. He said, "I see you're fixing to paint the skiff."

Cody stared. It wasn't about the singers. What then? He felt himself coiling, looking for chances.

"Thing is, Cody, here's my serious reason for being here. I dropped by to let you know that your alibi for noon day before yesterday did not pan out." Seb made his face solemn but sympathetic. He said, "Not a one at McDonald's could recognize you." He fished his phone from his front pocket, woke it, and showed the screen, a head and shoulders shot of Cody in the hot tub. Seb had not been to McDonald's.

"Not a one, Cody. So here I am again. This is not about singing. This is about did Cody Cooper rob and murder Leo Sackler."

"Give me a fucking break. Some counter guy at McDonald's is supposed to recognize me from a thousand different people?"

"Not a thousand. Several hundred. Police statistics show that recognition is common in similar circumstances. So that's strike one, Cody. I came to tell you that if you killed Leo Sackler over some sort of dispute, and he was trying to hurt you, or if it was an accident, which it seemed like, then speak up now."

"I don't know a thing about Leo Sackler. Or who the fuck he is."

Seb glanced over Cody's shoulder. He said, "Whoever keeps this garage keeps it neat. When I was a kid, my dad had his garage, and it looked like a grenade had gone off in it. I believe you had a grenade—no, it was an IED, wasn't it. Did I ever tell you I was in Iraq at that time? I was in Anbar, but we heard about it. One guy killed, another guy trapped until they cut him loose. Now here we are, two old Marines, facing off in normal life over a murder."

"I don't know a fucking thing about a murder."

"Well, maybe not." Seb stood and walked to the rear of the garage. He lifted the sodden orange tent and dropped it on one of the cardboard boxes. "I'm thinking your dad gave you this tent. It's wet too. Which is why no one at McDonald's recognized you, because you were not there. You were out in that storm. Which is why you got this boat up out of the water. Away from prying eyes."

Cody was looking over his shoulder. Now he turned away and held himself perfectly still. The Ka-Bar knife lay on the shelf ten feet away. It brightened in his mind. He tried to breathe.

Seb sat again. He placed his hands on his knees, hunched slightly forward. He said, "I wonder if you were out stealing Venus flytraps on the base when that storm hit. That makes sense, with this wet tent crammed in here. And also because I got a video. Look here." He thumb-searched his phone again, then started the video, holding the phone in front of Cody's face. Cody watched deadpan as the camera moved over the orange tent and blackened campfire. Seb slid the phone into his front pocket. He said, "That tent stands out, doesn't it. There was a guy they caught flytrapping over on the Orton Plantation last week, and they gave him a million-dollar bond. You hear about that? And you been arrested before for flytrapping. Right now, with this video, I bet I could appear before a magistrate and come away with a warrant to search your trailer, and if I do, I believe I will find an illegal harvest of Venus flytraps. That's a felony. And you're back to prison."

"You said you weren't interested in flytraps."

"I could call it in, stay here watching so you can't hide them."

There was a silence.

Cody said, "Go ahead." But his voice had tired.

"I'm not going to do it. In a way, I admire the ambition of it. That's got to be hard work, on your knees all day, digging. But then I think, no, Venus flytraps are one of the state's treasures, and they shouldn't go to benefit just one guy. Then I think, but here's a fellow soldier, and do I want to put his fucked-up ass back in prison?" Seb gripped the air with both fists. "That war was a clusterfuck, Cody. We went there to be men and came back animals." He replaced his hands on his knees. "I sometimes think if your life wasn't ruined over there, you were an animal to begin with."

Cody's eyes moved around the garage as if he was following a fly. They flicked across Seb's face, intelligent and watching.

Seb rose, stepped away from the chairs, and performed two jumping jacks. He said, "I do jumping jacks in the morning, and sometimes I'm like a cocked pistol and have to let off a few more." He lifted the Mylar-draped umbrella from the rafters and twirled it over his head. The Mylar curtains fell in a neat circle, enclosing him. He tilted the umbrella, and his face appeared through a seam. He said, "This is neat. What is this?"

"That's for a deer blind I'm working on."

"Pretty cool." Seb hung the umbrella back on the rafters. He sat again. He said, "Hate to say, but it's all adding up. Let me ask you this, Cody— are you a fucking terrorist?"

"No." Cody answered automatically, as if some invisible hand had pressed truth from him. Numbness came. Helplessness came.

Seb said, "That's what I had to think about. Is this fool gone straight-up crazy? Because I can break a major case here, Cody, a national case. This goes all the way to the White House. My ticket to ride, man. And all I have to do is ruin Cody Cooper's life. I had to do some deep thinking. Can you appreciate that?"

"I guess."

"I don't know what you were thinking. What I do know is we are in a serious predicament. Both of us. If they find you, and find out I didn't arrest you, I'll probably do time too. It'll be bad for me, since you're the brother of my old girlfriend. And you can't run. The feds are involved, and they are heartless in the name of justice and the national good. They won't know you from a bug. They found where you were digging the flytraps, and they're looking up arrests. They'll be here today sometime. So you go out there, and you get that stuff, and you leave it in plain sight. If they find it first, they'll find you, either through DNA or a fingerprint. Because I doubt you wiped it the way you wiped the trailer, because you hid it. So get it, wipe it, and leave it. If they find it, you're done. No help can come."

Cody's mouth opened. He was like a man on a raft who sees a ship and waits, tired of shouting.

Seb said, "I don't want a confession. That would precipitate arrest." He rose. He gestured at the umbrella. "This here's an interesting idea, but I wouldn't use it. You get caught with it, you can't explain it. I don't know if they're using thermal scopes, but if they spot you, might be better to be a guy out fishing."

Cody sat perfectly still, listening to the footsteps fade. He rose, moved to the front of the garage, and saw Seb get into his car and drive away.

Then it was panic hurry. Elton and Peener would be parked some-where, watching for Seb's car. Cody seized the bowline of the skiff and jerked it forward, collapsing the sawhorses. The paint can hit the concrete of the garage floor, popped open, and hurled a bloom of blue across the floor and an artful splatter across the boat's hull. He heaved the boat over, retrieved the motor and gas can from the rafters, and set them in with his laptop. Then he trot-lugged the boat across the lawn, blue-streaking the grass and leaving a wake of crushed pansies in a flower bed. He listened for a car, then ran to his trailer, found his phone, and ran back to the dock and kneed the boat into the creek, tied the bowline, set the engine on the transom, hooked up the fuel line. He listened for a car again, then ran back to the garage for his bicycle. He toted it to the boat yoke-style across his back and tumbled it into the bow.

What else? Money, for Christ's sake. His wallet, for Christ's sake. He ran to the trailer, found his wallet and keys and thrust them into his front pocket. Did he need keys? Fuck no. Fuck yes—for his bike lock, definitely, at Walmart, so he could definitely get back to the boat.

What else? Some fucking overlooked important absolute thing. But go go go! He pushed off. A rag. A fucking rag for fingerprints! Get that at Walmart, sweet great Walmart. He heard an engine, heard the slide of wheels on gravel.

He cast the bowline, hopped into the stern, and squeezed the gas bulb. The motor purred to life on the third pull. He nosed into the creek toward the inlet. His mind raced, his heart pounded, but the boat, an ordinary everyday scruffy-looking skiff, nudged slow across the calm water, just a white T-shirt guy out going somewhere, a guy with a bicycle in the bow, which was inter-esting but harmless, an ordinary guy doing some thing he was doing.

Behind him, he saw Elton and Peener come out on the dock and watch him.

THE DEAD KID

Seb glided his Honda to a halt in front of the lodge. He saw Deputy Randall Garland emerge from his squad car and approach fast across the gravel lot. Seb gathered his flashlight from the center console, wondering idly whether the eager Randall would need to backstep as the door opened, as he had done two nights ago when the investigation began. When he turned, Randall was at the side, waiting. Seb cranked the door open and got out.

"Morning, Randall. You holding the fort while they dig?"

"Yes, I am, Mr. Creek."

"Call me Seb. You track down any more clues?"

Randall smiled. "Not yet. Did you talk to DeWitt?"

"Yes, I did. It turned out he was the killer."

Randall's mouth opened.

Seb said, "I'm joking. I shouldn't be so convincing when I'm joking, but otherwise it's not funny."

"That's true. Are you here for the dig?"

"No, I'm going to look around again. I got an idea." Seb started toward the entrance to the lodge.

Randall followed. He said, "You do?"

This was an inquiry. At the lodge, Seb stopped, slipped on a pair of Tyvek booties. He said, "Yes, I do. I believe you're thinking about becoming a detective."

"I did start thinking about it."

"Well, here's what it is. Hard work, careful thought, and keen interest. That's it." Behind them, two vehicles entered the lot, Kate and Ernie in a car, and behind them, a white van marked FR MECHANICAL. "I believe your diggers have arrived."

Randall said, "See you." He started toward the vehicles.

Seb said, "What are the requirements for a detective?"

Randall turned, backpedaling. He smiled broadly. He said, "Hard work, careful thought, and keen interest."

Seb went directly to the master bedroom. His banter with Randall had been light and usual, but from the other world, the ordinary world where he no longer lived. He had, like Cody and with Cody, made a decision that could change his life. Really it had not been a decision. It came from a place beneath. But the ordinary world trembled.

The room was the same, the unmade bed, the dog-eared magazines, the looming rolltop desk. He switched on his flashlight. There were two columns of drawers in the upper section, left and right. He began pulling them, inspecting each and making a stack. He beamed the light into the cavities, looking for marks, tape, nails. He pulled the lower file drawers, inspected their cavities. He pulled open the main drawer, backing away as its nearly two-foot depth came free and swung toward his feet. He turned it over and placed it on the desktop. There were scraps of Scotch tape about a foot apart in a quadrant. A single piece of tape remained and held the corner of a Post-it note on which was written the word *under*.

She had left a note in the desk: *Look under here, find my testament.* Leo had found it, taped the note in its place, then hid the testament in his precious box.

Someone had taken it.

Outside at the wellhead, two men in gray coveralls had descended the ladder and were working with shovels in the well bottom. Kate and Ernie stood at the rim, each beaming flashlights into the dark.

Seb said, "Got a minute, Kate?"

They entered the house, and he followed her down the hall toward the bedroom. She was a generous-minded, amiable woman, a friend, and as they entered the bedroom and stood before the desk, he had the sudden strong impulse to embrace her, to reconnect with the ordinary world. He resisted. He said, "By the way, did you find a business card with Landman Realty on it?"

"I saw that in the case file. We didn't find it. It wasn't in the trash either."

He showed her the upturned drawer. He explained his theory of a missing testament, mentioned by the governor. He worked the case in the ordinary world. He said, "I got good photos. Probably don't need Barb. I'm hoping you can get some prints from the note. It should be Leo and Germaine. You might want to get prints from Josie Land too, who was her housekeeper. She lives over on—"

"Staunton. We did that this morning. We have Germaine's prints isolated."

"You are an on-the-ball detective."

"Oh yeah. Missed the phone, and now I missed the note."

"No, you found this note, Kate. There it is, and the honcho detective congratulates you. How'd they do in softball last night?"

"They won. My hubby clobbered a homer." She punched his shoulder. "You're a dude, Seb Creek. You are a dude."

Seb's phone rang. He looked at the screen. A call from Lieutenant Stinson.

"Go ahead, Lieutenant."

"You on the way in?"

"I'm at the lodge with Kate and Ernie. I'll be at the shop in fifteen minutes for the briefing."

"That's why I'm calling. It's canceled again."

"Okay. Why?"

"We got a dead kid at Cooper Farms."

"Who?"

"An eighteen-year-old Hispanic named Jorge Navalino."

ALLGONE

Cody swung the boat into a creek, then nosed in behind a willow that spilled into the water. He sat hunched, his hands folded into clams, thumbs out. He inhaled and exhaled, again and again, consciously. He had made a flash plan, and eventually he would have to move. He would have to examine the plan's bits and pieces, see if it was smart. Breathing was enough now, to fill with good air and its amazing free, important energy.

Great danger had come, then great goodness.

Except if it was trickery. And they were watching him. And they had guys in boats waiting to follow him to the missile stash, and Seb Creek was a way-smart actor, someone who knew him, who they sent to freak him—hurry hurry.

Later, in the eight-by-eight cell, he would think of Seb Creek, how convincing he was, how flawless in deceit.

Or later, with Keisha, watching their children, he would think of Seb Creek, how good he was, the man who saved him.

He sucked in air and burst it out.

Let it be the last Seb. Later, even if it was the eight-by-eight cell, and he trusted himself into prison. Trust was right. Follow trust. In the end, everything depended on trust, every heartbeat and breath and inch you went, you went on trust. He hardened in trust. He claimed it.

Also, Seb Creek was right, if they found the missiles, which they would someday with metal detectors or super space science, they would find his stupid stoner fingerprints. And DNA too, since the missiles had been heavy.

As he fished up his phone and typed *how to destroy DNA* in the browser search window, the flash plan came back and seemed good and right. First Walmart, see Keisha, a bunch of spray paint, a coat and a hat, rags and a cleaning agent, some fishing stuff. At the last second, before hitting enter, he remembered they could search his history, so *fuck fuck fuck!* use the tor browser. He set the phone as a hotspot and opened his laptop. The search came up with Cease, an oxidizing bleach, sold only in England, Australia, and India. Oxidizing bleach seemed to be the ticket for DNA destruction though, normal bleach being iffy. Then he found AllGone, which was Cease sold under a different name in America. Maybe his neatnik sister had had some, and Walmart would have some, and Keisha was there.

He nosed the boat through the willow branches, bending into the wet mossy leaves that stroked him. Peener and Elton would be on the water in an hour, say, or a half hour, maybe with binoculars. They would head for the islands, zoom here and there, or maybe the creeks, thinking he would hide until dark. Or maybe say, fuck it.

And he thought, if they don't find me, Elton will kill his nephew.

GAS CHAMBER

Seb arrived at Cooper Farms to find the other two investigation detectives, Marty Jerrold and Barb Addario, Barb with her two cameras slung around her neck, standing with the coroner, Walt Carney. All three were gazing into an eight-foot-deep trench. Randall Garland had gotten there ahead of him and now stood with another deputy beside his cruiser. The gravel lot was filled with vehicles, one of which was the blue van from the drone video. The trench was already staked with yellow tape. Hog stench was fierce and inexorable, mixed now and then with the smell of rotten eggs.

The trench was arm-width wide and fifteen feet long and slanted across a grassy slope between the hog buildings and lagoons. A small white shed sat at the high end where the muddy bottom had pooled with brown water. Three metal pipes emerged from the shed base, turned down, and descended the sheer face into the pool, where bubbles bloomed and burst. More pipes connected the small shed to a larger shed behind it. Beside the trench, two white socks were neatly draped over a pair of work boots. A yellow evidence marker lay beside them.

Below, facedown in the mud in the center of the trench, lay a man's body. He wore a short-sleeved blue shirt and brown pants rolled to the knees. The bill of his blue baseball cap knifed into the red-brown mud, and his feet were still submerged. His arms lay above his head in a diamond, as if he had begun a forward dive. A cell phone lay half sunk in the mud four feet from the body.

Seb said, "Where's Squint?"

Marty, whose section included Cooper Farms, and who had caught the case, said, "He's over with the father. The lieutenant's with him."

"His father's here already?"

"They both work here."

"Who else?"

"That's it. Two guys."

Barb said, "Amazing, when you think about. Thousands of hogs and two farmhands. Talk about efficiency."

Carney looked up at the detectives. He said, "Right here is the essence of income inequality in modern times. Two little bitty jobs and all this wealth. You're all Republicans, I bet. But now and then I must throw caution to the wind."

Barb said, "Not all cops are Republican." Carney looked at her. She said, "Don't ask. That's private."

Marty said, "She's a liberal."

Seb said, "So what happened?"

Carney said, "That trench is full of hydrogen sulfide."

Marty said, "Looks like he dropped his cell phone and climbed down to get it."

Seb said, "How do you know it's hydrogen sulfide?"

Carney said, "Because that's a hydrogen sulfide scrubber." He pointed to the small shed. "There's some kind of process in the little house there that cleans up the gas that comes off the pond, the one they got covered. The methane drives the generator in the big shed, but hydrogen sulfide is too corrosive to burn. The generator was howling away when we got here. Squint shut it down."

Seb said, "What's the trench for?"

"They're getting ready to cover the other lagoon and are connecting two scrubbers. They're putting in another generator."

"So if anybody falls in they die? Where are the people working on this?"

Marty said, "They're not here. They're waiting on a generator. They haven't even built the second generator house."

"It's a leak," said Carney. "They got a gas leak."

Seb pointed to the pipes that ran from the base of the small building into the brown water. He said, "That's bubbling. And there's a valve."

Marty said, "We noticed. But we can't check it until the masks get here."

"And the waders," said Carney.

Seb said, "Squint Cooper explained all this to you?"

Marty said, "He did."

"So the kid was out here by himself? No one saw him out here?"

"His dad was in number two building, dropping feed. Squint was up at his house. He's the one found him."

"Why'd he come?"

"Squint? It's his farm. I guess he was overseeing."

"And he wandered over here and looked in this trench?"

Barb looked at Seb. "Here we go. You think Squint pushed him in?"

Marty said, "There's tracks from the pipes to where he's lying. He climbed down there all by his lonesome."

An ambulance pulled up in the gravel lot behind them and parked alongside the other vehicles. Two technicians emerged, a man and a woman. They walked to the trench, the man carrying several pairs of green rubber waders, the woman with a canvas duffel.

Carney said, "Thanks, guys. Email me the receipt."

The woman unzipped the duffel and produced three face masks in plastic bags. Carney inspected one, thrust it under his arm, and began reading the enclosed brochure.

Marty said, "Tell you what, let me go down there first. Just in case."

Carney looked up. "I would appreciate that, Marty. Not from the danger. These are M95s. They'll do, as long as you snug them up. But if I go down there in that mud, someone will probably have to come rescue me."

Seb said, "Best thing though, Marty, is to go down with a rope around you."

Barb said, "Definitely, Marty."

Carney said, "You guys have a rope?"

The male technician said, "We should. But we don't."

"Get your waders on, Marty," Seb said. "I'll see if Squint has one."

A man wearing stained green coveralls was seated on a packing crate outside the number two building, his forearms braced on his knees, his head hanging between them. He raised his head at Seb's approach, showing a grimy tear-streaked face, then lowered it again. Stinson, bent forward with his hands on his knees, was speaking to the man. Now he straightened. Squint stood with folded arms and a thoughtful scowl.

Seb motioned for Stinson and Squint to approach. He said softly, "We got the masks, but it looks like we need a rope. As a safety precaution. Marty's going down."

Stinson said, "Why Marty?"

"He volunteered. It's his section. Walt said he'd get stuck down there."

"Walt would get stuck, and I'm thinking Marty could too. He's got a gut."

"I'll go. You tell Marty though." Then to Squint: "You got a rope?"

Squint said, "I got some chain out here, and some cord. But I got some rope at the house."

They drove in silence along the gravel road in the blue van. It was a working vehicle, with mud-crusted floor mats and a bug-splattered windshield. A red baseball cap was hung on a large bottle of water on the console between them.

Seb fished his phone from his front pocket and began searching his camera. He said, "Last time we talked, we talked about this boy." He glanced at Squint. "Never know what life's got in store."

Squint said, "I been knowing that."

"How'd you happen to look in that trench?"

Squint inhaled and blew his breath. He said, "I couldn't find him. Then finally I called him. I heard his phone ringing."

"It's a wonder that phone could still ring, down there in the mud."

"Well, it did."

"How do you suppose that trench filled with hydrogen sulfide? There's got to be end caps down there under that water."

"I bet there aren't."

"Seems like something was in the news not that long ago, a couple of guys in Ohio on a hog farm. One went down and passed out, and the other one went to help, and they both died."

"It was a family. It was three of them. They all died, one after another."

Seb opened Prince's video on his phone, surfed until the screen showed the farm, then leaned and held it up for Squint to see. He said, "This right here is Peter Prince's video of your hog disaster. What was it—fifty-three hogs? I got it anonymously, so I can't use it against him. But it might be evidence in the Leo Sackler murder."

Squint nodded and smiled. "Good." He glanced at Seb and flicked his eyebrows. He said, "Continue."

"How much of the video did you watch? Because after he showed the dead hogs, he kept going. It shows the van, this van right here, following the drone. All the way out to Ruin Road. You didn't watch that far?"

"I guess I didn't."

"What was Jorge going to do if he actually tracked him back to his LZ, by the way? Did he have the rifle?"

"He was going to call me, and I'd bring the rifle. And make a citizen's arrest."

Seb closed the video, then thrust a hip to tuck the phone into his front pocket. "Thing is, if you keep watching this video, you see he turns around and heads home. But guess what? The drone turns too and follows him. Prince says he was having fun, trying to catch back up. But Jorge didn't know that drone was following him. All the way back to the farm entrance. And what does he do? He drives right past the entrance. He does not return to the farm. That was around twelve noon, maybe half past. And Leo died around one, is what the coroner thinks. So what I think is, Jorge drives over to the lodge and robs and kills Leo Sackler, because he has heard about Leo coming into money. What do you think? Is that something the Jorge you knew could do?"

"No, it's not. He was a good kid. But who knows."

"Did he come back late that day?"

"No idea. I went back to the house. He was supposed to call me if he found Prince."

"He didn't call?"

"No."

"Well, that's where things are pointing anyway. I know his dad is pretty broken up. Lots of grief there. That's not proof of character, but it's a hint. If they were close. I mean he wasn't a hoodlum."

"They were close."

"Well, I hope we never find proof, for his dad's sake."

The road opened onto the landscaped lawn and the Cooper house appeared. Squint stopped in front of an open detached garage and got out. He returned a moment later with a coil of waxy rope. They started back down the road.

Seb hefted the rope. "This is a cowboy rope."

"That rope is forty years old. That was my rodeo rope."

"Did you ride bulls and all that?"

"I was a calf roper."

"Do any good?"

"Plenty good. Then I got drafted and joined the Marines."

"First time I ever heard your name was from my dad. Only Silver Star winner in the county."

Squint nodded. He switched the radio on, a man singing a song in Spanish.

Seb said, "Jorge drove the van a lot, I guess."

"It's our chore runner."

Seb switched the radio off. "Let me ask you this. Did you know Germaine Ford?"

"Of course, I knew her. She sued the shit out of me. Why?"

"I'm trying to get a handle on Leo Sackler. Did you know Hugh Britt?"

"I know he got killed."

"I guess it was big news."

"Not to me. I was in Viet Nam. I don't recall how I heard about it—probably when my dad bought this place. I definitely didn't run in that crowd. I was a farm boy from the western side of the county."

"Lot of people think Germaine Ford killed him. Because she gave the lodge to Leo. She went to see the governor too, to petition for clemency."

"Well, she was a strange woman. Who knows?"

"Beautiful back in the day."

"So I heard."

"You didn't know her back then?"

"Like I say, I was in Viet Nam."

"That whole time? Never got any leave?"

Squint looked across and said mildly, "Where is this going, Seb?"

Seb lifted the red cap from the water bottle and dropped it back in place. He said, "Whose hat is this?"

"Mine."

"On that video, the guy driving has got a red cap on. Jorge's wearing a blue cap. Stuck right down in the mud."

The farm buildings came in view. Squint parked the van beside the ambulance, lifted the rope, and got out. The group at the trench now included Stinson and the father. Squint waited for Seb to come alongside, then turned to face him. He said, "Because Jorge wore my cap, now your mind is working?"

"Don't be offended. I'm sure we'll find his DNA on the cap. But yeah, I do get a train of thought. It was you in the van, and you drove over and killed Leo Sackler—for some unknown reason, which was not robbery— then you hunted me down at Smitty's to complain about Prince, but really that was just a way to mention Jorge was chasing the drone. Because you got to thinking, that drone was taking pictures of a blue van out on Twice Mile, and the sheriff's going to want to know who was driving. Two hours ago, I told you I had that video. And now Jorge's dead."

"You motherfucker. You think I killed Jorge?"

"I don't really. That's just a particular train of thought. Anyway, Jorge went into the trench by himself. The train of thought would be, you turned a valve and threw his phone in there. Sorry, Jorge, I dropped your phone."

Squint, who had been slumping forward intently, now straightened. He laughed. "That's a mean-ass theory. Based on a red cap."

"Couldn't take it to a jury, that's for sure."

Squint started to turn. Seb said, making his voice casual, "I talked to DeWitt yesterday."

"Who's DeWitt?"

"The land guy. Didn't he come talk to you?"

"I don't recall anybody named DeWitt."

"No, I thought he must have come by, see if you were thinking of selling some land to pay for all this technology?"

Squint stopped. "I'm not selling any land."

"Well, he was in the neighborhood. He stopped off at Leo Sackler's to see if he wanted to sell the lodge. He told me he saw Leo was digging that well out. So that's how you knew, is what I'm thinking."

"Knew what?"

"That Leo was after something in that well. We're out there digging right now. When we find it, we'll have the mystery object, plus a red baseball cap. I wonder will that be enough?"

"I'm not going to talk to you any more about this, Seb. I can see you're aflame with a theory, and I will not collide with a mind made up. Any further communication with me will be done through my lawyer."

"I understand."

They started toward the trench again. Squint turned, stopped, laid the back of his hand hard against Seb's arm, stopping him. "Do not mention this shit in front of Manuel. That man is in pain, and I might have to break your fucking neck. We got a tragedy out here, in case you didn't notice."

Seb gazed at Squint intently. He said, "I definitely won't mention it." The ordinary world, which before had been trembling and distant, was now close, real, and completely interesting.

A NOW-AND-THEN DREAM

Cody didn't have a cable lock for his boat and motor, so it was, first, which boat ramp was closest to Walmart, and second, which one was safest from scumbags who might see a free motor, maybe even a free boat. He decided on the Dover ramp at the end of Clough Street, which was a nice neighborhood, without street people, and also, it was Monday and the high school kids would be in class. He tied the boat, wrestled out the bike, and started to pedal through a geography of broad lawns, curving walks, Grecian porticos, double and triple garages, hardly a car in sight. Cody had been raised in affluence, but now, after his rat life of prison and drugs and homelessness, this upscale neighborhood emitted an otherness field, like a hand in the face, so that he was out of place, peddling a rattletrap bike, wearing jeans and a moss-streaked white T-shirt, and which was why, it came to him, rat people rob each other, instead of these guys, where the money was. Not just because they stand out and look suspicious, but because the otherness field said, back, fool, you don't deserve to rob here. Which was why, if they ever did, they killed somebody or raped somebody or took a shit on the kitchen table.

Once out of the subdivision, he took out his phone and entered "Walmart" into the map, deciding on the twisty neighborhood route, since who knows, maybe Elton and Peener were cruising streets, and also the 24 bypass was narrow-shouldered and life-risky. Twenty minutes later he reached

Walmart and chained his bike to a shopping cart enclosure in the parking lot.

First it was find AllGone, and if they didn't have that, then something like it. Then it was rags, then paint and a raincoat and a wide straw hat, and a ready-to-go fishing pole and a few lures. Then it was Keisha, if he could find her and get her away somewhere. He couldn't call her, since Walmart was all about time theft and made everyone turn off their phones. Finding her, when he thought about it, was good besides just a last goodbye, since he could get her to stand in line to buy the AllGone, because of the security cameras. Why were you buying that AllGone, son? Trying to destroy some DNA?

The main door shushed open as he entered. He nodded past the greeter, an elderly black man, then turned back and touched the man's arm.

The man smiled. "Can I help you?"

"You know a girl named Keisha? She's a floating stocker. You know where she is today?"

"I don't. But I only come in an hour ago. But she works on Monday somewhere. You could ask in the office, but probably best thing is just find her. You know what I mean?"

"Thanks. I'll dig her up."

Cody made his way back to sporting goods, scanning. The interaction with the old man had given him a solidarity vibe. The old man knew her, that she was Monday working, and was thinking on her behalf, don't worry these Walmart managers with Keisha's personal business, the old man stepping out naturally for the good of the world. The good of the world was there if you could find it. It slipped in like a now-and-then dream between only certain people. Last night he had wept on Keisha's shoulder, and she kissed him and said, "Oh, honey," and it was the good of the world flowing into him. And Seb Creek knew about the missiles and advised him instead of arresting him, which was the same dream of good, the secret dream of *let's don't hurt each other*. If he came free, he could try to live well. He could tell Charlene, the leaf has turned. She would come home and find the boat gone and the spilled paint and abandoned flytraps, but when he got back, no matter what hour, he would wake her and tell her everything.

He found a cheap fishing rig and a packet of horsehair catch-anything jigs, then found a plastic hand basket and added a dark coat and hat, then, an inspiration, three cans of pink spray enamel, pink occurring to him as the perfect misdirection, since it was obvious and unsneaky.

Still scanning for Keisha, Cody went to the cleanser aisle and on a bottom shelf found a quart bottle of AllGone, but without a spray nozzle, which he had already decided was a must-have for crevice penetration. He knelt and read the contents of the bottle, which was mainly hydrogen peroxide and sodium hydroxide, then started reading the contents of the ones nearby with spray nozzles, none of which were exactly the same, then thinking maybe buy AllGone and also one with a nozzle and switch them, if they fit, so check, and, as he started to unscrew the spray bottle, a girl said over his shoulder, "Can I help you, sir?"

He looked, and it was Keisha, with her broad gap-toothed unselfconscious smile. He stood, grinning, and said, "Hello, miss. I'm trying to see if this nozzle here will fit on this AllGone product, which I want, but I would like to have it in a spray."

She said, "I can help you with that, sir." She took the spray-nozzle bottle and replaced it on the shelf. "Follow me."

He fell in beside her. "Are you taking me to a back room?"

She said, "Sir, do not be making naughty remarks." She stopped before a display of empty spray bottles and handed him one. "Just pour the AllGone into that and spray away."

He said, "I was looking for you. I was going to have to walk the whole damn store."

"Duncan told me. The greeter you talked to. I won't get a break for two hours. What is all this green on you?"

"Miss, that is moss. Also, miss, I need one more thing—some rags. Maybe shop rags, which I think you have."

"We certainly do. Come this way, sir. I'm calling you sir, sir, in case they reading lips on the cameras."

"Do they do that?"

"No. Unless they kidnapped a lip-reader. They wouldn't pay one."

They entered automotive, and Keisha handed him a bundle of pale-red shop rags. He said, "Any chance I could get you to buy all this for me?"

She said, "I could, but probably best not. Since, you know, I'm helping you, and you already picked this stuff out. I only get ten percent anyway. That's only a few dollars on this right here."

He said, "It wasn't that, it ..." He stopped, then said, "Well, shoot, I could have used that money." He smiled.

She said, "I guess I could do it on my break. If they talk to me, I could find something to say."

"Naw, forget it." Then he said, "What would they do if I just hugged you to my backbone and kissed you?"

She had a hand on her hip. Now she let her arms hang and said, "Well, go ahead, if you want to."

They watched each other, waiting. He said, "I won't."

She smiled, relaxing. She put her hand back on her hip and let her head slowly shift in inquiry.

He said, "Tomorrow I'm going to tell you a whole lot of stuff. We're going to celebrate tomorrow, if it ever comes. Remember I said that."

EASING TOWARD
OBLIVION

Squint's rope was a keepsake, so they had to devise a between-the-legs under-the-arms harness without cutting it. Seb took off his jacket, holster rig, and shirt and after ten minutes, they figured out a modified rappelling truss. Carney carefully applied Vaseline from his medical kit to the seal of the M95 mask, worked it firmly into Seb's stubbled beard, then pulled the straps tight behind his head.

He said, "If you smell rotten eggs, you're smelling death."

Seb slid into the chest-high waders and was lowered into the shallower end of the trench by Stinson, Marty, and Barb. At the bottom, he stood for a moment, breathing, then gave the okay sign. Carney returned it. Seb had sunk past his ankles and now began to slog toward the body, using his gloved left hand against the trench wall for balance, keeping his right hand aloft and uncontaminated for evidence, which was, in this case, as far as they could tell, only the phone. He knelt beside it and pulled it carefully from the mud, then slipped his arm into the waders and slid the phone into the plastic bag he had left protruding from his pants pocket.

He continued to the body, knelt, and felt for a pulse. Above him, he could feel Manuel Navalino's eyes. He looked up. He shook his head. Manuel moved away from the edge of the trench.

Marty tossed down the other end of the rope. Seb gripped it, drove his hands into the mud to pass it under the chest, then tied it tightly against the back and under the arms. As they pulled, he guided the body up, the back against the mud wall, until they had pulled it out.

He continued through the calf-deep clay to the pool that bubbled at the deep end of the trench. He squatted and felt under the red-brown water for the pipe ends. There were three elbows, all uncapped. He felt a continual pulse of bubbles from the center pipe. He stood. Above his head each pipe was intersected with a bulky blue-handled brass valve. He stripped off his muddy glove, tossed it up to Marty, and pulled on a fresh pair. He tried each valve handle, the center one last. It was partly open. He tightened it, and the bubbling at his feet stopped.

Above him, Carney said, "There it is. He climbed down those pipes and hit that valve. Probably turned it with his bare foot."

Manuel departed with the body in the back of the ambulance. Beside the trench, Seb sat on the grass and stripped off the waders, then the second pair of gloves. He had fended off the trench wall with his feet and hands as they pulled him up, and his pants and T-shirt were still mud-free. He used his shirt to wipe his Vaseline-smeared beard, but would need a bathroom to wash his face and mud-caked arms. They were only a hundred feet from the open lagoon, and the hog stench had no doubt permeated his clothes anyway and would mean a change.

Kate had arrived and was at the head of the trench dusting the brass valves. She looked up, appraised his mud-crust with a smile. She said, "Ever heard the song, 'Nice Work If You Can Get It'?"

He said, "I like Monk's version."

"All I know is the title, really. It always pops into my mind when I see somebody doing some kind of mean-ass work. You're a mess."

"You going to get anything from the pipes?"

"Too rough. Just giving it the college try."

"How's the dig going?"

"They're down about another two feet. It's starting to leak pretty bad now. We got a pump going."

Seb slid the bagged phone from his front pocket and laid it on the grass beside her. He said, "This is the kid's phone. It was stuck in the mud. It's probably locked. If you get it open, I need the calls for today."

Behind him, Stinson said, "Seb, let's do a briefing in the parking lot. Unless you want to get cleaned up first."

They gathered beside their parked cars. All three had heard that Seb's SBI investigation had been canceled, and they congratulated him, Marty and Barb enthusiastically, Stinson matter-of-factly. Seb held his arms akimbo, letting the mud cake in the light breeze, occasionally peeling a piece away. Marty and Barb reported their so-far dead ends, Barb about the store videos and warrants for the bank and phone records, which showed nothing promising, Marty about his visit to the prison, where he had discovered from guards and inmates that Leo Sackler was a domino champion, the manager-coach of the prison basketball league, an admired mechanic, and without enemies. He also learned that each month for more than forty years money had been deposited anonymously into Sackler's commissary account. The amount had increased over the years and was now $200 each month. Both detectives had reached out to their section's confidential informants, and so far nothing. Then they listened with comradely attention—and apprehensive glances at Stinson—to Seb's progress. Stinson folded his arms and lowered his head.

Seb went through the broken tibia and his subsequent theory of the murder, an accidental fall or push, someone on the surface with a rope, someone strong enough to pull a body up seven feet and tie it off on the ladder. This imagined scenario created silent consideration without endorsement. Then he recounted his long day of interviews, the extortion attempt— likely Elton Gleen, who denied it—then mentioned Randall's finding the realty agent, and ended with the drone video which showed the van proceeding toward the lodge.

Stinson looked up. He said, "Seb, that's good work with the drone. So we got two suspects, Elton and a dead boy."

Seb said, "We only have Squint Cooper's word it was Jorge in the van. You can't see the driver. I called Squint this morning to ask where Jorge was. Two hours later he was dead."

Stinson's enthusiasm stalled in a frown. He said, "So Squint killed Jorge to stop him from talking to us?"

Barb said, "Maybe Jorge turned that valve himself because he was feeling like shit after murdering someone. And threw his phone in there so it would look like an accident. For his dad."

Marty said, "How about he drove past the entrance to the farm so he could go get a pizza and never went to the lodge at all?"

Seb said, "Bottom line, we either got two accidents in three days, or we got two murders."

Marty said, "Or a murder and an accident."

Barb said, "This is why we do this, boys. This is kick-ass interesting."

Stinson unfolded his arms and laced his hands behind his head. He said, "We're getting the work done." He jabbed his chin at Seb. "What's next?"

Seb made assignments, Barb and Marty to look into Jorge, check for sudden money, check his background, then hassle informants and door-knock, starting in Coopertown—that last, a Stinson satisfier. For himself, there were a few last interviews. Then there was the well dig and whatever it turned up, if anything. Beyond that, it went unsaid, they faced the slow drip of snitch-waiting.

Seb gathered his shoulder rig and clothes and climbed the grassy slope to the hog buildings, looking for a bathroom to clean his arms. Hog noise swelled as he approached. He entered the end of the first building where a central aisle with pens on each side stretched a hundred yards into the interior. Fluorescent lights made glowing dashes on the low ceiling. Hogs teemed on the slated feces-encrusted floors, producing a racket of hoof-clatter, grunts, wheezes, and shrills. He found a small bathroom off the entrance, splashed water until his arms were clean, scrubbed his face and arms with powdered hand soap, dried with paper towels, then shrugged into his shoulder rig and jacket.

As he left the bathroom, Seb saw Squint inside the pens, walking toward him, high-stepping over the pen boundaries as he progressed, using a red plastic oar to fend away the hogs. Seb watched as Squint stepped over the last pen, laying the oar over his shoulder.

Squint said, "You know why I go through the hogs instead of down the aisle?"

"Why?"

"To condition the animals. If they're not used to a human being in amongst them, they spook when you load them for slaughter. Twice a day we make the walk, to ease them toward oblivion."

Seb nodded. He said, "Listen, I want to apologize for—"

Squint said, "About that red cap, I bet." He bounced the oar against his shoulder, then swung it down and tapped it on the concrete floor like a cane. "I figured that out. You didn't see a red cap, did you?"

"No, I didn't. That was my half-ass ploy to get you confessing."

"You were being a detective, and I admire it. The question is, did you tell your buddies I was a killer, and now I got trouble?"

"No, no. I was just swinging in the dark."

"Good. I damn sure don't need more trouble. Jorge's death is going to affect the hell out of this operation. Raleigh and the federal people are going to crawl up my butt. You headed to your car? I'll walk you out."

As they left the building, Squint swung the oar yoke-style across his neck, draping his forearms across the blade and handle.

Like a scarecrow, thought Seb, or a crucifixion.

Squint said, "You mentioned would I sell some land? I would not." They had reached the grassy slope. Now Squint stopped, turned, and pointed with both oar-held hands over the hog buildings. "My farm goes a mile back into those woods. I got a crew coming in a week to clear ground. I'm putting in organic Berkshires. Organic is the future of hog farming because rich folks like it, and they can pay. For smart farmers anyway. I might put in a prosciutto shed, if I can lure me off a prosciutto master. Berkshire prosciutto for the rich Chinaman."

They started toward the parking lot. Seb said, "I stopped by and saw Cody again. He had an orange tent all crumpled up in the garage."

Squint smiled across at Seb. He said jovially, "Well, you're a smart motherfucker. I gave him that tent for his birthday."

"I figured you remembered it. I think his flytrapping days are over though."

"You going after him?"

"I'm not."

"Well, I hope he appreciates it. I definitely do."

Seb touched Squint's arm and stopped. Squint turned.

Seb said, "You know what bugs me?"

"What?"

"It's that trench filling with gas so fast. I mean if he hit the valve on the way down, seems like that wouldn't have been enough time for the trench to fill up. It might have been though. The coroner thought so. But you know what would be good?"

"What?"

"You said you called Jorge and heard his phone ringing, and that's how you found him. So it'd be good if I could check your recent calls. On your phone."

"You're a hard-ass, aren't you?"

"I can't help it."

"Why would I kill Jorge again?"

"So I couldn't ask him if it was him in the van instead of you."

"And why the fuck would I kill Leo Sackler?"

"No idea. We'll see what comes up out of that well."

Squint swung the oar to the ground and leaned it against his thigh. He dug his phone out of his front pocket, entered the passcode, then offered it.

As Seb reached, Squint lifted the phone away. He said, "I'm not going to complain to the sheriff right yet, but if I have to, he'll damn sure listen. I wrote him a check last election." He handed the phone to Seb. "This better be the last I hear of this shit."

Seb smiled. He said, "I hope it is." He opened the recent calls. There was a call to Jorge at 9:16 a.m. He handed the phone back to Squint.

Squint said, "So what now? I'm a clever killer?"

"I guess I know you're clever. Now here's another thing. The guys said when they got here the generator was howling away. So you had to hear that phone over the generator."

Squint made a cold smile. He said, "I did. You come out here again, you better bring more than guesses."

Seb said, "Definitely," thinking, I'll bring handcuffs.

THE RIGHT CALL

Cody had gotten separate plastic bags, one for the rags and lures, one for the AllGone, and now tied them to his bike's basket, then slid the fishing pole under the brake cables. He unlocked the bike, wound and locked the cable to the seat post, and, as he swung a leg over, looked up to see Seb Creek walking toward him, both hands extended in an offer of mild surprise.

Seb said, "Damn, man. We meet again."

Cody felt his heart surge and felt also, wildly, that he must run, smash the bike hard into this cop, knock him down, and escape. He put a foot on the pedal. He looked down, past the handlebars, at the asphalt. He froze. Any instant, he might burst into tears. The man who had saved him had betrayed him.

He saw Seb's hand move to the handlebar, saw him halt beside the front wheel, heard his casual voice, "You're probably thinking, he's following me. Or I'm going to arrest you. Neither one. This right here is a chance meeting. I'm on the way to get a change of clothes. Can you smell that?" Cody saw a jacketed sleeve lift toward his face. His eyes darted. He sniffed. He said, "That's hog."

"Yes, it is. I been out to your dad's farm. I had to go down and get a dead boy out of a trench. I ruined my shirt, and I smell like hog."

"What happened?"

"Your dad has got some hydrogen sulfide equipment out there now. This kid, Jorge, got in a hole and got asphyxiated. Did you know him?"

"No."

"It looks like an accident. But I'm worried maybe your dad set it up."

Cody felt Seb's gaze probing. He did not lift his eyes. He said, "Why?"

"Let me ask you this. Did your dad, or maybe your mom, ever mention Hugh Britt?"

"No. Who's ... oh. The guy that was killed in the old boathouse."

"Right, that guy. Murdered with an axe years ago."

"By my father?"

"I'm just wondering. Anyway, forget it." Then: "You think I'm following you?"

"I guess."

"I promise I'm not. What do you have in the bags?"

"Just ..."

But Seb was already pressing the translucent plastic to inspect the contents.

Seb said, "AllGone. And some rags. And fishing lures for the fishing pole." Seb regarded him soberly. "I'd say you're on the right track. This is a huge relief, I can tell you that. I see this stuff, and I think, okay, Seb, good call. You made the right call." He found Cody's eyes. He said, "We're trusting each other. I bet if we get through this we'll be friends." He added, "And you can get your ass to Pass the Salt."

Cody half smiled. Seb started toward the Walmart entrance, then turned and said, "I was not following you, Cody. Nobody's following you. Be bold, bro."

THE TRUTH AND
JUSTICE WARRIOR

Seb sorted through the windbreakers, thinking about his parking lot encounter with Cody, whether it was chance or something the universe did. It was too complicated to think about.

Then he thought of how he had accused his father's hero of murder, wondering if there had been some hidden father-debunking going on. His father had once pointed Squint out on the street. He had been too shy to introduce himself, but had more than once recounted Squint's Silver Star bravado in Huế, how he had broken from cover to flank the second-story machine-gun nest, the double grenade attack, the knife fight with the survivor. So maybe a little father-debunking, which would be normal and natural and not important, not enough to color the facts, which were: Squint killed Jorge, and Leo, and probably Hugh Britt. At least Seb would be surprised if he turned out innocent. How to know? Maybe he never would.

He had come for a jacket but had forgotten to leave his shoulder rig in his car and would need a changing booth, or else shock the public with his chest-strapped nine millimeter. Since he couldn't find the changing booths, or a clerk, he decided on a windbreaker. He chose a green one, extra-large with an adjustable elastic bottom, and threw it over his shoulder, then found an extra-large three-pack of gray T-shirts, then wandered aisles until he found the cologne section and got a bottle of Aqua Velva. When he was a boy, in the mornings at the breakfast table, his father smelled of Aqua Velva.

In his car, Seb removed the holster from his shoulder rig and fastened it on his belt, then pulled off his stained T-shirt and put on a gray one and the windbreaker, tucking it over the holster. Then he splashed a handful of Aqua Velva over his hair, face, and pants and fanned with his notebook.

When he'd confronted Squint, throwing out the lie that the red cap had been visible to the drone, it had basically been a truth-and-justice move, with a little take-down-the-asshole thrown in, no doubt, and also the reflex fun of detective skirmishing. He had read about a warrior on a battlefield ready to plunge his sword into an enemy when the man spit in his face. The warrior sheathed his sword and let the man go, since he would not kill in anger.

His eyes fell on the cart enclosure where Cody had locked his bike. Had it been ego, a picture of himself as the honorable warrior, that prompted him to warn Cody instead of arresting him? Last year, Charlene had told him of Cody's bare-legged beatings with bamboo at the hand of his father, told him of the welts and cuts. Had it been stupid idealism? Maybe partly, but also partly compassion—which could still land him in federal prison.

He could tell the FBI it had been a technique, that he had sensed Cody's desperation, so had acted on impulse, turn the guy loose, let him recover the missiles. Besides, he only had suspicion. They would say, *Why not put him in the box and pound him?* At least set up surveillance. Releasing him was insane, maybe criminal. Since, as they knew, he was the brother of Seb's ex-girlfriend. But no, no, Seb would reply, the way of the truth-and-justice warrior is compassion and honor, and you are all baboons. And go to prison.

He googled AllGone on his phone. A powerful cleanser. Also there was a bundle of shop rags and the fishing stuff. Cody would be on the water all day, up some creek somewhere fishing, then after dark head for his stash and wash everything down. Then what? If he was smart, he would just leave everything exposed. If he was not, he would load them into the boat, try to move them into town, leave them somewhere public. And be caught. And say, Seb Creek gave me the idea. Especially after the chance meeting in the parking lot, especially if he started to think Seb had set him up. Life was dark and crisscrossed, and the flashlight of truth and justice was dim and clumsy.

His phone rang. It was the sheriff, who told him that the feds had taken over part of the sheriff's offices. Also, Agent Lowry wanted to talk to him. Also, his friend, Mia Fairchild, had been picked up by the FBI.

THE ONLY BONE

Seb drove with the blue light on top of his car, honking through inter-
sections. He got his NCIS compadre, Bill McAllister, on the phone, and
McAllister briefed him and said he would meet him in the sheriff's parking
lot. As Seb got out of his car, McAllister, still in his Stetson and wearing
the same clothes he had worn at the crash site, said, "First thing, Seb, my
man, you must settle down. She's not under arrest. Grayson Kelly is the
only one under arrest."

"She's not detained?"

"She's being questioned. They're picking fish out of a net, and she's in
the net. They got to look her over."

They started toward the sheriff's building.

"She's in the box?"

"Yes, she is."

"She's cooperating?"

"Far as I know."

They crossed the street, headed for the rear door of the massive red-
brick county building.

Seb said, "So the operative theory is, she and this Grayson guy figured
out a way to shoot down a Super Stallion, or two Super Stallions, so they
could make off with some Stinger missiles?"

McAllister laughed. "That's it. And we're the guys that caught them. An exciting career-builder."

"Is Lowry still the asshole in charge?"

"Yes, he is. We just call him the asshole. You know him?"

"I do. He fired me. Now he's got him a tasty bone."

"The only bone you got is always tasty, Seb."

Seb swiped them through the rear door. He stopped at the foot of the stairs. He said, "Run it down to me one more time. Piece by piece."

McAllister laughed again. "You're going to go up there and fight with Lowry, you pissant county cop?" He shook his head. He said, "Seb, Seb, Seb."

Seb waited, with a stare.

McAllister rubbed his eyes, red with sleeplessness. He said, "Look, these guys are jacked up. They got one more day until they disappoint the White House. Some guys, man, would shoot their mothers. Lowry would probably shoot his kids."

Seb waited.

McAllister sighed. He said, "Okay. Piece by piece. One, you told the sheriff that Jimmy Beagle rented boats. Which, by the way, means you started this line of investigation, and the country is in your debt." He raised his eyebrows. "Not funny?"

Seb did not smile. "Moderately funny. Go on."

"Oh, lord, he's getting that Sergeant Creek focus. Okay. Next, agents descend on poor Mr. Beagle and, what do you know, they find he has indeed rented a boat to the elusive Grayson Kelly, which is why Beagle was hanging out at his fish house last night, hoping Kelly would finally return his boat, which he was supposed to do the evening before. And, what do you know, while the agents are questioning Beagle and poking around the fish house, here comes Kelly in the rented boat and gets cuffed for possession of hand grenades."

"Did the boat show residue from the missiles?"

"No. But listen up to this interesting feature. How does Kelly know to rent a boat from Beagle, who doesn't advertise and is way in the boonies on a choked-up creek? He learned about Beagle from Miss Fairchild, who was hanging out with Beagle last night. Be honest, Seb. That's a hackle-raiser."

"Even if Kelly's the guy, which he can't be ..."

"How do you know?"

Seb stared. He could say, because Cody Cooper's the guy. He said, "Because even if he is the guy, he's just a guy in the right place at the right time that scavenged a dropped load. How is that a conspiracy?"

"Current theory, he shot the pilot. The chopper jerks around or something, which drops the load, or the load hits a tree. There's panic in the cockpit, which is why no one radios. Finally, they lose control, and the choppers collide."

"He shot the pilot in the fucking night in a fucking storm?"

"It would be a feat, but who knows? Except there are no machine-gun bullet holes in the wreckage. Which it would likely take to hit a chopper in the night in a storm. Unless you were an amazing rifle shot, which Kelly is. And you own a thermal scope, which Kelly does. Because we found one in his storage compartment."

"So he had two and hid the other one with the missiles?"

McAllister shrugged and smiled. "Must have."

"They find a bullet hole in the windshield?"

"The windshield is in tiny pieces."

"They find a hole in the pilot?"

"They're looking. The pilot's in pieces himself. And also burned up."

"So who knows? You guys maybe uncovered an amazing conspiracy. Or else everybody's innocent, which would be depressing."

"Also, ten minutes ago, we got two more pieces of evidence. One, they got a warrant for Mia's storage compartment and found three hundred pounds of ammonium nitrate. Which is plenty for a giant-ass bomb. Six fifty-pound bags. She had bags of clay stacked on top of them. Everything covered in dust. Plus, she's got five gallons of diesel in the back of her studio."

"What does she say?"

"No idea. I expect they're asking her right now."

"Does she drive a diesel?"

McAllister smiled and sighed emphatically. "Yes. A Jetta."

"That's probably just a coincidence though. Since the diesel's for making bombs."

McAllister joined Seb in a smirk. He said, "She's also got a record, Seb. She and a bunch of people chained themselves to a gate outside a nuclear plant."

"That's it?"

"That's it."

"So, hey, maybe Lowry's not such an asshole."

They started up the stairs.

McAllister said, "No, he's an asshole. But he might be a right asshole." At the landing, he touched Seb's arm. They stopped. McAllister said, "So what's the deal with this girl? Are you in love?"

"I am deeply in like."

"Well, don't do something awful, like take a swing at Lowry. I see you getting hot, I'm going to mace you."

"I'm in complete control. Because I am clear that no one could shoot down a helicopter going a hundred and fifty miles an hour. With a rifle at night in a storm. What I worry is, I'm the last sane person in this fucking building."

Besides, Cody Cooper has the missiles, Seb could say. But couldn't.

A FISHLESS KID

Cody handed his credit card to the gas jockey, a thin kid with an earring, who swiped it through his smartphone dealie. The kid said, "If you want a paper receipt you got to go up to the office."

Cody said, "Don't need one."

The kid gave back his card, then handed him the phone. He said, "Just sign on the line. With your fingertip."

Cody signed on the phone and returned it. Then he took out his wallet, fished out a five, and handed it to the kid.

The kid hesitated. He said, "Really?"

Cody said, "For watching the boat." Cody had forgotten groceries at Walmart and left the boat at the dock while he pedaled to the 7-Eleven.

The kid took the money. He said, "Wow. Thanks." He unzipped one of his fancy jean pockets, slid the bill in, rezipped. He said, "So what are you going after?"

"Blues. Specks. Anything."

"Specks are speckled trout?"

"Yeah." Cody unwrapped his bowline from the cleat and nested his grocery bag in the bow.

The kid said, "I'm from Nevada. I never caught one fish. I never even seen one. Maybe in a grocery store. Just fish pieces though. I might have seen a guppy."

Cody snugged the boat alongside the dock and stepped in. He said, "You never saw a fish in somebody's boat?"

"I just started yesterday."

"Well, you'll see one pretty soon. They look just like they do in the movies."

The kid laughed. "One day I'll go fishing, I hope."

Cody shoved the boat away from the dock. He said, "I'll take you fishing someday."

The kid said, "Really? That would be cool."

Cody pulled the cord, and the motor purred to life. He said, "If I'm not in prison."

The kid grinned and waved, and the boat nosed into the bay. Once out of the no-wake zone, he cranked it onto the plane. He had hauled the boat out on the Dover ramp, dried it with his rags, then sprayed it pink, using up all three cans in an unblotchy double coat. Which Charlene might like, if she got used to it. Then he sank the bike beside the ramp. Now, if anyone saw him through binoculars, they would see a straw-hat guy in a flapping raincoat and pink boat with a fishing pole. And not a fearful fugitive.

It was low tide. Now it was either lurk in the creeks or head for the islands and ocean inlets. Peener and Elton might cruise the creeks, and he would be trapped if they found him. So head to the islands, go half a tank south, fish the sandbar holes. At dark, turn north, pass the old wharf to reconnoiter, pass it several times, then haul up and make a fire and cook his weenies, a fisherman taking a break.

His talk with the kid gave him a good feeling, like his talk with the Walmart greeter, the sharing of vibes. Like with Seb Creek. Except with the kid he had made that dumb prison remark. If the cops decided to question all the gas guys, which they would, the kid could say, come to think of it, there was this guy that made a prison remark. He would take the kid fishing though. After all, take a kid fishing once in a while.

For some reason, even after Seb Creek braced him in the parking lot, Cody trusted him. A coincidence, said Creek. With his hog-smelling clothes and off-the-wall tale about his dad and a dead kid and Hugh Britt.

Creek had said, *your dad set it up*, and Cody had been so fuddled he hadn't asked anything.

He hadn't been fishing in five years maybe. Since before his homeless days. He had been plenty on the water, planting grass and flytrapping, but with no thought of fishing, and no inclination. Now he planned to fish all day, a day of boat-sitting and anticipation, in calm nature. Definitely, he would take the kid fishing. He would take Keisha and the kid, and joke around all day, be a big brother, make sure the kid went to college and felt confident. He let himself smile at his hokum, but the smile didn't penetrate. The wind whipped coolly around Cody's face. He inhaled it and sighed it out.

At Compass Inlet, he could see the horizon of sparkling ocean. He steered to the right and headed south to lose himself in the back-island sandbars.

TEA BREAK

The motorcycle squad was six deputies. Four were out riding funerals. The other two had been kicked downstairs to occupy the storage room beside the gym. Suit-and-tie federal agents, each with an open laptop, had taken over their desks. McAllister stopped at the first desk, occupied by a young agent intently paging through a screen.

McAllister, using a redneck drawl, said, "You finding anything, friend?"

The agent, a young guy with a comb-over and sharp nose, looked up, his gaze stopping in midair halfway to McAllister, face curt. He said, "What?"

McAllister gave Seb a should-I-fuck-with-this-guy eyebrow raise. Seb grimaced. McAllister said, "I need Lowry."

The agent looked back at his screen. "He's in one of the interview rooms."

As they started away, Seb glanced at the agent's screen. In one corner was a photo of a statuesque white vase, one of Mia's. He looked over the agent's shoulder at the URL—FairchildStudio.com. The agent darted him a sour look.

Seb followed McAllister down the hallway, then turned a corner to the investigations squad area, which had two interview rooms. Both doors were closed, the red lights above the doors illuminated. Between them was the door to the audiovisual control center. McAllister looked through its small window and knocked.

A moment later, the door opened inwardly. An agent leaned into the jamb and said, "What's up?"

Behind him, Seb could see another agent and a sheriff's deputy seated at the long narrow table gazing at a bank of screens. The agent wore headphones.

McAllister said, "Where's Lowry? This is Detective Creek."

"Interview two."

McAllister pushed the door and shouldered past the agent. He said, "Can you get him on the horn?" Seb followed him, acknowledging the agent and their transgression with a perfunctory smile.

The agent closed the door. He took his seat, the only empty chair. He said, "I'll interrupt, but you'll have to wait for a lull." He fitted a pair of headphones and returned his attention to the silent screen.

The screen on the right showed a large unshaven man in his twenties. A scarlet birthmark descended over his receding forehead like a wound. He sat head-tilted and open-mouthed. Then he seemed to rouse himself and began to speak with long lolling nods of emphasis.

The screen on the left showed Mia. She wore a sleeveless green top, and gazed evenly across the table at her unseen interrogator. Her elbows were propped on the tabletop, hands interlaced before her face, fingers extended like antennae.

McAllister looked at Seb. He said, "You know how to hit the audio?"

Seb said to the deputy, who sat between the two agents. "Chris, hit the audio on two."

The deputy glanced at Seb, then at the agent to his left. He made a dismissive grimace and flipped a switch on the console.

Lowry's voice said, "… Defense Authorization Act, Ms. Fairchild?"

As the agent turned, halfway removing his headphones, McAllister clapped him on the shoulder and said, "No sweat, buddy. NCIS has need-to-know."

The agent reseated his headphones and turned back to the screen.

On the screen, Mia said, "I know that you can detain me, but I know that you won't. As much as you may think the National Defense Authorization Act gives you that right, I trust you also know that lawyers on both sides would sue in a heartbeat, which is why it's not done." She reached below the table and brought out a smartphone. As she thumbed it, she said, "So fifteen minutes, Mr. Lowry. Then I leave this room, and you must either let me go or arrest me. I have been honest and truthful with you, and you have been devious and bullying with me, without giving me even the courtesy of telling me why I am here."

McAllister looked at Seb. He made a *wow* face and said, "I am also deeply in like."

The left-side agent held a console button. He said, "Agent Lowry, I've got Detective Creek in the control room."

"Detective Creek? Detective Creek is here, Ms. Fairchild. Will you give me a minute?"

Mia nested one hand inside the other. She said, "I'll give you fourteen."

They heard the sound of a door opening and closing. Then the door to the control room opened. Lowry said, "Let's talk out here."

Seb and McAllister joined him in the hallway.

Seb said, "You wanted to see me?"

Lowry said, "I need you to sign a written report. We'll write it, you sign it. We pretty much got the picture. You saw Miss Fairchild and Mr. Beagle last night on the barge, correct? And informed Sheriff Rhodes about that this morning."

"I did. I should have called last night, but it didn't occur to me."

"See Craig in our office area. Now I've got to—"

"Did she say how she knows Kelly?"

"Detective, I don't have time—"

"Did she say why she has the ammonium nitrate?"

Lowry inhaled patience. He said, "She has an explanation. Now if you don't mind …" He started to turn.

Seb gripped his arm. Lowry brushed the hand off, but stopped.

Seb said, "Thing is, you got a crap theory going, don't you? Which I expect you know, in the back of your mind. Because your theory is, first, some guy makes an insane plan to shoot down a chopper with a rifle and steal missiles, and two, he actually does it. In a hurricane wind at night. That's crazy, and believing it makes you crazy. This is some kind of impulse crime.

Probably kids. And what the hell would she have to do with any of this?"

McAllister said, "Seb, let this man work. He's only got twelve minutes left."

Lowry frowned at McAllister, then turned to Seb. "That's why we investigate, Detective Creek." He turned toward the door.

Seb said, "You're out of your depth, bro." As Lowry opened the door, Seb caught a glimpse of Mia. He said, "Mia, I'm out here waiting. I'll see you in twelve minutes."

Lowry turned, glared, and closed the door.

McAllister and Seb returned to the motorcycle squad room where Seb dictated his statement to one of the agents, then signed a printed copy. As he and McAllister turned into the corridor outside the interview rooms, Mia emerged, with Lowry behind her. She gave Seb a distracted glance and walked past him toward the elevators. Seb followed, glancing over his shoulder at McAllister, who offered a wan, good-luck shrug.

Seb caught up with her, touched her arm. Her head turned toward him a fraction. She offered a flick of smile. They reached the elevator, and Seb pushed the down button.

He said, "You're kind of freaked, I guess."

She studied the elevator door. He heard her long in-draw of breath, her long exhalation. She said, "I am."

He said, "How about this—we go across the street and get a nice window table at Debbie's. Have a cup of coffee. Or lunch, if you want."

She didn't reply. The elevator doors opened. They boarded and started down. She said, "I think I'll just go home."

The doors opened. He walked with her to the main door, opened it for her, and followed her onto the sidewalk.

He said, "Did you drive? You need a ride?"

She said, "I drove. With an escort of four FBI cars."

He said, "There's Debbie's, right there."

Mia sighed again. She said, "Okay."

They took the window table he and Prince had occupied. The same young waitress approached with two glasses of ice water. He said, "I'm getting to be a regular. Two coffees. Thanks."

The waitress smiled and nodded.

Mia said, "I'll have hot tea."

The waitress said, "Got it," and strolled away.

Seb gazed at Mia, who sat with her hands in her lap, looking down at the table. The table felt wide, like a chasm. He wanted to reach, to lift her chin, to lay a hand against her cheek, but saw she was in a vortex. She had been assaulted. He made his voice light. "You're probably thinking, damn, I meet this cop, and next thing the FBI picks me up."

Her eyes flicked to his face, then to the table again. She said, "I haven't gotten that far. But now that you mention it." Her voice was flat. Nothing was funny.

"So what happened?"

"What happened is, a dozen FBI agents arrived at my studio and asked to search it. Which I permitted. And my home. They were not neat."

"They're sort of freaked. They've got a deadline. From the White House actually."

Now she looked at him, without friendship, from the vortex. She said, "What were they looking for? They would not say."

"Right, they wouldn't say. They can't."

"Do you know?"

He hesitated. He felt her cool gaze as pain. He said, "I do know. The sheriff and I are the only ones right now that know. I mean of the local guys."

"Did you tell them to search my home?"

"Of course not. No, no."

"Then why did they?"

"Something went missing, and they're looking for it. They're completely on the wrong—"

"Something to do with the helicopter crash?"

He looked at her. His mouth opened.

She said, "I'm guessing, Seb. I didn't take it, whatever it is."

He said, "Christ, of course you didn't. I was just surprised you could guess that. No, that makes sense. Military helicopters, right?"

"Otherwise, you might suspect me?"

"I definitely do not suspect you, Mia."

"And they think Grayson Kelly took whatever it was?"

"Yes. That's the theory, and—"

"And because I know Grayson, then I'm part of it."

"Right."

He felt her gaze like a cage, enclosing him. She said, "You must ask me how I know him, Seb. Do you know that I have some fertilizer that can make a bomb?"

"I know that you are completely and absolutely innocent, Mia. I do."

She lifted her head from table-staring, sat straighter. She said, "No, you can't know that." She shook her head slightly, turned her gaze to the window, to the street, where there was light and space. She said, "I see you can't know that. It's fine."

He had the impulse to reach for her hands, but they were lost to him, hidden in her lap. Besides, she would resist. He said, "I do know, Mia."

She turned from the window, offered an effortful glance at his face, then again looked down. She said, "No, you can't. I met Grayson because he has the storage compartment across from mine. He sleeps there sometimes. He mentioned he wanted to go fishing, and I told him Jimmy rents boats. The ammonia fertilizer was in the compartment when I rented it five years ago. Left by the previous occupant. I didn't have a pallet, so I put my clay on top of it, in case water ever came in."

"Who was the previous occupant?"

"A farm store. But the records only go back three years."

"They'll get to it. They'll find that out."

"Did they tell you I was arrested in Ohio?"

"They did, yes. I'd like to hear all about that sometime. That must have been …"

A pained look crossed her face, stopping him.

She said, "Seb, look. You're a nice guy. But right now I'm …"

"I know. I know."

"Please don't say that. Maybe you know, but don't say it. I'm not good company right now. Besides my house is a mess. And I just found out they cut open every bag of clay in my storage compartment. I've got to get some tubs."

"Listen, let me help. I'll—"

"I don't want help. And really, I don't even have time for tea right now. Do you mind?" She stood. As he slid his chair back, she laid a hand on his shoulder. "Please. I'm going. Just stay here. That would be a favor. Thanks." As she walked toward the door, the waitress, bearing two mugs, lifted her face in question. Mia made a strained smile, shook her head, and left.

The waitress put the coffee in front of Seb. She said, "Should I take the tea back?" Then she saw his expression and stood straighter.

"Take the coffee back," he said. "I'll take the tea."

SADNESS IS DEEPER

Seb blew on the tea for a few long seconds, then drank it in three draws, still too hot. He dropped a ten on the table and walked outside. When Mia left, he had been stricken and hadn't turned to see where she was parked, and now quickly scanned the street and the public lot to his right for any sign of a Jetta. She was gone. He would get moving. Later he would think it through, when to call, what to say, maybe just drop by again. How much time to let go by. When she left, it was like grief. Tell her that.

He walked to the deputies' lot. As he opened his door, his eyes fell on a magnetic sign on the white car beside his, LANDMAN REALTY. Press DeWitt would be inside, giving his statement. He slipped his phone free and dialed Bonnie, the detectives' secretary.

"Investigations. Can I help you?"

"Bonnie, it's Seb. Did a guy named DeWitt come in to give a statement today?"

"Barb took it. He just left. Want me to catch him?"

"No, I'm outside right beside his car. I'll see him in a minute. What's he wearing?"

"A blue coat and some kind of cool hat. And a cool mustache."

"Okay." His eyes fell on the Walmart rose lying on the passenger seat. "Bonnie, you did me a solid by finding the governor's phone number.

You're definitely my gem. I have a gift for you, but you might have to wait until tomorrow."

"You're right outside, and you can't bring me my lovely gift?"

"It is lovely. And sweet, just like you. Also, one more thing."

"One more thing, of course. What?"

"I need a military record."

"Okay."

"I need to know what months or days a guy was granted leave during his enlistment. About fifty years ago."

"Dream on, Seb. Not a chance."

"I figured."

"Best you could do is find somebody who served with him and get testimony."

"Okay. Now I got one more. Kind of a hurry-up on this one."

"What kind of gift are we talking about?"

"A secret, thoughtful gift from my heart."

"Go ahead."

"There's a guy that used to write for the Raleigh paper forty years ago. Named Jeff Yates. During the murder trial of Leo Sackler he wrote an article for the *Observer*. I need to know if he's alive and how to reach him."

"Jeff Y-A-T-E-S?"

"That's it. This may increase the size of your gift."

"You got me flowers, didn't you?"

"I got you *a* flower. I'm only a corporal."

"Well, keep it in water if you don't get up here."

They ended the call. Seb watched the entrance of the sheriff's department. In a moment a man wearing the reported-about blue sport coat and a gray porkpie hat pushed open the doors, crossed the street, and entered the lot. Seb got out of his car, fished his ID badge from his front pocket. He held it up as the man approached.

DeWitt stopped and opened his mouth in annoyed surprise. A white mustache hid most of his upper lip and was waxed upward at the ends. He was in his fifties, short, fit, and irritated.

He said, "Is this about parking in the sheriff's lot?"

"No. I'm Seb Creek, the guy that sent you down here to give a statement."

"Oh. Nice to meet you. I gave the statement." He gestured toward his car door, which Seb was blocking.

Seb said, "You gave it to Barb Addario?"

"I didn't get her name. If you don't mind, I'm late, so ..."

Seb didn't move. He spread his hands. "I got to ask you a question."

"What?"

"Where did you go after you left Leo Sackler's place, before the Stillsons?"

"Oh, for God's sake. Am I a suspect?"

"No. But I need to know where you went. It's important."

DeWitt looked at the asphalt. "Where did I go? I have no idea." Then he looked up. "I went by Cooper Farms."

"What did you do there?"

"I talked to Squint Cooper. I go by his place every year or so, to show the mustache and keep my hand in."

Seb smiled. "That's a business mustache, isn't it?"

"Yes, it is. Now—"

"So what did you talk about with Squint?"

"Was he ready to sell off some land. He owns two miles of Sable River frontage."

"Was he?"

"No, but I keep asking. Then I went back to the office. I had a closing."

"Where did you talk to Squint?"

"In his house." He gestured toward his car again. "You mind?"

Seb said, "Did you tell Squint where you'd been?"

"What do you mean?"

"Did you tell him you'd been over to see Leo Sackler?"

DeWitt thought. "Yes. I did."

"Did you tell him Leo was digging out a well?"

"Yes, I did."

"Did he think that was interesting?"

"I have no idea. I guess he was a little surprised. I was, and that's why I mentioned it."

"Did you put that in your statement to Barb Addario?"

DeWitt hesitated, wary.

Seb said, "I just talked to her. You didn't."

"No, I didn't. So what?"

"You got to go back up there and put it in."

"Well, I certainly can't do it now. I'll have to—"

"You have to do it now."

"Or what? You charge me with obstruction of justice?"

"I give you a ticket for parking in the sheriff's lot."

DeWitt said, "Goddammit." He turned and walked quickly away toward the sheriff's department.

Seb said to his back, "I owe you, Mr. DeWitt."

DeWitt raised both hands shoulder height and let them fall. He did not reply.

Seb got into his Honda. He sent the window down, slipped out his phone again, and redialed Bonnie. When she answered, he said, "Bonnie, I just sent Press DeWitt back to redo his statement for Barb. He left something out. Is Barb still in the shop?"

"She's sitting at her desk."

"He'll be up there in a minute. Don't let her get away. Any luck with Jeff Yates?"

"Damn, you're pushy. But as a matter of fact, yes. He lives in Fort Wayne, Indiana, with his son. You want to write it? Or a text?"

"I'll write it."

He opened his notebook and wrote the address and phone as she recited. He said, "Any idea how old he is?"

"Eighty-four. No idea of his health, mental or otherwise."

"Thanks, Bonnie. Now one more thing. I could probably find this myself, but you're way faster than me. I need the number of Leonard Castle. He's the ex-governor's personal lawyer. He's still working in Raleigh as far as I know."

"So he might be in the phone book? Which almost anyone could access from the internet."

"Bonnie, you're up to two flowers. Definitely."

She said they better be roses, he said they were, and they ended the call.

He dialed the number of Jeff Yates. The call was answered on the second ring.

"This is Jeff." The voice had an elderly waver but was crisp with attention. There was a hissing sound in the background.

Seb said, "Hello, Mr. Yates. This is Detective Sebastian Creek with the Swann County sheriff in North Carolina. You got a minute?"

"I got more than a minute. Just a second." There was a mechanical *thump*, and the hissing ceased. "Had to turn off the shower."

"Let me call you back."

"No, I'm going to go right over here and sit down and listen. What's up? Was it Sebastian?"

"Call me Seb."

"Call me Jeff. All right, I'm sitting down."

"Thanks. I'm calling about a trial that you covered in Swann County, North Carolina, about forty years ago."

"That would be the Britt murder."

"It would. How did you know that?"

"I only covered one trial in Swann County, and that was it."

"You wrote an extensive piece for the Raleigh paper."

"For the Sunday magazine."

The man's mind was entirely lucid. Seb opened his notebook wrote *murder, trial, Squint, Germaine*. Things to cover. He said, "Did you hear that Leo Sackler was released?"

"I did. And he got that plantation or something. Are you folks reopening that case? I'd think double jeopardy would apply."

"No, not that case. This is a new case. Leo Sackler has been murdered."

"Oh, for God's sake."

"Two days ago. He was found down in a well he was digging out. He was hung."

"Oh, my. Now what can I do for you?"

"I'm not sure. I guess I want to hear about the murder. What people thought. Just anything you recall."

"Well, hell, that's a book. I was down there two weeks. Did you talk to the detectives? They might all be dead."

"They are."

"Well, I'm not. I'm creaky but able."

"Do you recall the details of the murder?"

"Of course. It was about magnets on a fishing scale. Leo Sackler pulled up with a boat of fish, and Hugh Britt came out and got him through the arm with a gaff and slung him around. He could have been prosecuted for assault if he hadn't been killed. Witnesses said he threw Sackler into pilings up and down the dock, one after the other. Bruised him up and severely injured his arm, which was the defense's main argument, that no one could use an axe after that."

"What did you think?"

"Well, he still had use of his left arm. Also, he was a basketball player and known to use both hands. But I'll tell you what, it was a hundred percent circumstantial case."

"You thought he did it?"

There was a silence. "I'll tell you what that case did for me. It was a lesson about the depressing ignorance of mankind. Like a fog that never lifts. Leo Sackler got up and testified, you know. He made a good impression too. I thought, well, if he did it, he's a terrific actor. What you did know was no white jury in Swann County in 1969 was going to let off a black man they thought might have killed one of their own. If they had to guess about it, they were going to guess against him. And they did. That case has come back to me many times over the years. Many times. You can't grieve about the injustice because you don't know if there was any. You grieve about not knowing. You grieve that twelve people made a decision, and they didn't know either."

Seb glanced at his notes. "How long was the trial?"

"Short. Two weeks. Testimony about the fight, testimony from the detectives. Then from Leo."

"Was it well attended?"

"Packed courthouse for the rich white man. Which is why I was there. Think about that. If you let that penetrate, you can get disgusted. We call it a justice system, but God knows what that would look like."

"Last two questions. Did you ever run into Squint Cooper?"

"The Silver Star winner?"

"Right."

"I never spoke to him, but I saw him around. You couldn't miss him. He was a great big boy and famous."

"I wondered if you might have written an article about him."

"I didn't. There might have been something in the paper though, probably not under the name Squint. You know how he got that name?"

"When he was a boy, he used to clench his buttocks, so his family called him Squint."

"Now there's a rusty nugget of memory."

"Where did you run into him?"

"At the trial. I sat behind him once and had my view obstructed by his considerable size."

"He attended the whole trial?"

"No idea. But that's where I saw him. Is he a suspect?"

"I'm looking at him. How about Germaine Ford? Did you know her?"

"I know that name. Who was she?"

"She was a beautiful girl that Hugh Britt was going out with. She's the one that gave the land to Leo."

"Oh, of course. I expect that caused many a rumor in Swann County."

"Many. Do you recall if she was at the trial?"

"I don't."

"Well, I'll let you get your naked self into that shower."

"I need to. Do one favor for me. If you solve this murder, please call me to let me know. I might not hear otherwise."

"I definitely will call you."

"You know what's deeper than disgust, Seb? This is wisdom from an old man. Sadness. Sadness is deeper."

ODD THOUGHTS

Cody tried to concentrate on fishing—casting, reeling, lifting the pole tip and carefully lowering it, feeling for bumps. Still, two full-blown futures kept floating through, with colors. One was gray prison. The other was Keisha in their yellow kitchen in the morning, with her bright brown smiling face, cooking eggs or whatever, or oatmeal, something healthy and forward-looking. Then, as corrective, he invited back the prison thought, and the vividness of gray concrete and shouts and smells and the unstopping trivial emptiness. But then the kitchen again, and Keisha, because he wasn't in prison yet, and might not be, and don't make a spot for prison in your mind, like a beaten fool, but don't think of Keisha either, like a childish fool. Think of fish, watch for cops, watch the currents and eddies where fish might swim.

He was ten miles south in the sandbar creeks. The tide was rising. He had taken the mushroom anchor from the anchor box and was now streamed behind it, casting into an eddy tail. He had caught three there, all different, a little blue and a little spot, but also a plate-sized flounder, a pole-bender. He had let them all go. When he let the flounder go, he had checked up and down the slough to make sure he was alone, having the odd thought that freeing a nice fish might be suspicious. He had been checking the water now and then for Peener and Elton, but checking it for releasing a big fish had to be a bad-mind odd thought. You let a fish go, so where're those Stingers? He was well-acquainted with odd thoughts, where you couldn't get a truth sense. They had pelted him since a boy, whipped into him first by his dad, then by the war, then by homelessness, where fear was right, but paranoia wasn't, and you couldn't tell them apart. Another bad-mind thought was the pink boat. He had painted his boat pink, which was insane, and would shout, what strange person would paint his boat pink, look at that person, and he had thought it would hide him by misdirection, his mind working in sections again. He was captured in a bad mind.

Then the kitchen thought came back, blooming hard against the nuzzle of depression, and painful hope came. She had stood in Walmart with her hands at her sides, ready to give up her job for a hug and kiss, if that's what he wanted.

He made a nice toss across the eddy and on the third lift got a strike, another pole-bender. The drag zipped as the fish streaked for deep water, so maybe a blue, long and strong. Lift, let fall and reel, repeat. He looked upstream for boats but caught himself before turning downstream.

Cody stripped off doubt. Anyone could let a fish go, any type of normal person, which even if he had never been, he sometime might be, and could be.

THE BOTTOM
OF THE WELL

Seb parked in front of the Ford lodge. Across the tall grass, he saw Kate standing at the rim of the well, saluting against the sun. He sent a hand lift and inquiring shrug. She shook her head. Seb nodded and fished out his phone. He had one more call to make. That would end the leads. Then it was the famous-rich-guy-murder-bust briefing with Stinson. He could endure it, since the investigation had been circumspect. Then the waiting. Unless he could get Squint to confess, or could devise a tricky Hollywood trap. Which first, why would Squint confess, and second, he couldn't think of a trap. And third, maybe Squint was innocent. Maybe, like cops and prosecutors he had read about and detested—and like some he knew—he had gotten mesmerized by a plausible false story.

He dialed. A woman answered and said she would see if Mr. Castle was available.

Seb had searched the internet and found a photo of the man, white-haired and broad-shouldered, seated behind his desk with the faintest of smiles, uttering for the camera the seasoned calm of accomplishment. When Castle came on the phone, Seb introduced himself, then said, "You were Germaine Ford's lawyer and wrote the will that gave her property to Leo Sackler."

"I was."

"Did you hear he was murdered?"

"I did. If you hadn't called in a week, I would have called you to offer what I can, which I'm afraid isn't much."

They spoke five minutes. In the end, Castle had nothing to add to the governor's statement, except that the psychologist he had enlisted was his daughter-in-law, and that Germaine had stated, both to his daughter-in-law and to him, that the truth would one day be revealed.

Seb thanked him, and they ended the call.

And Seb remembered, with excitement, and also chagrin, his earlier idea, which the latest death and Mia had driven from his mind: the forty-eight years of letters.

He found the number of the Amboise town hall on his phone and dialed.

"Amboise city. Can I help you?"

"Virginia?"

"Yes, it is."

"This is Seb Creek, the detective you spoke to yesterday."

"I want to thank you for arranging that call to my brother. Did you get the phone number I sent? For my mother-in-law?"

"I did, thanks. I called her, and she hasn't seen your husband for some months. The reason I'm calling is that I'd like to take a look at the letters Leo sent your mother. The ones in the precious box. I wonder if you can arrange that for me."

"I'll talk to my mother. We're having a service in the morning, and the burial."

"I wonder if it would be possible for you to call her now and ask her if I could swing by."

Virginia said she would, and they ended the call.

"Seb!"

It was Kate, waving from the well. He got out of the car and started toward her, then stopped, returned to his car, and sprayed his cuffs. When he reached the well, he offered Kate the can of repellent. She shook her head and pointed into the hole. She said, "They think it's an axe."

An extension cord ran from the V ladder and held a light which illuminated the two men below. They had dug five feet farther down and stood in muddy water. A black siphon hose descended beside them and made an occasional gulping hiss. One of the men had crouched and was feeling beneath the surface with bare hands.

Kate said, "It's wrapped in some kind of plastic."

Seb said, "If it's an axe, that's goddamn confusing."

"Why?"

"Forty-eight years ago, they found an axe thirty feet off the Britt dock. Which they concluded was the axe used to kill Hugh Britt."

One of the workmen below stood. He raised an object into the light. The handle was brown with mud and the head obscured with drapes of dripping plastic, but it was recognizable. It was an axe.

Kate said, "Way to go, Carter. Bring it up." She looked at Seb. "You think we're done?"

"Yeah. We're done. That's the axe that killed Hugh Britt. Otherwise it wouldn't be in the bottom of that well. And Leo wouldn't have been digging it out."

Carter, followed by the other workman, climbed up the ladder. He laid the axe on the grass. Kate knelt and with a pen pulled thin black plastic away from the metal, revealing a double-edged axe-head.

Seb said, "Think you can get anything?"

She said, "Never know. Maybe mitochondrial DNA. But I wouldn't get my hopes up. Tell me again, how did Leo Sackler know this was in here?"

"Current theory, she left a letter and someone robbed it from Leo."

"So Germaine Ford killed Hugh Britt?"

"I doubt it. I think she was there though."

"What about the axe they found in the water?"

"The killer threw it out there maybe. Or she did. Probably after Leo got arrested."

"My goodness. What a cool case. And the true murderer of Hugh Britt has now killed Leo Sackler. Is that the theory?"

"That's the theory."

"Well, Seb, dammit, who is it?"

Seb glanced at the two workmen, who were both listening intently. He fished up his phone, knelt, and took a close-up of the axe-head. He stood and smiled at the two men. He said, "Fellows, I cannot complete this mystery for you yet. Maybe tomorrow we'll get it tied up. But I really want to thank you guys. Hard work down there. Really good work."

Both of the men smiled and nodded. Carter said, "Well, damn."

On the way back to the squad room, Seb stopped at a flower shop and bought two more roses and a small vase. The vase was a stem of red glass, and he hesitated over it, since Mia made small vases too. Hers were a wrapped sheet of porcelain sloped up to a small hole, little clay buttons at the seam, reminiscent of a monk's cloak. He could swing by her studio, say remember that reminder *X* on my hand about the rose I had to get for someone? Have a light conversation. Which would be a bullheaded move. He bought the red vase, which was thin and tippy and seemed to represent the height of crappy design.

Bonnie was not at her desk when he entered the squad room. He filled the vase from the drinking fountain in the hallway and left it and the three-rose bouquet on her blotter. At his desk, he opened his laptop and notebook and began to complete the investigation summary. He had several interviews since he had last written and was immersed first in reporting, then in storytelling.

At one point he smelled perfume and there was a light kiss on his temple. Bonnie, broad-smiling, holding the vase of roses, said, "I don't care what they say, I think you are a sweet guy."

When Seb finished, it was past four. He ended with three theories. First, a person or persons unknown, but maybe Elton Gleen, robbed and killed Leo Sackler. Second, the unknown person was Jorge Navalino. The third theory was the elaborate Squint Cooper theory and had ancient roots, as in: Squint killed Hugh Britt in 1969 when he was home on leave, maybe, and probably over Germaine Ford, who was likely present at the murder. Then, a few days ago, Squint hears from the Realtor Press DeWitt that Leo is digging out a well at the lodge and concludes that Germaine has buried evidence there. He further concludes that she has left a testament informing Leo about the axe in the well. The next day, after chasing the drone in the van, Squint drives to the lodge and forces Leo to reveal the location of the testament in the precious box left by his father. Then he kills him, probably by dropping a lasso on him, which is why the arm was caught up in the rope. He left out the detail that Squint was a former calf-roper, since it might suggest confirmation bias. How Leo broke his leg was unknown, though it might have occurred in a scuffle. After killing Leo, Squint kills Jorge to prevent him from revealing that it was he, Squint, who drove the drone-chasing van.

Three murders in a zero-evidence package.

He felt a hand on his shoulder and turned. It was Marty Jerrold, reading the screen. Marty said, "I'm almost finished."

Seb waited. In a moment, Marty slung himself into the interview chair. He laid a two-inch-thick accordion folder on Seb's desk. He said, "Goddamn, son. You got my case, and now you're writing a mystery. What's your percentage on Squint Cooper?"

"Somewhere between a hundred and zero. What did you get on Jorge Navalino?"

"A nice kid, and everyone says so. No surprising money in the Navalino family bank accounts. But mostly we been knocking doors in Cooper-town. And there I have news. I picked up Lewis Krasner." He tapped the folder. "Remember Lewis?"

"Burglar?"

"Yes, Lewis the burglar. His sister is Carol Devon, and when we knocked up her trailer, she invites us in. And what do you know, right there sleeping on her couch is Lewis Krasner, who is her husband's bur-glar buddy. Her husband is Danny Devon, who is currently downstairs waiting on a better deal for armed robbery. They may take him to trial. Anyway, Carol jabs a bare foot right into Lewis' face and wakes him up."

"That's cruel."

"Oh, it was. He pops up and Carol says, 'Here they are. You wanted to go to jail, now's your chance.' It seems Lewis has been considering his future, and option one is go back to prison and see the dentist. He's got a terrible case of meth mouth, and it's recently gotten painful. We should start calling it zombie mouth. Or the mouth of hell. There's something about meth mouth that cringes me. It's worse than seeing a dead guy, because a dead guy, at least—"

"You're wandering, Marty."

"Well, it affects me. Anyway, he says he wants to make some confessions. Plural. So we bring him in, and he does. He didn't even have a warrant on him. He just craved a dentist and an orderly prison life. I just checked him in downstairs. I closed three burglaries."

"So what's the excellent news?"

"I cleared your case. The one you swapped me for, the pottery studio. And here it is." He tapped the folder. "It was one of Krasner's jobs."

Seb's mouth opened. He stared.

Marty said, "What? You look like I killed your dog."

Seb said, "No. That's great."

"Okay. Now then. Recall those motorcycle cases I swapped out to you?"

"That's Lewis?"

"No, not Lewis. But in the course of our interview he tells me about a couple of kids wheeling a motorcycle through Coopertown looking for a buyer. High school kids. He doesn't know them, but it's a clue. So since I solved your pottery case, how about you give me back those motorcycle cases?"

Seb opened his file drawer, sorted through the cases, and handed Marty a four-inch section of folders.

Marty said, "After all, if you arrest Squint Cooper, you won't need a few motorcycle busts. You'll be king of Swann County."

"Anything left in Coopertown?"

"About a dozen trailers. Barb's meeting me out there now, and we're going to finish up."

"So what did Lewis do with the pottery? There was a scale too."

"Gone to Mickey Christmas, the roving fence with the terrific name. Whereabouts unknown, but probably in Kentucky. How he intends to fence pottery I have no idea. Maybe he's a collector. Anyway, you got the doer. So my prediction is that the victim of this crime will feel emotionally generous. What? Did I kill your other dog?"

Seb had grimaced. He said, "Things got a little difficult there."

"Well, the course of true love never did something-something. Get married and forget love." Marty stopped, inspected Seb's face. "Well, goddamn, Jude, go out and get her."

"I'm looking for the right approach."

"What happened?"

Seb shook his head.

Marty said, "Never mind. I feel an avalanche of advice ready to pour out, so I'm out of here. I told Lewis to look for a visit from Detective Creek. He'll have his first appearance in the morning, so between now and then he's in lawyer limbo."

It took another hour to polish the report. Seb entered it in the log file and sent an email notice to Stinson. Then he sat at his desk, head down. He had a half-finished song, tuneless so far, a sort of love song to life. He could adapt it for Mia, make it an offering. Which might be too bold, since really they had only been together twice, at the café and on the barge. He thought of Ahmad, who had a boom box full of beats. The song could be a hip-hop thing, the love message hidden under the offsetting irony of a Southern white boy chant, expressing caution-to-the-wind trust.

His phone rang.

"Seb Creek."

"Detective Creek, this is Virginia Rubins calling you back about the letters you wanted."

"Right. Thanks. Did you get a chance to talk to your mother?"

"I did. She said she was planning to bring them to the funeral. Which is tomorrow at the Pilcher Cemetery. At nine in the morning. You know where that is?"

"I do."

"I was wondering if you wanted to …"

"I definitely will. I'll see her after the ceremony, if that's all right."

"I'm sure that will be fine."

They ended the call. If Seb called Ahmad, they could meet at Betty's Bar, or get a six-pack and sit by the inlet somewhere. They could work something up. Then knock on her door with the boom box, hey, I got a treat. And damn, sorry about the FBI. He opened Word and found the song. He read, *I used to be afraid of love* … He read to the end. It could work as a Mia song, definitely. Hip-hopping could add charm and ward off sentiment. Some of the lines were still stiff though. He needed long calm moments. He could go back to the barge, sit with Jimmy Beagle, talk about war and the FBI. And, by the way, Jimmy, what is Mia thinking?

He packed his laptop into his briefcase, then lifted the Lewis Krasner file and tucked it beside it. He took the elevator to the first floor and crossed the underground corridor to the jail. He checked his nine milli-meter in a weapon locker, passed check-in with the deputy at the entrance booth, and took a seat in one of the interview rooms. Ten minutes later a deputy ushered Krasner into the room. He wore the orange jail coverall and was trussed in full restraints, leg, wrist, and belt chain. The deputy locked him into the table ring and left the room.

Seb said, "Hooking you up is standard procedure, Lewis. I got no say."

Krasner said, "I'm used to it." He was a small man, in his forties, thin-faced and sharp-nosed, a variety of tattooed beasts, quotes, and insignias smattered like afterthoughts across his forearms. His long hair was wet and made brown curtains beside his face. The belly chain fell across one knee and *tink*ed as the knee bounced. He said, "So what do you want?" His teeth flashed black and tan as he spoke. He seized one of his ears and shook it determinedly. He tilted his head and thumped his temple with a palm. "You're Detective Creek, right?"

"Right."

"First thing you need to know, I'm taking my confession back. A hun-dred percent I take it back."

"Really? You didn't do the crimes?"

"I'm not saying I didn't do them. I'm just not confessing right now."

"You just confessed again."

"No, I didn't. I revoke that."

"You signed, Lewis."

"That's not my signature."

"We have videotape. I thought you needed a dentist."

"I do need a dentist."

"So what's the problem? You getting sick?"

"Yes, Mr. Creek. That's the problem. I'm quite sick."

"Did you see the nurse?"

"That's the problem. There's only one nurse, and she's a hard-ass."

"What are you coming down from?"

"Various ones of opioids. And heroin. I'm suffering bad, and this know-it-all nurse is absolutely unsympathetic. These people like her should not be serving the public."

"You drinking water?"

"I'm trying to. I have to drink from the goddamn faucet."

"So you hereby revoke your videotaped confessions?"

Krasner stared at him, absorbing the absurdity. He said determinedly, "Definitely."

Seb made a frowning smile.

Krasner said, "I'll come back tomorrow morning and re-confess, absolutely. How about that? There's no chance, is there?"

"No chance, Lewis."

"Get me some buprenorphine. Can you talk to the nurse?"

"I'll talk to her."

"Will you absolutely talk to her, without fail, and a hundred percent you will?"

"A hundred percent."

"It won't make a fuck of difference. I'm big-time fucked, man."

"You got to go through it, Lewis."

"I know it. I should have planned. I was thinking, I could have had a secret compartment installed in my ass or something." He leaned his head forward to reach his hands. He combed fingers through his hair curtains and let them flop. "This is terrific suffering, man." He sawed the handcuff chain back and forth through the table ring, making a zipping rattle. He said, "I know a guy that died in a jail cell. The nurse told me I was a baby."

"That was uncalled for."

"It was. Jail people basically have no inward sensitivity. What kind of people would apply for a jail job? Think about it. What do you want? I got to get going." He zipped his handcuff chain through the table ring again. "I'm getting claustrophobic."

"Tell me about the pottery studio."

"What about it?"

"You remember it?"

"Of course, I remember it. I thought there was antiques or something in there. It turns out it was all handmade modern stuff. I took some anyway, just in case."

"And the scale."

"Yes, I took the scale."

"How much did you get?"

"Very fucking nothing almost. Thirty for the scale."

"Mickey Christmas?"

"Yep."

"He take the pots?"

"What I had left. Five, I think. Ten bucks each one. A rip-off for sure. Some of those pots had price tags of like hundreds of dollars."

"Who told you there were antiques in there?"

Krasner alerted. He bobbed his head methodically, considering. He said, "I don't work for nobody. I do my own thing."

Seb waited.

Krasner said, "All right then. It was Elton Gleen mentioned it. We were shooting the shit around the tubs and someone said Mickey Christmas was coming, and it was like, damn, nobody's ready for that. And it came up Elton Gleen mentioned a place on Willow Road that he admired some of the art collection in there. So I borrowed Carol's car and hit it that night."

"You said you sold Christmas what you had left. Where did the rest of it go?"

"Just a teapot to Elton for twenty bucks."

"So he got first pick?"

"Yeah, because he admired it."

"Sounds like he got a bargain."

"Oh, hell yeah. That teapot had a price tag of five twenty-five. It was all modern though."

"You write all this for the other detective?"

"Fuck, man, I'm not writing again. I'm sick."

"I'll write it. You sign it."

A half hour later, as Seb left, Krasner lifted his head from his arm cradle and reminded Seb that he had promised to speak to the hard-hearted nurse, which Seb did, without avail.

It was past six. Outside, the sun had lowered and the air was cooling. Seb stopped at an Italian restaurant and ordered lasagna and a glass of wine. Then drank two more glasses. When he left the restaurant, the sun was golden through the pines. North Carolina sunsets were inferior to California's, where he had gone through boot camp and infantry training, because California had the western ocean. North Carolina had the eastern ocean, though, and notable sunrises. From his apartment window, he had seen many fine sunrises, each day different, like a changing painting. As he settled into the driver's seat, he decided to drive to a beach park and sleep in his Honda, wake to a pure sunrise, without rooftops and cars. I'm doing surveillance, officer. In case he spooked a ranger.

He turned the key, illuminating the dash, but did not engage the starter. Radio news blared, and he turned it off. The bottom difficult truth was that life was always one thing after another and no handle. The future swept into the past through the present, and things were infinitely complex, and there was nothing to hold on to—not in ordinary life, or in war, or after a war—unless it was a person, which he had lost.

He had fallen in love, was the truth. Love had attracted him, and he had needed it toward him, but his force had not been strong enough to keep it, and that was the true sad truth. This was wine thinking, his gloom-loving wine mind working, but truth anyway. At the beach, he could leave the car and sleep on the sand. Watching for drug runners, officer. He closed his eyes and saw her, and an ache pulsed.

On the drive to the beach, he made a six-mile detour down Willow Road all the way to the end, past Jimmy Beagle's fish house, dark in the moon-gleamed water, then to the turnaround in front of her studio, a dark bulk in the dark trees. He slowed and made a quiet circle in the turnaround. Then he drove away toward the beach, where the sun would rise and he could listen for a love song.

THE UNSEEN
POWERS OF LIFE

The sun was down, and the moon up and halfway open, like a sleepy eye. The silver haze on the water and the scrub and sand made Cody feel jumpy and exposed but didn't matter really, since the plan was to boldly build a weenie fire. He even had marshmallows. He had fished the west end of Cat Island, worked past the splintery wharf and the twin firepits where he had buried the missiles, then anchored at the eastern inlet until darkness closed. He was hidden in night now, so no longer worried about Elton and Peener, except to think now and then about what was coming there if he made it through.

He hadn't caught a fish for several hours. Which was fine, since the last one he had caught had swallowed the hook, and he had to stab its brain and cut it open to get the lure back. Now the fish, a ten-inch spot, lay butchered beside the weenies on the cooler ice, a fish formerly free to swim hither and yon in the ocean.

An insight bloomed. The insight was that the ruthless-feeling squeamishness he felt about the fish came from Keisha, which was how life worked and how you changed selves. She warmed his heart and his whole field of mind with happy sweetness, which didn't go with killing and also didn't go with insanely stealing Stinger missiles and getting snared in Elton Gleen's cold-blooded ways. They would call or come by tomorrow or the next day and Cody would say, I gave the missiles back. Do it somewhere public, so he wouldn't get hurt. He thought he had figured out how to handle it.

He had turned off the ringer on his phone, but now it vibrated in his pocket. It was Charlene. He thought of not answering. It would be about the paint and flowers.

He hit the button. "Hey, Charlene."

"Where are you, Cody?"

"I'm fishing." He looked up and down the black water. No lights or motors. Still, he laid the pole down and cupped a hand around the phone.

"Cody, what's going on?"

"Like what? What do you mean?"

"Like two FBI agents just knocked on my door and wanted to talk to you."

"What did they say?"

"About what, Cody? What did they say about what? What did you do?"

Cody had the sudden fierce paranoia that his phone was bugged, or that they were standing beside Charlene, listening. He said, "Nothing." Then he said, "Did they mention flytraps?" It made sense that he would ask that. Detective Creek said they were onto him because of flytraps. He pivoted the phone away from his mouth and inhaled.

"Yes, they did. They wanted to know if you were still poaching flytraps."

"Did they search the trailer?"

"They wanted to, but I didn't let them. I said since you weren't there, I didn't feel comfortable. Good thing I put your flytraps back in the fridge, because they looked in the windows. You left them all over the kitchen table."

"Before they got there, you did?"

"Yes, along with cleaning up the mess in the garage. I spent an hour scrubbing blue paint off the garage floor with turpentine. You dragged the boat right through my flowers, Cody. Why in the world would you do that?"

So far, if they were listening, it was about flytraps. It couldn't be about panic-dragging the boat and panic flight. He put apology into his voice. "Damn, Charlene. I'm so sorry. That paint spilled, and I just freaked I guess. I was so mad." That was lame. It was out though. He said, "I saw Seb Creek. He said you asked him to talk to me."

"Cody …"

"Also, he said Dad might have killed a kid that was working for him. Did you hear about that?"

"It's all over the news. But Dad didn't kill him, for goodness' sake. He fell into a ditch out at the farm, and it was full of deadly gas."

"You shouldn't have cleaned up. I was going to do it, definitely. But I was just so mad at the time."

"Cody, I'm not dumb. The FBI doesn't care about Venus flytraps."

"Well …" He held the phone away and breathed. He said, "What did they say?"

"Very little. Just where were you, and did you still go in for flytraps. I said you were out fishing, and you did not. They left a card, and you're supposed to call them. They want you to call them right away."

"Okay. Text me the number."

"What's going on, Cody?"

"Nothing. I bet I know what it is, Charlene. The state has got something going with the feds about endangered species. That's what it is. Look, do this. Go get the flytraps and take them to a dumpster. Can you do that?"

"Goddammit, Cody."

"Charlene, I told you I have turned the leaf, and that's the definite truth. But help me. Can you help me? They could be coming back with a warrant." There was a silence. His head went light and dizzy. He felt sudden relaxation. He had a thought: he could tip himself into the water and inhale and drift to the bottom and quietly die.

"Cody, I'm not dumb. You ran out of here like the wind."

"I wish you hadn't of cleaned up the paint. I'm going to replant every flower too."

"When are you coming in?"

"Not long. I'm trying for some drum. I been doing pretty good." If they checked his cooler, they would find one spot, which wasn't pretty good, if they were listening. He said, "Please dump the flytraps. In case they get a warrant. Text me the number. Don't worry. Everything's good."

"Christ. Fine. I'll be waiting up for you. We have to talk, Cody."

"Okay. Bye."

He ended the call. He sat, numb. It was like seeing a tidal wave a mile out there, small but coming and growing and too late to run. He turned sideways, locked his feet under the bench seat, and leaned over the water. First the cold shock. Then inhale.

He sat up and cranked the engine, then went to the bow and hauled in the anchor. His phone dinged with a text, but he did not look. He would call the FBI tomorrow, claim misunderstanding. They would probably bring him in. Where were you the night of the chopper crash? Where were you the night the missiles reappeared? They were the tidal wave. They meant to drown him. Or they would leave him clinging to a tree and recede. Wait and see. Indifference poured through him like relaxation, and behind it, center-chest, the hot longing for Keisha returned.

Later, past midnight, Cody nosed the boat into the sand in front of the firepits. He had the sudden dismal realization that he had forgotten wood. He had remembered matches but forgotten wood and must now either forage and leave footprints and have to brush them out and maybe miss some, or else abandon the fire idea, which he could not do because it was essential to his fisherman pose. Also, he had forgotten his Ka-Bar for digging and would have to twist off a brushing branch, which meant more fuck-up chances, missed footprints, DNA on a branch, something dropped in the dark. Depressing dismalness flushed through. He got a bad marijuana craving.

Cody pulled the boat snug, gathered his grocery bag from the bow, and went up toward the firepits to find a branch. As he neared them, he snapped his flashlight on and off to get oriented, and there, beside the left side firepit, he saw a bundle of brush, some still with leaves, and four arm-sized pieces of driftwood. He fell onto his knees in the sand and touched the small branches, then touched the driftwood, and it was like prayer, he thought, this gratitude for the unseen powers of life.

He found a straight branch and broke it into a wiener stick, then, using pieces of newspaper he had scavenged from a 7-Eleven trash can, built the fire and lighted it. He cross-stacked the four driftwood pieces over the jumping flames. The fire would signal his innocent fisherman's presence. They would come now if they were coming. Unless they were watching with thermal scopes, waiting to see what this unknown fisherman might do next. He roasted a weenie, then reversed the stick and toasted a bun on the other end, then clamped the weenie into the bun, doused it with ketchup, and ate it in four bites. He swigged from his water bottle. The fire had settled, was going to coals on the perimeter. He roasted another weenie and bun and ate them.

He broke the weenie stick and burnt it, then gathered the weenies and buns and ketchup in his T-shirt and brought them back to the boat. He retrieved his Walmart bag of rags and AllGone, then walked back to the fire, nearly flameless now, then turned and walked halfway to the opposite firepit, and then he was, best guess, directly above the missile stash. He fell to his knees. He was fully trusting now, trusting to the unseen power of the universe that would either deliver him to the ones watching with thermal scopes, or free him to live and have a happy future. He dug with bare hands.

When he was finished, he gathered the sand-heavy sleeping bag that had covered the missiles, the empty AllGone bottle and rags, and stowed everything in the bow. Then he made seven trips with the bailing pail to pour out his footprints. Then he pushed the boat off and clambered in. He made his way to the bench seat and sat and drifted away from shore into the moon-flecked calm, waiting for the search beams and the roar of boats. He drifted. He began to weep.

THE LETTERS

Traffic had stalled for a half hour, but the cops finally got a wrecker through on the shoulder, and things were moving again. When Seb crawled past the wreck site, he saw the three vehicles and out of habit deduced the scenario. The VW bug somehow went sideways, a blown tire maybe or it got rear-ended. Then it was T-boned by the SUV. The box truck was behind them and unable to slow. The bug was crumpled and had tumbled down the shoulder into the woods. The truck lay on its side. The SUV was already on the wrecker bed. As he edged by, Seb caught the eye of a paramedic he knew, made an inquiring gesture. With one hand, the man cut the air near his waist and shook his head. One death at least. From the look of the collapsed VW, possibly more.

That morning as he exercised Seb had turned on the TV news. Another bomb had gone off in Baghdad. The camera showed a crowd of Iraqis, men and kids mostly, but also women in burqas, milling at the perimeter of the wreckage, talking together, gesturing, some with cell phones. Their faces were blank. They seemed simply curious, like tourists, which in a sense they were. It was not their bomb or their deaths. No doubt invisible streams of grief were radiating through the city, but here, in this aftermath crowd, these at least had not died. They had gathered near the blackened cars and slumped building fronts to witness and absorb.

At the beach, he had worked on the song but not been able to sleep and had gone back to his apartment. His Mia gloom persisted through the morning and now, as he passed the wrecks, suddenly lifted. It was not just that there was life on both sides of death, it was that no one dies in his own life. Others die in theirs. So bravery. Then more bravery.

He fished his phone from his jeans pocket, surfed to Ahmad.

After five rings, Ahmad said, "Seb, my dawg." The voice was raspy loud, almost a shout. Behind the voice, Seb heard the chomping and gnashing of machinery.

"Ahmad, let's do a song."

"No shit?"

"The lyrics are pretty much done. It's a heart-rending love song, man."

"Heart-rending? That sounds pretty white."

"We get the singers doing some kind of backup. Some kind of talk-back or something. We'll figure it out."

"Let's do it, dawg. Give me the first line, let me get the line length."

Seb recited, "I used to be afraid of love, I hid my fear in pride."

"That's definitely white."

"I happen to be white."

"We might could black it up."

"We could."

"When can I get it?"

"I'll send it today."

"Beautiful, man. Say it again."

Seb repeated the line.

Ahmad said, "I got it. I'm a get to work on it today. I'm crushing, but I got my box right here. I might slip some car-crushing sounds behind it."

"Do your thing, Ahmad. What it is, it's a love song for this girl I know."

"The one you left the meeting for?"

"Yes. It's kind of a make-up song. Kind of an I'm-sorry song."

"You fucked up?"

"A little bit."

"Don't worry about it. This girl is cooked. She got no hope."

When he reached Pilcher Cemetery, he found the gathering had moved from the chapel into the graveyard. More than thirty people, all black, all in their Sunday clothes, had gathered at the grave and its mound of fresh earth. The casket was suspended above the cavity on two wooden planks. He watched as the minister gave the sign and eight men came forward to man the lowering straps. As they lifted, the minister and a young woman pulled away the planks, and the casket was haltingly lowered, with discreet discussion, by the eight men. When the straps were retrieved, a procession began moving past, some using the shovel to toss earth into the grave, some their bare hands.

The crowd began to file back to the chapel and parking lot. Seb stood on a grassy strip between two graves, nodding noncommittally to their polite glances. Last to leave were the minister and the family, Virginia Rubins, her three children, all boys, and her mother, June. Virginia said to the minister, "Dr. Packard, will you kindly take the boys ahead, and we'll be coming up?"

The minister murmured, and he and the boys continued toward the chapel.

Virginia and Seb smiled and nodded to each other. Virginia said, "Mama, this is Detective Creek."

June was a small woman. She wore a silky black dress and peered up at Seb under a black straw hat decorated with fabric flowers. She was in her late sixties, but her small face and neck were already rippled as a walnut. Her thin mouth made a quick smile without showing teeth.

Seb took her extended hand and said, "Sorry for your loss, Ms. ... I believe I do not know your last name."

"My name is Ms. Carson." Despite the aged appearance, the voice was clear and businesslike.

"Nice to meet you, Ms. Carson. I have been wanting to speak with you. If this is not the right time ..."

"This is a fine time because here we are, and our duty is done. What do you want to ask?"

"Mostly I want to ask whether there is anything you can tell me about the murder of Hugh Britt, anything that was not public at the time."

"You going back to Hugh Britt in case Leo was killed, and it had to do with it? So you for sure think someone killed Leo?"

"Sorry to say I do."

"Why?"

"The way we found him didn't make sense unless someone else did it."

Virginia said, "I told Mama I didn't think so either."

Ms. Carson said, "I can't say nothing about back then. It was all in the papers, and I was just a girl at home with my babies."

"Any idea why Ms. Ford named him in her will?"

"None whatever. I don't listen to talk neither."

"Did you happen to know a man named Squint Cooper?"

"Heard the name. Don't know the man."

Virginia said, "Why? Who is he?"

"Just someone I been talking to, trying to sort things out. He's an old-timer like Ms. Carson."

"Young man, I look more old-timer than I am. I'm a young-timer."

"I'm sure you are. Well, I won't take any more of your time. I have come, as I expect Virginia has told you, about the letters. I'm particularly interested in any letters he sent you after he was released. Did he contact you?"

June lifted her head and shook it slowly. "He was a faithful man in that. I'm sorry to tell you I have decided against it."

As Seb framed a reply, Virginia said, "Mr. Creek, Mama has buried the letters with my daddy."

"Really? You put them in the coffin?"

Ms. Carson said, "I did, and here come the burying man to put it all back in the earth. Where we all going and will meet again, Mr. Creek. And it all get sorted then."

The burial machine, a four-legged octopus with a massive bivalve bucket, was slowly pacing down a grassy corridor toward the open grave.

"Ms. Carson, did you happen to read any of his last letters?"

"I stopped long ago. I let the past die." She pointed a finger toward the grave, and her head jerked in a nod. "That man buried there is past caring, and we got to be past caring too. I'm the one at stake here, and I'm past caring. Let him lie in peace until it all get sorted."

She nodded, then turned and proceeded toward the chapel.

Virginia said, "I'm sorry. Mr. Creek. She has her certain ways." She started to follow her mother.

Seb touched her arm. "What will happen now is I'll get a court order, and we'll have to dig him back up."

"Those are heartache letters. They won't solve a murder."

"They might." The octopus had reached the grave and was positioning its tentacles. "Give me permission to retrieve the letters from the coffin. That's all I need."

"My verbal permission is all you need?"

"Yes."

"Okay."

"Please say it."

"I give you permission to get those letters. From my daddy's casket."

"Thank you. I'll be very respectful."

"Please do." She gave him a soft direct look. "You will not kick dirt on my daddy."

"I will not." Seb saw the octopus clamp its jaws into the hill of earth beside the grave. He ran, waving his hands.

THE TESTAMENT

Seb heard a racket of squealing as he entered the hog house and found Squint making another red paddle wade through the hogs.

Seb watched him scissor over the pen bars, then swing the paddle over his shoulders and drape his arms. He said, "Manuel quit me. I'm all alone unless I get some help, if I ever do. You look grim. If you want to talk, keep up." He swung the paddle down and carried it into the bright morning.

Seb followed. They started down the grassy slope toward the generator shed and the perimeter of yellow tape. Seb said to his back, "I been wondering if I got Jorge killed."

Squint stopped. They faced each other.

Seb said, "Then I thought, no, you had that planned, which is why you had to show up at the sports bar. You had to show me the video, make sure to tell me it was Jorge in the blue van. So he was dead from go. That's cold, Squint."

Squint made a distracted smile. He said, "Only a fool kills hot." He wheeled and continued toward the generator shed. Behind it stood the scrubber shed and the trench descending the slope toward the tarp-covered log lagoon. He spoke without looking back, to the sky. "Doesn't go with the life you think you're leading, does it?"

He stopped and turned again.

Seb stopped beside the trench, keeping a red paddle length between them. He ran his hand under the waist of his Walmart windbreaker. His left hand found the nut on the drawstring. He pulled it, loosening the hem.

"But it goes with the life you *do* lead. It goes with the life every weak-ass motherfucker on the planet leads and can't look in the face. Why are you here?"

Seb pulled his phone from his pocket. "I found her testament."

"Well, that day has come then."

Seb said, "I came to make you a deal."

Squint swung the paddle into a cane, turned, and walked toward the door of the generator shed. He cranked it open, reached the paddle inside, and propped it against the wall.

Seb dropped the phone and snatched at the windbreaker hem, but it snagged on the holster bottom. He tore it free and drew the nine millimeter, thumbing the safety as it came up, seeing the lever action rifle in Squint's hand now, seeing him bring it fast to his shoulder. He dropped to the grass as Squint fired. He brought up the pistol with two hands and fired twice. Squint ran sideways, levering the rifle. As the rifle came up again, Seb fired again, then rolled. Then his chest was in midair, and he twisted onto his back, preparing for the drop, heard the rifle shot, and felt a bullet pluck through his calf. He dropped eight feet and landed on the small of his back in the mud, his pistol held aloft with both hands. He lay for a moment, his eyes flicking around the perimeter of the trench. He needed to be at the deep end where the pipes descended, his back to the trench wall, the scrubber shed directly above, where there was no place for a man to appear and aim. Which Squint might anticipate. And it didn't really matter. From anywhere on the perimeter, Squint could peek Seb's position, then fire without exposing himself.

Seb sat up slowly, letting the mud reluctantly un-cling from his windbreaker, like a slow-motion dream, only the monster was not chasing him but had found him and was above him, anywhere at any instant on the perimeter. He sat, scanning and listening. He drew his feet toward his thighs, hunched forward, and with a single lurch was able to stand without releasing the pistol. He felt a stab of pain, saw the bloody blotch on the front of his tan pants. He pulled the leg free and stepped. Pain surged, but the leg held his weight. He slogged to the end of the trench, put his back against the pipes, pistol raised, his eyes continuing to flick around the perimeter. His calf throbbed. Against the cool of the mud, he felt the warmth of blood pooling around his ankle.

His position was hopeless.

He heard a scrap, heard the door of a shed close. He shouted, "Did I hit you?"

Squint's voice came from above him, close. "I'm afraid you did not."

"I told you I came to make you a deal, Squint. I can't make it if you kill me."

Seb heard a *clack* above him, raised the pistol and without taking the time to turn and look, fired twice directly overhead, then glanced up and saw the red oar clatter against the pipes two feet above him. The oar withdrew. Then he saw the valve, saw that one of his bullets had struck the swollen brass. The center pipe at his feet began to spew noisily into the muddy water.

Squint said, "I was fixing to turn on the gas, Seb. Looks like it's on now. I can hear it bubbling."

Seb said, "No one is going to think I fell in and shot the valve."

"I can change the valve. I believe I'll sink you in the lagoon anyway."

Seb smelled the acrid odor of rotten eggs, strong, then weak, then strong. He said, "You're going to want to hear this deal."

"I can't deal, Seb. I'm sorry about it." The voice had moved from the pipe end, was farther away and moving.

Seb said, "Cody needs a deal even if you don't."

There was a silence. Squint said, "All right, explain that." The voice was at the opposite end of the trench now. Seb leveled the pistol, aiming just above the perimeter where a man might peek.

"You heard about those choppers that crashed?"

"I did."

"If you'd been to town recently you'd have seen a bunch of federal investigators out and about."

"Go ahead."

Seb said, "The choppers crashed because one of them dropped a load out of its belly net and turned around and hit the other one. What they dropped was a trailer full of Stinger missiles. They dropped in a creek right in front of Cody's camp, and he found them and took them and has got them buried somewhere. If they get him, he's gone for good. So that's the deal. You confess and save us the trouble of a trial, and I'll let him slide."

Squint said, "How do you know he's got them?"

"I saw that tent on the video and figured it out. Then I went to talk to him. The feds will be up with him pretty soon, because they found where he's been digging flytraps, and he's got a record for it."

There was silence above him.

Seb said, "What do you think?"

There was another silence, longer. Then Squint said, "So what's the deal again?"

"I let him go. And you confess."

"You smell that gas yet?"

"I smell it."

Squint appeared at the edge of the hole opposite Seb, the rifle cradled. He said, "You're bleeding."

Seb lowered the pistol. He said, "It's through and through. No bone."

Squint said, "Can you climb?"

"I doubt it."

"Come up here to the shallow end, and I'll hoist you."

As Seb came forward, Squint uncradled the rifle and extended the barrel into the trench.

Seb said, "You got that on safe?"

"I do."

Seb holstered his pistol and seized the barrel with both hands. Squint pulled him from the hole with one powerful lift.

Seb said, "You want to hand me that rifle?"

"Not yet. Sit down and take a look at your wound."

Seb helped himself onto the grass with his hands. He pulled the muddy windbreaker over his head and drew up his filthy cuff. The hole was leaking but not pulsing.

Squint said, "Metal jacket. You're good." He sat crossed-legged on the grass, the rifle on his lap. He said, "You got her letter on you?"

Seb lifted his phone from the grass where he had dropped it. "It's on my phone."

"Where'd you find it?"

"Leo sent it to his wife."

"I figured a copy might be out there. But I didn't know who to strangle for it. I might could get out from under it. The thoughts of an old lady getting me back for fouling her creek. I wonder would a court hear it."

"Maybe not."

"Ah, well. The world is a vicious coward, Seb. Vicious to the bone and a coward to see it. The motherfuckers sent us to war where we killed our brothers like Cain. I know you killed, but I killed over twenty. I killed kiddos, and I killed women. And they raised me up for it, gave me the Silver Star. They said, strut on, big dog. You didn't kill Jorge. He had to go. And I liked him."

Seb waited.

"Pull out your phone. I want you to read her letter."

Seb removed the phone from his front pocket and woke it.

Squint said, "I loved that woman. I called it love anyway. She was a mile from me all the years, and I never could love my wife, which I think gave her cancer. Germaine could look at you and take you right inside her. Not just her body now. But God's at the bottom of the cesspool, says Seb Creek. Could be! Life did not open its secrets to me. Read that letter. Read it well, if you don't mind."

Seb read, "Dear Mr. Sackler. I have thought long about how to compose this letter. I am quite ill and hope I have not waited too long. I will get the facts out at least. I would also like to express my state of mind and heart, which I assure you I recognize and scorn as a selfish need. Your fate was to be imprisoned for forty-eight years for a crime you did not commit, plucked from a carefree life. My fate was to cause it and know it and live a coward. Here are the facts. As a girl, I recognized my beauty and its power and was first a precocious flirt and soon a wanton. I could blame the freedom of the age, but the truth is that I enjoyed men and took my pleasure there. When Rufus Cooper, known as Squint, came home on leave from Viet Nam a celebrated hero, I pursued him, and we began an affair.

I soon tired of him and began to return the attentions of our neighbor, Hugh Britt. The night of the murder, I arranged an assignation with Hugh, and Squint followed me to Hugh's boathouse where he found us in a state of nature. He flew into a rage, knocked me down, then took the axe from the wall, and killed Hugh before my eyes. Then he ran away and a few days later was back in Viet Nam. I have many times tried to recapture my state at that moment and have not very well succeeded. I was numb, terrified, and desperate. I took the axe and rinsed it in the water below the dock as if that might somehow conceal the crime and my involvement. Then I ran down Twice Mile Road to my home where I lifted away a board on the cover of an old well and threw the axe in. When you were arrested, I remained silent. I confess to you that I was relieved. I sometimes wonder if you had been sentenced to death whether I would have come forward. I take no comfort in thinking that I may have. I take no comfort anywhere, and never have, since the night of that murder. If you are vengeful, you could not wish me punished more severely than I have been. I acted for my reputation, and both our lives were wasted, and I am the cause. I have lived these long years walled in a prison as real as your own. I do not impose on you by asking your forgiveness, but if we meet again in the world to come I fervently hope it will be in a state where our earthly wrappings and desires will have fallen away to dust. The well is located on the left side of the house facing the inlet. It is thirty feet or so from the log wall and is ringed in brick. My father later filled it in. I was responsible for the anonymous amounts deposited in your prison account. I would have sent a thousand but did not want to create newsworthy attention. The lucidity of my writing should testify to my healthy state of mind. Your legal ordeal is over, but this document should be of some use for your reputation."

Seb looked up. He said, "And her large beautiful signature. Germaine Evelyn Ford."

"Can't you see why I was captivated?"

"She must have been quite a woman."

"She could swallow you whole. Hell, I was a farm boy. I didn't have no business with a girl like that, and I knew it. But the government made me a hero, and here she come. She figured me out pretty quick. She did like my war stories though. I believe sex and death are connected to the same appetite. Turn on your recorder."

Seb opened the recording app.

Squint said, "I'm glad not to kill you. I about got sick of it after Jorge. Ready?"

Seb nodded.

Squint said, "This is Squint Cooper of Cooper Farms on Twice Mile Road. I'm sitting here with Seb Creek, who is present and a witness. I confess that I killed Leo Sackler and Jorge Navalino, and also I killed Hugh Britt. Now I'm going to tell a few details. You had the main of it, Seb. Did you find that axe, by the way?"

"We found it yesterday."

"He was fucking her from behind, standing up. Oh, lord, that did for me. I smacked her down, then took that axe off the wall and put it right in his forehead. Down he went, and I hit him again for spite and hatred. She never made a peep. I believe she was waiting for me to kill her. I ran off and figured, well, that's the end of me. I killed my way to the end. I never spoke to her in my life again, not even when she sued me for spilling hog shit into her creek. I did go back to the boathouse later that night, when I calmed down. I started thinking, her word against mine. I'll deny everything, except I left the axe with my fingerprints on it, and I needed to get that and wipe it off. The axe was gone, so I took an axe out of my truck, dipped it in the blood, and threw it off the dock. Wearing gloves. And they did find it and draw conclusions. I saw footprints in the blood and on the dock, which I thought was Germaine. But it was Leo. When they arrested him, I thought, fuck it, I'm a free man. When my dad bought this place, first thing I did was start a lantern fire in that boathouse and burn it to the ground. On to the present day. Detective Seb Creek, you have been accurate in your conclusions. It was DeWitt with the mustache that alerted me to the fact that Leo Sackler, ex-con, newly released, was digging out a well on his property. I drew conclusions, which was, Germaine left a note telling him where the axe was and probably told him everything else to boot. So I took the van, and there he was, coming up with a bucket of dirt. I gave the ladder a shake, and you could hear the bone crack when he fell. He was dangling upside down in bad agony. I told him who I was, and I know it was like hell had opened up on him. Can't you imagine his state of mind? Out of jail, set for life, digging for the truth, and he stirs up the devil himself, gazing down without mercy. I made a lasso and told him to put it around his waist, and I'd pull him up. He started fumbling with it, and I snagged him. I hauled him up on his tiptoes and pulled the ladder up. I made him tell me the story, which he did. He told me everything, including where the letter was, in that metal box. I'll tell you a peculiar trait of the human mind. I wanted that letter halfway to protect myself, but a good deal just to see what she said about me. Just when you read it, I suffered again. Her entire remark about me was that she quickly lost interest. I took all those papers and photos in there too, just in case. I burned those, but that letter, I wired that motherfucker to a rebar and threw it in the hog shit along with his phone. Of course, when you think of it, she let that man go to jail for the sake of her reputation. So probably she wasn't worth much, which I take some consolation there. When I got back to the well, he was dead. On his way anyway. I hauled him up and tied him off. Jorge was dead exactly then. That was a had-to-happen. That fairly much soured me on killing. If it hadn't, I might have looked around for his kin. Leo swore he hadn't sent a copy on, but I knew he might have. What else?"

"How'd you kill Jorge?"

"The way you guessed. I turned on the gas, then borrowed his phone and tossed it in the ditch. I said, Jorge, I dropped your phone. And down he went like a good chap, which he was. Now answer this, Seb. Why do you want me? Revenge don't pay no bills. Why seize me up and throw me in jail, maybe execute me? I'm done killing. Don't say it's your job, or I'll fucking shoot you."

"I don't know, Squint. I guess if I knew what justice was, I would know something."

Squint said, "Cut the recorder."

Seb closed the recording app.

Squint said, "Cody's free?"

"I'm not going to catch him. They might."

"You took a chance."

"I did."

"Thank you for that."

Squint stood, offered his hand, and pulled Seb to his feet. He said, "Tell Cody I thought of him. Tell Charlene too."

He held Seb's hand for a long moment. He said, "God's at the bottom, says Seb Creek. We'll see."

He went to the edge of the trench, sat down, and dropped in.

JUSTICE, IF THERE IS ANY

The minister was black clad and tall and stood alone in the white chancel like an exclamation mark. He had read briefly from a text, and now lay the book on the pulpit, folded his hands, then let them fall, a gesture, Seb thought, expressing both reverence and relief. There were no pallbearers. The minister removed his reading glasses, glanced to the side, and made a faint nod. Two men in white shirts and ties emerged and wheeled the coffin into a side room. Cody and Charlene stood and made their way down the chapel aisle.

Seb, who had seated himself in the rearmost pew, rose to greet them. He took Charlene's offered hand.

She said, "You saw he didn't mention heaven."

Seb said, "I guess he didn't."

"I don't mind. It's nobody's business anyway."

Seb offered his hand to Cody who took it, looked away, then looked directly into Seb's eyes. "Hi, Mr. Creek."

"Good morning, Cody."

Charlene said, "Did you bring them?"

"They're in my car."

She said, "They're bringing the coffin out to the gravesite. We'll meet you there."

Seb said, "Okay. Cody, take a walk with me, will you?"

Cody said, "Sure."

Charlene said, "The grave's way over to the right."

Seb said, "There's half a dozen photographers out there. I told them to stay back, but they brought their football lenses."

"I could care less."

Seb, with Cody a half step behind, started along the sidewalk that led to the parking lot. Seb slowed, and Cody came alongside. Seb said, "They pick you up?"

"Oh, yeah."

"How did you do?"

"Pretty good, I guess. Here I am."

"How long did they keep you?"

"Just an hour about. Looked like they had a bunch of guys they were talking to. They had a whole waiting room full."

"They might call you back."

"I'll just tell them what I told them. I don't do flytraps anymore."

They had reached Seb's Honda. Seb opened the back door and removed the tin Phineas Brothers tobacco box. They started back toward the cemetery.

When they reached the cemetery entrance, Seb stopped. He said, "You know, when you think about it, you owe me big-time."

"Yes, I do."

"And you're a rich man now. You got two miles of Sable River frontage. You could sell half that, and there wouldn't be a bottom to your money."

Cody watched him, half-smiling. Something was coming, something not greed.

Seb said, "So you know what would be good?"

"What?"

"Something for the kids. Like a school maybe. Or a camp. Some kind of deep pocket community thing to give back for all the raggedy-ass worthlessness you have inflicted on society."

Cody laughed. He said, "We've been talking about it, Keisha and me. We're getting married. Charlene's excited too. It's going to be a community center. And definitely lots of stuff for kids, which is what Charlene does. She says we can probably get matching grants too."

"So I don't have to strong-arm you."

"Also, we're buying the Lands' house, for plenty enough so they can get a good place. We're taking the hogs out anyway. And guess what? I'm going to start a flytrap nursery, but kind of an eco-thing, to go with the community center."

They started into the cemetery.

Seb said, "Another thing you owe me is you got to join the singers."

"I'll come."

"Great. We're working up a special song. You like hip-hop?"

"Sort of. If I ever hear it."

"We're working on a hip-hop ballad sort of thing. For a woman I'm trying to get up with."

"I'll definitely come."

Down a lane, the gravesite came in view. The minister and his helpers were positioning the coffin under the octopus. Three lines of flat straps descended from its jaws. Charlene stood to the side, watching with folded arms.

Seb stopped, stopping Cody. They faced each other. Seb said, "One last thing. Why the fuck did you do it?"

Cody shook his head. He smiled. "It didn't occur to me not to. I kind of think it was fate."

Seb said, "Maybe so. I listened to the 911 call from the guys that found them. They said the Marines forgot some ammunition on the beach. They were reading all the numbers off."

"I left them standing up like a little forest."

Seb gave Cody a direct look. "One day all this will make a hell of a story."

Cody returned the look. He said, "Which I will never tell."

"So three of us, you, me, and Charlene."

Cody hesitated. Then he said, "Five of us. I told Elton Gleen, and he told his nephew."

"For God's sake …"

"He told me I was going to end up in an eight-by-eight cell unless I worked with him. I almost drowned myself."

"He saw money?"

"Oh, yeah. I was supposed to email the terrorists. Then he and Peener wanted to sell to the Mexican cartels."

"What's he say now?"

"Nothing. I met him at McDonald's and had my phone taped under the table. I called him later and played it back to him. He turned peaceful. Otherwise I would be dead. I think he killed my friend Harvey Clement."

"Yes, he did."

"That leaves the nephew."

"Carl Peener never made it back to Georgia. I think he's gone the way of your friend Harvey."

"Oh, man. I even imagined that, that Elton would do that."

They started toward the grave. A cluster of photographers stood at a respectful hundred feet and took pictures. The minister and the two men began to circle the coffin with the straps. Charlene spoke to them, and they stepped back.

As Seb and Cody approached, she said to Seb, "Tell me this. Did Virginia call you and say, I've got an idea? Or how did it come up?"

Seb said, "I called her to tell her I wanted to return them. They were supposed to be buried with Leo. When she heard Squint was going to be buried in the same cemetery, it just came up. She didn't insist or anything, just asked me to ask you."

"You tell her I said I'm so happy she asked. She's going to be our neighbor, and we're going to be good neighbors."

"I'll tell her."

Seb opened the end of the casket, exposing the legs.

Charlene said, "Open it all. Please."

Seb lifted the front of the casket, exposing Squint's waxen face.

Charlene said, "Let's put them all around."

Seb opened the tobacco box, and Charlene lifted a handful of the pink and green and white envelopes and spread them over the corpse, above and beside the head, on the chest, on the loins and legs. When the box was empty, she said, "I'll save the box for her. You can close it now."

Seb closed the rear section, then the front.

Charlene said, "Tell Virginia I know it's not vengeance. It's more like justice, if there is any. Tell her we're sisters now. We're neighbors and sisters."

Seb said, "I'll tell her." Then he said to Cody, "You ever been in Elton Gleen's trailer?"

"Once."

"You ever see a teapot in there?"

FROM THE HOUSE
TO THE HOME

Seb could have entered the studio without knocking, as he had before, as any customer might, but a knock would bring her to the door, which was the plan. He knocked three times and listened. He peered through the panes of the door window into the studio. He knocked twice more. Since it was Memorial Day it was possible she was gone, maybe with friends to the beach, except it was raining, and also Gloria, their soprano, had called an hour ago, and Mia had answered. He waited and listened, resisting another knock. On the right, the display lights in the gallery were bright.

He had spoken with her twice on the phone since their unhappy meeting at Debbie's Diner. The first call had been to inform her that the FBI had confirmed that Grayson Kelly had been with his grandmother—and been seen by neighbors—on the night of the helicopter crash. Kelly faced federal charges for the possession of hand grenades, but the conspiracy theory had been dropped. The FBI had not recalled Mia, but also had not called to put her at ease or apologize. She expressed concern about his gunfight and sympathy about his wounded calf.

The second call had been to let her know that her burglary had been solved and a teapot recovered.

The first call had been awkwardly formal, the second more cordial, but both calls brief. She offered that she recalled that particular teapot, liked it especially, and would be glad of its return. Her reserve, he sensed, had become more protective than angry. She was hesitant, seeking a flow, but unable yet to find it. He had been working hard all week with Ahmad and the Pass the Salt singers to help her.

A shadow fell across the door's window. Mia opened and stood before him in tan shorts and a white, clay-spotted T-shirt, drying her hands on a towel, which she wore tossed across her shoulder.

"Hi," she said. "You don't have to knock." Her smile was faint and waiting. She would open and receive him, if he had the proper key.

He said, "I know, I guess." He fished up his phone from his front pocket, opened the photo he had taken that morning in the property room. Her teapot. "We found it in the home of a dangerous felon. He's going to prison for receiving stolen goods. So that's good at least."

She said, "You want to come in? How's your leg?" She stepped back.

He said, "Can't right now. The leg is good."

She delivered a curious look and stepped forward again. She said, "I've been reading all about your famous case. It was in the *New York Times* this morning."

"Right. One of their reporters wants to do a book."

"No kidding. You going to do it?"

"At first, I thought no, but then she said it won't just be a crime story, but it'll be about the whole context, and justice, and race, and be a crimes-of-the-father type thing. Plus it'll give me a chance to talk about Pass the Salt. So maybe. I'm considering it."

She nodded and waited.

He said, "Me and the singers have been busy all week, working on a new song. Remember I told you about Ahmad, the hip-hop guy who came up with the name Pass the Salt? He's been bugging me to do some rap."

"Are you going to do a hip-hop song?"

"Sort of. It's sort of a hip-hop ballad. Ahmad says it's pretty white."

She nodded. Her hands went to the towel across her shoulder. She waited.

He let a long pause go. He gave off a faint shrug, a direct look. He said, "Want to hear it?"

She smiled. "Sure."

Seb stepped backward down the wet stone walkway into the drizzle. He motioned for the singers, who strode fast from their concealment around the side of the building. There were eighteen of them, free on Memorial Day, under a moving cascade of colorful umbrellas, one of which was handed to Seb. Eight of the men, Cody included, carried a four-by-eight-foot sheet of plywood, dropped it on the lawn with a *whump*, and arranged themselves on top of it. They were the rhythm section. The rest of the singers made a semicircle around them. Ahmad had the boom box strapped around his neck and, after a four count, started off a quiet rain of snares, toms, and cymbals, neatly combined with a little *shush-shush* car-crushing sound. The rhythm eight started a booming stamp-back response on the plywood, then settled into a half-note groove. A boom box organ began a droning melody. The singers snapped their fingers in a syncopated popping.

Mia came forward from the doorway and stood on the sidewalk with folded arms. Her mouth opened. She beamed.

The organ went silent, and Seb began his white boy chant-singing over the stomps and pops.

> *"I used to be afraid of love, I hid my fear in pride.*
> *All I felt was loneliness when I looked inside.*
> *Now I'm facing up to love like a shadow on the wall.*
> *Love is getter brighter, and the shadow's getting small."*

The organ started. The singers sang:

> *"Everybody's traveling from their house to their home.*
> *Some go together. Some go alone.*
> *All I'm trying to say, girl, is I want to walk you home."*

Seb took up his chant.

> *"I had a head full of differences and a heart full of pain.*
> *But when you find love there's nothing else to gain.*
> *When you find love, it's like a candle in the night.*
> *If you get lost, just head for the light."*

The singers sang the chorus to the organ. Seb chanted.

> *"I know love's for the chosen few, maybe I don't belong.*
> *But a broken heart's a small price for something that strong.*
> *So I'm standing here outside your door. Hurts like a prison wall.*
> *But I'll be right here standing, till the last shadow falls."*

The singers sang,

> *"Everybody's traveling from their house to their home.*
> *Some go together. Some go alone.*
> *All I'm trying to say, girl, is I want to walk you home,*
> *just walk you home, back home, back home."*

The organ faded, the stomping slowed, and four finger pops ended the performance.

Mia put her fists against her temples, opened her hands, touched her heart. Her eyes had wet and overflowed. She went to Seb. She kissed him, holding, then stroking his cheeks. She drew back. She laughed. She bowed and touched her heart to the chorus. The chorus laughed and beamed. She embraced Seb again. She kissed him again. The singers milled and commented. Wine bottles appeared. Mia led them into the studio, where she gave a tour and several singers bought goblets, bowls, and vases. Eventually many toasts were drunk, to Seb, who they treasured, and to Mia and Seb, who they had hopes for, and, since it was Memorial Day, for soldiers they had loved and lost.

Then, in twos and threes, goodbyes were said, and the singers left. Mia closed the door, then led him back through her studio and across a small yard to her home, where she showed him her living quarters, with pots from many potters and with colorful paintings from many art fairs, and the patio and herb garden and the forest behind and this and that.

And things went on from there.

ACKNOWLEDGMENTS

Lots of people contributed to the research behind this novel, and I'm truly grateful to all of them. I needed to learn about police procedure and Marine MPs, the hog farm fiascoes of North Carolina, and make a thorough study of PTSD. I read books and combed the internet. I talked to cops, lawyers, professors, hog farm researchers, and lots of Marines. I'll name them in no particular order: Sheriff Hans Miller, Major Don Baker, Deputy Philip Crider, Sergeant Todd McAllister, Nat Fahy, Louis Lapointe, Kerry Mason, Mike Surles, Mike Saniford, Sam Kellum, Jane Preyer, Mike Williams, Daniel Wallace, Tom Demmy, Bill Showers, and Don Lloyd. Lieutenant Brian Williams, my go-to guy for cop life, deserves special mention. He always responded cheerfully and fully to my many inquiries.

I'm grateful to Fred Chappell for getting me started in the world of agents; to my captain in the sea of publishing, agent Peter Rubie; to my editor Madeline Hopkins, who tracked down all my missteps; to my editor Ember Hood, who sweetened the writing; and to Kurt Jones, who devised a cool cover.

Lastly, and chiefly, I'm grateful to my wife, Cynthia Drake, whose glad support and sensitive critiques shaped both me and this novel.